THE GOOD HUMOR MAN,
OR, CALORIE 3501

ANDREW FOX

The Good Humor Man, Or, Calorie 3501

TACHYON PUBLICATIONS | SAN FRANCISCO

Cover design by Ann Monn
Interior design & composition by John D. Berry
The typeface is Chronicle Text with Chronicle Display

Tachyon Publications
1459 18th Street #139
San Francisco, CA 94107
(415) 285-5615
www.tachyonpublications.com

Edited by Marty Halpern

ISBN 10: 1-892391-85-6
ISBN 13: 978-1-892391-85-8

Printed in the United States of America
by Worzalla

First Edition: 2009

9 8 7 6 5 4 3 2 1

For Dara, Natalie, Levi, Asher, and Judah, with love;
and for Ray Bradbury, J. G. Ballard, and Barry Malzberg,
with affection and admiration.

THE GOOD HUMOR MAN,
OR, CALORIE 3501

3500: the number of food calories which, if consumed and not expended to support bodily functions, will add one pound of fat to the human body; conversely, the number of calories which must be burned to lose one pound of fat.

New American Dictionary of Nutrionics
Edited by Richardson, Avis, Carter, et al.;
Putnam, 2015; page 8

PART I

*The Good Humor Man's
Very Bad Week*

CHAPTER 1

I remember cheese.

I remember pizza; *real* pizza. Deep-dish, Chicago-style, four-cheese pizza, fresh from the oven, the cheese steaming and bubbling on top like cooling lava.

We go over a sharp rut in the road. I'm in the Good Humor van, heading for Mex-Town. My balls have shrunk to the size of raisins. Whatever we're about to be faced with, it won't be a cake walk, like this morning was.

Two call-outs in one day. It's almost beyond belief. Our squad hasn't responded to more than one outbreak per quarter in nearly fifteen years. What in God's name is going on? It's almost as if an epidemic of gluttony has broken out in Southern California.

"Hey Lou, you feel comfortable handling one of these?" Mitch, my partner, my best friend, fondles a sawed-off shotgun in his lap like a favorite grandchild.

"No. I don't." The thought of using a gun terrifies me almost as much as the thought of having to make a show of force in Mex-Town.

The van is crowded with twice its normal complement. Mitch called in the San Clemente squad for backup. We've never worked with them before. I glance at their unfamiliar, nervous faces in the rear-view mirror and feel perspiration gather on my palms.

We're all old men. Alex, Jr., at forty, is the baby of the group, a quarter-century younger than most of us; he only suited up this morning because his father passed away two months ago and left us a man short. We belong out on a golf course, playing the back nine... not in the most anarchic part of the county, hunting for dangerous contraband.

Thousands of pounds of genuine American cheese, left over from before the nutrition laws, before the geneticists got their hands on the food supply, before the Second Great Depression. If they could manage to sell it, those Mex-Town thugs would end up the nation's wealthiest men. They've got a prize worth killing for.

This morning's raid was different. It felt like carnival time, like the old, good times. A couple blocks away from the community gym, our target, Mitch turned on the recorded calliope music, and I'd smiled. I appreciate tradition. We were going to make a show of it. We were going to show the young folks, the ones who'd never seen us pull off a raid, what the Good Humor Men were all about.

Mitch pulled the truck into the parking lot of the Rancho Bernardino Municipal Gymnasium. It felt bizarre that we were about to raid the gym; engaging in gluttony on these premises was like trying to snow ski on the rim of an active volcano. But it was nearly Christmas time, and the holiday season has always been when the weak-willed are most likely to take stupid risks.

We barged through the entrance, "Camptown Races" still blaring behind us. Sweaty faces of all ages turned in our direction, eyes wide. Mitch took the point. Seeing him in front of me, lugging his dragon, his miniature flamethrower, over his shoulder, thrilled me with a shower of memories. For a few seconds, I was a young man again, a commando fueled by delicious resolve. A zealot for a good cause. A believer.

Once the shock began fading from the onlooking faces, it was replaced by hesitant smiles, then a few thumbs-up signs. They were going to get to see a spectacle. Many of them had never seen us on the job; they'd only seen us driving our truck in the Thanksgiving Day parade. One young woman, dressed in gray, shapeless exercise clothes, began clapping. Her smile only accentuated the painful thinness of her face.

As we walked toward the offices in the back, the applause spread. *Pour it on,* I thought. This was the sound I'd been anticipating even more than the calliope music. Applause, public approbation, the affirmation of the good I do in the world.

Brad bashed in the doors that led to the main office with the butt of his rifle. An old pro, like Mitch, he knew when to play to his audience. We crashed an old-fashioned office Christmas party. Sheet cake, red and green Christmas cookies, and some cloudy liquid substance in a punch bowl, probably a rough analogue of eggnog. Some idiot had opened the rear window and was frantically tossing potato chips, chocolate, and cartons of some sort of ice cream into the lot behind the building. As if that would do him any good.

"Brad, collect their health insurance cards," I said. It felt like reciting words from a script, playing a character. *This isn't really me,* I wanted to explain to the dozen county employees in the room. Soon to be *ex*-employees.

One man stared at Brad and me with pleading eyes. "I — I didn't get a chance to eat any of this stuff. I just got here. Ask them —" he gestured to his coworkers "— ask any one of them. They'll tell you. I didn't eat *none* of this stuff. Can't you, maybe, let me off *easy?*"

"You know we can't," I said. I despised him, as if he were a cockroach scurrying across the toe of my shoe. Someone always thinks they deserve special treatment. "Down the gullet or not, just being in the same room with this contraband makes you an accessory."

"But my health card — I *need* it —"

"Stay clean and you'll get it back in five years."

When the man refused to hand over his wallet, Brad dug it out of his pocket. It was as though he'd plucked out the man's heart. "But you don't understand — I get these seizures, and I need my pills — you *gotta* understand, there's no way I can afford the pills without my health card —"

My contemptuous feelings toward him evaporated. I'd prayed I could dodge the gut blow this one time, but I couldn't. Every damn raid within the past five years, I've hit this damn wall. I'm a physician. A healer. How could I deny a man his meds? But if I weakened, the whole edifice would collapse.

Mitch came to my rescue, as he always does. "Mister, you should've thought of that before you dug your fingers into the sheet cake."

"Everybody lock and load," Brad says from behind the wheel. "Welcome to Cheese City."

I tug on my Kevlar vest, trying to keep it from pinching my neck. It smells musty. They're relics, dusty fossils from the old wild days, from before our raids ossified into run-of-the-mill fire shows.

I glance warily at the three barrels of gasoline stuffed into the back of the van. Whatever happens this afternoon, it sure as hell won't be a run-of-the-mill fire show.

Empty government surplus food cartons litter the street. Dozens of residents loiter in the square surrounding the post office. Four pallets of cartoned cheese sit at one end of the square. Several men are distributing boxes.

"Mitch, you're the man," Brad says. "Do we stop here?"

"Not right now," Mitch answers. "This is penny-ante stuff here. We've gotta see how far this crap has spread. Remember those directions I gave you for the warehouse? Drop me and Lou and the gasoline off there first. If we're lucky, the bulk of the cheese is still down there. Then the rest of you do a recon, sniff out the worst spots. Split up and go to work."

The leader of the San Clemente squad stares out the window, slack-jawed. "Jesus... I hope like hell we don't have to go house to house. That'd take a month and a day..."

No one scatters when we drive past. A couple of old-timers scowl and raise middle fingers. The younger residents only shoot us curious stares.

"Doesn't look like they're used to seeing Good Humor Men," I say.

"They aren't," Mitch answers. "We've never screwed with them much. They want to fuck up their own health, that's A-OK by me. Most of 'em aren't real Americans, anyway. But this time, they've crossed the line."

A kind of no man's land separates Rancho Bernardino from what's now called Mex-Town. The whole area used to be part of the same municipality, the city of Rancho Bernardino. But twenty-two years ago, the lighter-skinned, upper-middle-class portion of the city split itself off from the darker-skinned, working-class portion. The no man's land is an empty, late-twentieth-century commercial district of abandoned strip malls and rubbish-strewn gas stations. Sad shells of old Dairy Queens and Taco Bells are tattooed with obscene graffiti.

The retreat of suburbia has emboldened the local wildlife. Two deer block our path. A buck and a doe. They hold their ground, not budging an inch as Brad is forced to slow down and swerve around them. They're starving. The flesh papering their protruding ribs looks thin as cheap aluminum foil. Once they're sure we won't stop to feed them something, they return to their feeble grazing of the tall weeds alongside the road.

"Poor things," Mitch mutters. "If I had my deer rifle with me, I'd put them out of their misery. They'd be my twenty-third and twenty-fourth kills this month. No sport's left in it anymore. They practically beg me to shoot 'em."

"You've shot twenty-two deer so far this month?" I watch the emaciated creatures dwindle behind us and finally disappear into clouds of road dust. "I always thought there were limits on how many deer you could kill in a single season."

"Not this year," he says, his tone forlorn. "Or last year, neither. In fact, hunting season's been extended to practically year round, ever since neighborhoods all over started getting overrun by deer. Deer that look just like those two poor bastards back there. Haven't you had some come begging around your place?"

"I haven't been able to keep flowers or vegetables in the ground in my back garden for months. I thought the problem was rabbits. What's behind this? I wasn't aware that Southern California's been suffering a drought."

"We haven't been. Rainfall's been normal. Ain't been a shortage of any of the vegetation deer normally feed on. They're eating. But from the looks of them, they might as well be eating air."

Eating air... "Have you asked your friends in Parks and Wildlife about this? Maybe it has something to do with pesticides, or runoff from crops getting into streams?"

Mitch shook his head. "Smart folks have been looking into this for over a year now. They ain't come up with a thing. The deer eat as much as they always have — more, in fact; the poor bastards spend every waking minute eating, but not a bit of it sticks to their bones. These past six months, my kills aren't even worth dragging home."

Would deer eat cheese? That old-fashioned, semi-organic stuff now floating around these parts has to be the highest calorie-per-ounce foodstuff left in North America. "Mitch, what do you know about this ex-government warehouse?"

"Most of it is underground," he answers. "An old federal facility. Hasn't been actively used since the mid 'teens. The old Department of Agriculture built it to store surplus dairy commodities — butter, powdered milk, and cheese."

"You say it's underground?" Brad asks, not looking away from the rutted, dusty road ahead.

"Not all of it. Just the main part. The feds took advantage of a system of natural caves to save some money. The temperature in the caves stays a steady fifty-eight to sixty degrees Fahrenheit, year round. Saved 'em a mint on electricity costs. The only portions they had to cool down were the chambers where they stored the butter and the cheese."

"But Mitch," Alex says from behind me, "you say this place hasn't been actively used in twenty-five years. Wouldn't all that stuff have gone bad years ago?"

"The butter, yes," I interject. "But the cheese... the cheese wasn't a completely natural product, not even back then. Federal surplus cheese was heavily laced with preservatives. So long as the refrigeration equipment remained functioning, there's no reason why that cheese, sealed in air-tight plastic, wouldn't be perfectly edible, even now."

"So who's been paying the electric bills all this time?" Alex asks.

"The feds have," Mitch answers. "They just haven't been aware of the fact. Four miles from the underground warehouse, there's a military base. The base has its own generating plant. When the warehouse was built, the Army let the Ag Department run an underground line from the base's electrical plant to the cold-storage facility. Lot of water under the bridge since then. The military forgot about the line, but it's been humming along, keepin' all that cheese nice and chilled these past twenty-five years."

"Our tax dollars at work," Brad mutters, speeding through a red light. "So if the feed line and the cheese were so forgotten, how'd they get remembered all of a sudden?"

"A technician uncovered the feed line while he was making repairs on a generator. He and his partner couldn't locate the line on any of their schematics, so they decided to follow the line and see where it led. They followed it right to the warehouse, and eventually it led them into the caves. Where they found the coolers. And the cheese."

"How do you know all this?" I ask.

"If things had gone right for that technician and his partner, I wouldn't know nothin'. Neither would anybody else, except maybe their black-market connection. It didn't take them long to realize they'd stumbled on a gold mine. That cheese — thousands of five-pound bricks of it stacked twenty feet high — was worth millions to the right people. Those two perps started sneaking it out of the warehouse in the middle of the night, a pallet at a time. Only problem was, the warehouse was situated in the wrong kind of neighborhood; pussy-footin' around at three in the A.M. don't help you if half the town sleeps during the day and stays up all night. Real fast, their conspiracy of two started growing; they were having to pay off more and more of the local characters in blocks of cheese. In a situation like that, a secret's got the shelf-life of raw meat at a dog-fighting match."

The lead man of the San Clemente squad speaks up. "So who tipped you off?"

Mitch smirks. "Even in Mex-Town, there're still folks who believe in what us Good Humor Men stand for."

The sun hovers low in the west, a shimmering blood-orange. I tell myself I should be happy Mitch has selected me for his partner. He's definitely the handiest with a firearm. But the notion of going underground with a wagon-load of gasoline isn't comforting at all.

Brad turns off the main thoroughfare onto a side road lined with tiny bungalows the color of mud. "That it ahead, Mitch?" he asks. "Doesn't look like much."

"Yeah. It's like an iceberg. Ninety-nine percent of it's beneath the surface."

We drive through open, rusted gates. I can still make out part of a sign that hangs askew: PROPERTY OF U.S. GOVT. The buildings are unimpressive — a low-lying office complex constructed of cinder blocks, and three taller warehouse structures made of sagging corrugated metal.

There's another truck parked by what looks like a main entrance. A big, unmarked truck with a thirty-foot box on back. Inside the box are five or six pallets of cheese.

I climb out of the van and stare at the contents. Six pallets, with each pallet holding maybe sixty cases of cheese... I'm looking at close to a half-million dollars of black-market contraband.

"Mitch, what do you want to do with these pallets in the truck?"

"They can wait until we come back out," he says, climbing down. "You got your radio on you?"

I check the box hanging from my belt. It's old and dusty. Who knows whether it still works? "Got it."

"Aren't you missing something else?"

Am I? I've got my medical bag slung over my shoulder. I shake my head.

"This, dummy." Mitch holds up a second shotgun that he's taken from the van. He motions to toss it to me.

"I don't want it, Mitch."

He scowls. "I don't care whether or not you *want* it, Lou. You're taking it. Everyone carries a gun on this mission. No exceptions."

He hands me the shotgun. I feel like a little boy handling a stick of dynamite. "The shells — they're loaded with plastic buckshot, right?"

Mitch smiles his lop-sided grin. "Heh. Yeah, right, Lou. Right." He turns back to the other men in the van, who've finished unloading the gasoline into the cart I'll be pulling. "Plan to be back here in forty-five minutes to pick us up. I'll radio when we're all done."

"Sure thing, Mitch," Brad answers. "Good luck. And have fun." A minute later the van is generating a dust plume that floats lazily back in our direction.

"Leave the gas out here for now," Mitch says. "The men who're loading up this truck are probably inside, pulling down more cheese. Let's go inside, real quiet-like, and hopefully catch those boys daydreaming of all the shit they're gonna buy."

We head inside. Rows of old metal desks are still covered with obsolete computer equipment and thick sheaves of printouts. It's ridiculously simple to follow the trail of the men below us; all we need do is walk the five-foot-wide path in the dust created by the pallet jack. The black marketeers have made our job easier in another way, too — they've lit the corridor with kerosene lanterns.

We walk around a bend, and the hallway takes on a gradual downward slope. Three minutes later, we reach a pair of fifteen-foot-high sliding steel doors. The walls are rock now, no longer corrugated metal.

After we pass through the doors into the caves, the floor's slope becomes steeper. The space between the floor and ceiling gradually increases as we descend.

"You feel how cool it's gotten?"

The sudden sound of Mitch's voice makes me jump. It *has* gotten cooler. The temperature must be at least fifteen degrees lower than it was outside. I begin noticing a slight vibration in the floor, a vibration which becomes an audible humming. We must be getting closer to the refrigeration units.

Ahead of us, barely discernable in the lantern light, are stacks of pallets, piled four or five high. The top cases are at least thirty feet off the floor. The floor levels off, and the passageway widens into a tremendous open space. I look up, wondering whether there are limestone formations hanging high above my head, in the darkness.

The cardboard cases stacked onto the pallets are marked "NON-FAT DRY MILK; DONATED BY THE PEOPLE OF THE UNITED STATES FOR FOOD ASSISTANCE PROGRAMS; NOT FOR RESALE." Worthless on the black market. We walk past what seems like acres of it. The humming grows louder. Finally, we come to a sweating steel wall. The trail of disturbed dust leads to tremendous insulated doors. One of them is partially open; a blast of winter's air escapes. The humming is very loud now. Still, Mitch signals for me to be quiet. He motions for me to follow him through the partially open door. Inside, we immediately duck behind a stack of pallets.

I can see two men. One is using the forklift to lower pallets to the floor. Mitch signals for me to sneak behind the other man, who's operating a pallet jack. I sense the weight of the shotgun in my hands. This isn't anything like this morning. I could get my head blown off.

Mitch pokes the muzzle of his shotgun into the back of the Mexican manning the forklift before I can take a single stride. All I have to do is step out of the shadows with my gun, and my target, the man with the pallet jack, immediately puts up his hands.

"What — what is this?" he blurts. "Who are you guys? Cops?"

I see Mitch smile. "Worse than cops. We're Good Humor Men."

"Shit," I hear the Mexican mutter.

"Look, we don't have a problem here," my man says very fast. "Take a look around you. You see what's there?"

I do. Cheese as far as the eye can see. An Arab oil sheik's ransom.

"My partners and I, we aren't greedy," he says. *"Look* at all this shit. This could last us for years and years, right? We'll cut you in for a slice. Make you millionaires a dozen times over —"

A gob of Mitch's spit lands near my man's shoes. "We're Good Humor Men," Mitch says. "We don't do deals."

I think about the half-dozen Nestlé bars I have hidden away inside my vest pockets, souvenirs of this morning's raid, intended for my ailing father.

Now my man looks genuinely frightened. "So... so what are you gonna do, then?"

Mitch's eyes twinkle. "Heh. Nothin' much. Just make the world's biggest grilled cheese sandwich."

I drag the cart loaded with drums of gasoline down to the refrigerated room. Mitch has handcuffed the two perps. The fair-skinned one looks like he may've soiled his pants.

I stare at the three barrels of gasoline. "Mitch. Is this legal? Isn't the cheese the property of the federal government?"

My friend and partner looks up at the hundreds of pallets. "This isn't federal property, Lou. If the feds abandon a facility for more than fifteen years, said facility reverts to the ownership of whatever state it happens to be in. So all this cheese is the property of the State of California. And under the California State Criminal Code, we've been given the authority to use whatever instrumentalities that are necessary and proper for the confiscation and destruction of contraband foods which menace the public health."

"But 'necessary and proper' doesn't necessarily mean that we set this entire facility on fire. Couldn't we just cut off the power to the refrigeration units, or disable the condensers?"

Mitch grips my shoulder hard enough to make me wince. "Lou. When I'm in charge of a mission, 'necessary and proper' is whatever I *say* it is. And I say that it is *necessary* and *proper* for us to set this goddamn warehouse on fire. Teach every cheese-eating fucker within five miles a lesson they won't never forget."

My God. He's never spoken to me this way before. There's no friendship in his eyes.

"Hey, you old peckerwood!" Mitch's grin returns. "What are we arguing for, huh? Just spread the damn gasoline around so we can get the fuck outta here. We'll go have us a beer after we get back home, just the two of us."

Mitch is my best friend. I don't think I could've made it through the first five years after Emily died without his companionship. Without the Good Humor Men. I open up the spigots on the gasoline drums and pull the cart along the corridors of cheese, spilling gasoline in pungent trails.

Mitch ignites his dragon. The blue and orange flames that race along the floor look like living things, luminescent serpents that whip each other with long, deadly tails. The cardboard cases catch quickly and easily.

What I did this morning, when the dragon was in my own hands — were my actions of a different kind than Mitch's, or merely of a different degree? I'd thrown the confiscated cookies and cartons of ice cream into the disposal tubs Alex, Jr. held across his shoulders. Then the sheet cake. It was almost a shame to destroy it. Someone had taken a great deal of time arranging the faux icing into those little roselike swirls. And the words "Merry Christmas," spelled out in red and green cursive lettering, surrounded by fat red Santa faces... it almost made even my Jewish heart melt.

"Are we going to burn the stuff in here?" Alex asked.

"No. Follow me out into the gym. We'll do it where everyone can see." It was important that we give our audience their show, their spectacle. Over a hundred pairs of eyes focused on us as we exited the offices. I gestured for Alex, Jr. to set the tubs down, then walked over to the first one, the dragon nestled in the crook of my arm. I stuck the nozzle within the rim of the first pot. Then I pulled the trigger and kept it pulled, just like Mitch had taught me.

The blast was sudden and startling. The skin on my hands and face tightened in the reflected heat. The sheet cake was consumed almost instantly. I smelled the familiar stench of carbonized grease. Tens of thousands of calories burned in less than a second. Hundreds of dollars of contraband going up in wispy smoke, all due to a tiny squeeze of my forefinger, the personal expenditure of a fraction of one stored calorie.

In the weeds by the back of the gym, I didn't find much to destroy. About a half-dozen bags of chips; a few cartons of unmelting "ice cream"; some scattered chocolate bars. Sunlight glinted off the wrappers of one of the candy bars. I picked it up. Gold letters spelling "Nestlé Chocolate" were embossed on the wrapper. The small print read: "Product of Switzerland; imported to Great Britain under authority of Confections Importers, Inc." Of course, every cheap counterfeit made the same claim. But the quality of the embossing made me suspect these might be the genuine article.

I stared at the hand holding the chocolate bar. My hand, dotted with liver spots, flesh loosening into papery folds, the hand of a sixty-eight-year-old man who maybe had no business doing all this anymore. A bully's hand?

I checked behind me to make certain I was absolutely alone. Then I stuffed four of the chocolate bars into the pockets hidden inside my Good Humor Man vest. Not for me. For my father. Nearly a hundred years old, warehoused in a giant nursing home, with hardly a memory left... and the only thing he pleads for anymore from me is sweets.

So who's worse? Mitch, the overzealous soldier? Or me... the hypocrite, the physician who saw the dangers in this program years ago, but never spoke up because he was present at the creation, because he's as implicated as any man alive?

My eyes sting now as we hurry back toward the surface. The stench of acres of processed cheese, cardboard, plastic liners, and wood combusting smells much like I imagine the odor of burning human flesh would. It must be all the fat within the cheese.

Outside, the late afternoon sun is harsh. I look east, toward the scrub land that covers the underground warehouse. Already, plumes of white smoke escape from buried vents. The van arrives.

"How'd things go underground?" the leader of the San Clemente squads asks Mitch.

My best friend grins. "Smooth as a baby's keister."

"What're you planning on doing with those two characters?" Brad asks, gesturing at the two handcuffed men we've brought up with us.

Mitch bounces the handcuffs' keys in his palm. "Figure I'll chain 'em up to that post over there. We'll radio the cops to come get them. In the meantime —"

He unholsters his dragon, points it at the open box of the delivery truck, and holds the trigger down for five seconds.

"Mitch, what —?" A wind blows sudden, terrible heat into my face. "The truck —" It might not even belong to these two men. It might belong to some total innocent, miles from here, who'd never dream of selling contraband. This is vandalism, pure and simple. I touch my friend's shoulder gingerly, like he's a bomb I need to defuse. "Was that really necessary?"

He whirls on me, his eyes hot as the tip of his flamethrower. "Jesus Christ, Lou. Will you calm down already?" His face softens some, but it retains a veneer of angry incomprehension. "Get a grip on yourself, Doc. Let the fire do your thinking, okay? Works for me."

The truck explodes.

They drop me off four blocks from the post office. Cheese distributions are going on in five locations, so we've split up, hoping to mop it all up before sundown. I take a peek around the corner to see what I'm up against. There are about two dozen of them, gathered around several pallets of cheese in the parking lot of a ramshackle McDonald's building.

A woman is doing the organizing, a formidably stout matron dressed in a flowing orange skirt and blouse. She talks loudly in Spanish and paces between the pallets, kicking a teenaged boy when he doesn't follow her instructions fast enough. She's not just giving the cheese away; she's organized a bartering system. Some bring offerings of clothing, others bring pots or toys or electric fans. She pays for these offerings with cheese, then redistributes the bartered items among members of the crowd.

I take two deep breaths, then step around the corner.

"*Hola!* My name is Dr. Louis Shmalzberg." They stare at me, then stare at my shotgun. "I'm a Good Humor Man, legally deputized in the State of California to confiscate and dispose of contraband foodstuffs. Such as that cheese."

I hear several of them mutter, *"Queso,"* then glance down at the USDA-branded blocks in their hands.

"That's right. *Queso.* That cheese is illegal. It's no good for you. Bad for your health. There is other cheese, other *queso,* the kind that you can buy at the store, which *is* good for you. This cheese that you have here, it's old, it's very bad. That's why it's illegal." I gesture toward a pile of discarded cardboard cases. "I must ask you to place your bad cheese on that pile of trash."

They look at me with silent hostility so electric that I'm actually relieved Mitch made me take this gun. None of them move toward the pile. The matron in the bright orange outfit seems to be in charge here, so I walk toward her, taking care to point the barrel of the shotgun at the ground.

"*Señora.* Please. Be the first to put away this bad, illegal food."

We lock eyes. The fierceness, the stubbornness in her face reminds me of my mother's mother, who escaped from Communist Romania as a girl and forever afterward had an uneasy relationship with authority. "Throw the *quesos* on the pile of trash there."

She curses me beneath her breath. But she does as I tell her. After all, I'm holding the gun. She doesn't respect *me.* She respects the gun. I'm merely its bearer. I'm Cortez, stealing Aztec gold. A conqueror. An invader.

Now that she's acceded to my authority, the others should follow suit without much fuss. "Come on now," I say, wishing I could remember some of my high school Spanish. *"Rápido."*

The older ones drop their illicit treasure onto the pile, their mouths compressed into thin, bitter lines. The younger ones, wanting to retain some scrap of self-regard, stay farther back and toss the blocks so that they land near my feet.

I begin to breathe more easily. I'm going to get out of this all right. It's just another roundup. Just another day's work for this part-time Good Humor Man.

There's just one cheese-holder left. Standing beneath the tilted

Golden Arches, a small man, can't be taller than five-two, but with broad shoulders, a laborer's shoulders. Probably over sixty, like me. He clutches his five-pound block of cheese tightly, like it's his most beloved child.

"Sir, please place your cheese on the pile."

He doesn't move. His thick fingers tighten around the cheese.

I curse under my breath. I take a step closer to him, gesturing with the muzzle of the gun. *Damn him* — it had been going so smoothly. I feel the sweat begin to trickle down my sides again.

I try to make my voice as hard and cold as the gun I've been given. "Put the cheese on the pile. I won't repeat myself again. Do it. *Now.*"

It's not that he doesn't understand. He understands — even if Spanish is his only language, he knows exactly what I'm saying.

He digs his fingers beneath the lip of the cardboard carton and tears the top off. The block of cheese, a quarter of a century old, glistens in its transparent plastic inner lining. What is he doing? Placing the package against his mouth — is he kissing it? No. He rips the plastic open with his teeth. I hear the crowd gasp like a single organism. He opens his mouth wide, wider —

And takes a gigantic bite of cheese.

Oh no. No. Everything's falling apart. "Don't do that! Consuming contraband substances is a direct violation of the California Health Code —"

His only answer is to take a second, more voracious bite.

"Sir —!"

I'm losing it. The whole situation is slipping through my shaky fingers, like I'm a fucking amateur. What would Mitch do? He'd bash in this joker's cheese-eating face. But I can't do it.

"Stop! Stop eating it! Spit out that contraband *immediately!*"

The matron in the orange outfit starts laughing. A nasty sound, like the braying of a donkey. It frees the others to begin laughing. A couple of the younger ones take tentative steps toward the pile of cheese, testing me, smirks spreading on their brown faces.

The galloping gourmet beneath the Golden Arches plays to his adoring audience. His movements become theatrical, the grand gestures of a circus ringmaster. He takes his biggest bite yet.

And chokes on it.

His eyes go wide, first with surprise, then with panic. His jaw drops open. He forgets about the cheese, dropping it as his hands reach for his own clogged throat.

My long-ago training in emergency first aid warns me not to interfere with a choking victim if he is able to utter a sound. So I hang back, waiting. I can't help feeling a small surge of satisfaction that this man's antics have led to this.

But he doesn't make a sound. He's suffocating.

Shit.

Old reflex kicks in. I haven't had to perform a Heimlich maneuver in ages. Discarding the shotgun, I knot my fingers together near the pit of his stomach and yank, hoping I'll see a yellow wad shoot out his mouth. No go. *No va.* I plant my feet better, square my shoulders, and pull again. Still nothing.

Damn that cheese! Pull! Nothing. Pull again! The cheese laughs at me... my heart is beating too fast. One. More. *Time!*

Failed... it's not coming out. I'm too weak. Too old.

No. Can't think that way. Been a doctor for, what now, forty-three years? No fucking hunk of cheese is going to beat *me*. Lay him down on the ground. His face looks like a radish. I tilt his head back. A simple change of angle might be enough to partially open his windpipe. I lower my ear to his mouth, praying that I'll sense a gurgle of air.

Nothing. I have to put my fingers in his mouth, see if I can grab hold of the mass. Good way to get a finger or two bitten off. His eyes are still open. I hope he understands.

"I'm going to put my fingers in your mouth, try to get that blockage out. I'm a doctor. Don't bite me, okay? Do you understand?"

His eyes flicker, turn up in his head, then close. He's out. Great. Now I'll have his automatic reflexes to deal with. A cool desert wind blows grit into my eyes. I pull his jaw down, stick my fingers into his mouth. He's missing most of his upper teeth on the left side; I try to stay to the left as I probe the upper reaches of his throat. There. I feel it. A claylike lump blocking the passageway. Nothing to grab hold of. Squishy. Slippery. There! I've got it! Gently, gently pull it out. Slowly —

I feel my fingerhold tear away. I remove a piece of mucous-covered cheese the size of a squished marble. A piece the size of a plum remains in his throat.

I have to cut a hole in his windpipe, a hole below the cheese. An emergency tracheotomy. I did one on a mannequin once. Almost fifty years ago.

I grab for my bag, rip it open. My supplies spill out. A scalpel, a knife — didn't I pack one?

It's all useless. Just purgatives. A few bandages and antiseptic lotions. Not even a pen knife.

I stare into the faces surrounding me. "I need a knife. I'm a doctor. A *médico*. I need to make a hole in this man's throat so he can breathe. Can any of you give me a knife?"

They don't understand. Knife — what's the Spanish word for knife? No time for this. I grab my radio from its holster. Only now I notice the stains near its base. Battery leakage stains. Dead. The damn thing is dead.

"Mitch!" I scream in the direction of the caves, the last direction I remember them heading in. "I've got a man down! I need a knife!" My voice, thin and hoarse, bounds back to me from the derelict McDonald's. "A knife! Mitch! Brad! *Mitch!*"

Something glints near my left knee. A pen. A chrome-plated Cross pen. I'd forgotten it was in my bag.

I straddle the unconscious man's chest. This will be clumsy, brutal, and messy. The flesh of his neck is loose and wrinkled. Pushing the pen through it is like pushing a broken needle through leather.

I'm rewarded with a sudden spurt of blood. Someone to the right of me screams. The bleeding is worse than I'd anticipated. I reach for where my cloth bandages are spilled on the ground.

The matron grabs my arm.

"Let go! I need to staunch the bleeding —"

Others in the crowd move in. The sight of blood has freed them. Freed them to tear into me. I shake my arm loose. They're on me, four of them, trying to pull me off him.

"You don't understand — I'm a doctor — I need to *save him* —"

The first blow skips off my shoulder blade. The second lands square. I think my nose is broken. I try covering my face.

Boot in my ribs. A young man's picked up the shotgun. He's holding it by the barrel, like a baseball bat. Winding up like a major-league hitter. Emily, it'll be soon now...

Aahhh! My *ears!* A shotgun blast. From behind me.

"— *off* him! You fuckers get off him, or the next shell goes between your goddamn eyes!"

Mitch. He's here. The angry faces scatter. I see the fading sun again, over the Arches. Someone hoists me off the ground. Brad. My patient is still bleeding from the hole I made in his throat. I see his chest move up and down, lungs pumping air. At least I accomplished that much.

Brad gently but insistently pulls me away from him. "Brad, let go. He'll bleed to death. Let me finish —"

A man from the San Clemente squad turns his dragon on the pile of cheese. "I've got to finish. Mitch, make him let me go —"

Mitch responds by grabbing my legs. "Lou, you're out of your head." The two of them hoist me like a piece of lumber. "Let's get him back to the van, pronto."

My words rise from the bottom of the ocean. "... but... but he'll bleed to death —"

"Who? The brownie? Fuck him. Fuck all those miserable cocksuckers. We did what we came to do. Now we're getting the hell out."

It's all out of my hands.

Upside down, the Golden Arches look like a pair of teats. They bob up and down, just out of reach, the breasts of a golden woman. A giant maiden who will suckle me on nourishing, fattening milk, if only I'd let her.

The candy bars I stole for my father, crushed, broken, slide out of my vest pockets. I feel them slither down my torso and watch them fall into the street. I'm sorry, Dad. You won't get your goodies. I'm sorry. Even though you were an absentee husband, an absentee father, always chasing after your latest celebrity client, I still love you. Everybody deserves a little pleasure. Even Dr. Walter Shmalzberg — the liposuctionist who killed Elvis Presley....

CHAPTER 2

I'm being carried... haven't been carried since I was a little boy... this doesn't feel real, almost like a session of *Realité Magique*...

I'm with my wife. Emily and I just made love. She caresses my face with her fingertips, the way she used to. Before she died. I don't want to think about the helmet or the migraine headache that will be coming soon. I don't want to think about what I might be doing to my brain. Emily is here now, and she's stroking my face.

I'm in my examination room at the West Hollywood clinic. My plastic surgery practice gone, I put in a few shifts a week here as a general practitioner to make my rent. This room stinks of mold. The wood paneling has warped and pulled away from the wall, a result of a ceiling leak that's never been fixed. The intercom buzzes incessantly. I was supposed to see my first patient an hour ago. But I've got better things to do.

Emily and I have just finished breakfast. We're on the veranda of the Monteverde Inn, enjoying the spectacular scenery of Costa Rica's Central Valley, sipping the most delicious cups of coffee we've ever tasted. The mold scent is distracting, but a bit of extra concentration and it's obliterated by the aroma of brewing coffee. The space between my eyes throbs. But this is worth it.

Her breasts are as full and lush as the fruits of the tropics, radiating health and wholesomeness. No disease could ever maim such radiant globes —

"Doc?"

The mold smell returns. I'm back in the examining room. Humiliation and fright clear my head like a bucket full of ice water. I yank the RM helmet from my skull, turning to see who's come into the room.

It's Mitch Reynolds, a sportsman who wrenched his knee. I've been giving him weekly shots of cortisone. "Doc? I'm sorry to, uh, disturb you. But I've got this business interview I can't be late for, and those shots you give me are all that've been keeping me walking..."

He stares at the RM helmet, illegally reconfigured, hanging from my hand. He's no babe in the woods; he knows what it is. His eyes are equally surprised and pitying. The pity makes the rush of nausea worse than it normally would be. "That's one of them *Realité Magique* gizmos, huh?"

I nod, feeling the room begin to polka.

"Uh, Doc," he says, slowly, "I don't mean to tell you your business or anything, but that can fuck you up pretty bad —"

I stumble past him and vomit into the sink.

"Lou, you can do it. Knock 'em dead, pal. You're about to kick the Good Humor Man movement in California into high gear."

Mitch follows me as I enter the State Capitol chambers and await my introduction. The confidence in Mitch's voice helps dispel some of my stage fright. Some, not all.

"Honorable ladies and gentlemen of the legislature. My name is Dr. Louis Shmalzberg. I work as a doctor of general medicine in a low-income neighborhood of West Hollywood." I grip the lectern tightly, trying to keep my legs from shaking — I feel thrilled, empowered, more whole than anytime since Emily died. "Every day, I treat dozens of patients hobbled by obesity and the maladies it causes: pulmonary heart disease, cancer, diabetes, arthritis, asthma, and spinal strain. Every day, the State of California, now running annual deficits in the tens of billions, spends millions of dollars it doesn't have treating these diseases. Diseases caused by the endless rivers of processed sugars and hydrogenated fats we all consume.

"What can be done? Decades of public health education campaigns have failed. As a nation, we get fatter and sicker — and poorer — every year. Our bodies, trained by thousands of years of scarcity, are hooked on cheap, ubiquitous, empty calories. When citizens are unable to stop harming themselves, government has a moral duty to step in. Opium was once legal, readily available, and almost universally abused. Society made the choice that it not remain that way. We as a society can make the same choice regarding anti-nutritious, high-calorie foods."

I have the attention of every lawmaker in earshot. GD2, the second Great Depression, has frightened and demoralized them, bled California's business community and government white. They're eating from the palm of my hand. "I've heard many political leaders state that California can't afford another experiment in Prohibition. That police forces, already strapped by shrinking tax bases, don't have the resources to enforce a ban on obesity-generating foods. This is not a burden that government needs to take on alone. Just as the Minutemen rose from the citizenry to secure American independence, so today a legion of volunteers stand ready to secure our independence from the slavery of obesity."

Time to close the sale. "Deputize the men and women of the Good Humor Man movement, just as the lawmakers of Massachusetts and New York did three months ago. Let us make California strong again, both physically and fiscally. Let us make our home once more the Golden State, not the state of the Golden Arches."

Mitch is beaming. The bill will pass. We're in.

I wake up on a familiar-feeling sofa. It's the sofa in my study. I'm home.

I feel a hand on my shoulder. Am I still inside a dream?

"You look like crap," Mitch says. "How do you feel?"

"Like... crap."

"You've got visitors."

"Who...?"

"Group of school kids from Jerry Brown Elementary. They're here for their nutrition history lesson."

My appointment for this semester. I'd completely forgotten. "Damn... I'd hate to disappoint... Karen Dissel."

Mitch smiles. "Yeah, I'll bet you would. She's been carrying a torch for you the size of the Statue of Liberty's, and everybody in town knows it. She's a little young for you, but that's all right, you old dog. Long past time you got saddled back up again. Don't worry — that busted nose gives you character."

I close my eyes and see Karen Dissel's face, cheekbones protruding like the womanly breasts she never developed. Once upon a time, when I was still a plastic surgeon, her appearance was a look I gladly accepted tens of thousands of dollars to sculpt on a patient's face. But now her gauntness makes me shiver. Karen looks like a tribeswoman from an old news show about an Ethiopian famine, only she's the victim of a famine we've willingly brought on ourselves. A thirty-six-year-old woman dwelling inside a prepubescent body... I wonder if she's ever menstruated. I wonder if she suffers at all from the thought she'll never bear a child.

"Mitch... I'm in no shape to go in front of those kids. Could you... do it for me, this one time? Do you know how to work the vid-9 unit?"

"That old contraption? Yeah, I guess I can figure it out. Sure, Lou. I'll fill in for you, don't you worry none. Get some more rest. You've earned it."

I listen in as Mitch introduces himself to the class in the meeting room next to my study, answers a few questions about being a Good Humor Man, and then starts the vid-9 program. It's sponsored by the MannaSantos Corporation, and it's meant to be a sort of "Scared Thin" for the under-ten set. I'm rather fond of the ludicrous title: *Beware the Fat Monster!*

"In the days before your parents were born, the people of the rest of the world looked at America and laughed at 'The Land of the Fat'..."

MannaSantos's image-archaeologists did one hell of a job. Somehow they got their hands on a print of a nearly fifty-year-old German porno film which was marketed to European fat fetishists. Essentially a home movie of suburban American life, circa 1990, it features three-hundred-pound women wearing tank-tops and bright pink polyester shorts, exiting a neon-lit Krispy Kreme Doughnuts shop, their arms filled with bags of fried, sugar-coated dough. The filmmakers always shot them from behind, framing the view so that the screen overflows with jiggling buttock flesh.

"America, land of the free and home of the brave, was suffocating

beneath a sea of ugly, unhealthy fat. Something had to be done. Just
as they had so many times before in the history of our country, hopeful
Americans turned to science for an answer —"

Here comes the bullshit. MannaSantos and the other chemical
companies didn't create genetically modified foods in response to
some obesity crisis. They created them to more effectively market
their own proprietary brands of herbicides and pesticides. They created them because they thought shoppers would pay more for bananas
that could sit on supermarket shelves for months without rotting.

Bread basket of the world... we thought we'd always keep that
title, that it was our birthright. But we somehow forgot that the customer gets a vote, too. People around the world revolted against
being forced to consume what they called "Frankenfoods." Punishing
tariffs spiraled into trade wars, which spiraled into the Second Great
Depression, the worst years of my life. If it hadn't been for the treasure my father gave me, his vacuum-packed legacy, I'd have lost this
house, this clinic. And these children wouldn't be sitting here today,
absorbing these half-truths under my roof.

I want to tell them the truth, *my* truth. I want to tell them that they
are the first generation in American history who will be shorter than
their mothers and fathers. I want to feed them the whole milk and
whole cheese and natural fats their growing brains and bodies need.

How did I get sucked in? Why did I let myself be seduced?

As if it can read my mind, the vid-9 program offers an answer. It's
reached the part about Hud Walterson. The very first Good Humor
Man. The founder of my guild.

I've seen this program often enough to have memorized every
frame. At the beginning of the public part of his story, Hud was the
reluctant owner of nearly a thousand pounds of flesh, trapped in his
own bed by immobilizing weight. He'd been an overweight child, his
widowed mother's only happiness, and by the time he'd turned thirty,
his mother and aunts had fed him to the point where he weighed an
estimated nine hundred pounds.

Hud's rescuers were a wealthy Beverly Hills dietician, whom
my father knew socially, and the dietician's partner, a washed-up
Hollywood starlet who had gained new fame following her own dra-

matic weight loss under the dietician's care. Emily and I saw Hud's extrication from his bedroom (paramedics used a forklift), televised live on *The Geraldo Rivera Show*. Video simulcasts over the internet documented his stomach-stapling surgery, his various lipectomies, and the experimental drug treatments.

As a TV stunt, his Beverly Hills handlers arranged for Hud to burn the small mountain of junk food his relatives had stockpiled during his years trapped in his former home. Hud insisted that the producers let him carry out the burning with a military flamethrower. I see him again, still mountainously impressive at just over five hundred pounds, his face flushed with passion, holding the nozzle of his flamethrower in both hands like a priest preparing to drive out the Devil. America witnessed the birth of a new hero when Hud waded into the pile of snack cakes, corn chips, candy bars, and chocolate bunnies, his eyes flashing with an almost-palpable hatred as he incinerated his former treats.

Hud Walterson was the right man with the right gimmick at exactly the right time. The country was desperate for a new craze, anything to divert attention from the international economic meltdown. The national mood was ripe for a big, fat scapegoat. And Hud Walterson, making as many as five or six paid appearances a week to burn up heaps of junk food, pointed his accusing finger at a juicy one – the notoriously gluttonous eating habits of the average American, bankrupting the American health system with a plague of cardiovascular disease, joint degeneration, and cancer.

Emily and I saw Hud in person, at an event sponsored by a Los Angeles chain of body toning spas. She had recently been diagnosed with breast cancer; I hoped that taking her to this presumably goofy event would help lift her spirits. Hud was down to three hundred pounds then, a third of his peak weight. The hundreds of dollars' worth of snack foods he was to burn had been donated by local grocery stores; I remember thinking how bizarre that was. Hud Walterson attacked that food, incinerated it with the frightening, total conviction of a Crusader leading the charge to recapture the Holy Land from the infidels.

Emily remarked that if she could manage to fight her disease with just half of Hud's emotional dedication, the cancer would shrivel inside her like a box of MoonPies bathed in napalm.

Things began going downhill for Hud not long after we saw him, however. His body betrayed him; it fought to regain the pounds he'd shed, lowering its metabolism and increasing its production of insulin. With every pound he regained, he lost another paid endorsement, another donation of snack foods to burn. But having captured the national spotlight, he refused to let it go. Following in the hallowed footsteps of Bonnie and Clyde and Billy the Kid, Hud Walterson became an outlaw.

Snack food warehouses in California and Nevada burned to the ground. An ice cream factory in Seattle lit the night. Neighbors of the destroyed building swore that just as the fire started they'd heard a tinny calliope playing children's songs. Urban legends quickly sprang up — Hud Walterson had hijacked an ice cream truck in Las Vegas to use as his getaway car; Hud was being secretly financed by Jane Fonda and the Turner media empire; he'd bought a whole fleet of second-hand ice cream trucks to use on missions; Hud and his gang would not rest until all of America had been purged of junk food.

Hud returned to the big time just three weeks before Emily died. I was with her in her hospital room when accounts of his latest provocation exploded onto all the national news channels. A man with a video camera had caught Hud in the act at a McDonald's in Salinas. Hud was back up over the five-hundred-pound mark; his jowly face was tired and strained as he ordered employees and patrons out of the restaurant. In true Robin Hood fashion, he tossed a five dollar bill to every patron he'd deprived of a meal. He no longer had his famous flamethrower; instead, he dragged two huge gasoline cans around the restaurant, splashing the liquid on grills, deep fryers, cash registers, and rows of cheeseburgers pre-assembled for the lunch hour. Emily and I saw the videotaped fire replayed on dozens of newscasts during the next two days, endlessly repeated on CNN and Fox News. The hypnotic images temporarily distracted us from what lay ahead for us.

That incident was the spark that ignited dozens of copycat arsons around the nation. By that time I wasn't paying attention. Emily was going very quickly. Her double mastectomy had failed to halt the advance of the cancer. Chemotherapy and radiation treatments provided only temporary roadblocks. I was a physician. But I was unable to do a thing to save my own wife. Three months later, the future we'd planned for and everything I'd loved about my life were buried along with her.

Five months after she died, the law finally caught up with Hud Walterson. And I was there in person, just as I had been at his start. It was around seven in the evening. I was walking back to the garage where I'd parked my car, following a shift at the McHardy Clinic in West Hollywood. I remember very little about that time. I sleepwalked through most of my shifts, writing basic prescriptions for the flu, diabetes, and hypertension, hazily witnessing how chronic neglect and poor habits led to crippling chronic disease.

I was walking through a shabby, garbage-strewn neighborhood when I saw that the street had been blocked off by police cruisers. A large crowd of neighborhood residents, pushed back from orange barricades by police, had surrounded a candied popcorn factory. Media vehicles were just beginning to pull up, large vans topped with telescoping satellite antennae, magic wands pointed at the collective subconscious of an audience of billions.

I asked a young black woman what was going on. "They got him trapped inside," she said. "The Good Humor Man."

"Who?"

She sighed impatiently. "You know. The guy who burns up junk food. Hud Walterson."

It was the first time I'd ever heard him called that. I joined the crowd and waited for things to happen. Negotiations were not going well. Every few minutes a police captain with a bullhorn repeated his demands that Hud come out; the captain promised Hud would not be harmed. The crowd eagerly scanned the factory's windows, hoping for just a glimpse of the gargantuan outlaw. The entire cordoned-off area took on a carnival air.

The SWAT team fired tear-gas canisters through the factory's windows at nine o'clock. The crowd tensed as we heard the soft *chuffs* of the canisters being fired, the tinkling crashes of the windows breaking. Something would happen now — Hud and his followers would appear on the roof; they would rain flaming candied popcorn down on the heads of the police before escaping in a helicopter playing calliope music...

Black smoke billowed through the broken windows. The smoke had a strangely sweet, nauseating odor, like burning motor oil mixed with caramelizing maple syrup. The SWAT team used battering rams to break down the doors, but the fire quickly grew too intense for them. Fire trucks arrived quickly. Soon dozens of hoses were spraying the building down, but the inferno refused to be quenched. We waited for Hud to appear. Surely he would find a way to escape. All around me, people gulped their cheap wine and chewed their greasy, fried snacks while they watched the doors.

Suddenly, all eyes (and video cameras) darted to a large window on the third floor. He was there, flames backlighting his mountainous silhouette. Would he try to climb out? Would he jump? He didn't move, even as the fire came closer. It was inhuman, that he could stand so stock-still. He stared down at us, a weird look of triumph on his face, as if he'd transcended all failures, all pain. Then there was a sound of beams breaking. He looked up at the roof that was poised to collapse. When he looked down at us again, the triumph in his face was gone, replaced by a despair that chilled me.

The roof fell. A collective gasp went up from the crowd. Hud wouldn't be coming out. This time, he was burning with the hated snack foods. We looked at the flames, and then we looked at each other. I had the eerie sense of the crowd seeing itself, truly seeing itself for the first time. More than half of them held bags of potato chips or fried pork cracklings in their crumb-coated hands. Next to me, the young woman I'd spoken to earlier shriveled under accusatory gazes — her mouth was stuffed full of candied popcorn, the same brand that had been packaged at the burning factory.

At first, she seemed embarrassed and afraid. But then her eyes acquired a new determination, a fiery conviction that I'd seen before, in Hud Walterson's eyes. She spat out her mouthful of candied popcorn, then threw the box on the ground and trampled it. She stomped on the box, each leap more furious than the last.

Her gesture spread like wildfire through the crowd. Soon dozens of people were throwing down their bags of fattening snacks, spilling high-calorie beers into the gutters, stomping on chips and pies and pork cracklings until the crumbs were ground into the filthy asphalt. Even though I had no junk food of my own to destroy, I joined in the destruction, caught up in the communal electricity, feeling my blood run through my veins for the first time since Emily had died.

And a hundred TV cameras captured our savage celebration of Hud's mission, our annihilation of our artery-clogging enemy. Captured it and broadcast it to a nation of people hungry for an easy victory, for a foe they could smear into the dirt. Hungry for something to set fire to.

I hear the children clapping in my meeting room. According to the story they've just seen, poor Hud Walterson won a posthumous victory far larger than any he'd ever achieved in life. A happy ending for us all. The makers of this little fat-umentary, as if abruptly realizing that they've spent too much time obsessing on Hud Walterson's martyrdom, manage to squeeze the following quarter-century into less than four minutes. The establishment of hundreds of local Good Humor Men chapters, officially sanctioned by state governments eager to rein in health care spending; the chaotic mass layoffs that followed the breakup of most multinational corporations during the trade wars... All of this races across the screen as quickly as a commercial for Leanie-Lean meats.

Now the lumbering fatties from the first segment return, only this time they're greeted by smiling cartoon MannaSantos scientists carrying platters of fresh fruits and vegetables. Eating this bounty, the fatties magically morph into glowing, toothpick-thin demigods. As the music swells, all the children applaud again, even louder than before.

"So never forget — you ARE what you EAT! The Fat Monster can't hurt you unless you INVITE him into your mouth. And avoiding the Fat Monster has never been easier, thanks to the MannaSantos family of fine food products — Lep-Tone fruits and vegetables, Leanie-Lean meat products, and the NEW Metaboloft line of fresh corn, corn sweeteners, corn starch, and other corn derivatives."

The program's over. Normally, this would be the time for my grand finale, my unveiling of my "show-and-tell," a preserved example of the program's archaic societal nemesis, my method of permanently imprinting the children's impressionable minds with an enduring horror of the Fat Monster.

But *I've* been the monster. How could I have done that thing, so many, many times? Make children scream at the sight of what is more precious to me than anything else left in this world?

I won't do it. Not ever again. I'd rather rip out my own bowels and eat them in front of those kids, if traumatizing them is so imperative. How could I have blinded myself so completely? How could I have let myself become something I should have despised, some foul-smelling bit of excrement I'd scrape off the bottom of my shoe?

"Lou? I need to finish up the class. Where's the jars of fat?"

It's Mitch. His request ignites a blush that burns my whole body. I shake my head with all the force I can muster.

"C'mon, Lou, the jars of human fat. I want to knock those kids dead, just like you always do. Where are they?"

I force myself into a sitting position. The room swims around me. "No," I say. "You can't... I won't let you touch them..."

"What's the matter with you? All I wanna do is the same thing you've always done —"

"No! It's — it's *obscene!* A desecration of her memory!"

"What are you talking about? Are you out of your head, Lou? Pipe down, the kids'll hear you —"

"The whole, the whole *world* should hear me! Should hear me *damn* myself!"

Mitch grabs my shoulders and forces me back into a prone position on the couch. "Yeah, you're out of your head, all right," he says. "Damn. I knew I shouldn't have let them discharge you so fast. They patch you up and shove you out the front door, bad as it was in the Army —"

"Get them *out* of here!" I scream. "The children! Karen Dissel! I won't have them absorbing any more poison in my house!"

"Okay, okay, I'll clear 'em all out. Then you and I are going back to the hospital, pal —"

"I don't need to be in a hospital! I need to be in the innermost circle of Hell! Just — just let me be, Mitch!"

"Lou —!"

He tries grabbing me again, but I pull away. "Just, just leave me alone, Mitch. Just *go*. I'm all right. I... I need some time. By myself." I stare into his worried face. "Really, I'm okay, Mitch. But I need to think. Everything that's happened recently... I have to sort things through. As my best friend, can't you give me that? Just a few hours to think?"

He chews his lower lip, then nods his head. "All right, Lou. I'll leave you alone awhile. But I'm coming back later to check up on you. Whether you like it or not. Get me?"

I nod. "Thanks, Mitch."

I hear him usher the school group out, then he closes my front door behind him. I want to look at them again... the jars of human fat I'd refused to let Mitch touch. I need to beg Emily's forgiveness.

I sit up again, more slowly this time. There's a bandage on my nose. I touch it, lightly. *Owww*... no need to try *that* again anytime soon. My nose isn't the only thing that smarts. I discover two large bruises, one on my right hip and the other on my lower rib cage. There's a dull throbbing at the back of my skull. The room goes out of focus.

I wait for the colors behind my eyes to clear, then try to stand. I fall back onto the couch. I'm a doctor; I should give myself hell for trying to stand so quickly.

I'm a doctor. Right. I'm a healer, and I killed a man today. Not by plunging a pen into his neck. No, that was just the proximate cause. I killed that man twenty-five years ago, the day I convinced the California Legislature to deputize the Good Humor Men.

I see the Mexican's face again, his eyes rolling up in his head, his broad, tanned face turning red as a ripe tomato. I see Emily's face, impatient for the local anesthetic to kick in, eager for the touch of my cannula, my magic wand. And then, suddenly, I understand.

That night in Los Angeles, the night Hud Walterson burned to death... maybe it wasn't junk food I was stomping into the asphalt. Maybe it was *cancer*. Maybe it was cancer I was trampling, and guilt.

My God. I've never let myself make this connection before. Of course. Everywhere, in the journals, in the newspapers, there were stories about the correlation between significant weight gain and various types of cancer.

Our private game. Emily's serial weight-gain, followed by tender, erotic sessions of liposuction. It was a game that evolved over time, that we groped toward and embraced in a mostly wordless fashion. It wasn't something I made her do. But she helped invent the game and eagerly surrendered her body to it primarily for my pleasure.

I wasn't willing to smash myself into the concrete. So I took out my vengeance on the implements some part of me believed I'd used to kill my wife. And I've continued on my path of vengeance for the last twenty-five years. Trying again and again to slay the dragon, but never getting it right. Because the dragon I was really trying to slay was *me*.

Me.

My front doorbell buzzes. It's probably Brad or one of the other squad members, not realizing I've just pleaded with Mitch for some privacy.

It buzzes a second time. I wait for them to go away. They don't. Another buzzing, followed by a prolonged knocking. I hear footsteps retreating down my driveway, but just as I'm on the verge of relaxing, the knocking begins anew, this time at my kitchen door out back.

Crap. I'll need to tell them to go away myself. I make another attempt to stand. This time, I stay up. The nausea's still there, but not as bad. I slowly walk to the kitchen, steadying myself against the walls, irritation building with every difficult step.

I peer through my back door's spy glass, stealing myself to give Brad or whomever a radioactive piece of my mind. My persistent visitor is a dark-skinned man, and a stranger to me. I'm surprised, and that surprise reminds me how much America and Southern California have changed since I was young. He's dressed in a conservative dark gray suit, wearing some kind of government ID badge, which he holds up to the spy glass. Turning away from the door now would be too rude, even given my condition.

I open the door partway. "Yes? May I help you?"

His intelligent, intense blue eyes immediately connect with mine. His half-smile is neither kindly nor antagonistic, but somehow detached, and a bit superior. First impression: I don't care for this young man.

"I am seeking Dr. Louis Shmalzberg. Would you be he?"

His accent lets me place him. He's Indian, or from one of the nations of the Indian subcontinent. I haven't had the opportunity to speak with many Indians these last twenty-five years. We haven't been a land of immigrants, or a land friendly to visitors, since before GD2.

"I'm Dr. Shmalzberg," I answer cautiously. "What can I do for you? I'm afraid this isn't a good time —"

"I am Ravi Varuna Muthukrishnan, from the United States Department of Agriculture. My office is the Agricultural Research Section of the Food and Nutrition Service." He stiffly sticks out his hand. Just as mechanically, I shake it. "I have traveled all the way from Alexandria, Virginia, to see you, Dr. Shmalzberg. I believe you have an artifact in your possession which my office would be most interested in examining, and perhaps acquiring."

"An artifact?" My heart jumps — my initial, absurdly paranoid thought is that he's referring to those Nestlé chocolate bars I pilfered during the first of yesterday's raids, the ones I lost in Mex-Town. "I'm sorry, I have no idea what you're referring to —"

He smiles a cool smile. "Of course." He glances into my kitchen. "Is there somewhere private where we may talk? I waited until after your visitors had left."

"Look, Mr. Muthnoo —"

"Muthukrishnan."

"I'm not well. I, uh, I was in a car accident yesterday. Got pretty badly banged up. Can't you come back another day?"

His smile loses some of its forced wattage. "I am afraid that I am not at liberty to wait very long. My staff and I are working on multiple projects during our stay in California. The project which concerns you, it is of a highly speculative nature, but it also has potential national security implications of the greatest magnitude. If you would telephone me as soon as you are feeling somewhat better —"

"I could do that."

"We are staying at the Hotel Nixon, in San Clemente." He removes a business card from his breast pocket and writes a telephone number and room number on the back. "Can I expect a call from you later this evening?"

I don't like being pressured, not even for "potential national security implications of the greatest magnitude" — he's from the goddamn

Department of *Agriculture,* so how vital can this be? "I truly doubt that. Look, I can hardly stay on my feet right now. I'll get back to you when I can —"

"Please do so as soon as possible." He hands me the card. "This is a matter of great importance, Dr. Shmalzberg. Both to your government, and to you, personally. You see, I am not the only party who is seeking this artifact. And I believe you will find the others to be much less polite than I am."

"If you would just tell me what it is you're looking for, I might be more helpful."

He glances over his shoulder, taking in the hedges and trees which surround my patio and garden. "I'm not at liberty to discuss specifics in an unsecured area such as this. We must follow proper protocols. I will leave you to your rest. But I trust I will be hearing from you soon, Dr. Shmalzberg?"

Dizziness assaults me like a swarm of gnats. I manage a weak nod, then close the door.

I sink into one of the chairs at my kitchen table. What on earth could the Department of Agriculture want with me? And who's to say this Muthukrishnan fellow is even *from* the Department of Agriculture? Phony business cards are easy to come by. Judging from his accent, he's not native-born, and America's had a strict anti-immigration policy since the time this snot-nose was in diapers.

What could he be after? An artifact... What do I own that could be called an artifact? My Sony CD player, circa 2002? I suppose *I* could qualify as an artifact, being an ex-practitioner of an extinct medical art.

I don't want to think about it, but the thought refuses to go away. There's only one "artifact" I ever owned that was really worth the title. My father's bequest to me. The Elvis (or, as I named it when I was little, "Elvis-in-a-Jar"). And if that's what Muthukrishnan's after, he's shit-out-of-luck; I haven't had the Elvis in my possession in twenty-seven years. I sold it back to its place of origin. In return for a truckload of cash, most used to finance Emily's cancer treatments, I promised never to reveal that it had ever existed. They didn't tell me what they planned to do with it. In all likelihood it's been locked away in a bomb-proof vault, more secure than the Dead Sea Scrolls. Hidden away from America's memory forever.

I stumble into my study, managing to make it to my desk. I pull my keys from my pocket and open the credenza cabinet. And there they are, the two glass cylinders, each filled with between four and six pounds of human fat, stabilized by xenon gas. Mottled, yellow, oily lipid tissues; to an unfamiliar observer, they'd look somewhat like tubfuls of margarine, partially melted in the sun. In some spots, the yellow fat is stained pink by the blood that was unavoidably extracted along with the lipid tissues. Fat and blood, all of it protected from the corrupting air, preserved forever, so long as I keep it free of ultraviolet rays and heat.

Those two cylinders are why the school board relies on me for health education. No one else can show the children what I can. I wasn't always a humble General Practitioner. I'm a rare bird. My specialty, like my father's before me, was liposculpture, also known as body sculpting, or liposuction: the surgical extraction of excess fatty tissues.

I place the two cylinders on my desk, handling them as gently as I would the golden eggs of a phoenix. And when I look at them, my heart soars higher than any fantastical bird of legend. The precious tissues preserved inside are all I have left of my Emily.

I spread my trembling arms around them and lay my bruised cheek on my desk, then pull the cylinders tightly against my skull.

Emily. I'm so sorry. I'm so sorry.

I'm so terribly, terribly sorry...

I'm awakened by a rustling outside my window, in the bushes.

I remain very still, listening. There isn't any wind. Maybe I didn't hear it; maybe it was a product of this bump on my head?

No. There it is again. The rustling lasts longer this time. Something is poking into my hedge, crawling beneath my window. Something large.

I feel my palms begin to sweat. It's a Mexican in my bushes, one of the cheese hoarders from Mex-Town, come to avenge the man I killed. Or maybe Muthukrishnan, come to steal the Elvis-in-a-Jar?

Rustling again. I can't take it anymore.

"Is anyone out there?"

I open the window a crack. "Is there *anyone* out there?"

The only way I'll know is to turn on the back floodlights and look out the clinic's back door. At least, sneaking into the kitchen, I'm much steadier than I was a few hours ago. Opening the door, I smell something musky and frightened.

It's a deer. A terribly thin deer, haggard and weak as the two I passed on the road yesterday. It's eating berries off my hedges.

I wait for it to jump away from me and run off. It doesn't. As soon as it sees I don't have any food to offer, it returns to its meal of bush berries.

I sit down on my back steps and watch it eat. While I'm trying to think what I might have in my pantry to feed it, my phone rings.

The machine can answer it. It might be Brad or Mitch. They're the last people on Earth I want to speak with right now. But the voice that leaves a message isn't any voice I was expecting. It's hesitant, befuddled by the series of beeps. My father's voice.

Oh, *hell*. I'm not together enough to deal with him right now. But a nagging sense of filial responsibility makes me pick up the phone.

"— Louie? Louie, are you there? It's late. You should be home. So pick up the phone, Louie, okay? Okay?"

I click off the answering machine. "It's okay, Dad. I'm here."

"Hello? Who is this?"

"It's me, Dad."

"Did I wake you? It's late, right? It's late where you are?"

"It's the same time for me as it is for you." I check my watch. "It's one-thirty in the morning. What are you doing up? Are you all right?"

"I'm not all right, Louie. You have to come get me. They're not doing right by me here."

He almost never complains about the home anymore. Why now? Has his dementia taken a turn for the worse?

"What's the matter, Dad? What's going on?"

"Come get me. Can you come get me, right now?"

"No. Not right now, Dad. You have to tell me what's the matter first."

"What's the matter? What's the matter? They're starving me here, that's what's the matter."

"What?" I hear the deer outside. I feel the weight of hooves walking on my grave.

"I said, they're starving me here. Weren't you listening?"

The food. He's complaining about the food. The most common, natural thing in the world is for rest home patients to complain about their food.

"You don't like the food there? They aren't feeding you enough?"

"No!"

"I could talk to your doctor, get them to put more spices in your food —"

"No! You aren't listening! They feed me plenty. Three, four times a day. Soon as I finish one tray, they got another one waiting for me. But I'm always hungry, Louie. I never used to be hungry all the time like this."

My palms begin sweating again.

"Louie, son, I can see my ribs."

CHAPTER 3

The smell of disinfectant. The smell of old men, moldering in their narrow beds like piles of rags. The smell of my own fear.

Someone's let all the air out of my father. Looking around the room at his ward-mates, either sleeping or fixated on silent vid-9 screens... someone's let the air out of them, too. I'm standing in the middle of a ward of starving men.

A nursing aide enters the room with a stack of fresh sheets. In seconds I've backed her into a corner. "What the hell are you lunatics doing to the men here?"

She drops her sheets. "What —?" She stares up at me with wide, terrified eyes, like *I'm* the lunatic. "Do — doing to them? What do you mean?"

"Don't you have *eyes?* These men — my father — they're wasting away! I demand to see the physician in charge. Immediately!"

"But — but Dr. Abramson is at a conference out of town —"

"I don't care if he's gone to Mars. Get him for me. Or get me whoever's in charge of this chamber of horrors."

I try to get my emotions under control while I wait for the attending physician. Feeding captive old men those goddamn diet foods... it's so perverse and monstrous, I have a hard time believing they've actually done it.

I haven't seen my father in nearly four months. My list of excuses stretches as long as the road between my house and this rest home: I've been too busy; the three-hour round trip is too tiring; seeing my father depresses me; there's nothing I can do for him. About a third of the time, he either thinks I'm his old medical partner, Isadore, or he fails to recognize me at all. He was never that good a father to begin with, and he was an even worse husband to my mother, and he wasn't there for me after Emily died.

All my excuses aren't worth a pile of shit.

My father was always a husky man. In his later years, prior to the onset of his dementia, he caught the national fever for exercise and diet regulation, and he managed to lose much of his spare tire. Yet even four months ago, when I last saw him, he was still a substantial man.

Not now.

I watch his rib cage rise and fall with the regular rhythm of sleep. He never had cheekbones before; the puffy flesh of his face had kept him looking younger than he was, almost boylike. Now he has the craggy cheeks of a mummified ballerina.

Two people advance on me — a uniformed man, presumably a security guard, and a woman, an administrator or head nurse. She's scowling like I've just taken a king-size bite out of her posterior and she's eager to return the favor.

"Can I see your visitor's pass?" the guard asks. I yank the pass out of my pocket. Before I can launch into my tirade, the woman cuts me off. "Sir, if you persist in making wild accusations against my staff, I'll have to ask you to leave. If you'd like to talk calmly about whatever's disturbing you, do so."

"And you are —?"

"I'm Anne Posely, nursing supervisor. I'm in charge while Dr. Abramson is off-campus. May I ask who *you* are?"

"I'm Dr. Louis Shmalzberg. My father is Dr. Walter Shmalzberg. One of your patients."

"I see. May I ask what's gotten you so upset?"

I fight down an impulse to shake her like a rag doll. "Look at him. Just take... a look."

She walks to my father's bedside and picks up his chart. "I see your father has been with us nearly four years now," she says, trying to placate me with a calm, upbeat tone. "According to these notes, he's been doing quite well. He was admitted with a diagnosis of McCrowley's Dementia; there's not much we can do for that, unfortunately. I see that he's suffered from rheumatoid arthritis since he's been here, but he's responded very well to drug therapy, and he hasn't complained of any joint pains for the last six months."

She hangs the chart by its cord on my father's bedpost again. "Overall, Dr. Shmalzberg, aside from the dementia, it appears that your father is in remarkably good health, particularly for a man of his age."

In. Remarkably. Good. Health. I feel a chill at the base of my spine. "Nurse Posely, I don't mean to question your professional judgment; but wouldn't you have to agree that my father is suffering from... clinical *malnutrition?*"

She looks at his chart again. "Hmmm... according to this, he *has* lost some weight over the past few months. But he's still well within the limits of the recommended weight tables for his age and build. In fact, his weight loss should be considered a positive outcome. There'd be much more cause for concern if he'd started gaining —"

I grab the chart from her. "According to this, my father has lost nineteen pounds in the past four months. And in the six months before that, he lost an additional ten. Do you consider that *normal?*"

The security guard steps toward me, but the nurse waves him off. "It's not necessarily *abnormal*. Some long-term-care patients' weights are known to fluctuate. Generally, this isn't a sign of ill health, unless the fluctuation is markedly upward —"

I don't know whether to laugh or scream. "Listen to me. You said 'some' long-term patients' weights fluctuate. What does it mean when *all* of their weights are fluctuating, and all fluctuating *downward?* Check their charts! I know what these men looked like four months ago! Every single one of them is losing body mass at a frightening rate!"

She frowns, finally taking me seriously. "What are you implying, Dr. Shmalzberg?"

"I want to see my father's menu charts. Complete with a list of ingredients used to prepare his foods. And I want to have a look in your kitchen and talk with your food preparation staff."

"May I ask why?"

"It's within my rights to see those things."

"I know it is. But again, I ask why?"

My fingers tighten around my father's chart. *"Why?* You've been pumping my father full of diet foods, that's why. For some reason completely beyond me, you've been lacing your patients' meals with that MannaSantos weight-loss crap."

Her eyes widen behind her glasses. "That's an absurd allegation, Dr. Shmalzberg. Why on earth would we be feeding these men weight-reduction foods, unless they were dangerously overweight to begin with?"

"You tell *me.* Is this Dr. Abramson of yours that eager to free up beds for new patients?"

She gasps. "I have worked with Dr. Abramson for the past eighteen years, and no one — *no one* — is more dedicated to the well-being of these patients than he is. Come with me, Dr. Shmalzberg. I want to set your mind at ease. Let's go take a look at the kitchens."

I spend the next ninety minutes searching for some speck of evidence that my suspicions are true. Nurse Posely takes me to all three of the large, institutional kitchens. She lets me question the cooks and other workers without her being present. I examine the kitchens' menu plans. I search their pantries, refrigerators, and freezers for the MannaSantos-produced foodstuffs I'd been so certain of finding. The head dietician even shows me her food order invoices for the past year.

The only tie to MannaSantos I find is a single order, eleven months old, for a small shipment of Leanie-Lean meats and breakfast products. The red flag I'm searching for just isn't there. No one is hiding anything.

When I return to my father's bedside, he's awake. He tries sitting up in bed, and I help him by rearranging his pillows. He squints as he struggles to focus. "Iz... Izzy? Am I in the hospital?" His voice is tremulous and hoarse.

These first few minutes are always the worst. "No, Dad. You're not in the hospital. You're in the convalescent home. Pacific Vistas."

He stares at me with sudden surprise. "You're... not Izzy."

"No, Dad. I'm Louis. I drove up from Rancho Bernardino this morning."

"Louie?" His eyes finally focus on my face. "What happened, you fall off your bicycle? Your mother seen that shiner yet? She'll be worried as hell."

He reaches up and gently touches the puffed up tissues around my left eye. I realize what I must look like. "Don't worry, Dad. I, uh, I slipped in the shower last night. It's not as bad as it looks. I'll be fine."

He relaxes. "Good. I wouldn't want your mother getting all upset." My mother's been dead since my third year of medical school.

I pull a chair to his bedside. "Dad, do you remember calling me last night?"

I see the fright in his eyes, and it stabs me through the soul. "What, ah, what did we talk about?" Before I can think of how to answer, he grabs my hand and says, "No, wait, don't tell me — I remember. You went over to your cousin's, right? For Passover Seder. Your cousin Cindy. Buddy's little girl. It was just like old times, right? The dinner, I mean. Matzoh balls. Potato kugel. Baked brisket with gravy. You were wondering where the hell she and her husband got the money to feed all those people that kind of food. See? I remember!"

He *does* remember. But that Passover Seder was last spring. My father and I had this conversation more than six months ago.

I pat his hand. "That's right, Dad. I told you all about the seder at Cindy's house. But that's not what we talked about last night. You called to tell me you were hungry all the time. That you felt like you were starving."

"Well... I *am* hungry all the time. *All* the damn time. The food around here is *shit!* No taste at all! Say..." he says, his voice turning suddenly sly and whispery, "you bring me any of those, y'know, those candy bars you pick up?"

Damn. No, Pop, they're crushed into the dirt on some street in Mex-Town. "Uh, no, Dad. I forgot. They're still at home." *Home.* The question I've been dreading asking him all morning. "Last night you told me you wanted me to take you away from here. Away from Pacific Vistas. Do you want to come home with me?"

But he's not paying attention to me anymore. He's staring at the vid-9 set mounted in the corner. Hazy black-and-white images flicker past. Wayne Newton's mustachioed face. Some kind of documentary on Vegas lounge singers...?

"He looked great, didn't he?" I turn back to my father. He has a tremendous grin on his face, just like when he'd brag to my mother about the latest Hollywood heiress who'd signed up for a "nip and tuck." "Man oh man, didn't he look *great,* when I was done with him?"

"Who, Dad?"

He frowns quickly at me. "Oh, *you* know who!"

I remind myself to be patient. "No, I don't."

He props himself up on his elbows and looks around to make sure no one else is listening. Only then does he tell me, in a stage whisper worthy of Lionel Barrymore. *"Elvis!"*

Oh Lord, here we go again.

"I wish to God that man was standing right here in front of me," he exclaims, his wavering voice choked with emotion. "By God, I'd like to shake his hand! He *made* me, you know that? He made me who I am, the most successful plastic surgeon in Beverly Hills. He had more to do with it than all my professors combined. More even than Dr. Illouz, my mentor, the founder of the liposuction industry! Those last four weeks of his life, after my procedure, everybody who saw him said, 'Doesn't Elvis look *wonderful?* It's as if someone's taken twenty years off him.' You've seen the photos. Didn't he look great? Didn't he look better than any time since his big 1968 comeback?"

"Yes, Dad. He looked *great.* You did a fabulous job."

"Fabulous? That's all? It was the first liposuction procedure performed by an American physician on American soil — I was a *pioneer!* Like — like the first man to land on the moon, or Columbus. Sure, there was that little post-surgical fuck-up... but hell, it was my first time. Didn't NASA blow up a rocket or two on the way to sending Armstrong to the moon? Shit, if Elvis hadn't been scarfing down a goddamn private pharmacy, he probably would've pulled through just fine. My job was to make that man look like a Greek god again, and by God, I *did* it! Nobody was supposed to know. But I made sure the right people knew what I had done. Pretty soon they were *lining up!* That's right — lining up to have their bodies sculpted by the man who'd made Elvis look like *Elvis* again!"

I pull a thermometer from my bag. "Open wide, Dad."

He eyes the thermometer suspiciously. "You gonna stick that up my ass?"

"Only if you want me to." The days when he could make me curl up with embarrassment are gone. At least the excitement, the memories have made him more coherent; I might actually be able to have a real conversation with him now.

"Okay, Dad, no more fooling around. Be a good patient, open wide, and lift up your tongue. Or I *will* put this in the other end."

He does as I say. But as soon as I get the thermometer beneath his tongue, he starts talking again.

"Yu... yu shud tank him, too..."

I reach out quickly to keep the thermometer from falling to the floor. "Dad! This'll only take a minute. Just hold on to whatever you want to say."

I can see it's a struggle for him to stay quiet; I realize how scared he must be to lose the thread of his conversation. But he holds on like a good soldier. After two minutes I remove the thermometer.

"What I was saying before — *you* should thank him, too. Elvis, I mean. If it wasn't for him, I wouldn't have had the stash to send you to medical school —"

Ninety-nine point one. My father's temperature is half a degree above normal, the slightest low-grade fever. To make absolutely sure, I stick the thermometer in his mouth again. The reading remains the same. A minuscule fever. What could be causing it? Some sort of minor infection? If it were chronic, that might help explain the weight loss... but his charts show that he's been eating normally all along — ravenously, even; certainly not the typical response to an infection. And besides, he's not the only one here who's lost a considerable amount of weight. Are they *all* running elevated temperatures? What would Nurse Posely say if I popped this thermometer into another few mouths?

I could ask her. Here she comes.

"Well, Dr. Shmalzberg, are you satisfied now that we aren't filling your father's dinner tray with weight-loss foods?"

"Yes... I'm satisfied. Thank you for giving me such full access to your staff and records. And I'd like to apologize for my tone earlier. I don't know if you also have an elderly parent, but it's very easy to become overprotective."

Her stern expression softens. "Apology accepted, Doctor. We're very proud of the quality of treatment we provide our patients. Is there anything else we can do for you?"

"A few minutes ago, I checked my father's temperature. He's running a slight fever."

She retrieves his chart from his bedside and examines it. "Yes... his aide has made note of it. It's not high enough to be of serious concern, though." She flips through several more of the pages, then skips back to an earlier section of the chart. "Looks like your father's been running this slightly elevated temperature for some months now. We've tried bringing it down with antibiotics. But none of our regimens has had any effect. Still, he hasn't seemed to be any the worse for it. Minor fluctuations in basal body temperature aren't that uncommon."

I consider asking her if I might examine the other patients' charts for records of their temperatures, but then another idea strikes me. "I'd like to check one more thing before I leave, if it's possible. Do you have a metabolometer?"

"Yes. We have one stored in one of the labs." She gives me a sly little grin. "I can assure you we haven't been having your father run any cross-country races."

I force myself to grin back. "I'm sure you haven't. But I'm a doctor as well as a son, and I won't be able to sleep unless I check out every little hunch. You'll indulge me?"

She smiles again. "I'd hate for you to lose any sleep, Doctor. I'll see if I can get one of the lab technicians to bring the metabolometer over."

I return to my father's bedside. He's wearing a conspiratorial grin. "If you're gonna play, son," he says, "play to *win*. You get me?"

"Uh, Dad, what is it we're playing?"

He scowls. "Christ, Louie, it's a good thing I was around to teach you how to wipe your ass. Otherwise, you'd *never* have learned." His face takes on that conspiratorial veneer again. "They've been coming 'round to see me. Like bees drawn to honeysuckle. They really want it."

"Want *what,* Dad?" Suddenly the pit of my stomach goes sour. "Who's been coming around to see you?"

"Strange men. Foreigners. They want — y'know, what we've got. What you and me got." He smiles up at me, his eyes brighter than

I've seen them in a long time. "The Elvis."

Muthukrishnan. *Damn* him! How *dare* he come here and bother a helpless old man! "This visitor — was he an Indian? An Indian from India, I mean? What did he say to you?"

"An Indian? Coulda been, I guess. But there wasn't just one guy. There were two."

"Two men visited you together?"

"No. At least — at least, I don't think so. I think it was two different guys, on different days. It's, ah... ah, Jesus, sometimes it's so damn hard to *remember* —"

"Can you tell me what they said to you?"

"They — well, he knew all about what I'd done. With Elvis. He knew about, y'know, the souvenir I kept —"

"'Elvis-in-a-Jar'."

"Yeah. That's what you called it when you were a kid, right?"

I smile. "Go on, Dad. You're doing great."

"He wanted to know if I still have it. Didn't say I do; didn't say I don't. So he wanted to know if maybe *you* had it. I didn't say anything then. But maybe... I dunno, maybe I grinned a little..."

I'm stunned as it sinks in. He thinks I still have it. I never came out and told him that I'd sold it. But he must've suspected — with my practice melting away to nothing, and Emily's health getting worse... He knew. I'm sure he knew. And now he's forgotten.

"I want you to take this schmuck for all he's worth," he says, squeezing my hand. "Fancy-shmancy French accent... he's probably loaded. They all want a piece of America, these foreigners. And that's what we've got — a real, *authentic* piece of America. But whatever you do, Louie, you've gotta promise me —" He pulls me closer, his eyes wide. "— *promise me* you'll never let it go. You've still got your cannula, don't you? Use it on a pig. Pig fat's probably the closest to human fat. Fill up a vacuum jar with pig fat. Stupid fucker won't know the difference. He'll go back to India or wherever figuring he's taking a piece of America back home with him. Well, he *will* be. Just not the piece he figured he had."

I smile weakly. "So you told him I have the Elvis..."

"Not in so many words, no. But that doesn't matter. What matters, what *matters* is..." I see the fierce light behind his eyes begin to dim; his brief spell of lucidity is waning, and he knows it. "Louie, what *matters* is that you never let it go. No matter how much they offer. It's what made our family what we are. It's what made *you* and *me* what we are. Promise me, son. Promise me you'll never let it go..."

Shit. "I... I promise, Dad."

His grip on my hand tightens. For a second, he's as strong as he was when he used to lift me onto his shoulders. But then his grip fades along with the light in his eyes. A metallic clattering approaches from behind me. A lab technician rolls a cart with a metabolometer on it next to my father's bedside.

"This what you need?"

I give the device a quick once-over. It's not the newest or most advanced, but it should tell me what I want to know. "Thank you. This should do just fine."

"You know how to work it?" He's a balding man in his midfifties, with a kind face.

"Thanks, but I can manage." He plugs it into the wall before he leaves.

"Dad, I need to run another test on you."

"More... more thermometers?"

"Not this time. I'll need to put this mask over your nose and mouth for a few minutes. What I want you to do is breathe in through your nose and exhale through your mouth into the mask. Can you do that for me?"

Confusion falls over him like a gauzy blanket. "Izzy? Are you putting me to sleep now? Is there something wrong with me?"

"No, Dad. There's nothing wrong with you." I hope. "And I won't be putting you to sleep. All this machine will do is measure how well you're breathing."

My answer seems to calm him. He doesn't protest as I place the mask over his mouth and the oxygen feed tube over his nose. An aide comes onto the ward as the metabolometer hums into life. "Oh! Hello!" she says. "I'd heard that Walter had another visitor." She leaves her cart near the door and walks over to shake my hand. "You're Walter's son, aren't you?"

"Yes. I'm Louis." I shake her hand. She's attractive, in a plain kind of way.

"Good to meet you. I'm Barbara. Your father's one of my favorites. What a character! You should hear some of the things he says to me when he's in a certain mood. Your father's been exceptionally popular these past few days."

"Oh?"

"He's gotten as many visitors in the past week as most of the patients get in six months. There was that man from the government, then the other one — he was kind of *rude,* that one — and now you. I wish all my guys here had so many family members and friends looking after them."

Two men. Two separate men visited my father; he wasn't lost in a fog when he recalled that. "Barbara? These two other visitors — did they come to see him together?"

"No... that man from the government I mentioned — young guy, kinda good looking — he was here only two, maybe three days ago. The other one, the guy who acted like some bad-ass out of a movie... let's see, he must've come to see your father sometime last week."

Why is the Elvis suddenly so important? "Every non-employee who comes into the building has to sign in, don't they?" I ask.

"Sure. No one from outside walks past that front desk without signing —"

The metabolometer chimes loudly. I undo the straps from around my father's head as the unit's printer hums. "I'll let you get back to what you were doing," Barbara says. "Nice talking with you. You've got one hell of a dad. Come see him more often, okay?"

"Thank you. I — I'll try to do that."

She walks back to her cart. I look down at my father again. "Izzy, isn't she *something?*" he says, eyes comically wide. "Look at the size of those tits! That gal must have saline implants the size of grapefruits —"

"Dad! Please!" Even though she's across the room, she obviously heard him. All she does is ruefully smile and shake her head.

I hide my embarrassment by pulling the readout from the metabolometer. As soon as I see the number, all thoughts of shame vanish.

Eight-point-seven Kelvinic units.

Eight. Point. Seven.

My hundred-and-two-year-old father, who spends all day lying in bed watching the nursing aides bend over, has the metabolism of a forty-year-old marathon runner.

CHAPTER 4

"Dad? I have to ask you something. Something important."

"Izzy? What?"

I lightly grasp his shoulders, hoping the physical contact will help him connect to the here-and-now. "No, Dad. It's not Izzy. It's Louis. You have to help me make a decision."

"Oh —" His eyes focus on my face, and I feel him return to me. "Okay, Louie."

Every instinct screams at me to yank my father out of this place. But with who-knows-what stalking the Elvis, I have to wonder whether I'd be placing Dad in greater jeopardy by taking him home with me. Muthukrishnan certainly didn't *seem* dangerous, but there are too many unknowns — particularly with another mysterious party involved, someone Muthukrishnan warned me about. Also, this place has become home for Dad; at his age, suddenly changing his environment could possibly push him into the grave faster than an elevated metabolism could.

"Last night, you told me that you wanted me to take you away from here. To take you home. Is that still what you want?"

"Take me home? But, but Louie... *this* is home — my friends are here... Besides, you've got your own life. Look, son, I don't want to be schlepped around like some old suitcase. Just leave me be."

His eyes are clear. He's all there, for this brief instant. "Okay, Dad." I guess that makes up my mind for me. At least for now. "Okay."

At first, Nurse Posely refuses to believe the results of the metabolometer test. Until she runs it again herself. Threatening to exercise my rights as my father's legal guardian, I convince her to put him on a regimen of high-calorie powdered dietary supplements, the sort usually prescribed only for AIDS Complex 8 or 9 sufferers. He'll start receiving an extra fifteen-hundred calories a day, on top of his normal meals.

I sit at my father's bedside for a few more minutes, holding his blue-veined, fragile hand. I can't be an absentee son anymore. I can't let months slip by without seeing him.

The afternoon is fading into evening. I've got a ninety-minute drive ahead of me; considering the shape I'm in, it'll feel more like a ten-hour haul. "I guess I need to be getting home," I say. "But I'll come back to see you soon. I won't let so much time go by. I promise."

"Good." He cocks his head and stares at my face. "You take care of that shiner, okay?"

I smile and pat his hand. "I will. Thanks."

"And remember what I said about the Elvis, okay? Jew a good price out of them. But don't you *dare* let it go. Okay?"

Why does he forget the things I wish he'd remember but remember the things I wish he'd forget? "I'll, uh, remember, Dad." I kiss him on the forehead.

He grabs my wrist. "Louie? Son?" He's staring at me very intently now. "You look different. You look like you've lost some weight."

I have to laugh. It's the perfect end-note to this insane symphony of a day. "I'm fine. I'm the same as I've always been. You take good care, all right? And don't cause Miss Barbara any trouble."

But he's gone again, his attention recaptured by the video screen. Despite everything, this has been the best visit I've had with him in years.

At the front desk, while the receptionist is distracted by a phone call, I leaf through the visitors book. Two days back, I find Ravi Muthukrishnan's signature. He signed in as Division Director, U.S. Department of Agriculture, and he listed my father as the person he'd come to visit.

I leaf back through the previous three weeks' worth of names, searching for another foreign signature or another listing of my father's name. But there are no indications in the book of anyone else having come to see my father.

*

God, I hate this drive.

It's like a midnight walk through an eighty-mile-long graveyard. These eighty miles of Orange County between my father's convalescence home and Rancho Bernardino used to be some of the most densely populated land in California. All the concrete and steel and stucco are still here. The only thing missing now are the people.

I'm out of my depth. A good doctor knows when to turn to his colleagues. I personally know only one colleague who's anything of an expert on regulating human metabolism... Harriet Lane. But so far as asking her a favor, she's got two strikes against her. One, she's worked her entire career for the MannaSantos Corporation. And two, fourteen years back we came within a hair's breadth of being lovers.

Night's fallen. I roll down my window and turn the radio on. The voice that pours from the speakers is a familiar one. "How Great Thou Art," sung by a middle-aged, bloated, drug-addicted, but still gloriously gifted Elvis Presley.

I was only four-and-a-half when Elvis died. I remember President Carter's brief eulogy. I remember my father's black, volatile mood, which lasted for what seemed like months. One of my earliest memories is of going to the airport to see my father board the jet to Paris. It was 1976, the Bicentennial year. My father won the opportunity to become the first American physician to study under Dr. Yves-Gerard Illouz, the great French plastic surgeon who had invented the technique of liposuction. And it was this distinction which brought my father into the orbit of Elvis Presley.

Elvis's handlers were planning his third great comeback. The only problem was, by 1977, their boy was in pretty sad shape: addicted to a pharmacy's worth of pain-killers and other drugs, and inflated to a bloated caricature by years of lavish living. Crash dieting could only accomplish so much. Elvis needed to lose the jowls, he needed to lose the paunch, and he needed to lose both before he lost the spotlight.

That was where my father came in. He'd been back from Paris barely four months when the call came from Colonel Parker. Not long after their conversation, my mother and I took my father to the airport again. This time, he was flying to Memphis. He told me he was leaving to help a very important, very famous man. After this, my father would be famous, too, and we could all live in a bigger house in a better neighborhood and I would have more friends than ever.

Years later, in bits and pieces, I found out what had happened in Memphis. The planned liposuction procedure on Elvis was guarded as carefully as the blueprints for a nuclear bomb. Functionaries rented clinic space in Oxford, Mississippi, utilizing one of the many false-front corporations which Colonel Parker had set up for shady contingencies. Elvis's handlers booked him into a concert in Syracuse, which he supposedly canceled at the last minute due to a bout of food poisoning.

My father was completely confident he could handle the operation, in superb style, and he lost no opportunities to impress this upon Colonel Parker and Elvis himself, who was understandably nervous. Actually, Elvis was the first patient my father was to perform a liposuction procedure upon by himself, unsupervised; all of his earlier procedures had been performed under the direct supervision of Dr. Illouz. My father never revealed this fact to his clients. Had there been no complicating issues, there is every likelihood that my father's first solo procedure would've been a total success; he later proved himself to be a very careful and skilled surgeon. However, three factors mitigated against success. The first was my father's understandable jitteriness. The second and third were on Elvis's part. The King was indulging in an orgy of legal and illegal drug-taking, which made his body's reaction to a major surgical procedure unpredictable. Also, my father instructed Elvis to eat absolutely nothing during the twenty-four hours before the procedure. However, eating, along with drug-taking, was one of the major ways in which Elvis dealt with stress. Suffice to say, when Elvis went under my father's knife the next morning, he did not do so on an empty stomach.

My father told me the removal of excess fat from Elvis's neck and jawline went flawlessly. It was when he tackled the King's beltline that he hit trouble. Under guidelines established years later, my father wouldn't have attempted to remove nearly the volume of fat that he did that morning. But Elvis certainly had no shortage of belly adipose, and my father went at it with gusto. Too much gusto, as it turned out. Forty minutes into the procedure, the volume of blood traveling through the suction tubing increased dramatically. And it was mixed with a plethora of foreign substances which my father at first failed to recognize.

His sharp-edged cannula had accidentally punctured Elvis's stomach cavity. The fatty lipid tissues and blood which filled the vacuum container were quickly mixed with the partially digested contents of Elvis's midnight snack and his large, furtive breakfast. My father caught his mistake very quickly, immediately halting his liposuction procedure and opening up Elvis's abdomen so he could suture the hole in the King's stomach. The emergency repair seemed successful. Elvis was brought out from under anesthesia shortly thereafter, and he spent the next week in hiding, convalescing in a rented antebellum mansion in Oxford.

Unfortunately, my father's specialty wasn't gastrointestinal surgery. He had done a workmanlike job, but he wasn't completely confident that he had stanched all the internal bleeding, or, even if he had, that it would stay permanently stanched. He strongly recommended that Elvis see another surgeon for exploratory surgery on his abdomen.

But Elvis was in no mood to risk going under the knife again. Cosseted in his numbing blanket of pain-killers and other drugs, he was feeling no pain. And once the bruises and scarring of the operation began to fade, he was extremely happy with the results of my father's procedure. He was so grateful that he showered my father with gifts, including an engraved gold ring which he'd worn throughout many concert tours; a gem-studded belt with a massive gold buckle; and an autographed copy of the famed photograph with President Nixon.

My father was paid very well. As part of his work agreement, he'd signed a contract which swore him to secrecy; Colonel Parker didn't want the world to know that Elvis's new-found svelteness was due to anything other than rigorous self-improvement. But, in addition to the personalized gifts Elvis gave him, my father kept another souvenir of his brush with fame. He'd assured Colonel Parker and the others that he would properly dispose of the fat, blood, and stomach contents he'd extracted from Elvis. Nearly eleven pounds of it had been suctioned out by my father's cannula and captured in a large vacuum jar. Unable to carry it with him on the plane back to Los Angeles, he boxed up the jar very securely and shipped it to his office. "Elvis-in-a-Jar," stabilized by an infusion of xenon gas, joined our household a week after my father arrived back home.

Three weeks later, Elvis died in a bathroom in Graceland. My father received another urgent call from Colonel Parker and flew back to Memphis immediately. Although my father's signature is not the doctor's signature on the death certificate, he performed the autopsy, and he was involved in the ensuing coverup.

The world learned that Elvis had died of heart failure. But the real cause was internal bleeding of the stomach cavity, exacerbated by the disastrous interactions of his unregulated drug regimen with the antibiotics and coagulants he'd begun taking after his surgery.

In the public eye, the deceased Elvis was quickly transformed from an over-the-hill pop star to an American deity. And my father's purloined souvenir suddenly became the most incalculably valuable relic since the Holy Grail.

The medley of Elvis gospel songs on the radio comes to an end. I turn the radio off. The night air has changed from pleasantly brisk to chilling as I speed past shopping malls, car dealerships, and movie palaces as deserted and guano-stained as Mayan ruins. I turn the heater up another notch and try to ignore the desolation outside my windows.

When I arrive home, blinking red diodes on my answering machine tell me I have three messages waiting. There's a strange odor in the room, faint but unpleasant. Maybe a vial of medication leaked in my examining room?

The first message is from my cousin Cindy, reminding me about the Hanukkah dinner she's having at her house tomorrow night. She hints that I should expect a plateful of her famous *latkes,* her holiday potato pancakes fried in natural, full-fat oil.

The second message is from Mitch.

"Hey, Lou? Look, I'm just calling to check in on you. You gave us a real good scare in Mex-Town, buddy. That's the closest we've come to losing somebody since that dust-up near the county border eighteen

years back. I know you were out of it yesterday, said some things you probably didn't mean. Hey, give me a call when you're feeling up to it, okay? We need to talk."

After pressing the Delete button a second time, the third message comes on. I recognize the British-tinged voice immediately.

"Hello, Dr. Shmalzberg? This is Ravi Muthukrishnan from the Department of Agriculture. I am calling you on Thursday at twenty minutes before five in the afternoon. I did not receive a return call from you either yesterday or today. I passed by your home this morning, hoping to find you available. I was supposed to return to Virginia this evening, but I have delayed my flight by one more day in hopes of speaking with you personally. I cannot impress upon you too forcefully the importance of our speaking. Once again, my telephone number at the Hotel Nixon is..."

My first impulse is to delete the message. But I find myself fumbling for pen and paper, then jotting down the number. I need to tell him to stay the hell away from my father. And maybe I'll have the energy to squeeze some answers out of the officious young prick. Tomorrow. After I've slept for a month.

But Mitch... him I need to draw a line with. Tonight, while I still have the will. I can't talk with him in person. I'm at my lowest; he'd only have to exert a fraction of his intensity to argue circles around me. So instead of calling his home, I call the machine at his shop.

"Mitch... this is Louis. I wanted to let you know I'm all right. I was up north earlier, when you called, visiting my father. Look... this isn't easy for me to say. I'm resigning from the Good Humor Men. What happened in Mex-Town... I don't want you to think I'm resigning because I got hurt, because I'm afraid. I *am* afraid, but not of that. I'm more afraid of the kind of man I've let myself become."

I start shaking, and I'm not even talking to him in person. "Mitch, I'm supposed to be a doctor. Tuesday... Jesus Christ, the day before yesterday I killed a man. Not directly. But if I hadn't been there, he wouldn't be dead. I just... I don't believe in what we're doing anymore. This has been building for a long time.

"Don't call me tonight or tomorrow morning. I've got to rest. I'm sorry, Mitch. I hope this won't come in the way of our friendship."

I hang up. *There; you've committed yourself.* My head is pounding. Better gulp down some Tylenols before I retreat to my bed.

There's a bottle in the medicine cabinet. The bathroom is even cooler than my office. Strange.

I stare at myself in the mirror above the sink. Have I lost weight? My face looks the same to me. The same bags beneath the eyes; the same loosening folds of flesh beneath my jawline.

I keep a bathroom scale next to the toilet. Stepping onto it, I wait for the numbers to swirl around to 177, my steady weight since I was forty years old.

The needle stops at 168 pounds.

If I were to shrink at the rate of one inch per month, and the rest of the world were shrinking at the same steady rate around me, I'd never notice.

It's cold in this room. I feel a breeze where there shouldn't be one. In the mirror, the gray-checked shower curtain flutters behind me.

I pull back the shower curtain. The window above the tub is broken.

The strange, unpleasant odor I noticed before gets much stronger. I recognize it now. The aroma of a lit clove cigarette.

"I've been waiting some time for you to return, Dr. Shmalzberg. I hope you will forgive that I have not straightened up the clutter I created in your bathtub. Americans of your class usually employ domestic help for such things, I believe."

He's standing in the doorway. Turkish-looking — copper-colored face, thick black mustache, hair like glossy black plastic. Head shaped like a block of granite; no neck, or maybe it's hidden by that silk scarf/necktie. Shorter than me, but much broader across the shoulders, and younger. He's wearing a finely tailored suit of expensive sharkskin silk. Flecks of ash from his cigarette fall onto my hallway carpet.

"Who the hell are you?" Useless question — I know who he is. He's the second man. The visitor who didn't sign the visitors log. His French-tinged accent is the clincher.

"My name is unimportant." He smiles, revealing teeth that seem too white and too large, and flicks a long ash into my sink. He douses it with a quick burst of water from the faucet. "Think of me as an emissary. My home is a European province of the glorious, restored

Caliphate. My master is the ruler of that province. He has sent me to acquire a cultural relic, a relic which I have every reason to believe you possess. The means of this acquisition he has left entirely in my hands."

I stare briefly at those hands. His nails are manicured and clean, obsessively so. But the fingers those nails are attached to are thick as blood sausages, and the knuckles are as weighty-looking as bolts on a bulldozer. I can't imagine those hands playing a violin, or probing the delicate, fat-laden inner reaches of a woman's thigh with a cannula. But I can imagine them doing less pleasant things.

Still, a man can only be pushed so far. "Get the hell out of my house, before I call —" *He could crush my fingers before I dial 911.* "— before I *signal* for the police to come. I'm a very important man in this town. With important friends."

He smiles indolently, then takes a long, leisurely drag off his cigarette. Surprisingly, he takes care to exhale away from me. "This signal — that would be the Bat Signal, yes? You have a hidden button beneath your desk — or perhaps here, next to your lovely porcelain toilet — that you press, and a large man dressed in a black costume arrives quickly, bursts through the door, and renders me senseless with a severe beating? Would that be correct?"

His eyes flash in a manner not unfriendly. "Please forgive me, Doctor. I am a great admirer of your American cinema heroes, ever since I was a lad. I did not mean to belittle you."

"What *do* you mean to do?"

"What I mean to do, Dr. Shmalzberg, is entirely up to you." His small, intense eyes, filled almost entirely by black pupils, never leave mine. "My purpose is to return to my country bearing the last preserved remains of the Noble Blessed Troubadour. Reports gathered by my country's Ministry of Intelligence, added to my own investigations, have led me to you. Cooperate, and it is within my power to make you a very wealthy man. Refuse to cooperate, and it is within my power to make you a very sad man, indeed."

There's no sense in playing dumb. Unlike Muthukrishnan, he's not being coy about what he knows. But he doesn't know everything. "I don't have it."

"Really? Your father made it quite clear to me that you do."

His mentioning my father makes my adrenaline rocket. "My father... suffers from McCrowley's Dementia. Anything he said to you was thirty years out of date."

He appears to consider this, twisting the tip of his mustache. "During my many years of service to my Emir, I have become a keen judge of men and their truthfulness. Your father may not possess all of his mental faculties. But what he did not say, and the manner in which he did not say it, was most revealing. The faces of old men are exceptionally expressive."

He interlaces his fingers and tenses them. Cablelike tendons on the backs of his hands protrude through hairy, dark flesh. "You have the Troubadour's preserved remains, Doctor. One way or another, I will obtain them."

"Damn it! I'm telling you, I *don't have them.*"

"Then please do me the favor of telling me what you have done with them."

His question, so obvious, brings me up short. When I sold the Elvis to the Graceland Foundation, the agreement I signed stipulated I would never reveal the preserved fat and stomach contents had ever existed. I could get myself off the hook so easily. But I can't bring myself to tell this Franco-Ottoman that he needs to book a flight to Memphis.

My hands are shaking. I ball them into fists. It's not just fear I'm feeling – it's anger and *pride,* family pride bound up inside an intense patriotism I haven't felt in decades.

My gut decides for me. I don't want the Ottoman to have it. Nor Muthukrishnan. They're foreign vultures come to pick America's bones clean – devour the last bit of fat, pillage the final storehouse of treasure. I want to split his leering face with an axe labeled "Made in America."

Don't you dare let it go, my father said. I never should've sold it. It belongs in the bosom of my family. The only one who is going to lay hands on the Elvis is *me.*

"I sold it," I tell him. "Twenty-six years ago, to a Canadian software magnate. He was living in Vancouver then. I recall reading that he died a few years ago. If you give me a few minutes to go online, I might be able to dig up his obituary."

"Ah. I see." He puffs on his cigarette. This time, he blows the nauseatingly sweet smoke directly into my face. "Tell me, Doctor... why do I not believe you?"

His words freeze my spine into brittleness. I prepare myself for pain. "Believe or disbelieve anything you want," I manage to say. "You're in a free country."

I watch those hands. I imagine what they can do to my profoundly exhausted body. For the moment, all they do is stub out the butt of his cigarette on the edge of my sink. "For a man with so much formal education, you show a shocking lack of wisdom. I have been watching you. You have built your life on fragile foundations, much like — what is that charming American expression? Like a 'house of playing cards.' All I need do is remove one of those cards, and the entire edifice of your existence comes crashing down. You would be wise to be thinking of this."

He offers me a curt bow. "Until our next meeting, Doctor. Please conclude your business in the lavatory. I will let myself out."

He leaves. I lean against the sink, all strength gone, feeling as feeble as the starving deer from last night.

But my mind is afire. Strangely, part of me looks forward to the coming conflict. My life has grown stale, tired. So much of it a tissue of lies. Let him blow part of it away, if he can. I hardly know myself anymore. And what I know, I don't like.

But one thing I do know. "Touch one hair on my father's head..." I hear myself say —

My next words amaze me.

"... and I'll kill you."

CHAPTER 5

I'm in the forest. Surrounded by starving deer. Their wavering legs are barely strong enough to hold them up.

Mitch and Brad are here with me, armed with rifles. They've come to put the deer out of their misery.

The woods explode with machine gun fire. Deer parts fly like confetti.

Mitch and Brad are gone. Replaced by Muthukrishnan and the Ottoman. They're the ones with the machine guns, the ones slaughtering the deer.

A man walks out of the woods. The firing stops. He kneels by the dead deer, places his hand by each dead animal's bloody muzzle, and puts something in its mouth. The deer stir, then rise. Now they're as plump as pampered zoo specimens.

The man looks at me. It's Elvis.

I open my eyes. It's past one in the afternoon. My alarm clock has been bleating for the past three hours.

I'm stiff and sore, but less so than yesterday. A glance at my phone tells me there've been no calls since last night. Surprising. I'd have expected Mitch to try reaching me several times by now.

I limp back to my bedroom to pull on a robe. This old terry cloth robe is the most comfortable piece of clothing I own. It was a birthday gift from Harri.

Harri. Harriet Lane... I'm not looking forward to talking with her, but I should take advantage of this lull between crises to call her.

It seems like a hundred years ago when she was my lab partner, before she switched programs to molecular biology, with a concentration in human nutrition. There was always a certain... *something,* a sexual tension, between Harri and me. If Emily hadn't already been in the picture — who knows?

Harri got into the gene-splicing game with one of the half-dozen biotech and chemical firms that later became corporate parents of the MannaSantos combine. We went years without being in touch. Then, fourteen years ago, she reappeared in my life. I was a widowed country doctor trying desperately to keep my clinic afloat, hawking MannaSantos weight-loss products on the side to bring in some additional cash flow. Harri was project director for several of the products I was selling, and she saw my name on a list of distributors. She had never married. We were both in our midfifties then; perhaps the phrase "better late than never" drifted through her mind when she read my name.

Harriet lived in the outskirts of Vegas. We began seeing each other, commuting between Rancho Bernardino and Las Vegas several weekends a month. Despite the distance, it might have worked. It might have worked, except for a legacy of my marriage, a family peculiarity which made it painfully obvious that I was my father's son.

One evening, after we had eaten dinner at my house and then fumbled through a session of heavy petting, Harri wanted to have a smoke outside. She went looking through my closets for a coat to wear. She found Emily. Rather, she found what I'd retained of Emily — the two vacuum jars filled with the fat I had lovingly liposuctioned from my wife's hips, thighs, and buttocks over the final six years of our marriage.

Perhaps if I'd been more quick-witted, I could've come up with some semi-plausible lie which would've satisfied her — after all, liposuction had been a major part of my medical practice before GD2, and I could've rationalized holding onto the two samples of my work for the giving of historical lectures and so forth. But the clumsy, embarrassed foreplay we'd shared a half-hour before left me feeling vulnerable and open. The word "pervert" didn't even occur to me.

I told Harri everything. I told her all about Emily's minor weight-gain during her midthirties; how we'd joked about my providing her a body-sculpting treatment for her birthday; how these little jokes had segued into reality; and how our sexual life together had come to revolve around unending cycles of self-encouraged weight-gain on Emily's part, followed by loving, intimate, tender sessions of liposuction on mine.

I should've expected Harri to react the way she did. Perhaps one needs to be part of my family not to feel a sense of revulsion; maybe my father and Emily are the only two people who could ever understand. Harri and I haven't spoken since that night. Fourteen years ago.

Her work and home numbers are still in my address book. I call Harri's MannaSantos office number in Las Vegas. An unfamiliar man tells me he thinks she may be managing a different department. He transfers me to a receptionist, who recognizes Harri's name without hesitation; she's now the Technical Information Director for the Department of Customer and Community Relations. A few seconds later, I hear her voice.

"Hello? Harriet Lane speaking."

Her voice hasn't changed. It's still nasal, oddly sexy, flavored with a strong dose of Long Island. Hearing it brings back a flood of memories — some exciting, some embarrassing as hell.

"Harri? This is Louis Shmalzberg."

A heart-shriveling pause. "Louis Shmalzberg? As in *Doctor* Louis Shmalzberg?"

Oy. Vey. "Uh, yes."

Another pause, icier than the first. "Is this some kind of apology call? After, what, fifteen years? Fifteen years without a *peep* from you? You've got a *shit*-load of nerve."

Huh. The anger I expected. What's behind it — well, *that's* unexpected. "Harri... I thought you'd never *want* to hear from me again. It's not that I've never thought of you —"

"So why are you calling now? Just find your long-lost little black book?"

"You're an expert on human metabolism. There are things I need to ask you —"

"Let's keep this conversation short. *Yes,* I'm still single, goddamn it. *No,* I won't go out with you again. All your questions answered? Good. Have a nice life, Louis."

"Harri, that's not what I'm calling about. Look, please listen. I never meant to hurt you. I never had the chance to explain what you saw. To *really* explain. But *please* believe that if you and I had gotten... closer... I never would've tried anything with you that you would've been uncomfortable with. I mean that."

I hear a hint of a sigh. "All right, Louis. That's probably as close to an apology as I should expect to get from a man. Aside from that one night of... weirdness... you were a pretty nice guy. A gentleman. And God knows, there sure as hell aren't that many of *those* around. Go ahead. Say whatever you called to say."

I tell her about my father. About the thousands of starving deer. I begin telling her about my own surprising weight loss when she cuts me off.

"Louis. Stop." Her voice is abrupt, but not from disinterest. "Don't tell me anymore. Not right now."

"Is anything wrong?"

"I need to get off the line. I'm not trying to blow you off. I promise. I'm heading to lunch off-campus. Let me give you a call back in a half-hour. Okay?"

"Do you have my number?"

"I've got it recorded."

"I'll, uh, I'll be waiting by the phone," I say.

"Good. Take care, Louis."

She sounded almost afraid. As if hearing me out could get her in trouble. Did she think someone was listening in on our conversation?

Normalcy is slipping away from me, breaking up like an iceberg that's meandered into the Gulf Stream. Maybe normalcy is a chimera. Maybe nothing in my life has been truly normal since Emily died. Or maybe my life has been *too* normal — too scripted, too predictable? Could this turmoil be a blessing?

But I'm afraid. What will be left of *me* when my life becomes unrecognizable? I head into my study and unlock the cabinet where I keep the vacuum jars. I lift them from their resting place, as gently and quietly as if I were waking her from a long sleep.

These gently mottled swirlings held in stasis — I can stare at them for hours. The patterns are as pleasingly lovely as the thick whorls of paint with which van Gogh formed his starry nightscapes.

Beautiful. But how could they be anything *less* than beautiful? Every cell within each globule of fat contains its own perfect map of Emily. Linked together, those supple lipids formed the substrata of the soft, gentle surfaces through which she experienced the world and the world experienced her... her face, arms, belly, breasts. Lips.

I'm not at all surprised that the cannula, primary instrument of the liposuctionist, was invented by a Frenchman, long before the absorption of La Belle France into the realms of Islam. A long, slender cylinder, inserted by male hands into fresh apertures created within the most tender portions of a woman's body — the cannula was the creation, not of a corporation, but of an artist. My mother always detested my father's work. As soon as I took up that work myself, I quickly understood why. I timidly sensed the sexual electricity underlying each procedure I performed. Yet I forced myself to think of the living, female flesh I was shaping as inert clay. Until the day I first wielded my cannula within the flesh of my own wife.

I had always been aware, from the time I first began to adore Emily, of a fierce desire to consume her, to completely possess her. Merely embracing her, merely kissing her, inserting myself inside her... how sadly inadequate such actions seemed. But by extracting the physical substrata of my wife's femininity with my cannula, by suctioning that physical essence into a glass enclosure where I could directly experience it, even touch it, if I wished — this moved Emily's infinitely precious physicality from the stark category of "hers" into the shared category of "ours."

I never asked her to replenish her curves. Her increased eating regimen, she undertook that of her own sly, sexy volition. The first session was the only one we ever performed in my clinic's operating room. After that, Emily would only allow my cannula to touch her when she was nesting in our silk-covered bed.

A much less pleasant memory surfaces. I put the two containers of Emily back on the shelf. Silk sheets and darkness... While my father was out of town, as he so frequently was, my mother would lie in her bed for days at a time, in total darkness. Maria, our housekeeper, would feed me my meals. I spent the rest of my time at school or reading. How old was I — seven? Eight? When Maria was busy elsewhere, I'd take a book and a flashlight and sit outside my mother's door, so I could try to protect her from whatever was making her so sad.

How quiet that room was. My mother never turned on the television or radio. I never saw the light of a reading lamp beneath her door. My young imagination was consumed with thoughts of what she could be doing during all those daytime hours spent in complete darkness. But there were times... times when, if I listened as hard as I could, I could hear my mother crying.

It was the most frightening sound. It meant that nothing was safe. Only the most powerful magic could make the world right again. So I would sneak into my father's study and take the Elvis down from its place of honor behind my father's desk. And then I'd carry the Elvis into my mother's bedroom. And I'd crawl into her bed and put it near her feet. I'd hold my breath until her crying stopped, waiting for the Elvis to work its magic. And her crying would stop, for a while.

The phone on my desk rings. "Okay, Louis, I'm back," Harri says when I pick up. "I just gobbled down lunch. We can continue our conversation."

I force myself to focus on Harri. "How was lunch?"

"Vaguely disgusting. I'm calling from a little burger shack at the edge of the desert."

That's surprising. Harri was always a strict vegetarian. "How are the veggie burgers there?"

"They don't have any. And I wouldn't eat one if they did. My diet's about eighty percent animal proteins nowadays. Not that it'll do me much good in the long run."

"Harri? What's going on? Why the secrecy?"

"Louis, I'm going to tell you things that could have very bad consequences for me. Things that could get me fired, end my career, or... or worse. I'm telling them to you because I may need a whistle-blower down the road, somebody not under the company's thumb. And weird as you are, I'm pretty sure I can trust you."

The sound of her breathing mingles with other sounds, cars or trucks speeding by on a nearby road. I don't suppose she's using her portable phone; transmission over airwaves would probably seem too insecure. I try to picture her standing at one of those retro pay phones, exercises in nostalgia planted by maverick telecoms in places outside cell range, next to a run-down burger shack alongside a Nevada desert highway. I wonder what she looks like now.

"One of our products has gotten out of the box."

"Products?" I picture an ear of corn with tiny legs crawling out of a cardboard shipping box.

"The Metaboloft corn strain. Our newest and most profitable line. It's a drifter. A big-time, high-plains drifter."

"I don't get you."

"How much do you know about agri-engineering?"

"Not much. Just what I read in MannaSantos press releases when I was one of their salesmen."

"Then you know the basics. The companies that merged to form MannaSantos were among the pioneers in recombinant DNA manipulation. The corporation's strategy has always been to field the widest variety of weight-loss products, so that nearly all consumers can find at least one variety that works for them. Metaboloft corn was simply the latest step. Do you have any idea what proportion of items sold in the typical grocery store contains some form of corn derivative?"

"I imagine it must be pretty high."

"Extremely high. The corporation saw an opportunity to sell proprietary, metabolically active corn to every food processing company in America. Companies would pay a huge premium to MannaSantos for the privilege of labeling their items 'Metaboloft.' Consumption of three standardized servings of product per day will raise a customer's metabolic rate by an average of two-point-three Kelvinic units. Like the Lep-Tone line of fruits and vegetables, Metaboloft's effect isn't permanent. But unlike Lep-Tone, it has an atypical cumulative aspect over time. The body tends to become more sensitive to the Metaboloft effect with continued exposure, in contradiction to most drug effects, which attenuate with increased exposure. And Metaboloft is effective with a much wider range of the population than Lep-Tone is."

Jesus. I'd thought Harri would give me a little advice for my father. I wasn't expecting to hear this. "How was Metaboloft ever approved as a general-use product? Sticking it into toaster pastries and corn flakes... it's as irresponsible as spiking tap-water with antibiotics in order to wipe out sinus infections."

"Money talks, Louis. You know that."

"But this still doesn't explain what's happening to my father. Or the deer. I haven't read reports of deer breaking into grocery stores and chugging down Metaboloft diet sodas."

"They don't have to. Metaboloft has come to them."

"This 'drift' you mentioned before... the engineered strain has migrated to wider fields of corn? That still wouldn't explain the deer —"

"Shit. Louis, I've gotta go."

"But we're just getting to the meat of all this —"

"It'll have to wait, okay? A pair of security guards from MannaSantos just pulled up. I'll call you back. Either tonight or tomorrow."

"Are you in trouble? Do you need —?"

She hangs up before I can finish. How much trouble is she in? Did the guards follow her? Maybe they were just stopping off for lunch, and she's just being paranoid?

I don't need more tumult in my life. I called Harri hoping to begin clearing up an existing crisis, not to expose myself to a whole new can of worms. Now there's nothing I can do, except wait for her next call. Damn it.

Shit. I'm late for Cindy's dinner party in La Jolla. Apart from my father, she's the only family I have left. Worse, I forgot to get out to the store to buy a gift. I search the kitchen for something to bring. The best I can find is a bottle of California table wine. I wrap it in tin foil and hope Cindy won't notice that the top fifth of the bottle is empty.

I squint in the harsh daylight and lock my front door. Useless ritual. The Ottoman has proven he can come and go whenever he damn well pleases. He could be watching me right now, as I climb into my car. Maybe it wouldn't hurt to ask Mitch or Brad to spend the next several nights at my house. For that matter, as a Good Humor Man, I've amassed a bucket-load of chits from the Rancho Bernardino police. It's time to start calling in some favors.

At least I don't have to contend with traffic on the way south. As little as twenty years ago, a rush-hour drive through Orange County to La Jolla would've been an ordeal. Today, I'm free to push my diminutive Nash as fast as its skinny tires will go. The luxurious suburbs between the highway and the Pacific never emptied out. But Los Angeles and San Diego are mere shadows of the megalopolises they were at the turn of the century. The nation's center of gravity has been shifting eastward for decades.

The sign for Cindy's exit looms suddenly. Her home, a handsome Reagan-period split-level ranch, sits on a hillside above the boarded-up remnants of a middle school. Her son and daughter-in-law are planning a child. I'll have to remember to congratulate them.

Buddy answers the door. I've never much cared for him. According to Cindy, he's been an emotionally removed husband and father, burying himself in his engineering business. It's probably the resemblance to my own father that irks me. But he's certainly provided my cousin and their son with a comfortable home.

"Hello, Lou. Cindy was just wondering whether you'd make it."

"Hi, Buddy. How are you?" We awkwardly shake hands. I catch him looking curiously at my black eye. "You haven't fed the last crumbs of the *latkes* to the dogs yet?"

"Not yet. Cindy's just taking them out of the oil now."

"The *latkes* or the dogs?"

No smile. "The *latkes*."

"Good. I understand Will is scheming to make you a grandfather?"

"Yeah. Isn't that a kick in the head?" He almost smiles. "He and Blair are out in the solarium, if you want to go congratulate them."

"I'll do that. Here's a little something for the party."

He takes my wine and mumbles his thanks. The rich aroma of frying *latkes* greets me. I exchange nods of familiarity with several of the other guests. Many of them must have heard I'm a Good Humor Man. I wonder how they feel about that, sipping their fat-laden matzoh ball soup at Passover and eating their *latkes* at Hanukkah next to a man with the power to revoke their health care privileges.

I find Will and his young, painfully slender wife sitting on a cushioned bench near the edge of the solarium. I put my hand on his shoulder. He turns around and grins. "Louis! I'm so glad you made it! Mom'll be thrilled!"

The three of us hug. They notice my bruises. "Say," Will says with obvious concern, "what'd you do to your face? You aren't taking up kick boxing at your age?"

"It's nothing," I lie, "just a stupid accident. I'm much more interested in hearing about *your* big news."

Will looks expectantly at his wife. "Go ahead, honey. Tell him."

"Well," Blair says, clutching her bony knees with pent-up excitement, "just this week I started my hormone therapy. I'm terrified of the weight gain, of course, but the doctor says if I tough it out, I should be ovulating within four or five months. Which means that, God willing, they'll be able to extract a viable egg by summertime."

I hug her again. "That's fabulous! I'm so glad you two decided to go through with it."

Will scoots closer to Blair and puts his arm around her. "The costs would swamp us if it weren't for Mom and Dad pitching in. The government grants help, but because we've decided to go full designer, they're only covering about thirty-five percent. It's a shame you're not an embryologist, Louis. It'd sure be terrific to get a family discount."

I'm so proud of them. Their announcement is the only good news I've heard in what seems like a century. "You know your mother and I have always been close. You're about as near to a son as I'll ever have, Will. So let me put something on the table. Whatever the government and your parents aren't paying for, how about you let me make up the difference?"

Blair shrieks with excitement and throws her arms around my neck.

"That's awfully generous," Will says. "But it could end up being a lot of money. Are you sure —?"

"You let me worry about that," I say, feeling wonderfully benevolent. "I haven't had anyone to spend money on for years. Make me happy. Let me do this for you."

"He *wants* to help us, Will," Blair says, pulling his arm and smiling. "Don't you want your cousin to be happy?"

"Well..." The wavering disappears from Will's face, and he vigorously shakes my hand. "Okay, then! This'll really help us get started on a good footing. Hey — maybe we'll have a second one!"

Blair takes both my hands in hers and stares into my face. I can't help but think how beautiful she would be with another thirty pounds softening her bony frame. "Louis, we'd like you to be the baby's godfather. As godfather *and* a doctor, would you help us pick out its features and personality traits? Our embryologist is down in San Diego. We'll be working with her this spring."

"I'd be absolutely delighted," I say. Even though the notion of pre-selecting a baby's sex, height, and skin tone, along with attributes such as musical aptitude and mathematical skills, gives me an old-fashioned case of the willies.

I leave the two of them alone with their excitement, then find Cindy in the kitchen, wrapping her *latkes* in paper towels to absorb the excess oil. I sneak up behind her and put my hands on her shoulders. "Miss, tell me the name of the black marketeer you bought that oil from," I say, "and it'll go easier on you."

She turns around. "Lou! You made it!" Her bright-eyed smile immediately turns to shock, however. "Jesus Christ! What happened to your *face,* honey?"

Cindy's nine years younger than me. Despite the age difference, we were close growing up. She was a lifeline for me after Emily died. I've never been able to lie to her. "A bad day in the food confiscation business," I admit.

"Shit," she scowls, pulling off her cooking mitts and lightly touching the bruises around my eyes. "They beat you up? Where were those macho pals of yours? Aren't they supposed to protect you? You're too old for all that crap, Lou. How long have I been begging you to give it up? It's not as if you believe in it anymore."

She'll certainly be happy to hear my next bit of news. "I resigned. Just last night."

Her eyes go wide. "Really?"

"Really. I've confiscated my last chocolate bar."

She hugs me tightly. "That's *great,* Lou. That's really great. That's the *best* news I've heard since — well, the *second*-best news, after Will and Blair deciding to have a kid."

"I told them I'd pitch in for the embryologist's fees."

"That's awfully sweet of you. But can you afford that?"

"I'll do whatever I can. I figure it's my patriotic duty to help grow the population. Although it sure would be wonderful, not to mention enormously cheaper, if they were willing and able to get pregnant the old-fashioned way."

"Heh. Yeah." She smiles ruefully, multiplying the tiny age lines around her eyes. "But you can't expect kids today to put up with what our generation did, Lou. Blair's seen the pictures of me pregnant with Will. I was El Blimpo, remember? She's heard how long it took me to drop all that excess blubber. Asking her to get pregnant *au naturel* would be like asking her to cut off her arm." She doffs her apron and puts her arm around my waist. "C'mon into the dining room. The kids are about to light the candles. Then we'll eat."

The guests are all gathered around the ornate brass menorah, the ceremonial candelabra with its branches for each of the eight days of Hanukkah. Although I've never been particularly religious, I have warm feelings for this holiday, with its symbolism of ever-increasing light. Tonight six candles will be lit.

Blair, the youngest person present, sings the ancient prayers of praise in Hebrew and then in English, while touching the wick of each candle with the flame of the *shamas,* the lead candle. The sixth candle, the one for tonight, isn't seated firmly enough. Blair jostles it with the *shamas* while trying to light it. The burning candle falls onto the tablecloth.

Blair's face goes white. *"Damn —* so clumsy —"

Not wanting Cindy's heirloom tablecloth to get burned, I reach for the wick. "It's all right —" My fingers burn as I snuff out the fire.

"Lou, your fingers — let me get some first aid cream," Cindy says.

"Not necessary. I'm fine." I take a knife and dig the excess wax from the candle holder, then reset the candle in the menorah. "Go ahead, Blair. Finish the prayers."

Cindy makes an ice pack for me nevertheless. The guests and I sit ourselves around the dining table. The long table is covered with platters of fruits, vegetables, and prime cuts of Leanie-Lean meats. Cindy emerges from the kitchen with the *pièce de résistance* — a heaping tray of steaming, crispy *latkes*. We all applaud. Especially this ex-Good Humor Man.

The oldest among us look the happiest. I watch guests in their six-ties or seventies eagerly place three or four *latkes* on their plates at a time. Blair, however, quivers with distaste as she reluctantly spears one small potato pancake, then cuts it in half and quickly shoves the other half onto her husband's plate.

I take three, plus a generous helping of the sour cream Cindy has managed to conjure up. If there are any *latkes* left over, I may ask Cindy if she'd wrap some up for my father. The aroma... it's as if I'm standing in my mother's kitchen again. I dip a *latke* in the sour cream and take a bite. It's just as delicious as I remember. Maybe more so this year, because this is the taste of hope, of fresh beginnings.

The room is quiet. The only sounds are the crunching of *latkes* and faint music outside, coming from somewhere down the road. It gets gradually louder, as if it's coming closer.

That first *latke* goes sour in my stomach.

The approaching music is the false cheer of a calliope.

CHAPTER 6

I glance around the table. The pit of my stomach begins to churn. Some of the others hear the music, too. I see the anticipatory dread in their faces. And worse, accusation, aimed at me like a blowtorch blast.

Maybe the truck is going to another house? The calliope gets louder. Cindy catches my eye. I feel sick. I desperately shake my head, struggle to wordlessly convey *I don't know a thing — this has nothing to do with me...*

I hear the truck come to a halt, then the clatter of doors being shoved open, men grunting beneath the weight of equipment, disposal pots banging as they're unloaded. It's all so familiar. Only I've never heard it from this side of the equation before.

Blair spits out the piece of *latke* and hides it in her napkin. Her act unfreezes everyone else at the table. Plates clatter and water glasses spill. Guests rush to the kitchen garbage disposal or bathrooms. Many will force themselves to vomit; I've seen all this before.

But it's too late. Already the Good Humor Men are smashing in the door. I stay at the deserted table, eating my last two *latkes*. I know better than to try to hide the evidence of my "crime." I have my credentials on me. Perhaps by confronting these men calmly, as a colleague, I can convince them that nothing illegal has occurred, that Cindy obtained a special religious exemption for using the oil... even though no such exemptions exist.

An axe blade bursts through the front door. The first Good Humor Man enters my cousin's house. And my world is plunged into queasy, inexplicable nightmare again.

It's Mitch.

"Aww, fucking hell," he says when he sees me. "I didn't want to believe you'd really be here."

He can't be here. This is thirty miles south of the edge of our district.

"You — you have no enforcement powers here," I say. "You don't have... what is your authority to make a raid outside our district?"

"*My* district, you mean. Didn't you just quit us?"

"Yes. I did." The anger and hurt in his voice hit me like burning arrows. But again I ask, "What is your authority?"

"Special dispensation," he says slowly, his eyes tracing the trail of *latkes* crushed into the carpet. Brad and Alex, Jr. enter, Brad carrying the dragon, Alex bowed beneath the weight of the clumsy disposal tubs. Brad sprints into the other rooms to round up the guests. His eyes don't meet mine. But Alex's eyes do. He stares at me with the shocked, stung look of a little boy who has caught his father making love to a mistress.

"The local crew gave us permission to operate on their turf," Mitch says. "When I explained it might involve a case of corruption inside our unit, they didn't have any choice but to say yes."

Brad ushers the guests back into the dining room. Several of them stare fearfully at his flamethrower. Grown men playing soldier. Why didn't I ever let myself see it before? Because I was one of the toy soldiers.

Someone is hanging back in the hallway. Brad grabs her arm and pulls her roughly into the room. It's Blair. The poor thing wipes flecks of vomit from the corners of her mouth.

"Brad!" I shout, standing. "Don't be rough with her. With any of them. It's not necessary."

"Lou?" Cindy stands at the edge of the crowd, an oven mitt still dangling from one hand. "Lou, these are... friends of yours? Can't you make them go away?"

"Cindy, please believe me, I don't have anything to do with this —"

Her voice is plaintive, quivery, almost childlike. "Can't you make them go away?"

I turn to Mitch, my oldest friend, hoping I'll find some pity in his weathered face. I don't see what I'm hoping to see. He jerks his head toward the door. "Lou. Let's you and me step outside a minute."

Out on the porch, Mitch whirls on me, his face distorted with fury.

"Lou, how could you *do* this to me?"

I'm momentarily wordless, stunned that he can view himself as the injured party. He sticks his contorted face close, too close, to mine. "Do you realize the position you've put me in? What the fuck do twenty-five years of friendship mean to you? Don't you have a single goddamn thing to say for yourself?"

"Who was the informant, Mitch?"

"What?"

"Who told you I'd be here, and that *latkes* would be on the menu?"

My unexpected question deflates his anger. Fury gone, he looks like a graying sixty-six-year-old man again. "Hell, I can't tell you that. You know better than to ask that, Lou."

I nod. He chews his bottom lip, twists the axe handle in his hands. "Lou... I don't understand any of this." He stares at the ground. "Why you quit. Why I found you in the middle of this crime scene. Maybe you're hacked off at what happened the other day in Mex-Town. About me and the boys not being there to back you up when you needed us. Maybe this is your way of gettin' even. I don't know." He looks up, and his voice gets stronger. "But what I *do* know is that we've been friends for an awful long time, Lou. I don't like throwin' friendships away."

"I don't either."

"Good. I'll make you a deal. Come back inside with me and help finish up the raid. Let's pretend this quitting business of yours never happened. Agree to come back to the unit, and I'll explain to the other guys that this was a sting operation, that you were on the side of the angels the whole time. How about it, Lou? Can we make these last three days just disappear?"

Becoming a Good Humor Man again... that rates dead even with necrophilia and cannibalism on my "to-do" list. But I'd eat my own arm if it would save my family from humiliation and financial hardship. "I'll rejoin the unit, Mitch, on one condition. You let the others know this was all a mistake. The three of you leave those people in there alone. My family and all their guests."

His eyes fall to the ground again. He shakes his head slowly. "You're asking too much."

"Why? Why too much?"

"That should be goddamned self-evident, Lou." His fury reawakens. "Brad and Alex saw what those people dumped in the toilets. They watched those girls in there make themselves throw up. What do you expect me to tell them, huh? How am I supposed to keep their respect, their allegiance, if I tell them some bald-faced lie? It'd mean the end of the unit!"

"You'd be lying to them anyway," I say as calmly as I can manage. "You want things between us to go back to how they were? I've told you what I need."

His half-hissed obscenity barely reaches my ears before he swings his axe in a violent arc, embedding its blade in one of the porch's wooden posts. "It's *impossible!*" he shouts. "Why are you being such a suicidal asshole? Those people in there — they're going down no matter what you do. You can save yourself, save your reputation, and they're going down. Or you can sacrifice yourself, like some fuckin' *idiot,* and they're *still* going down. So what's the goddamn *difference,* Lou?"

He doesn't see it. He doesn't see the difference, and that is terribly sad. "'Those people' are my family, Mitch. If you can't see a difference between my betraying them and my standing with them... then our friendship is done."

I see something break behind his eyes. I've done it. I've stepped into the abyss.

I follow Mitch back into the house. Cindy's guests are doctors, engineers, and architects. Most of them have probably never even been issued a traffic citation, and now each of them will have this century's scarlet letter permanently affixed to their record and reputation: "G" for Glutton. Their eyes beseech me for mercy, as though I control their fates. But I'm plummeting through the abyss right alongside them.

"Collect their health system cards," Mitch says to Brad. He indicates me with a twitch of his thumb. "His, too."

I open up my wallet and remove the laminated card. Sixty-eight years old. I'd better pray for good health.

Cindy watches me hand over my health card. Her last shred of hope that I might be able to stop all this dies. Tears begin flowing down her sunken face.

I can't bear to see it. "Cindy, I did all I could. I tried..."

My pleas die in my throat when I see her look to Will and Blair. They haven't lost only their health cards today. All chance of government grants for child-bearing just evaporated. Without those grants, their hopes for children have evaporated, too.

Oh, God. I'm dragging the future down with me. I need more than anything in the world to comfort them. But Buddy, Will's father, blocks my way.

"I never did like you," he says in a clipped voice, "you son-of-a-bitch."

His fist in my abdomen comes almost as a relief.

Home again, home again...

The cedar trees that line my driveway look like towering wraiths in the moonlight, monoliths waiting to fall and crush me. My flood-lit house beckons to me, an oasis of sanity and safety. It's an illusion. None of this will be mine much longer. Without the lease payments from the city, denuded of income, it won't be very many months until the bank forecloses and I'm put out on the street.

As soon as I open the front door, it hits me — the sickly sweet odor of clove cigarettes. He's not wasting any time.

"I know you're here," I cry, turning on all the light switches within reach. I'm on my own — no Mitch or Brad to back me up; no friendly San Bernardino police.

"I was not making any attempt to conceal myself, Dr. Shmalzberg." The Ottoman steps into the light, a grinning battle tank wrapped in emerald silk. "I trust you enjoyed a pleasant holiday meal with your family?" His voice, falsely sweet as poisoned syrup, wraps itself around a brief chuckle.

"You should've left my family out of this." I pray my voice isn't as tremulous as it sounds inside my head.

"I 'should have'? Ahh, but Dr. Shmalzberg, you 'should have' cooperated more fully. Actually, I must tell you that I am very pleased with the way events have unfolded. There is great pleasure to be had in squeezing the testicles of the arrogant. And you were arrogant, Doctor. Did I not tell you that your life was no more secure than a house of playing cards? But did you pay heed to this most considerate warning? You did not. And so I applied a slight tap of my fingertip to a card on the bottom tier." He makes a fluttering, falling motion with his fingertips. Glowing ashes from the tip of his cigarette land on my waiting-room chairs, etching black burn marks in the upholstery.

"You've accomplished nothing," I say, sounding unconvincing even to myself.

"Nothing?" He raises half of that single thick eyebrow which borders the top of his face. "I have rendered you more receptive to bribery by severely decreasing your ability to earn income. At the same time, I have made threats of personal harm more credible."

"Bribery?" I say, grasping desperately at any tangent which might give me time to think. "So you're still willing to discuss payments?"

He takes a long, slow drag from his cigarette. "Although I personally would not extend the graciousness of an offer of remuneration to you a second time, my master has directed me to demonstrate the benevolence of his regime by granting you the opportunity to efface your initial misjudgment. However, please understand that even such benevolence as his is not infinite. A second error on your part will free me to apply my... discretion." His black pupils gleam with anticipatory happiness.

"How much money are we talking about?"

"That depends entirely on the value of your service. Accurate information which leads me to the recovery of the Noble Blessed Troubadour's preserved remains — information which will be validated by my continuing custody of your person — will result in a substantial reward: either a wire transfer of forty-thousand golden dinars from my master's treasury, or a less valuable but more immediate cash payment of one hundred thousand of your American dollars. The actual handing over of said remains will increase your reward by a factor of three."

"The dollars — you have them on you?"

The Ottoman grins broadly. "The voraciousness of your greed is pleasing. Be assured that the precious dollars are most readily available. I take it that you will be providing information which will allow us to take a productive journey together?"

I could drive with him to Graceland. I could turn him loose on the

King's heirs, then take his filthy reward money and run. Maybe it would be enough for me to start over with again.

But I can't do it. Selling the Elvis to Graceland was one thing — I did it to pay for Emily's treatments. But selling him to a foreign government... the "Noble Blessed Troubadour" is as much a part of America as Mount Rushmore. No matter how powerful the French Caliphate has become, no matter how rich, they don't have the right to tear away a chunk of America.

I won't be a traitor to my country. And I won't betray my father again. I already sold my birthright once.

The stiffening tendons of his hands provide evidence of his growing impatience. "I can do better than provide information," I say. It's crazy, this ember of a plan. It's reckless and crazy and painfully disrespectful to my wife; but it's the only plan I can think of.

"Better than information... I can provide the Elvis."

"I thought as much, Doctor." The hands relax. "How much the better for you. Lying is a blot upon the soul."

I walk into my study, the Ottoman a step behind me. I unlock the cabinet where I keep Emily, only sliding it far enough open to reveal one of her two vacuum jars. I remove it and hand it to him.

He slowly turns the jar in his enormous dark hands, peering into its depths like a fortune teller consulting a crystal ball. "I am greatly surprised. To keep such a valuable possession in such an unprotected hiding place..."

"I wanted to keep it close and handy. I had no reason to think anyone besides my father knew it existed." He's keeping both the vacuum jar and me in his field of vision. I've got to get him to turn away, just for a few seconds, long enough for me to find something to clout him with.

"This artifact... it is not all that I expected." He holds the jar higher, closer to the dim overhead light. His voice grows colder. "My sources told me I would be acquiring between ten and twelve pounds of the Noble Blessed Troubadour's substance. I judge this container to hold no more than six pounds."

"Then your sources obviously knew next to nothing about liposuction procedures. Any old-time practitioner would've told you that six to eight pounds is the maximum volume of fat that can be safely removed during a single procedure. And Elvis only had time for one session before he died."

He sets the vacuum jar down on my desk. "I must warn you, Doctor... it is not necessary for me to rely upon your word alone that the tissues preserved within this jar are, indeed, the tissues I have sought. My master thought it prudent to provide me testing equipment. The hair of the Troubadour was less difficult to acquire than the fat has been. Having a few strands in my possession provides a fool-proof insurance against wasting my ruler's treasure upon counterfeits."

"You have a genetic analyzer with you?" He says nothing. If only I could get him to turn away — "Running the hair and fat through the analyzer is completely unnecessary. Proof of the fat's identity is easily visible. Surely you're aware that my father's cannula accidentally punctured Elvis's stomach cavity. Take a closer look at the fat in that jar, and you'll see partially digested chunks of Elvis's breakfast mixed in."

He picks up the jar again. This is my chance. "Here, let me turn on that lamp so you can see better."

I turn on the standing floor lamp next to my couch, then back away as he steps into the light. He holds the jar beneath the lamp shade, searching for what I described. Finally, his back is turned. I reach onto my desk for the commemorative plaque from the city, a gift celebrating my twentieth anniversary as a Good Humor Man. It's marble, heavy as a bowling ball.

"I do not see any particles of food matter, Doctor."

"Look closer," I say. No good; he's turning back toward me. There's a spare remote control for the vid-9 unit near the edge of my desk. I punch the Play button. The voice of the unctuous MannaSantos narrator blares from the meeting room next door —

"Beware the Fat Monster! In the days before your parents were born, the people of the rest of the world looked at America and laughed —"

His face jerks away from me. "What trickery is *this?*"

I lift the marble plaque above my head and clout him with all my strength.

Got him! But he drops Emily's jar — the thick glass bounces off the lamp's edge and shatters on the floor. I hadn't thought — oh God, Emily's remains are all over the carpet, mixed with broken glass...

He fell onto the couch. He's lying still. Not dead — he's still breathing.

Emily. I'm so sorry. No part of you ever deserved to be used like this. But you saved me, darling. You saved me.

At least for the time being. I nudge the shoulder of the man who has deranged my life. He doesn't stir. But he's brutally strong; he won't remain unconscious forever.

Killing him now would be easy... technically easy. In this house, scalpels are more numerous than spoons. And I know exactly where to cut him. But I just can't do it. If I had anesthesia equipment... no, leaving him unattended while under anesthesia would be the same as killing him. What else do I have in my clinic?

My examining table has restraining straps. I could strap him down. And shunt him with a glucose feed so he wouldn't starve to death while he's waiting for someone to find him.

But before I move him, I have to take care of Emily. I couldn't bear to smear her adulterated remains into the carpet while dragging the Ottoman to my clinic. I fetch a flexible spatula, soup ladle, and bowl from the kitchen. I know she'd be laughing if she could watch me scooping her up like spilled pieces of jellied gefilte fish. I wish I could hear her laughter right now.

Thank heaven my examination table has a hydraulic adjuster that lets me lower it to knee level. The three straps seem unnervingly thin as I draw them tightly across my captive's broad chest and legs, securing them with angry yanks. I reluctantly clean and dress his head wound. Then I rig up a glucose drip. His veins are clearly delineated, steel blue like a map of rivers feeding into the Black Sea.

I bury the bowl of Emily's exposed remains in the back yard, beneath an elm tree we planted together. She loved the night sky, tracing the constellations. The cool desert wind quickly dries my sweat, leaving only the salt behind on my skin.

They expect me to have the Elvis. Maybe the only way for me to stay alive will be for me to actually have it again. But more important than having the Elvis as a potential shield is this: Nothing has been right, nothing has been good since the day I sold my birthright. Selling it didn't save Emily. Nothing I bought with that money has brought me satisfaction or joy.

I used to bring the Elvis into the daytime darkness of my mother's bedroom, hoping that its invisible rays would somehow banish the wraiths draining her spirit. And they did. For at least a little while, its magic returned a living, caring mother to the scared little boy who needed her. I want to call on that magic again.

I *need* to call on that magic again.

My old life has withered into a dried scab on the back of my hand. New, unseen flesh has grown underneath. It's time to pull the scab away and learn my new skin.

PART II
All the King's Fat

CHAPTER 7

"I'm going to Graceland
Graceland
In Memphis, Tennessee
I'm going to Graceland..."

Paul Simon's been spinning on the car's stereo for the last five hours. I pull into Albuquerque well after dark. The first three exits off the highway into the city are blocked, so I take the fourth, the Central Avenue exit. Which takes me onto a still-living portion of old Route 66. The Mother Road. Adobe motels with glowing Art Deco neon signs beckon to me, images from sepia-toned postcards.

The snowfall's gotten much heavier. Good thing I've acquired a sense of how to drive on the white stuff. Growing expertise or no, I'm beyond eager to get off the road. Any of these motels will do. I choose the Pueblo 66 Motor Inn, based more on the quality of its neon sign than anything else. Just three cars are parked in the central court-yard. At least I won't have any trouble getting a room.

I expect to see a Native American waiting for me behind the reception desk. But the man behind the desk is tall and blond, maybe ten years younger than me, with a pinched, severe face.

"'Evening," he says. "Bet you're happy to be getting off the road."

That's an understatement. "Hello." I brush flecks of snow off my shoulders and stare enviously at the fireplace. "Do any of your rooms have fireplaces like that one?"

"Some do. Fireplace rooms cost a little more — ten a night more than our standard rate."

"Which is?"

"Twenty-nine ninety-five double occupancy. Local calls free. Special movies extra. Will you be paying cash or charge?"

Out of habit, I almost pull a credit card out of my wallet. But I hesitate. Charges on a card can be traced. Besides, the money I took from the trunk of the Ottoman's car gives me an extremely generous cash cushion. At least until the time comes to bargain for the Elvis.

"Cash," I say. "And I'll take a room with a fireplace."

"It's worth it. Staying one night?"

I nod. "Unless this storm doesn't let up." I'm bone-tired and hungry. "I need dinner, but I don't want to get back in the car. Do you serve meals here, or is there somewhere I can walk to?"

"We only do breakfasts here. There's a place called Mona's a block-and-a-half away, to the right up Central. Food's decent, nothing fancy."

"Thanks. I appreciate it." I take my key and walk toward the door.

"Hey, mister? You gonna want a woman? For later, I mean."

I stop and turn around, thinking maybe I misheard. "I'm sorry —?"

"I can get you a woman for the night, or just part of the night." His expression remains dull and matter-of-fact, enlivened a little by expectation of extra profit. "Indian or white, your choice. Good rates. I could have her waiting for you when you get back from dinner. It's a cold night."

We're shrinking back to our roots, the whole country. Albuquerque has become a rough-edged frontier town again. "No, uh, thank you. The fireplace should keep me warm enough."

The food at Mona's smells much better than "decent" as I walk through the door of the small, dimly lit adobe diner. I don't need to read the menu; I'll indulge in the enchiladas, tostadas, and taquitos I remember so well from lunches with my father in downtown Los Angeles... even if the beef is flavorless Leanie-Lean, and the cheese is denatured.

While waiting for my dinner, I peruse the dusty bric-a-brac for sale in the back of the restaurant. Lots of vintage Southwestern kitsch: Lone Ranger Big Little Books, beaded necklaces, kachina dolls. Something metallic and familiar-looking sits near the back of a shelf.

A portable *Realité Magique* unit. God... I haven't seen one in years. I pick it up, look for the place of manufacture. Lyons, France. It's one of the early ones. Not only that — it's been illegally jacked, just like mine was; the unit that Mitch made me throw away when I first became a Good Humor Man. Whoever owned this wanted to create his own private fantasias. Despite the risks of addiction, despite the dangers to his brain.

Holding this thing brings back so many memories. Not all of them bad, but all dangerously seductive.

The food, when it comes, is tasteless as sand. Not the fault of the cook, or even the ingredients... guilt doesn't make for a pleasant dinner companion. And I've got two: the guilt of having just purchased the RM unit, and the guilt of having not driven directly to Harri. This morning, when I awoke in Yucca, it would've been a straight shot north to Las Vegas. Maybe three or four hours at most. But I told myself I didn't want to bring my troubles down on Harri's head, in addition to her own problems.

I'll call her as soon as I get back to the motel. It's not too late to turn around and go north to Las Vegas. If she needs me. If she wants me.

Her voice on the phone is fogged with sleep. "Louis... is that you? I tried calling you back last night... left you a message to call me... let me call you back in a little while, okay?"

I'm so relieved to hear her voice. "You're all right?"

"Sure I'm all right. Why wouldn't I be?"

"You cut our conversation short yesterday. When those men drove up —"

"It was nothing," she says quickly, all traces of sleep gone from her voice. "Let me call you back in a few, okay?"

"I'm not home."

"Where are you?"

"New Mexico." I could tell her I'm on vacation. But just like fourteen years ago, I can't lie to her. "I had to leave Rancho Bernardino."

Her voice reverts to cautious distrust. "What's going on?"

How do I explain without sounding like a psychiatric patient? "I got in trouble with my Good Humor Men squad. An enemy ratted out some family members of my mine —"

"Since when have you had enemies?"

"Let me finish... when I tried to protect my family from having their health cards taken away, the other members of my squad turned against me. I've lost my practice. I've been publicly disgraced. So I'm taking the opportunity to... well, to recover a family heirloom."

"What! All this in *one day?* What deity did you piss off?"

She doesn't want to talk anymore on her home phone. She doesn't say why, but I'm sure she's afraid her line is tapped. Waiting for her to call back, I end up staring at the Remington print hanging on the wall. A Plains Indian hunts a bison with bow-and-arrow in the glow of a glorious purple sunset. Another ten years of population melt and it'll seem like white settlers never set foot on the Plains.

I wonder how they're doing. The Indians. So much of their traditional diet is made up of corn. So are they wasting away faster than the rest of us? Or has their high communal incidence of obesity provided them a shield, a temporary bulwark of flesh against the workings of the Metaboloft gene?

The phone rings. I pick it up before the first tone fades. "You found a safe phone?"

"Safe in one respect, at least," Harri answers, a strained laugh in her voice. "I'm at a pay phone outside a titty bar, about two miles from my house. I didn't think I'd be much competition to the girls inside, but most of the 'guests' here are about your age, and, well — you should see the wolf-looks I'm getting from these men as they walk to their cars!"

"If they're staring at you, they at least have good taste."

Her laugh is more full-bodied this time. "Flattery will get you *nowhere,* Louis. Now, how the hell could you get yourself run out of town? Didn't I always tell you you had no business being involved with those Good Humor roughnecks? I *knew* something evil like this was bound to happen!"

Oh *really?* Someone is engaging in a little selective memory adjustment. When we first started dating, Harri was perfectly happy to be hooking up with a Good Humor Man. "Thanks so much for the support and sympathy."

Nervous, I flip through the pages of a Gideon Bible I found on the nightstand. It falls open to a bookmark. No, not a bookmark; a business card from one of the local "warmth" girls.

"Okay, guess I deserved that," Harri apologizes, more quickly than I expected she would. "It sounds like you've gone through a real shit-storm. I'm just disappointed..."

"Why?"

"Well, to be perfectly honest, if I end up needing a whistle-blower, you'd be a hell of a lot more useful to me if you hadn't become a disgraced fugitive."

"I get you." I take a closer look at the card. The drawing of a vulva is explicit in a raw way, but also very well done. "It certainly wasn't my intention to ruin my reputation."

"I know. I know."

I put the card back and close the Bible. "You never finished telling me about the Metaboloft gene."

"In for a penny, in for a pound, I guess. Where did I stop yesterday?"

"We were talking about starving deer. I caught one knocking over my trash cans. How are the deer being affected by Metaboloft? Corn isn't normally part of their diet."

"No, it's not. Your deer aren't eating corn. That's the most frightening aspect of this infestation. It's gone way, way past the corn fields."

Although what she's telling me isn't unexpected, my stomach feels like I'm spinning out on snow-covered I-40. "How far? It's gotten into the *grass?*"

"At this point, I don't have any idea how far. The geo-genetic map of the infestation changes month to month, and we haven't even begun studying how far insects and wind currents might be spreading it outside the United States. What I *do* know is that the Metaboloft gene — we lifted it from an Amazonian blowfish — is exceptionally social. The little son-of-a-bitch really sleeps around. Its ability to finagle itself into the genetic structure of other plant forms is like nothing I've ever seen."

"What about safeguards? Surely MannaSantos must've known about their creation's proclivities before they put it into the hands of farmers?"

"Of *course* we knew, Louis! We aren't *idiots*. The project managers recognized what the new gene could do, and they built a virtual fortress-wall of inert proteins around its location in the altered gene-string, to ensure it would be neutralized if it was ever carried to other plant forms. Sort of a custom-fitted condom. Not only that, but the company directed that all farmers approved to grow Metaboloft corn could only grow the product on limited acreage, and that acreage had to be surrounded by thick belts of non-related crops, like soybeans, wheat, or cotton."

My father's eyes float in the shimmering air above the fireplace, seeming to grow bigger as the flesh around his eye sockets melts away. "So what happened?"

"What else? The unexpected. The confluence of X-factors that nobody was able to foresee. All of the field testing on the Metaboloft corn was performed in hermetically sealed environments. The scientists tried to make these sealed environments as nearly identical to natural growing environments as possible. And these trials only took place after months' worth of simulations had been run on the company's bank of supercomputers. Everything looked dandy. Normal precautions kept the blowfish gene from spreading, and in the exceedingly rare instances when it did, the protein condom sat on top of it like the Rock of Gibraltar.

"Three years ago we signed up our first farmers. They made record profits. Public acceptance of the new brand was quicker and more enthusiastic than that of any other product in MannaSantos's history. Our stock price took off like a rocket. Everybody was happy as pigs in perfumed shit. Yours truly included, since my bonus was composed entirely of preferred stock options.

"But a funny thing happened on the way to paradise. You remember that ozone hole that appeared over parts of Iowa two summers ago?"

"Vaguely... I remember reading something about a billion dollars' worth of corn getting a bad sunburn."

"Yes. Well, the Metaboloft corn actually proved to be hardier than standard varieties. The intensified dose of ultraviolet rays didn't seem to harm it at all. Not visibly, at least. But later tests showed the product had undergone internal changes. The protein condom surrounding the blowfish gene had been weakened. Just enough to be susceptible to one other environmental factor we'd thought we'd guarded adequately against — the B3Z9 secretion found on the legs of local bees. That's the stuff which helps make bees 'sticky' and more effective at carrying pollen from one plant to another. Under lab conditions, the B3Z9 secretion hadn't degraded the protein condom at all. But the combination of elevated UV exposure and B3Z9... well, let's just say our condom broke, but good."

My ear aches from the pressure of the receiver against it. "What happened when MannaSantos discovered the breakout?"

"Harvest was virtually over by then. The company directed that any remaining Metaboloft corn be cauterized with special herbicides. They promised to reimburse the affected farmers with an improved variety of the product for the following season, cost-free."

"How benevolent of them —"

"Look, MannaSantos took the outbreak very seriously. They bought up and destroyed all the produce from the crop belts that had surrounded the Metaboloft corn in southeastern Iowa. Our investigators believed the rogue gene hadn't had time to spread farther than the belts. They tested samples of corn and other crops all over the state. All the samples were clean. They thought they'd nipped the outbreak. Our gene engineers then spent the rest of the year working on strengthening the protein condom and building in even more safeguards. The Metaboloft corn planted the third season, and all the product planted since, is completely environmentally inert."

"Am I wrong to assume a great big *'But...'* enters the story now?"

No laughter. "The 'but' is that the bees carried the gene to places the investigators hadn't thought worth looking. Weeds and wild flowers; flora outside the human diet. Once it insinuated itself into these plants' seeds, the blowfish gene was entirely unencumbered by any protein condom at all. Its spread was only limited by the speed at which insects and the wind could carry it. Our drifter doesn't discriminate at all. It's equally happy to infest grasses, feed grains, tubers, legumes..."

"And MannaSantos has managed to keep this all a secret?"

"The government knows. Their researchers discovered the outbreak about ten months after ours did."

"Why hasn't the public – or at least the medical community – been informed?"

"Oh, why do you *think,* Louis? MannaSantos is one of the wealthiest firms in the country, not to mention the most aggressive. Plus, the feds recognize that the only organization with expertise and resources even barely adequate to begin attacking the problem happens to be – big surprise! – MannaSantos. Can you imagine what would happen to the company's stock valuation if word got out? Forget for a minute the public's loss of confidence in the company. Why would Joe and Joanne Public pay a two-hundred-percent premium for Metaboloft-branded products, once they realize they're getting the same weight-loss benefit from any loaf of cheap, generic white bread? Word of this gets out, and MannaSantos could potentially face bankruptcy within a year. No company, no technical help for the government."

"If word leaking out could be so catastrophic, why tell me any of this?"

"I'm telling you all this because... because even though right now MannaSantos has every reason under the sun to get this mess back in the bottle, there may come a time when the company's interests and the interests of, you know, humanity at large... won't be in synch anymore."

I don't want to think about that. "Are you making progress, at least? Surely, with both MannaSantos and the government pooling their scientific talent... you'll get this cleaned up, won't you?"

My feeble show of confidence merely makes her sigh. "You can only work with the tools you have at hand. We've got, at most, maybe thirty percent of the biodiversity we had fifty years ago. The most incredibly frustrating part of this whole project is that when promising genetic blocks appear in the databases – records we have of pieces of genetic material that could potentially help us build a counteragent to the Metaboloft gene – the donor organisms are gone. Kaput. Extinct.

"Huge chunks of our databases go back to the 'teens. International scientific agencies were falling over themselves, trying to catalogue the genomes of thousands of plant and animal species before they disappeared. They tried rescuing viable mating colonies, too, or at least preserving cell samples. But in the middle of GD2, there wasn't any money for that massive a preservation effort. Data was much cheaper and easier to preserve than tissues or organisms. So data's all we've got left. Enough data to make me scream."

The bison in the picture looks so fat, healthy. Even the Indian looks positively stout. But when the Indian eats the bison which eats the grass which carries Metaboloft... "You're not saying it's hopeless?"

"Hopeless? No. Fresh data banks have arrived in the past month from India and China. But even taking these new data pools into consideration, we've already mined close to three-quarters of the known stocks of genome information. And we're shooting blanks. You want to know what kills me? Our best lead, the source of a gene strand that could slap the Metaboloft gene silly and send it crying for momma? You know where that gene strand comes from? The common, domesticated banana."

I don't understand. "But Harri, I just bought a bunch of bananas at the market last week."

"No, you didn't. You *thought* you were buying bananas. But what you actually bought was a banana-like fruit, genetically modified to be a delivery system for a whole range of vaccines. You're a doctor, Louis. When was the last time you gave a kid a vaccination shot for polio, chickenpox, influenza, or even tetanus?"

I remember articles in medical journals years ago about the advances in worldwide vaccination techniques. "You mean to tell me there aren't any plain, ordinary bananas grown anymore?"

"Nope. The new, genetically altered varieties brought in such tremendously higher profits that growers all over the world yanked up their root stocks and switched over. It didn't hurt, too, that the altered strains produced fruit which was hardier and took twice as long to rot. You want to know when the last 'plain, ordinary bananas' were harvested? I looked it up. It was 2022, in a remote mountainous province in the Philippines.

"And here's the kicker, Louis. What company brought the genetically altered bananas to market?"

I don't need three guesses. "MannaSantos."

"Bingo with a capital 'B'. The banana project was one of the very first things I worked on. When I was young and altruistic and wanted to help save the world."

The self-loathing I hear in her voice pains me. "Tell me what I can do. Do you want me to come be with you? I could be in Vegas by tomorrow night."

Part of me wants her to say yes. Another part prays she doesn't. "That's very sweet of you, Louis. But no. You'd be a distraction. And I can't afford distractions right now."

When I ask again what I can do, she tells me to stay in touch. And then she surprises me by asking what she can do for *me*. I ask if she can send someone to visit my father and tell him that I'm all right, that I'll come see him as soon as I can. She tells me she'll go visit him herself, as soon as she's able to take a day off.

I hardly have time to thank her before she gets off the line. I don't get a chance to wish her good luck. Or ask her to be careful.

Loneliness settles heavily on my shoulders. I open the Bible to look at that business card again. Some adolescent fumblings with Harri fourteen years ago... that's the most intimate contact I've had with a woman since Emily died. I'd hardly know what to do anymore. Maybe letting a professional do it all for me is best.

I feel myself blushing like an adolescent as I dial the front desk. The clerk I spoke to earlier answers. "That offer you made before," I say. "I'd like to take you up on that."

The next few minutes are an ordeal of panicked anticipation. Too late, I realize I didn't specify an Anglo or Indian companion. I hope she'll be an Indian woman. I don't care how young or old; I just want a bed companion with solid flesh on her bones.

My companion knocks just as I finish drying myself from a fast shower. I open the door. She's an Anglo woman, in her fifties or sixties, dressed in an ill-fitting blonde wig. I can tell from the angular lines of her face that she'll make even Miss Dissel look voluptuous by comparison.

"Mr. Berg?"

"Yes. Please come in."

She takes off her winter coat and tosses it onto a chair. Her form-fitting knit dress makes her painful to look at, accentuating the jut of bone where the curve of pliant flesh should be.

She reads my face. "So I'm not what you were expecting, huh?" She shrugs her shoulders. "That's all right, honey. Turn out the lights and it's all the same. Nice fire; it's *cold* outside!"

I don't want to be cruel. But the thought of seeing her without her dress on... "I — I'm so sorry. I thought I was ready for this, but I'm not —"

She sits on the edge of the bed and rubs her ankles. "There's no rush. You having equipment problems? I'm pretty good with that."

I shake my head.

"Okay. The customer's always right. But I don't make house calls for nothing, not on a night like tonight."

I send her away with seventy-five dollars of the Ottoman's money. The RM headset sits on the dresser, near the second — and last — jar of Emily's remains. I haven't let myself use an RM in over twenty years. But everything's changed now. Why deny myself her company, or the shadow of her company?

I put it on. The leatherette straps feel clammy on my bare scalp. The brief slide through vertigo strips two decades from me. I'm a young widower again. Only the pain isn't as fresh.

"Louis? That's a lovely fire you've got going. I've always wanted to see the Southwest in wintertime. This vacation was a wonderful idea."

I slide into bed next to my wife. Her hips have rounded noticeably in the nine months since the last time we used my cannula together. Her eyes grow playful. "I may've overshot my mark just a bit, weight-wise. Do you think?"

Pulling her toward me, I watch a log crack in two and fall into the fire, causing a brief flurry of sparks. A throbbing gathers behind my forehead. I sense my metabolic fires burning hotter as the flames in the fireplace begin to slowly die.

CHAPTER 8

Q: So, Dr. Shmalzberg, if the world were about to end, what would you do? Take a trip to Jamaica? Study the Torah? Get laid?

A: I'd drive sixteen-hundred miles to buy or steal a jar of Elvis's preserved belly fat.

"Dr. Shmalzberg?"

The window slid open without my noticing, nudging me from my musings. "Thanks for being patient, sir. Mr. Swaggart will be out to see you shortly. Please have a seat in the main reception area. And thank you so much for visiting Elvis's Graceland."

The receptionist murmurs the pleasantry with all the genuineness of a talking toaster. This Tennessee blonde with the adorable chin cleft and mechanical delivery is the fourth functionary I've introduced myself to since my arrival at the Graceland complex. Six and a half hours ago.

My persistence must finally be paying off, however. From the look of my surroundings, I've gotten closer to the center of things. This waiting room is a replica of the famous Jungle Room. I saw the original this morning, in the main house. It was enclosed in walls of glass, protected from dust and temperature shifts like a da Vinci painting. I almost laughed, seeing dreck that even my grandmother would be ashamed of protected with such care. Lime-green shag carpeting. Sofas upholstered with fake monkey fur. Smiling tikis embedded in the shiny dark wood of every lamp, cabinet, coffee table, and chair.

"Louis Shmalzberg?"

I turn around. A diminutive man in a gold suit waits to shake my hand. "Thank you for your patience. I'm Daniel Swaggart, Associate Director for Acquisitions and Exhibits."

His tall, hairless forehead pegs him at middle-aged. But his short stature and smooth, unlined face almost make me believe he's a pre-teen wearing a suit and a rubber bald-head for a school play. "Thank you for meeting with me," I tell him. "Mr. Greenaway isn't available?"

He smiles. "Mr. Greenaway retired twelve years ago. I took over his job when he left."

Greenaway was the man I dealt with when I sold the Elvis. I shouldn't be surprised he's retired. We conducted that transaction a quarter-century ago, and he wasn't young then.

"I realize this may sound somewhat rude, Doctor. But before we begin our discussion, I must ask you for some proof that you are who you claim to be. The Graceland Corporation's greatest asset is the unquestionable authenticity of the artifacts it shares with the public. Preserving and enhancing the sanctity of Elvis's memory is our business." He smiles that unsettlingly delicate smile again. "Not that I have any reason to believe you aren't *you*. But I have to stick to protocols, you understand."

"No problem at all," I say, handing him my driver's license and my Good Humor Man badge. Plus, I have something else with me that should establish my bona fides even more effectively.

I unzip the large canvas satchel at my feet and pull out a smaller case made of worn black leather. I set it on my lap and click open its tarnished brass clasps. Inside are my cannula and vacuum pump, unused in two decades. A pair of antiques, manufactured in Heidelberg, Germany, in 1998. Outside of medical museums, there probably aren't more than a few dozen of these left in existence.

I watch his eyes grow big behind his glasses as he realizes what I'm showing him. He reaches out tentatively. "Is that... is that the instrument your father used? What was inserted into, ahh, the belly...?"

His reverent tone masks what must be an acquisitive mania in his curator's soul. It's my turn to smile. "No. This isn't my father's cannula. His is even older than this one, one of the first ever made."

"Do you have it?" he asks quickly, hunger creeping into his voice.

I close my black bag and place it back in the satchel. "It's not with me. But I can put my hands on it. If we're able to arrive at a deal."

"I'm afraid I don't understand, then. I was told you were offering unique artifacts for immediate sale. Items that I could properly evaluate and authenticate."

"I only mentioned my father's cannula as a possible sweetener." My fingertips glide along the top of the satchel. "I have other items with me which should interest you greatly. Although I'm afraid I *did* misrepresent myself, somewhat."

His eyebrows arch slightly. "Oh? How so?"

"I implied I was interested in a straight sale of my goods." I fold my hands on my lap. "But it's a barter I'm interested in. Several of my artifacts for one of yours."

His eyes remain unreadable. "I see. I'm rarely presented with a proposal of this kind. Would you mind taking a walk with me? I'd like to continue our discussion in my office. It won't take us more than a few minutes to walk there. You'll have a chance to see some of what we've done with the Graceland complex."

"I'd like that very much."

We exit the office complex and enter a glassed-in, climate-controlled walkway. Ahead of us, a set of escalators lift pedestrians to a glass and neon bridge that crosses high above Elvis Presley Boulevard.

To our left is the Graceland mansion itself. It looks unimpressive, almost puny, hardly more monumental than the doctors' and lawyers' homes in the neighborhood where I grew up. It doesn't help that the house is dwarfed by the hotels, retail malls, and amusement parks that surround it. I try to imagine the mansion as it appeared back in the mid-1950s, when the thoroughfare that later became Elvis Presley Boulevard was hardly more than a dirt road. It must've seemed much more impressive back then.

Riding the escalator to the bridge above the boulevard, I stare up at the gray, angry sky. It might snow at any moment. It feels so strange, rising through a column of seventy-five-degree air while surrounded on all sides by raw, unpredictable winter. Like I'm in the midst of a 3-D movie; and any second now the clouds will peel apart, unzipped by celestial fingers, revealing blue blue ocean and Elvis on a surfboard strumming his guitar, singing to a chorus line of mermaids.

Swaggart gestures for me to join him at the guard rail. "I think you'll find this one of the most impressive views in the whole complex," he says. Six lanes of traffic flow beneath our feet, passing block after block of what appear to be — churches? Can that be right? I'd expected to see souvenir shops, miniature golf courses... and I do see some, but they are vastly outnumbered by the neon-striped spires and towers of houses of worship.

"The churches have sprouted up just in the past five years," Swaggart says. "This place almost went under thirty years ago. Elvis's original fans were beginning to die off. Attendance at the house was declining ten, fifteen percent a year. The area surrounding Graceland had become a slum.

"My father began the process of changing all that. He wasn't a member of the family or the inner circle. His rise in the corporation was purely on the basis of talent and vision. He was one of the first to realize how Elvis's protean nature could be harnessed to ensure a growing profit stream, no matter how radical the shifts in the psycho-emotional needs of the American public."

I was hoping he'd talk more about the churches. "I'm afraid you've lost me..."

His smooth face becomes more animated as he warms to his subject. "More than any other major American figure, Elvis is a Rorschach blot. His persona, music, and influences encompass an astoundingly wide swath of the American experience. A viewer can chose to see virtually whatever he wishes when he stares at a reproduction of that famous face. For far too long, cultural historians chose to focus exclusively on what they saw as the *duality* of Elvis's persona — the 'momma's boy' who worshipped his mother and sang gospel music, versus the 'rebel,' the sexual adventurer who introduced the pelvic thrust and black culture to the white teen masses.

"But his ability to encompass opposites goes far beyond that. Even during the most emotionally charged years of the Civil Rights era, he was able to appeal to both sides of the racial divide. In 1957, polls revealed that he excited black teen girls and white teen girls nearly equally. Yet the hardcore Southern white audience never held this against him, because Elvis was so clearly one of their own.

"He also bridged both sides of another of his era's social chasms, the issue of drug use. At the same time he was collecting police badges and petitioning J. Edgar Hoover and Richard Nixon for status as an undercover Federal narcotics officer, Elvis was slowly poisoning himself with vast quantities of stimulants and depressants."

"So you're saying Elvis was some sort of... super hypocrite?"

"Not a hypocrite, no. A hypocrite believes and acts one way while espousing the opposite. Elvis was able to fully encompass contradictions."

Maybe it's the glow of all that churchy neon, but his enthusiasm is infectious. "I think I see. You're talking Louisiana Hayride versus Las Vegas Hilton. *The Complete Sun Sessions* versus the soundtrack to *Clambake*. Skinny Elvis versus Fat Elvis."

Light from the neon Elvis silhouettes mounted on the bridge glints off his glasses, making his eyes look bright pink. "That's in the spirit of what I'm telling you, yes. Although as you well know, 'Fat Elvis' has no place in the current *zeitgeist*."

"You said the churches have only been here five years. What was on all that prime land before they were built?"

"Remnants of past efforts to align ourselves with the American *zeitgeist*. When my father first began working here, the company was strictly a purveyor of nostalgia. A nostalgia too narrowly focused to be economically viable. My father's initial impulse was to broaden the company's focus to include nostalgia for Elvis's *era*. Utilizing Elvis as the fulcrum for an entertainment experience which immersed the visitor in the glories of the 1950s — years when American might was second to none, when our families and churches were strong, when our economy was bigger than the rest of the world's combined output — during the awful years of GD2, this was a *masterstroke!* Virtually overnight, my father's strategy made Elvis relevant again.

"A few years later, when the rise of young world powers like India made our relative decline painfully apparent, he shifted his strategy to focus on Rebellious Elvis. The Elvis with the constant sneer, who dared combine all the *gauche* forms of American vernacular music into something brazenly new, who flaunted his incendiary sexuality even on *The Ed Sullivan Show* — *this,* my father recognized, was the persona to anesthetize America's wounded pride."

He still hasn't answered my question. "So what was out there — museums? Theaters? Roller coasters?"

"All of that, and more."

"And it's all gone now? Knocked down?"

"Some of it still stands. But times and needs have changed. Ten years ago, our prognosticators concluded that America is on the cusp of another Great Awakening, a spiritual revival of the kind that occurred during colonial times and again in the Civil War era. Your Good Humor movement has been a foreshadowing of this — the masses seeking to purge their bodies of evil. We seek to predict such gathering waves, then position ourselves to ride them. In the most profitable way possible."

"But how do you make money off of churches?"

Swaggart's laugh is startlingly loud. "Was that — was that a *serious* question?" He regathers his composure. "I'm very sorry," he says soberly. "To answer your question, the Graceland Corporation owns all the land within a two-mile radius of the mansion. The dozens of churches, synagogues, and temples you see all pay rent to the Corporation. The Corporation provided loans for the construction of said edifices and will be making money from interest for many decades to come. The religious institutions raise money in all the ways such institutions always have: weekly collections, televised appeals, tithing, et cetera. The Corporation takes a flat twenty percent. And we benefit in other ways. The pilgrims all need to eat and sleep, and the Corporation is happy to provide restaurants and hotels."

I can't help wondering what Elvis would think about this spiritual commerce being carried out in his name. "I can see what Graceland gets from the churches. What do the churches get from Graceland?"

Swaggart stares at me like I'm a simpleton. "That should be obvious," he says. "They get *Elvis*. On a strictly licensed basis, of course." He turns back to the panorama below our feet. "Those churches, they're like a hundred petri dishes. Each one an experiment by a different preacher, all praying that his particular mix of Jesus or Moses or Krishna and our Elvis will bloom and spread through the country like a burgeoning epidemic."

He turns back to me. "It's easier to show you than tell you. Would you like to visit one of our most promising churches? It's not far from my office."

"I'd be very interested, thank you."

My host leads me out of our bubble of artificial warmth onto the western side of Elvis Presley Boulevard. My lightweight California overcoat is immediately overmatched by the weather. At least the church isn't far.

"Welcome to the Church of the Third Resurrection," Swaggart announces grandly. From the outside, the building isn't all that remarkable. Apart from Art Deco neon fins, its traditional Protestant architecture wouldn't look out of place on any Midwestern suburban street.

It's empty and quiet inside, and much bigger than I thought it would be. They can probably squeeze between six and seven hundred pilgrims in here. I follow Swaggart toward the front stage. We pass stained glass windows depicting what I recognize as the Stations of the Cross. After the window of Jesus on the cross, there is one with his disciples surrounding an empty tomb. Then a taller window depicting what can only be a young Elvis on stage, his sideburns and pompadour looking oddly Byzantine when formed from hunks of colored glass. The final and tallest window doesn't depict any figures at all; only an abstract flame or radiance.

Swaggart watches me trying to puzzle out the story behind the windows. "The worshippers here consider the first resurrection to be Jesus's emergence from his tomb. Can you guess the second and the third?"

"The second resurrection must be as Elvis. The third... I couldn't even hazard a guess."

He climbs onto the stage and stands beneath a sculpted representation of this church's trinity: the cross, the face of Elvis, and a stylized, abstract radiance. "Jesus died on the cross to free man of his sins. Three days later He appeared to His disciples and promised He would again return. With His second resurrection He appeared to the world as Elvis Aaron Presley, whose mission on this earth was to free man of our false dreams, which had accrued in our souls during the centuries since the cross. Elvis lived all our darkest fantasies for us so we wouldn't have to — the worldwide fame; the fawning multitudes; the love of any woman he desired; mastery of his chosen art; freedom to alter his consciousness; enough wealth to acquire anything that he wanted, and more. He had it all, and the world watched it poison and kill him. A lesson worth heeding, Dr. Shmalzberg."

The smug little hypocrite. The evils of wealth — as if he isn't swimming in preferred stock options. I glance up at the stylized flames above Swaggart. "So the third resurrection — he returns as a 'hunka hunka burning love' and redeems the world?"

"A very inventive pun, Doctor. No, the exact nature of the third resurrection is kept deliberately vague. Whatever the actual nature of the third resurrection, it will serve to free mankind of our fleshly bodies, the source of all sin. To reduce us to our most basic essence, that of pure spirit."

To free mankind of our fleshly bodies... A chill slithers up my backbone. Swaggart's "third resurrection" sounds frighteningly like the ultimate denouement of MannaSantos's runaway Metaboloft gene.

He leads me toward the exit, oblivious to the fact that his treasured third resurrection is much closer than he could dream. "Our Protestant sects have been the most creative when it comes to theology," he says. "Not to denigrate what our rabbis or Hindu or Muslim clerics have tried. You're of the Jewish faith, aren't you? We're especially happy with what Rabbi Goldblum has come up with. The way he's been able to translate traditional Presleyan recipes into strictly kosher meals has been nothing short of amazing. And the rabbi himself is a very credible Elvis replicant."

We reenter the heated walkway. Snow flurries have begun falling. They melt on the glass overhead. He points the way to a large, warehouse-like building. "My office is in there. In the Collections Overflow Annex."

He punches in a security code at the door. We walk past a pair of what appear to be Elvis-themed Mardi Gras parade floats, each a hundred feet long. One is a tableau from *King Creole,* another from *Blue Hawaii.* A bit farther in, one of the demons of my childhood grins down at me from a thirty-foot-tall photograph. Oh, how my father hated Richard Nixon. There he is, shaking hands with Elvis in the White House. Elvis is wearing the belt, the gold World's Championship Attendance Record belt presented to him by the Las Vegas

International Hotel; the belt he gave my father as a gift. The one I have with me in my satchel.

The wall-length windows of Swaggart's office provide a spectacular view of Elvis Presley Boulevard. He motions me to an overstuffed velour chair, then showers me with a smile that could pull the gold from my teeth. "Can I offer you a fried peanut butter and banana sandwich? One of Elvis's favorites."

Although I'm hungry, I shake my head no, not wanting to consider what "peanut butter" is made of nowadays. He pulls several forms from a drawer. "There are substantial tax benefits for donating artifacts to the Graceland Heritage Foundation, our non-profit branch. Given your family's connection to our founder, I'm certain that my Board would be happy to valuate your donations most generously."

So that's what this whole show-and-tell has been about. Without even knowing what it is that I have in my bag, he's tried to dazzle me into giving it away. "I'm not interested in making a donation, Mr. Swaggart. I'm interested in a trade."

He leans toward me. "What is it we have that you want?"

I take a deep breath. "I intend to reacquire what I sold your predecessor twenty-six years ago. The jar of preserved adipose tissues my father extracted from Elvis in 1977."

To his credit, Swaggart doesn't immediately react. "I see," he says at last. "May I ask why?"

"My father is dying. The 'souvenir' he kept from that experience was possibly his most precious possession. Until he entrusted it to me."

"And you sold your birthright for a mess of pottage."

"Yes." Should I tell him about Emily, her cancer? No; he doesn't need to know. "My father's memory is dying faster than the rest of him. Having the Elvis near him, where he can see it, could restore his glory years to him."

He leans back in his chair. "That's admirable, Doctor. Truly. I was very devoted to my father, myself. But surely you must realize the extraordinary nature of what you're asking. You're asking me to surrender a piece of *Elvis Aaron Presley*. I don't know how religious you are, but wouldn't you say that those ten pounds of fat your father extracted should rightfully rest in the same place as the body they were taken from?"

My heart stops. "So you buried the fat?"

His lips part, but he pauses before answering. "No, we didn't bury it," he says. I begin breathing again. "An extraordinary request. What you have there to offer me in exchange must be equally extraordinary."

I place my satchel on my lap. I'll start with the ring. "These are both tokens of appreciation Elvis gave my father. This ring was originally given to Elvis by the Jewish members of his Memphis Mafia." I hand Swaggart the ring, a weighty chunk of twenty-one-carat gold surmounted by an oversize *chai,* symbol of a happy life; the Hebrew characters are outlined by rows of diamonds. "His friends had their names engraved on the inside."

He retrieves a jeweler's loupe from his desk and examines the ring closely. "I'd have to authenticate this, you understand."

"Of course."

He hands it back to me. "What else do you have?"

"This." I pull the belt from the satchel. I get a much more noticeable reaction out of Swaggart. His hands tremble as I hand it to him. He flips the gargantuan gold belt buckle over and brings it very close to his face. I'm sure he's looking for some minute flaw, some tiny identifying mark that only he and his staff would know should be there.

When he lowers the belt to the desktop a minute later, his expression is both enraptured and wary. "This... this is authentic," he says. "From the opening of the first museum, back in the 1980s, we've always had a reproduction on display. No one ever knew what had become of the original."

"Keep in mind that I'd be able to make my father's cannula available for your collection, as well." He's still staring at the belt, but there's a twinge of sadness around his mouth. "The jar of fat — I'd like to see it now, if that would be convenient."

His voice is flat, airless. "We don't have it anymore."

"What?" A sudden pain makes me clench my eyes shut. "But you said you didn't bury it —"

"We didn't. My predecessor stored it in a vault, away from public view. It was... stolen. A disgruntled ex-employee. We're virtually certain of that."

Of all the ironies — here I was, contemplating somehow stealing it myself if Swaggart wouldn't deal, only to learn someone beat me to the punch years ago. "If you're so certain this employee did it, why didn't you ever go after him?"

"Her."

"Her. It's not as though Graceland doesn't have pull with the authorities. You must fund half the Memphis Police Department —"

He cuts me off with a forlorn sigh. "There were... complications. Matters I'm not at liberty to discuss. The likely thief was cognizant of the fact that her knowledge of certain internal matters effectively shields her from legal pursuit on our part."

"So she's still alive? You know where she is?"

"We have kept tabs on her, yes. In case she should ever decide to attempt to harm or embarrass the Corporation."

I thought this "Chase for the Great Whatzit" would end here. But I guess this is an E-ticket ride. "Maybe you all are constrained from going after her. But I'm a free agent, with no connection to Graceland. Tell me where to find her, and I'll go after the Elvis."

I see one of his eyebrows arch. "You're serious about this?" he asks. "Your father's handiwork means that much to you?"

"It does."

His fingers caress the belt. "Information is a commodity like any other, Doctor. And all commodities cost."

"No." I reach across the desk, scoop up the belt, and stuff it back into my satchel. "The belt is no longer on the table. Not in exchange for information that may or may not prove useful. I may need it for when I negotiate with your ex-employee."

Grabbing the belt was a good move. The sweat on Swaggart's lip has gotten beadier. He dabs at it with a crisp white handkerchief. "When you... ahh, *if* you are able to reacquire the artifact, you realize that, legally, it will still remain the property of the Graceland Foundation. However, as I said before, I'm fully sympathetic with your dying father's emotional needs. I see no reason why we shouldn't be able to work out a shared custody —"

"I'll think about that. When and if the time comes." *Like hell I will.*

"But surely you can't expect me to release the information to you for no recompense..." His face regains some of its self-possessed slyness. "Actually, I've thought of a trade neither of us would object to. You were once a very highly regarded plastic surgeon. Do you still retain your old skills?"

Swaggart certainly doesn't look like someone in need of a liposuction procedure. "You'll have to be more specific. My 'old skills' cover a lot of territory."

"I'm speaking of facial reconstruction. Back when you were practicing, it was available to anyone with enough money. Now the law limits it to people with medical necessities, or accident victims. Can you still do it?"

I take a closer look at Swaggart's face. There's nothing wrong with it. Good bone structure, normal musculature... not perfectly symmetrical, but then again, no one's face is. "It depends on what you have in mind. Some procedures were extraordinarily involved. Others were relatively simple, and I did them hundreds of times. I'll bet even my father could still perform a passable nose job."

His lips press themselves into a tight smile. "Good. It's a nose job I'm thinking of. Does my surname mean anything to you, Doctor?"

"Your surname?" Actually, it had seemed faintly familiar. *Swaggart.* Some news story from a very long time ago... a sex scandal in some socially backward Southern state, Mississippi or Louisiana. "Wasn't there a preacher, a televangelist... *yes.* Jimmy Swaggart, wasn't it? 'I have sinned against you'?"

"Correct. The Reverend Swaggart was my great-grandfather. Which means The Killer was a cousin of mine."

"The Killer?"

"I'm sure you're familiar with the musical rivalries of the early Presleyan period. During the first half-decade of his career, only one other rock 'n' roller challenged Elvis for preeminence. My great-grandfather's first cousin, Jerry Lee Lewis. If Jerry Lee hadn't married his own thirteen-year-old cousin, scandalizing the nation... who knows? He could've been crowned King. Perhaps you remember when a coterie of music critics tried to rehabilitate my cousin at Elvis's expense?"

I do recall a *Time* magazine cover with the caption, "Who's the REAL King of Rock 'n' Roll?" It featured snarling portraits of Elvis and Jerry Lee Lewis, both dressed in boxing garb.

"My father had nothing to do with any of that," he continues. "But the Board of Directors always looked upon him with suspicion after that damnable *Time* article appeared."

He turns so that I can look at his profile. Portentously, he taps his nose with his index finger. "This is my genetic curse, Doctor. The spitting image of The Killer's nose. At every Board meeting, I have endured the unwavering, hostile stares of Elvis's descendants, all aimed at this traitorous protrusion."

Swaggart pulls some strings. The next morning we drive to a municipal hospital where he's managed to rent a surgical suite for the day. A nurse pins up photos of Elvis's profile, photos Swaggart brought to guide me in my work. Just before we put him under, I learn the name of the city where I'll be traveling next: New Orleans.

When Swaggart removes his shirt, I see the results of an earlier attempt at ancestral renunciation. His entire torso is covered with tiny square tattoos. Photo-quality reproductions of dozens of Elvis's record covers, each exquisitely engraved in his flesh.

The grid is interrupted only on his solar plexus. In that place of honor are the cross, the face, and the flame that will consume all flesh.

Breaking Swaggart's nose isn't the hardest thing I've ever done.

CHAPTER 9

New Orleans was once one of America's top tourist destinations. Now the only tourists who still come are connoisseurs of ruins and scavengers of illicit foods. Hurricane Katrina flooded eighty percent of the city decades ago, and then Hurricane Edwin flattened much of what was left.

A damp, cold breeze makes me step inside a boarded-up doorway. The man I'd spoken to on the phone told me to stand in front of the abandoned Catholic church opposite my hotel, the Fairmont, a once grand hotel just outside the Quarter. Clumps of homeless men and women are burning trash fires just up the street. The wind blows gray smoke in my face. My escorts should be here soon, the men who'll take me to see Oretha Denoux. It didn't take too much prodding of the leads Swaggart gave me to locate Denoux's organization. Just mentioning the name "Elvis" on the phone was enough to make her people take me seriously.

A black limousine turns off Canal Street, taking the corner much faster than it should. It skids to a halt in front of the church. The limo's doors pop open. Three young black men, faces mostly hidden by wide-brimmed hats and dark glasses, swiftly approach me.

"Are you with Oretha Denoux?" I ask, feeling both foolish and afraid.

Two of them grab my arms. "Get in the car, Graceland," the third says.

The ride that follows isn't the most pleasant I've ever taken. I spend it immobilized between two towers of muscle, blindfolded, my ears battered by a bizarre fusion of speed ska and Louis Armstrong.

I'm led inside a building, walking blind. I'm still blindfolded when a woman introduces herself as Oretha Denoux. "You come to see me at a very inconvenient time, Dr. Shmalzberg. Carnival season has just begun. Tonight is our first parade."

Her voice is pleasant enough. Melodious, but with the submerged steeliness of someone who is used to the exercise of unquestioned authority. The bodyguards remove my blindfold. Somewhere outside, a brass band rehearses.

"My men examined the contents of your wallet," she continues. "Jerome tells me he found a Good Humor Man badge with your name engraved on it. Member since 2017. That is bad. Very bad. And very indiscreet. Can you give me one reason why I shouldn't have my men cut out your liver and toss the rest of you in a bayou?"

I should've been more prepared for something like this. But Swaggart didn't tell me Denoux would be a gang leader of some kind. She's sitting in an oversized chair, virtually a throne. She is... substantial. Not obese by any means, but a woman of presence. Behind her throne is a gigantic plume of peacock feathers, matching the crown of feathers and gemstones nestled in her dome of wiry black hair.

"I'm waiting, Doctor. Patience is not foremost among my many virtues."

The henchmen holding my arms (in old detective novels they would've been called "torpedoes") snicker. Swaggart stated that Ms. Denoux is a canny businesswoman. I'll try to take advantage of that. "One good reason you shouldn't toss me in the bayou?" I say, my voice stronger than I expected it would be. "I'll give you several. One, I understand you appreciate a good profit; I intend to provide you with one. Two, although I still carry the badge, I'm no longer a Good Humor Man. I was officially expelled as of five or six days ago. You can check that out with the Rancho Bernardino government in Orange County, California, or directly with the town's Good Humor squad. Three, if the Good Humor Men are your enemies, I'd make a very valuable ally. As a founding squad leader, I know their tactics and procedures as well as anyone. I know most of the state chapter heads personally. And every principle the movement stands for makes me want to puke up the same liver you so dramatically offered to remove."

She laughs at this, a full-bodied laugh; not mocking, but appreciative. "You speak very well for yourself. However, I still find the badge most disturbing."

"If I'd wanted to hide my past association with the Good Humor Men from you, why would I have carried the badge in my wallet? The only reason I've kept it at all is because of the doors it might open for me while I'm trying to reacquire my family heirloom. In most parts of the country, being a Good Humor Man earns me a lot of deference."

"Agreed." She leans slightly forward on her throne. "But who is to say that you did not keep your badge in an easily findable place exactly so that you could appear disingenuous and nonthreatening?"

"Call my references. I'll give you the numbers and names. They'll tell you how traitorous I am."

She laughs again, but this time a mocking tone is wrapped within her mirth. "Oh, I intend to call them." She nods to the henchman on my right. "Jerome, be sure to take down the good doctor's contacts." He pulls out an electronic notepad and thrusts it into my hands. "But rest assured that any information I obtain from your acquaintances will be taken with a large amount of salt... say, the amount suspended in the Gulf of Mexico."

I place the notepad back in Jerome's large paw. "Ms. Denoux, why not listen to my offer, weigh its profit potential, and then decide whether the profit outweighs any possible risk I might pose?" Her face remains shadowed, hard to read. "Honestly, if the Good Humor Men wanted to send someone to spy on you, why would they send *me?* I don't exactly blend in." I'm the only Caucasian, as well as the only person over forty, in the room.

She laces her fingers and leans her chin on them. "The time I can spare for this interview grows short. I agree that there is little possible harm in listening to your offer. But before we talk business, you need to explain to my full satisfaction one other matter. When you first contacted my offices, you mentioned an artifact that exceedingly few persons are aware exists. Who pointed you in my direction?"

There's no sense in trying to lie. Even if I could come up with a lie I thought was plausible, she'd see through it in an instant. "Daniel Swaggart of the Graceland Foundation."

Jerome's grunt is almost sympathetic. His boss looks anything but pleased. "Ahh, Dr. Shmalzberg," she says, her mouth betraying a genuine sadness. "And here I was almost beginning to like you. I am surprised. I truly believed Mr. Swaggart would never be foolhardy enough to risk upturning our proverbial apple cart. But now I have no choice but to do serious damage to his beloved Foundation. Not to mention its elderly messenger boy."

"Swaggart's not coming after you," I say, quickly. "Even more than you, he wants to keep things quiet. I'm an Elvis collector, not a cop or an investigator of some kind. Swaggart only agreed to tell me where you are because I'm harmless, and because he knew I'd offer you a good price for the Elvis. And because I offered him a bribe he couldn't pass up."

"And that was?"

"I'm a plastic surgeon. I gave him a nose job. Changed his nose from a Jerry Lee Lewis beak to something more closely approximating the Presley proboscis."

Her icy countenance thaws into something close to a grin. "Really? Swaggart had you do that? For *that* he gave you my name and risked upsetting our truce?" She throws her head back and laughs. When she looks at me again, her eyes sparkle. "I believe you, Doctor. I finally *believe* you. I know that walking pustule too well to not believe that is exactly how he would behave. The worm! The toady! He would give them his balls in a box if they'd make him chairman!" She gestures dismissively to her men. "Leave us. Dr. Shmalzberg and I will be discussing business in the parlor."

The parlor is decorated with expressionistic paintings of what look to be Mardi Gras parades. Ms. Denoux invites me to sit on a plush leather sofa, then offers me coffee. She surprises me by serving it herself, even steaming the milk for me. The coffee is richer than any I've tasted in years. A prime culprit could be the foamed milk, which tastes suspiciously (and deliciously) natural and creamy.

She invites me to tell my story. I repeat all that I had told Swaggart, adding in the events that led to my resignation/expulsion from the Good Humor Men. I finish my account by offering an opening bid on the Elvis: seventy-five thousand dollars.

She presents neither a counteroffer nor even a reaction to let me know she has heard my proposal. Instead, she sips slowly from her cup and eyes me as she might an interesting insect specimen. "Where is home to you, Doctor? Do you miss it very much?"

Not the question I was expecting. "Home?" The realization hits me like a slab of meat dropped from a third-story window. "Right now, I'd have to say I don't have one."

"Then I am most sorry for you. Home has always meant everything to me. Family. Neighborhood. I was born in New Orleans, and apart from the few years I worked for the Graceland Corporation, I have always lived here. Are you aware of what happened to New Orleans during the years of GD2?"

I shake my head.

"There is an old saying: 'When the rest of the nation sneezes, New Orleans catches pneumonia.' For many years the city's entire economy rested on tourism and international trade. So what do you think happened here when the international trading system collapsed and the average household income plunged by over sixty percent?"

"I'd say the rest of the country caught pneumonia, and New Orleans went into cardiac arrest."

"Precisely. Tourism evaporated. The French Quarter became another of our above-ground cemeteries, quiet and empty. Even our petrochemical plants, affected by the decline of the rest of the nation's economy, were shuttered. The only people who remained were those without the resources to leave. Or those who, like my family, refused to leave.

"This was in addition to the devastation brought by two major hurricanes, Katrina and Edwin. More than two thousand people drowned. Tens of thousands more were left homeless. After Edwin, there was no money to rebuild. The federal government cut us loose. That was when I made my decision to go to Memphis, to join the Graceland Corporation."

"Why Graceland?"

Her face takes on a self-satisfied glow. "A family connection. My grandmother had been one of Elvis's retinue of servants at the mansion. The heads of the Graceland Foundation always had a soft spot for anyone who'd had personal relations with their King. I did not want to leave New Orleans. But I saw the potential to return someday and uplift my home with the skills I would acquire."

Interesting as all this is, I'm concerned that I didn't get even a glimmer of a response to my offer. "I don't mean to be rude, Ms. Denoux, but I thought we were talking about the Elvis."

She pats my hand condescendingly. "Oh, but we are, Doctor. You see, I want to make you understand that Elvis Presley means very, very little to me. Fats Domino means more to me than Elvis Presley. Louis Armstrong, *far* more. I am not a cultist or a collector of 'holy' artifacts. I am a pragmatist; Elvis was never more to me than a means to my end."

The meaning behind her words sinks in. The slippery fat is sliding from my grasp again. "So what you're telling me is, you sold it."

Her dark brow furrows with concern. "I'm sorry to cause you such disappointment. But of course I sold it. I sold it within weeks of obtaining it, after putting forth word of its availability to trustworthy elements within the collectors' community. The proceeds provided the initial capital I used to build the organization I now head."

I sigh. "And who did you sell it to? Space aliens who wanted to clone Elvis and populate an entertainment satellite with hundreds of copies of him? My next stop is a hundred billion light years from here?"

She laughs. "Oh, I doubt you'll have to travel quite that far. Do not look so depressed; it makes me sad. There is no reason why we cannot still conduct business."

"Only now we're negotiating for information, rather than fat?"

She hands me a second cup of coffee. "Information is what this world is built upon. That, as well as family and fine food. But before you offer me a revised sum, let me make you a proposal. Cash money is a fine thing, but as you can see, it is not something of which I am bereft."

She places her soft hand on my thigh. "However, there may be something you can offer which would be of far greater benefit. Before you can do so, you'll need to take a little ride with me. You should find it quite illuminating."

*

I'm still not completely trusted. As soon as we leave the parlor, the two torpedoes slip the blindfold on me again. Ms. Denoux remains close at hand.

"I apologize for the return of the blindfold, Doctor. But I'm sure, were you in my position, it is a precaution you'd take, as well."

I hear car doors being opened. "Jerome, please make sure Dr. Shmalzberg doesn't hit his head." Then I smell tanned leather, cannabis, and foreign tobacco. The engine rumbles to life, almost certainly an old-style gasoline or diesel internal combustion model.

"We're heading for our den," Ms. Denoux tells me. "How familiar are you with the customs of New Orleans Carnival krewes?"

"Uh, not familiar at all."

"In the old days, a krewe was basically a social aid and pleasure club. Each krewe held several balls and social events during Carnival, and most also sponsored a public parade. Carnival was always central to the city's idea of itself. It was one of the things that made enduring the humidity and poverty and hurricanes worthwhile."

We round a corner faster than I would've thought possible. I'm thrust against Ms. Denoux. She rights me without any fuss and continues. "With the abandonment of Carnival during GD2, a part of this city died. A vital part; the part that gave those who stayed here the will to resist adversity, to stay the course —"

"To ride out the storm?"

"Yes. My overriding goal, even before I left New Orleans for Memphis, was to somehow resurrect Carnival. Ahh — our den is just ahead."

As soon as the car door is opened and I'm guided outside, I suck in a lungful of pungent nostalgia. It's like being on the old Santa Monica Freeway at rush hour — diesel fumes choke me, make my eyes water even behind their partially protective blindfold. One after another, large displacement engines cough and rumble into wakefulness.

"This is one of several warehouse complexes where we create and store our fleets of parade floats," Ms. Denoux says. I can barely hear her. Hands push and pull me up a short set of steps, then across a metal deck that vibrates like the cockpit of an ancient biplane. I'm pushed against what feels like a padded pole. Something is wrapped around my legs and midsection. Hands grasp my wrists, pull my arms behind me. I feel cold steel closing around my wrists, squashing my watch into my tendons.

"Why am I being handcuffed?"

Ms. Denoux's voice comes to my rescue. "There's no need to fear. You've been cuffed for your own safety. The streets are badly cratered, and there's a good chance our driver will need to employ violent evasive maneuvers. Far better you should endure some discomfort than be thrown beneath the wheels of this float. I am right here next to you, secured to a harness post only five feet away."

The deck beneath my feet begins vibrating at a higher frequency. The whole structure shudders and moans as we begin rolling forward. The diesel stench recedes from my lungs. I smell other odors in the breeze: ripening garbage, raw sewage, and, incongruously, the aroma of freshly baked cakes.

I hear voices, excited cheers, chants, and loud music. As if in response, loudspeakers somewhere behind me thunder into life. The back of my body is pummeled by mighty vibrations, the heavy syncopation of a brass street-jazz band.

"There is music all over the city tonight," Ms. Denoux says, her voice barely reaching me through the thick blanket of sound. "Word has spread. The street knows that tonight is the first parade. The music is both celebration and camouflage."

"Camouflage?" I yell back at her. "How so?"

"If there is music everywhere, your friends cannot use remote sound triangulation equipment to pinpoint the route of our parade. They are forced to create roadblocks in many different neighborhoods, man checkpoints all over the city. The more thinly we can force them to spread themselves, the less chance there is of a confrontation."

"But why would they be trying to stop you? What do the Good Humor Men have against a parade?"

"That will quickly become apparent."

We aren't moving very fast. As my ears adjust to the music, I can hear other sounds, packages being torn open on the float, shouted exclamations from float riders, voices below us calling out —

"Turtles!"

"Kingkake!"

"Creoles! Here! Over here! Creoles!"

"Throwmesomethin, mister!"

"Kingkake! Kingkake!"

"ThrowME*somethin!*"

Something is shoved into my mouth. Something soft and spongy. I gag violently, but then the flavor hits my taste buds. It's sweet. Delicious. My tongue detects different layers — crunchy glaze, chocolate, angel food cake, caramel swirled with raspberry sauce. This pastry is the best thing I've had in my mouth in a quarter-century.

I open my mouth wide, hoping my benefactor will insert another one. My gesture is greeted with friendly laughter and pats on my shoulders.

My blindfold is removed.

The first thing I see is fire. Dancing fire, jets of flame gyrating ten feet above the street, swooping and spinning. The flames are held by human dancers. They clutch tall metal poles which terminate in what look like huge candelabras. The flambeaux are the only illumination on this street. No street lamps; or, if there are, all their bulbs are burnt out or broken. Glancing around, I see that my float and the floats ahead of and behind us carry their own lights, hundreds of multicolored lights draped in strings. The floats look like toppled-over Christmas trees.

I glance at Ms. Denoux. She looks like a warrior princess from a Wild West Show, her feathered bonnet and soaring peacock cape making it hard for me to tell where her costume ends and the float begins. "What was that your friends stuffed in my mouth?" I yell.

She's busy waving at the crowds and tossing gold coins from a box at her feet. "That was a turtle. One of my staff's special concoctions, a re-creation of an old delicacy. Did you like it?"

"Yes!" I feel like a kid on a carnival midway. I want to drive the float, gun its engine to full throttle. The crowd surges around us, rapt faces lit by swaying firelight, arms held above their heads, open palms grasping, beseeching. "I loved it, I want another one!"

She laughs, and I hear the sound of a delighted little girl in it. She kneels and reaches behind her into another box, then carefully steps across the shuddering deck, holding onto a series of grab-handles.

"Open wide, Doctor."

I open my mouth as wide as it'll stretch. Ms. Denoux doesn't shove it all the way in. She waits for me to take a bite, chew, savor the flavors, then swallow; then she inserts the turtle just a little more. "Is this what you wanted to show me?" I ask as soon as the pastry is gone.

"Only part," she says, stepping back to her own harness post and rearranging her straps. "The rest will come soon, once your friends find us."

"They *aren't* my friends," I say, frustration rising. Rounding a bend, I count eight lumbering floats behind us. "Selling the Elvis couldn't have possibly paid for all this. How do you fund your Carnival?"

She smiles sardonically. "When I returned to New Orleans, the city was replete with economic niches lying unfilled. The food industry here was crippled by a lack of traditional ingredients, thanks to the food fascists. I brought it back to life by restoring the flow of those traditional ingredients, now entirely sourced off-shore.

"And all this? This is my way of giving back to the city that sustains and shelters us all year long. Most of the people you see can't afford our delicacies at market price. But during Carnival, all is given free for them. This season, the crowds are even more voracious than normal. Rumors have spread of a wasting disease that attacks the old. Many people you see are gathering what they believe are life-saving foods for their elders."

So the Metaboloft effect has reached even here. Our procession turns a corner onto a wider boulevard. The crowds are ten people deep, spreading back to sidewalks broken up by the roots of giant live oak trees. Riders hurl a continual fusillade of small packages. Some fly only a few feet before being snatched from the air, while others soar and spin, food missiles aimed at those poor unfortunates trapped at the back of the crowd.

Our procession slows, then comes to a complete stop. Ms. Denoux speaks rapidly into a radio headset, an angry look on her face. "You know my rules! Stopping is not permitted for any reason! *Any* reason!

I don't care *how* thick they've built the roadblock! That lead float of yours is built to handle it! Use it — or I'll shove you out of that driver's seat so fast you'll have friction burns. Are we in *complete* understanding?"

Thirty seconds later, the parade's music is overwhelmed with sounds of breaking wood as the lead float crashes through some sort of barricade. I look more closely at the front end of this huge vehicle I'm handcuffed to. Its prow comes to a sharp, armored point. As the float ahead of us begins moving forward again, I notice the tremendous girth of its tires, the massive suspension that wouldn't look out of place on a desert assault vehicle. The parade resumes, but for me, at least, the helium has been let out of the balloon. This is less a bacchanalia than a hurricane party. We're waiting for the storm to roar in.

It doesn't take long for the first gusts to arrive. I hear the keening of calliope music, growing steadily closer. In response to Ms. Denoux's exhortations, the parade splits apart. Our float veers sharply left, its engine emitting an urgent, powerful whine. My right shoulder and head are bashed against the harness post as we climb a weed-strewn median. The float crosses this obstacle with the ease of a supercharged millipede. Five or six other floats behind us follow our lead, towers and turrets dislodging oak branches that shatter on the broken asphalt. Other floats follow the lead vehicle, which accelerates in its original direction.

We turn onto a wider street, taking the corner so fast my stomach lurches. The tossing of pastries from the floats hasn't stopped, not even for a second. Gas shells erupt amidst the people on the sidewalks. The Good Humor Men are close. My eyes begin tearing as wisps of gas reach the float. The crowds scatter. Children scream as their mothers drag them away.

We pick up speed. The first of the Good Humor trucks darts out from a side street. It races along on the far side of the median, weaving to avoid debris, heading against traffic, which, luckily for them, is nonexistent. It's no match for us on a straightaway. We quickly begin pulling ahead — but not so quickly that I don't see the rifles in the hands of my old comrades.

I hear the cracks, then the pings of shots ricocheting away from metal side-skirts. And the thuds of bullets striking home, puncturing tires. We don't lose any speed — the tires must be run-flats.

My eyes, still teary, are suddenly flash-blinded by a pair of head-lights. Another truck, this one lying in wait alongside a darkened syn-agogue, darts onto the street. Its windshield is barely five feet from my legs. The road's hardly wide enough for the float alone. The truck's body panels scrape against our side-skirts in a shower of sparks. One parked car could mean disaster — they'll have to stop. Pastries aren't worth dying for. Are they?

Hands push fire through opened windows. Incendiary bombs? I look backward, craning my neck to see where the weapons land. One bounces off a deck and flares briefly on the street. Another catches against an empty harness post, ignites the straps and nearby boxes. A rider blasts the flames with a burst of chemical spray.

Half a block ahead, a huge sport utility vehicle sits half-on, half-off the sidewalk, squeezing the truck's path to zero.

"Pull off!" I yell at the Good Humor Man driving. Doesn't he see? "Pull off! Stop! *Stop!*"

The truck slows, but not nearly enough. Looking down, for an instant I see a middle-aged white face, a face that could be Brad's, or Mitch's. Or mine.

The smashup savages the night. Our float shudders violently to the left as part of the Good Humor truck gets trapped beneath our wheels. I feel the whole mammoth vehicle fishtail. Then we lurch back to the right as the wheels free themselves of wreckage.

And still the pastries continue to soar, their cellophane packages glinting in the light of gasoline fires.

Enough. Let's turn around. Enough of this *Road Warrior* Mardi Gras. It isn't worth this. Not a life.

There's a barrier up ahead, a jumble of Dumpsters and old cars. Turning off would mean slowing down, maybe leading the parade into a cul-de-sac, a trap.

We don't slow down.

Twenty yards from the barrier, I see another panel truck lumber-ing toward us. This one from the left, from the far side of the wide median. The driver — what's he doing? He's jumped out of the truck onto the street — he's launched it at us like a giant clattering cannonball. If it's loaded with explosives or gasoline, it'll explode against our side and I will helplessly burn...

Our driver takes evasive action. But pinned in by trees and utility poles, he only has a narrow pathway in which to swerve. Here it *comes* —

Impact! No explosion, thank God. The truck rebounds off us like a billiard ball hitting a bowling ball. We rock violently but right ourselves. The driverless truck careens off our side in a blaze of sparks, bounces off an overturned Dumpster and a pair of utility poles —

...and topples onto a group of children watching us from the far sidewalk.

We hit the barrier. The clamor of screeching metal blots out any screams I might otherwise hear.

"Assassins! Lunatics! *Kamikazes!*"

We're back in the den. Ms. Denoux's fury could melt lead. One rider on my float had his legs crushed when that driverless truck careened into the float's side. Another man, riding on a different float, was killed by a stray bullet.

And then there were those children on the sidewalk.

"*Now* do you see why I need your help, Doctor?" Her eyes drill holes through me, as though she considers me partially responsible for the carnage.

"Tell me what you want me to do," I say quietly. "And I'll tell you if I'm able to do it."

"Make. Him. *Stop*. This Martin Severald — damn his hairless skull! Guns! He dares to introduce *guns* into our contests! What sort of a lunatic is he? Doesn't he realize that in a competition of who can buy the deadliest weapons, he will lose? And in the escalation, people will die?"

"What about the local police? You must have them sitting in your pocket. Can't they pressure Severald to back off?"

"Our local police," she hisses with contempt, "are ineffectual. *We* provide more security in the neighborhoods than they do. The Good Humor Men were ineffectual, too. Until Severald arrived two years ago."

I decide to risk her wrath. "You want to give back to your community? I saw children crushed out there tonight. Crushed to death because they wanted a pastry. Don't lure them into danger. Cancel your parades."

"That is *not* an option. Do you think I don't *mourn* for those children? But I cannot — I *will* not let that shake me from my course. Carnival is vital to this city. Carnival will *never* be canceled."

So much for that suggestion. "But how do you expect me to get Severald to stop? Local squad leaders aren't appointed; they're elected by their men. If Severald has solid support from his men — and judging from the almost fanatical dedication I saw out there tonight, he most certainly does — the only way to get rid of him, short of killing him, would be to convince him to voluntarily step down."

"I do not want him killed," Ms. Denoux says. "I want him neutered. Martin Severald is a beginner, an amateur. Before Severald, David Brock was our Good Humor Man. Brock knew how to play our game. When he and his men pursued our parades, it was theater. Pastries were confiscated. Some citizens lost their health cards. But no one was ever hurt."

She places her strong hand on mine. "If you wish to learn the name of the buyer of your Elvis fat, you will convince Martin Severald to step down. And you will return David Brock to authority."

I can't recall ever having met Martin Severald. But I've been introduced to hundreds of Good Humor Men over the years. At various conventions, I've addressed thousands more. My biggest hope of pulling this off is that, even though I don't remember him, he'll remember me.

His office is located on the eighth floor of a shabby downtown office building. The elevator rattles ominously as I ascend, making me wish I'd taken the stairs. The decor is about what I expected it to be. Paramilitary. Copies of vintage Good Humor Men recruiting posters are displayed prominently, reeking of macho self-righteousness.

Someone steps into the outer office. He's wearing jungle cam-ouflage and combat boots. In the middle of downtown, it looks silly. "Yes? Can I help you?"

I hand him my Good Humor badge. "Show this to Martin Severald, please. Tell him I need to speak with him. Privately."

He glances at the badge, and I see his eyebrows rise as he reads the initial service year. He disappears into the inner office. About two minutes later, another man emerges. He's an inch or two shorter than me, but much broader, almost as broad as the Ottoman. His grip is strong, aggressively so. "I'm Martin Severald, squad leader, South Louisiana Good Humor Troop One."

"Doctor Louis Shmalzberg, squad physician, Good Humor Men of Rancho Bernardino."

"It's an honor to have you here, sir. I heard you speak in Tucson, at the 2038 national convention. Your speech meant a lot to me. What brings you to my office? We don't usually get unannounced visitors from National."

"Let's talk privately, Mr. Severald." He leads me into his office and shuts the door behind us.

Once we're both seated, he pushes my badge across the desk to me. "We've been having a rough go of it recently," he says. "Is National planning to back us up? I was hoping —"

"Where is Mr. Brock?" I say, cutting him off. "This matter concerns him, too."

"David Brock? He's not in leadership anymore. After the men voted him down three years ago, he pulled out of the squad."

"Then you'll need to contact him and communicate the dictates of this meeting."

His expression sours in a barely perceptible way. "And just what are the 'dictates' of this meeting?"

I force my face to remain blank. "We in National had hoped it wouldn't come to this, Mr. Severald. Squad autonomy is very impor-tant to us. But your activities have crossed the line. Your aggressive-ness threatens to unravel an undercover operation more than fifteen years in the making. An operation that could deliver the entire con-traband food trafficking network into our hands."

He squints. "I don't understand —"

"You've become a liability, Mr. Severald. I hate being so blunt. For us to have allowed you to oust Mr. Brock was a mistake. We now intend to rectify that mistake."

"Mistake?" His hands curl into fists on his desk. "My men elected me. Who the hell are *you* to be telling me a goddamn thing?"

"You want to know who I am?" I turn the badge around so that it faces him. "I'm member number one-thirty-nine. My squad was one of the founding dozen. I saw Hud Walterson with my own eyes the night he died; I was only half a block from the candied popcorn factory while it burned. I didn't see it in a documentary — I was *there*. That's my authority, Mr. Severald."

The starch goes out of his bearing. "So what is it you want me to do? Cut back our patrols? Kiss that goddamn bitch Oretha Denoux on the ass?"

"You will have to step down. Mr. Brock will need to be reinstated as squad leader. You will be allowed to stay on as a member, but not in any leadership capacity."

"You can't *do* this," he says, a vein on his forehead pulsing violently. "My men won't stand for it —"

"We can disband your chapter. Have the State of Louisiana remove your legal protections. We will then institute a fresh chapter, install Mr. Brock as head, and recruit new members."

"I'll fight this —"

"You don't want to do that. Not unless you crave public humiliation and the end of any standing within this organization."

It begins to sink in that he's not going to win. "Why are you doing this? None of this is in the charter, the bylaws..."

I smile as sympathetically as I can. "There are charters above the charter you know. I respect you, Mr. Severald. I respect your dedication, your devotion. It's tragic that things have come to this. Because I respect you, I'm going to tell you something you aren't supposed to know. Repeat this to any other officer from National, and it will be vehemently denied. Even my meeting with you here today will never be acknowledged. Insist that it occurred, and you'll be ostracized.

"That bitch Oretha Denoux? She's one of ours. She has been from the beginning. And she's worth more to us than a hundred of you."

*

Five days after my visit to Mr. Severald, Ms. Denoux invites me to join her in her parlor. The glowing smile on her face tells me she is pleased.

"You appear to be a man of your word, Doctor. Last night's parade occurred without incident. No shooting, no pursuit. No Good Humor Men at all. My sources tell me that David Brock has been convinced to return to his old post. A cash gift from my corporation helped him make that decision. You've done much. What are your plans after you regain this Elvis fat? My organization has a place for a man of your knowledge and talents."

"I'm taking things one day, one place at a time. So tell me, where am I heading for next?"

She hands me an envelope. "Miami Beach. That is where my buyer was living at the time of the sale. But there is something else you should know. Something that could impact your transaction, perhaps in a dangerous way." She didn't mask the concern in her voice.

"What are you telling me?"

"This buyer told me much about himself. He was a plastic surgeon, too, like you and your father. He knew your father professionally. This is why he wanted the Elvis fat."

I search my memory for a possible match but come up empty. "Why is this a problem?"

"Because his hatred for your father burned like a flambeau's blue flame."

CHAPTER 10

I'm sitting in my car, windows down, sipping a papaya-grapefruit juice near Biscayne Bay, not far from the Miami Beach Convention Center, where Elvis performed in 1970. According to Oretha Denoux, Dr. Eric Trotmann has the Elvis.

Trotmann. My father's worst enemy. The disgraced colleague my father tried to send to jail, but only succeeded in getting temporarily disbarred from the practice of reconstructive surgery.

There's no chance he hasn't held onto it. Having it in his possession, knowing that my father was denied it, would be worth more to him than any conceivable sum of money. I sense it's here — the Elvis is somewhere within a two-mile radius of where I'm parked, hidden in this tangle of century-old hotels, megalomanic architecture, and pumped-in sand. Ms. Denoux and Trotmann exchanged business correspondence not more than nine months ago. He's here. I feel it.

GD2 provided him some cover by deranging the nation's medical network. The economy's thousand-car smashup opened innumerable cracks in the sidewalk where scurrying cockroaches like Trotmann could live and flourish.

Now I just need to shine a bright flashlight beam into the right crack.

Checking the local phone book is easy enough. But also useless. The copy of his recent correspondence that Ms. Denoux provided me isn't helpful; the return address is a post office box, closed six months ago. In a library branch near City Hall, I rummage through old phone books going back two decades. I find a few Eric Trotmanns listed in the earlier volumes, but all without a "Dr." attached to the name.

Knowing Trotmann's ego, none of these could've been him.

I have better luck at the main Miami-Dade County office of NHMS, the National Health Maintenance System. NHMS doesn't pay for any cosmetic surgery beyond reconstructive procedures deemed medically necessary, so I figure Trotmann would've been providing most of his services outside their purview. But he might've at least signed on to the NHMS physician rolls, in order to lap up any legitimate work that might be thrown his way. He's four or five years younger than my father, which puts him in his midnineties. He could still be plugging along.

Thanks to the Freedom of Medical Information Act and my status as a physician, NHMS's bureaucrats allow me relatively unhindered access to their files. Trotmann is in their database, but his record was marked "Inactive" five years ago. No contact information is available.

Playing a hunch, I switch from Referrals to Complaints. *Bingo*. A Ms. Julia Bonnabel filed a complaint against Trotmann only twenty months ago. She's local. There's an address listed: 53 Sunset Lane, apartment 451. In Overtown.

When I leave NHMS headquarters, I spot a long black sedan, windows darkly tinted, slowly winding its way through the streets of the municipal complex. I'm pretty sure I've seen a similar vehicle, possibly that same car, on the highway between New Orleans and Miami. I might've even seen it on the road between Memphis and New Orleans. The black sedan pauses at a stop light, the hum of its motor like the watchful purr-growl of a panther. Then it drives away.

No one needs to ask for directions to Overtown. Not even a newcomer like me. Like Manhattan's skyline, Overtown is visible from twenty miles away. It sits suspended like a gigantic Sword of Damocles above the relatively low-rise structures of the South Beach Historic Art Deco District. This city-above-a-city was planned and built when Miami Beach's city fathers believed the world couldn't get enough of their island. The boom years, just before GD2.

Overtown, "two-point-seven square miles of brand-new real estate, with spectacular views of ocean and bay, minutes from the famous Deco District, available for luxury retail and residential development," was built in the shape of a gargantuan table. Its deck, the foundation for dozens of once-planned skyscrapers, hovers eighteen stories above beach level. In order not to throw the denizens of the original city completely into shadow, Overtown's designers specified that the deck be constructed of translucent glass-polymer, strong as steel, fortified by a web of titanium rods.

The engine of my little Nash, burdened by the weight of my belongings and the food I've brought from New Orleans, whines pitifully as I ascend one of the long spiral rampways that leads up to the deck. Overtown's builders camouflaged the deck's four main supports with statuary. Four grand colossi now appear to support Overtown on their massive shoulders — Christopher Columbus, "discoverer" of the New World; Carl Fisher, the developer and impresario who founded Miami Beach; José Martí, liberator of Latin America from Spain; and Elian Gonzalez, liberator of Cuba from Castroism. Winding around and around the spiral ramp, my windshield is filled first with Columbus's boots, then, more distant, Elian's Nike sneakers; Columbus's oilskin tunic, then Elian's bony adolescent knees; Columbus's sextant, Elian's handheld Nintendo game console; Columbus's flaring Roman nose, Elian's halo of angelic curls, befitting a miracle child who was rescued from drowning in the Florida Straits by dolphins sent by Jesus... or so the story is told.

The parking garage at the top of the ramp is eerily deserted. I count only seven other cars. Three of those sit on flat tires. From what I've heard, much of Overtown has devolved into low-rent housing for the service workers required by the relatively thriving Art Deco District below.

I'm at the edge of a vast construction site, frozen by GD2 in a permanent state of incompletion. The skeletons of gigantic towers rise from the yellowed glass of the deck, awaiting concrete and chrome skins that will never come.

In the sheltering shadow of a derelict trolley car, I check my map for 53 Sunset Lane. It doesn't look to be too far away, maybe three or four blocks. I walk alongside a grid of moving sidewalks that haven't moved, in all likelihood, since the year I sold the Elvis to Graceland. Ahead of me, a flock of seagulls hover, their beaks flecked with red, screeching murderously as other birds try to snatch their prizes. They scatter as I walk closer. My nose tells me what they're fascinated with before my eyes do. It's a dead cat, its hind parts caught in some rusting machinery.

The four-story apartment building at 53 Sunset Lane appears to be in much better shape than its neighbors. This isn't saying much. The security gate is permanently open, its hinges reduced to brown metallic flakes. The building's foyer is partially filled with reeking trash bags; either garbage pickup is extremely irregular in Overtown, or the building's tenants are trying to discourage squatters.

I climb the worn stairs to the fourth floor, find apartment 451, and ring the bell. I hold my physician's identification card up to the peephole and wait for Ms. Bonnabel. I can't get my father's voice out of my mind, the bile in his voice as he described Eric Trotmann's crimes. They had been friends and roommates in their med school days (Trotmann had been one of the youngest students ever admitted to UCLA's Medical School). They both opted to specialize in reconstructive surgery. Not long after I was born, they established a practice together in Beverly Hills. But their partnership didn't last long. It dissolved over a dispute regarding billings and record-keeping.

This was just a minor speed bump in my father's career. When my father's practice took off like a Saturn V rocket, his ex-partner was left very much on the ground, breathing rocket exhaust and hating it. He, too, went to France to learn liposuction. But by the time Trotmann returned to Beverly Hills and reestablished himself, the one-time boy wonder found himself relegated to the minor leagues of the plastic surgery business, forced to witness my father's major league triumphs.

Still not a peep from Julia Bonnabel. Just as I'm beginning to wonder whether I should return later, I hear footsteps from the other side of the door. A woman's voice asks, "Who is it? What do you want?"

"Ms. Bonnabel? Julia Bonnabel?"

"Yes..." the voice answers, warily. "Who are you?"

"I'm Dr. Louis Shmalzberg. With the American Society of Plastic and Reconstructive Surgeons." I hold my physician's ID closer to the peephole. "I'm part of a team investigating allegations of malpractice made against Dr. Eric Trotmann."

A chain latch clinks loudly as Ms. Bonnabel pulls the door open three inches. I'm only able to see half her face. The one eye I can see floats in a dark, sunken socket. "Sure as hell took you long enough. I put in the complaint on that bastard a year and a half ago."

"I'm sorry it's taken so long for someone to contact you. I'm not connected with NHMS. My organization is a professional standards body, a kind of self-policing agency for plastic surgeons. We're seeking to build a case to strip Dr. Trotmann of his license and keep him from harming any other patients. But he's been very hard to catch up with. Would you have a few minutes to answer some questions?"

The eye on the other side of the chain twitches briefly. "No one's come to see me for a very long time." Another few seconds of silence. Then a sigh. "Give me a minute. I'm not... just give me a minute to put some things on."

I wait ten minutes in the dim, musty hallway, staring out a dirty window at the stunningly blue winter sky. Rehearsing in my head what I'll ask her. Wondering how difficult it will be to steal the Elvis away from Trotmann, once I find him.

So many advances in medicine have resulted from the obsessive tinkerings of isolated eccentrics. After my father became a minor celebrity in Beverly Hills, Trotmann emerged from his workshop with a brand new type of cannula. Traditional cannulas relied upon a prior injection of hyaluronidase and salt water to loosen subdermal tissues. Trotmann's cannula supposedly made the chemical injections superfluous; he designed the cannula with a mechanical cutting head, a miniature grasping claw, each pincher sharp as a scalpel. Liposuction was passé, he declared in television interviews. The wave of the future was lipo*sculpture*.

At first Trotmann did quite well. Plastic surgery is a trend-driven business; by appealing to the media's baser instincts, he was able to attract a sizeable clientele of cocktail party braggarts and worshipers of the new. But problems with his technique soon became apparent. Serious problems. Women who had extensive procedures on their thighs or stomachs developed hideous furrows where the fat had been excised. A good part of my father's practice in the early and mid-1980s consisted of corrective work on Trotmann's patients.

I hear a dead bolt sliding clear. Ms. Bonnabel gestures for me to enter. Her eyes look less sunken than they did before; but looking closer, I realize this is due to a careful application of heavy makeup. I wonder if she's put on a wig. Her flowered dress hides her from neck to toes. Her computer record listed her as thirty-eight; she looks to be in her sixties.

Drapes are pulled tightly shut across her windows. Her apartment reeks with the mothball-and-cough-syrup odor of a sickroom. She limps heavily to a leather reading chair, but she hesitates before sitting down. "There was a time," she says, "when I would've spat in your face if you told me he'd done anything wrong. But that's what cults are like. Meat. Stupid, stupid meat. That's all I was to him."

I've never seen one of Trotmann's patients before. My father told me some developed immune system disorders similar to those suffered by some recipients of silicone breast implants. Ms. Bonnabel appears to be one of those unfortunates.

My father served as an expert testifier at Trotmann's first and second malpractice hearings. Later, he participated in an effort to bring criminal charges against him. But the profession was notoriously reluctant to permanently censure one of its own. Trotmann refused to abandon his innovation, clinging to it like he would a favored but sociopathic child. He avoided the proliferating lawsuits by vanishing. Every few years he resurfaced in a new place. The Bahamas. West Palm Beach. Barbados. Always staying close to open waters and escape.

"I'm so sorry, Ms. Bonnabel. I hope that my organization will be able to help somehow. Or at least prevent him from hurting others." The deeper I head into this, the more lies I tell.

"I'm sorry," she says, "what was your name again?"

"Dr. Shmalzberg. Louis Shmalzberg."

"Please sit. Like I said, I'm out of practice having guests. Out of practice seeing people, period."

"Thank you." I settle myself onto a worn leather sofa. "When was the last time you had any contact with Dr. Trotmann?"

"*Doctor* Trotmann?" She half sits, half falls into the chair. "That man's no doctor. A witch doctor, maybe." She laughs weakly.

"Have you spoken to him since you filed the complaint? Can you tell me where he is?"

She blasts me with a sour look. "Aren't you going to ask what he did to me?"

Her question brings me up short. "Of course. Please describe your full history with Doctor, uh, Eric Trotmann."

"It was a bad time in my life," she says, staring at a shapeless glass paperweight on the coffee table. "My marriage and business had just fallen apart. I didn't have anyone to turn to. Family — who the hell has any *family* anymore? I remembered reading somewhere that chocolate has this magical anti-depressive effect on women. *Real* chocolate; it had to be the real stuff. So I went looking for it. I found it at Lansky's. One of those 'eat-easies' that sometimes get raided. And that's where they found me."

"Who? Trotmann?"

"No. Trotmann's women. Two of them. I guess they could smell the despair on me. They came over to my table, sat with me. They seemed so sweet, so sympathetic. Like angels. I was too far gone, too goddamned *needy* to question their motives. By the end of my second visit to Lansky's, they'd dug my entire life story out of me. At first I thought they might be Jesus freaks. But I liked their company, needed it, so I ignored the alarm bells. They told me my coming to Lansky's was a sign. That without knowing it, I'd already started on the path to redemption. A power greater than me had guided me onto the right path."

Religion. I live the bulk of my life ignoring it, and now, these past three weeks, I can't escape it. "But what does this have to do with Eric Trotmann? What was he getting out of all this?"

My hostess sighs, then smoothes her dress across stick-thin upper legs. "What does he get? He gets money, for one thing. As new church members, we had to tithe fifteen percent of our gross incomes. That could get reduced later, depending on how many new 'converts' we could drag in. And he gets bodies, women's bodies, to play with. To abuse and mutilate. He hates women, did you know that? But it doesn't matter. They worship him like he's a god, that sadistic, horrible, withered old man. I'm one of the only ones to ever get out."

She fixes me with an unyielding stare. "Would you like to see just how much he hates women? How much he hated *me*?"

Before I can say a word, she painfully rises from her chair. She lifts her dress slowly, a few inches at a time. Queasy anticipation makes me sweat. Her long calves are marked with a web of blue varicose veins. It's when the dress rises to the thighs that the damage begins. Even though I've seen dozens of burn and accident victims, seeing this premeditated violation of a human body makes my gorge rise.

Gullies. Fissures. Dry riverbeds. It's easier on me to reimagine those legs as geological features than to see them with the eyes of a man. Trotmann really did a job on her. She turns around so that I get the most complete view. The subdermal damage clearly extends above her thighs, crossing her buttocks, winding around her hips. Even his incisions were crude, the work of a beginning med student. Or a surgeon who simply doesn't care.

She lets her dress fall to her ankles. If I had months to spend, and if she were wealthy enough to have her own fat tissues cloned, I might be able to fix half of what Trotmann has done.

"Tell me where to find him," I say, "and I'll try to ensure he doesn't repeat what he's done to you. Tell me where his church is."

"I... I don't know, not anymore. I'd tell you if I knew. But he was always moving it around. Do you know how many empty auditoriums, ballrooms, and social halls there are in Overtown? Owners are desperate for any rents at all. And half the buildings up here don't even have owners anymore; just squatters."

"Can you put me in touch with any of your old friends? Women who might still be members of the church?"

"I told you before. I'm black-balled. I'm not a person to them anymore."

"Would any of them still go to that Lansky's you mentioned?" Ms. Denoux told me about Lansky's. She has contacts there.

"Probably. They have to keep putting on weight if they ever want a shot at one of that old bastard's 'cleansings'." Her gaze turns hard and purposeful. "I might have a photo of me with one of the girls. One of the younger ones. Would you like to see it?"

"That would be very helpful, thank you."

She returns from her bedroom a few minutes later and hands me a photograph. "Here. Keep it. I can't stand to look at it anymore."

In the photo, a much younger-looking, healthier Ms. Bonnabel stands on the beach with her young friend. Both wear two-piece swimsuits. I think I can see one of Trotmann's trademark jagged incisions on Ms. Bonnabel's left inner thigh. Her companion appears unmarked. The younger woman has an unusual combination of features — dark olive skin, bright red hair, and green eyes. Her figure is coltish, pre-adolescent, with negligible breasts and boyish hips. She wears her hair shoulder length, with prominent curled bangs, just like Emily did.

"What's her name?" I ask, beguiled by the younger woman's smile.

"Margo. I never knew her last name."

"You think she still goes to Lansky's?"

"I have no doubt. Lansky's is the only place that can get her big enough for one of Trotmann's... mutilations."

She grasps my hand and presses it onto her thigh. I feel her scars through the cheap dress. "Find her," she says. "Stop him before he makes of her what he's made of me."

CHAPTER 11

I check into a room in a nicer part of Overtown; "nicer" being purely relative. According to Ms. Bonnabel, the crowds don't begin hitting Lansky's until after eleven P.M. I still have a few hours. I want to talk to Harri, hear how she's progressing in the fight against Metaboloft.

She picks up just after the fourth ring. "Harri, it's Louis."

A sharp intake of breath. "Good. I was wondering when you'd check in next."

"Is this a good time for me to be calling? Do you need to get back to me?"

"It's all right, Louis. It's all fixed. I got a friend to doctor up my phone. If anybody's listening in, all they're hearing is static and bits of prerecorded conversation."

"Wonderful. Have you had a chance to see my father?"

"Last Sunday. He wanted to know when you'd be coming by to see him."

"Are they giving him the high-calorie supplements I prescribed? Is he still losing weight?"

"They're feeding him the supplements, even though he hates the taste. He's still losing, but the rate of loss has slowed considerably. That head nurse you spoke to has started giving the supplements to all the patients on the ward. It scared me to see them. I've been fighting the spread of Metaboloft for the past eighteen months. But I've never seen the vanguard effects so up close and personal."

I try to sound upbeat. "How's the fight coming?"

"Honestly? Like shit, Louis. I feel like a quadriplegic who's been ordered to perform a trapeze act. We still don't have the tools to even *begin* working."

"What about those databases that were supposed to come from India and China?"

"We got them..."

The hanging pause at the end of her reply makes me nervous. "And?"

"They're useless."

"I thought you said those databases would take months to completely mine?"

"You don't have to examine every object in a Dumpster to know what's in there is garbage. Almost a third of the records in the databases were stripped. Empty of useable data. Another fifteen to twenty percent were corrupted with viruses. It's out of our hands now. The State Department is reviewing their options. The Chinese and Indians aren't exactly our bestest buddies. State's trying to decide whether this was an official provocation."

"What do *you* think?"

"I don't think the Chinese or Indians had anything to do with this. Metaboloft may not be an immediate threat to them, but give it three, four years, some of those spores are going to make their way across the ocean and take root."

"Then who? Who would want to do this?"

"If I knew that, I could alert the authorities and we'd be on our merry way, wouldn't we?" The sarcasm and fear in her voice sting. "I think it's someone inside, Louis. Inside the company. This isn't the first time 'accidents' have slowed us down."

"Have you reported your suspicions to anyone above you?"

She snorts with a derision that shoots straight through the phone line. "Think about it — I'm breaking every corporate secrecy policy talking with you, on the chance that the company that prints my paychecks could be doing something potentially genocidal. Doesn't that tell you I might not know who to trust?"

A horrible thought strikes me. Swaggart's church. I was struck by the connection between their theology and the silent deadliness of Metaboloft. It seemed a fanciful link then, a game the mind plays to frighten itself. Now, I'm not so sure. "Harri, are any of your co-workers involved with a church called the Church of the Third Resurrection?"

"What kind of question is *that?*"

"Humor me. Their teachings could condone what's happening with Metaboloft. Is there a branch of the church in Las Vegas? Have you ever heard anyone talking about it?"

"We're a bunch of scientists. Nobody here talks much about religion. We're lucky if the managers remember to shut down for Christmas."

"Just... keep an ear open for it, okay? It might be a lead, it might be nothing."

"Sure, all right... Look. There's something else I need to tell you. Someone here is looking for you."

For the second time in as many minutes, my blood goes cold. "From MannaSantos?"

"No. A fed. From the Department of Agriculture. Somebody I haven't worked with before. Last name is Muthukrishnan."

Shit.

"Louis? You still there?"

"Did you tell him anything?"

"No. He insisted it was very important he reaches you. He said he's already spoken with you once. He had an FBI agent with him. Does this have anything to do with your getting kicked out of the Good Humor Men?"

This is a nightmare. How far do I have to run? "For God's sake, don't tell him anything. Tell him you haven't heard from me in fourteen years."

"Don't worry. I'm spreading my trust very sparingly these days."

"How did he know you knew me?"

"I don't *know,* Louis. Guys from the government have a way of finding stuff out. Except the really useful stuff, like how to deactivate the Metaboloft gene. Can you at least give me a hint why the feds are after you?"

"Muthukrishnan's not a fed. At least, I don't think he is. He's an Asian Indian, and he's not the only foreign national who's been after me."

"Wait a minute. Why can't he be Indian and a fed? Plenty of these USDA and National Institute of Science guys I've been working with are from India. They've got a surplus of trained tech bureaucrats, and we've got a shortage. So we give them special work visas —"

"It doesn't matter. Just don't tell him about me, okay?"

"Louis, this doesn't sound like you. You're in worse trouble than you've been letting on."

"I'm *fine*. Just don't say a word. Can you promise me that?"

"Oh... all right. I promise."

"Good." My breathing begins returning to normal. "Thanks for seeing my father."

"De nada."

I tell her to watch out for herself, then we hang up.

Muthukrishnan. Black sedans tailing me from Memphis to Miami. The Ottoman — is he still strapped to my examining table? Or is he riding in one of those black sedans? Sabotage inside MannaSantos...

Just because you're paranoid doesn't mean they aren't out to get you.

Stay focused. Grab hold of your anchors. There are two of them now. Margo — finding her, saving her from Trotmann's butchering. And through her, finding the Elvis. Reclaiming it. Redeeming it.

I've descended from Overtown into the Deco District. Miami Beach has turned traditional cosmology on its head. Above me, Heaven is the low-rent district. But the underworld of the Deco District thrives, dynamic and alive despite the shadows imposed on it. The underworld is where the action is.

Cars are banished from much of the District, so I park near the boardwalk and unload my rolling sample case from the trunk. Samples of new products from Ms. Denoux's organization should help get me through the door at Lansky's. They may also help convince Margo to be cooperative.

Walking into the Deco District is like shedding a century. Neon is everywhere — blue and pink neon scripts that spell out the names of elderly hotels: Cardozo, Avalon, Breakwater, Delano. Virtually every other block has been transformed into a film set. Crowds of vid-11 technicians and their equipment make maneuvering my sample case along narrow sidewalks a chore. Actors and models, most in mid-twentieth-century costumes, are making commercials for everything from the newest Hudson runabout to a line of perfumes that double as anti-wrinkling agents.

A couple more blocks from the ocean, the intensity of street life falls off dramatically. I check the map Ms. Bonnabel drew for me. I've just crossed Cleveland Avenue; Lansky's can't be too far away.

Something rustles in the alley between two stuccoed hotels. I instinctively step away into the street. A pair of filthy hands thrusts a battered carton into the light. "Chocolate!" a voice hisses. *"Real* milk chocolate! Good prices!" I quicken my stride. If he knew what I have in my case, the poor wretch would kill me for it.

I turn left at Essen Lane, a winding little alleyway of closely bunched storefronts. I see the store I'm looking for up ahead. "Nostalgia Ltd." An innocuous antiques emporium, albeit one that stays open curiously late. Staring at the modest window display, I see they specialize in late-twentieth-century electronics: Nintendo games, clunky laptop computers, a microwave oven that looks like a hand-built nuclear bomb.

A drop of water, heavy as a marble, hits me on top of my head. More fall in the lane, clattering on the cobblestones like widely scattered hail. How can it be raining here, with Overtown between us and the clouds? But then I think about caves. It's night, cool and humid. We're between an ocean and a bay. The underside of Overtown, a gigantic pane of plastic, must provide its own nightly rain showers, a phenomenon probably unforeseen by its builders.

I push open the front door. Except for the single employee, playing an old Nintendo next to the cash register, the shop is empty. "Help you with something?" he mumbles, not looking up from the tiny screen of his game unit.

"Can you recommend a good place to eat?"

"Depends," he says, finally looking up at me, then down at my wheeled case. "What's in the bag?"

"I'm a salesman. These are samples from New Orleans."

"Let's see."

He whistles with appreciation when I unlatch the case. "Okay. Go through the door in back, the one marked 'Management Only.' Mr. Lezarro'll want to have a look at your goods."

He presses a button beneath the counter, which buzzes me through. Behind door number one is a much more solid-looking door number two. An eye-level panel slides open. I can see two gun-metal gray eyes and a partially flattened nose.

"Mr. Lezarro?"

"That would be me. You, I don't know from nobody. Julio says you've got goods for sale. Let's see what you've got, Mr. New Orleans."

I open the case again, lifting several of the pastries closer to the panel. I explain that I work for Oretha Denoux. After making a quick phone call, Lezarro lets me through. He ushers me down a steep set of carpeted stairs, assisting me with my case.

Halfway down the stairs, I'm nearly overwhelmed by a voluptuous odor — the sweet scent of melting butter. The dowdy antiques shop upstairs in no way prepared me for what awaits down below. Crystal chandeliers. Private booths outfitted in red leather. At the center of the intimately lit dining room, slowly revolving glass towers show-case Lansky's supreme attractions: cheesecakes, Black Forest cakes, puddings, and tarts. Cream puffs and éclairs, wedges of fudge as big as my fist; all glistening with hundreds of grams of fat and thousands of sugar calories. All undoubtedly authentic. What an incredible bust this would be for me, if I were still a Good Humor Man.

I'm in luck. At the far side of the dining room, Margo's red hair stands out like a neon bomb burst. I check the photograph to make certain it's her, but it's not necessary; I'd already memorized her features. She's in a booth near the back, alone. I gesture to the maitre d' that I'd like to sit at the booth in front of hers. He says that Mr. Olmas, the manager, will be over to see me once I've had my dinner, compliments of the house.

I slide onto the red leather seat facing her. It's hard not to stare. She's reading her menu, so I examine mine. My eyes widen as I scan the prices of steak tartar, salmon almandine, and eggs Benedict; each entree costs about as much as a night's stay in a fine hotel. How can Margo afford to eat here regularly?

A waiter asks if I've made my selection. I see an item that's an old, half-forgotten friend. Sliced corned beef, imported from Argentina, well marbled, on rye bread dressed with mustard. I could buy a week's

THE GOOD HUMOR MAN | 153

worth of supplies for my old clinic with what it takes to buy this sandwich. Good thing it's on the house.

Margo's food arrives. She's skipped the entree, gone straight for dessert. Her server unloads four large pastries — a towering hunk of chocolate layer cake, a sugar-crusted bear claw, a fudge pyramid, and a slice of cheese cake drizzled with strawberry sauce — plus a cup of coffee. I watch her pour pure cream into the coffee, filling the cup until the glistening liquid nearly overflows. Without stirring it, she leans over and carefully sips off the excess. To my surprise, she eats stoically, without any sign of pleasure.

How can she eat all this and still remain so slender? My best guess, judging from her age (late twenties) and unusual combination of features, is that her parents custom designed her, probably specifying an elevated basal metabolism. So now she's eating like a demon to negate that. I may not understand why she's chosen to be involved with Trotmann and his cult, but I can't help but admire her sheer pluck, her grim tenacity.

My sandwich arrives, so overstuffed that I can barely fit my mouth around it. It's beyond delicious. I'm only able to finish half of it, which makes my respect for Margo's will power grow even more. My waiter removes the remaining half-sandwich and returns it to me in a pressure-sealed plastic go-box. Soon thereafter, Mr. Olmas joins me at my table. After some amiable small talk, I open my case and arrange my sample pastries on the table, making sure Margo can clearly see them.

I catch her sneaking glances at my samples, even as she scoops up the last crumbs of her pastries. Olmas and I agree to have starter quantities of the new items dropped to him, using couriers he trusts. I intercept another of Margo's fleeting glances, nod and smile, but she looks away.

How do I start a conversation? I could offer her some of my samples. But the thought occurs to me that I've brought something even more appealing to her. My cannula. After all, pastries are merely a means to an end — the hollow end of a liposuction instrument.

I remove my old cracked leather valise from the wheeled cart, unbuckle the frayed straps and lift out the long, slender tube of stainless steel — more slender, even, than Margo, whose eyes grow wide as she begins to recognize what I have in my hands. The cannula is coated with a light film of dust. I unzip an inner compartment and take out a yellowed packet containing a sterile wipe. I glance at her as I wrap the damp cloth around the cannula tube. A flood of emotions plays across her face. Indecision. Reverent desire. Wary uncertainty, slowly beaten down by desire's heat.

She rises from her booth. I don't look up until I feel her standing next to me.

"Peace... peace be unto you," she says, her voice cracking slightly. "May your sins be scoured away, removed forever."

She thinks I'm part of her cult. Wish I knew how to play along. "That's very kind," I say, smiling but allowing my confusion to show. "Do I know you?"

She instantly blushes. "I'm sorry — I thought —" She stares at my cannula again. I place it back in its case. "It's just that... I've never seen one of those before, outside of where I — outside of one other place. I didn't think there were any others."

"You mean this antique of mine?" I touch the faded red velvet inner lining cradling the cannula. "Not many living people have seen one of these. Years ago, I used to perform a procedure called suction-assisted lipectomy, or liposuction. But nobody's done one of those in decades. Where on earth would you have seen a cannula like mine?"

She bites her lip. "My... my pastor has one."

"Really?" I say, smiling. "How fascinating. Is he a collector?"

Her gaze remains riveted on my cannula. "No... not really..." Just to see how she'll react, I begin to close the valise. "Wait! Please —" I'm surprised by the genuine panic in her voice. "Can't I take a closer look at it? Please?"

"Of course."

I reopen the valise, then pull the table lamp closer. The light glints off my cannula's stainless steel tube. Its shape is as familiar to me as the contours of my hand: blunt-ended, eighteen inches long, a third of an inch in diameter, tucked neatly into the space next to its detachable suction unit.

Her hand reaches for it, then pulls away. "May I —?"

I nod.

A tiny sigh escapes her lips as she reaches inside the case to touch the cold, smooth metal of my instrument, the sword of my obsolescent profession.

We walk along the boardwalk at the edge of the dunes. The night tide is coming in. The sound of the waves and the warm neon glow of Ocean Drive make me feel almost at peace, like I'm on vacation, hoping for a new romance.

I've told her Trotmann, her "Reductionist," is an old colleague of mine. I've mentioned that he once sought to buy foods in bulk from Oretha Denoux, and that as one of her representatives, I'd be curious to find out if he's still interested. She senses there's more to it than that, but I'll stay vague until I have a better sense of her loyalty to Trotmann. So far, she's remained equally vague about offering to take me to him.

I decide to broach the subject of Julia Bonnabel. "I recently met someone you may know."

"Who?"

"Julia Bonnabel. She's been suffering from medical complications, and I was called in to consult. She was operated on by Dr. Trotmann a few years ago. While she was a member of his church."

I watch her face closely. I can't be certain in this dim light, but I think she blushes. "Poor Julia," she whispers.

"So you do know her?"

"Yes," she says quietly. "We used to be friends, sort of."

"Have you been by to see her recently? A visit from a friend would do her a world of good."

"I can't... it's, it's complicated."

"What's so complicated about visiting a friend?"

"Can't we just drop this?" She glares at me like I've jabbed her with a fork. But then her gaze falls to the ground. "Julia... she was one of the church's first members. She helped bring *me* in; I haven't forgotten that. She received as many sacraments from the Reductionist as anybody did. I... I know she got hurt. The others said it happened because she'd stopped believing. Then we found out she'd gone to the authorities. She shouldn't have done that — the Reductionist had told her her problems were minor, that he could fix them if she'd, y'know, just have faith again."

"Do you believe that?"

She looks away. Her reply is almost muffled by the surf. "I don't know... sometimes I don't know *what* I believe anymore. Sometimes I'm scared."

"Margo. Tell me something."

"Yes, Doctor?"

"Why do you do it? What's the attraction? You've seen what the consequences of those 'sacraments' were for Julia. Why risk the same? Especially when virtually every woman in the country strives to achieve the kind of body you already have."

She scowls. "This *perfect* body?"

"Maybe 'perfect' is too strong a word... but open any magazine, turn on any vid-11 program, and you'll see yourself reflected in every depiction of feminine beauty."

"Just like what my parents wanted," she mutters. She picks up a broken seashell and tosses it into the water. "My parents designed me from some menu. How tall I'd be, how smart I'd be, how well I'd sing. Point and click. Like they were ordering a suit of clothes from some goddamn online catalog. My mother didn't even put me in her own body. She didn't want to get *fat*. I was made in some industrial park."

We approach one of the colossi that supports Overtown on his shoulders — José Martí. "Do you know what a burden 'perfection' is?" she asks. "How do you live up to it? It's fucking *impossible*. But they still expect you to." She sits cross-legged on the boardwalk, facing the ocean. "And what good is perfection? It only leads to its own corruption." Her voice is different now, like she's reciting from rote memory. "Leave a perfect bowl beneath the sun. It fills with dust, and the rain turns the dust to mud. But the bowl is perfect, you see. It can't drain. Once corrupted, it stays corrupted forever."

"But you aren't a bowl."

She stares up at me, her face seething with frustrated fervor. "Aren't I? Every day sin settles on me like dust. The food I eat in Lansky's... it's *real,* it's made of *real* things. Not all that bioengineered crap from MannaSantos. When I eat it, it scours me, scours my insides... it makes all the sin settle in places where I can see it, feel it, pinch it. Then the sacrament siphons it all off. I can watch it all being sucked away, into a prison of glass."

I try to imagine what kinds of sins are so weighty they cry out for Trotmann's bloody cutting cannula. He's created the perfect retirement package for himself, living on young women's money while continuing his sadistic "liposculpture" experiments on patients who literally beg him to violate their bodies. And he's set himself up as a god, or at least a prophet. I almost admire his achievement.

The breeze from the ocean brings a whiff of ozone. "My food bill is breaking me," Margo continues, her voice drained of its earlier emotion. "I'd go down south if I could, to the Latin countries. They don't have Good Humor Men or Metaboloft, and normal people eat stuff like I get at Lansky's all the time. But I wouldn't want to leave the church for that long, and traveling outside the U.S.A. can be hard."

She stands, using my case to help hoist herself up. She runs her fingers along the edge of the bag, up its handle. Then she glides her fingertips lightly across my knuckles. The sudden contact, our first, makes me shiver. "I feel like I'm on an endless treadmill, but I don't have a choice," she says. "The Reductionist... he won't do me yet. It's been almost two years since my first and only sacrament. I've tried as hard as I can to gain the inches back, but he says I'm still not ready. I think he plays favorites. It could be —" Her voice breaks. Do I detect a note of calculated distress? "It could be *years* before I'm big enough to satisfy him."

"Margo. Don't go back to him."

She stares into my eyes, removes my hand from the case, and squeezes it between both of hers. "Why shouldn't I?"

Behind us, the neon glow of Ocean Drive begins sputtering out. High above, the scattered lights of the few occupied Overtown towers blink and die. "What's happening?" I ask, grateful for a chance to think of an answer.

"Don't worry," she says. "It happens all the time." She points to a floating power generation plant close to the horizon, barely visible in the moonlight. "It's the old wave-energy generator. It's cranky. The lights will come back on sometime before morning."

In the sudden absence of city light, the stars blaze with renewed radiance above the ocean's darkness. Margo's hair looks black in the distant celestial light. As black as Emily's was. "Tell me where he is," I say.

I sense her nearness, the warmth of her skin. "How do you know the Reductionist has what you're looking for?" she asks.

Can she read minds? "I haven't said a word about looking for something."

"You didn't need to. I can just tell. Your being in Lansky's the same time I was — that wasn't an accident. And tracking down Julia Bonnabel. You wouldn't have gone to all this trouble just to make some dinky sale."

How much do I tell her? How much is *safe* to tell her? When her parents selected her traits, they didn't skimp on the cunning. While I'm debating how to regain the initiative, she takes my hand again and steals the initiative for herself. "I'll tell you how to find him," she says, her breath scented with chocolate, "if you'll do a certain something for me first."

It doesn't take the wisdom of Solomon for me to figure out what that might be.

CHAPTER 12

"Did you find everything you need?" Margo asks as I open the door.

I feel like a reborn adolescent, horny and raw with anticipation, as I walk into my hotel room with a bag full of supplies. "Yes. We're all set." Scalpels, gloves, and topical anesthetics were easy to find. Hyaluronidase required a lot more looking, but I found that, too. I reach into my shopping bag and pull out a loose white robe, the closest surrogate for a hospital gown I could find. "Here. Put this on in the bathroom."

She frowns. "The Reductionist operated on me while I was naked, like Eve before the Fall."

"I'm not the Reductionist. Go change."

While she's in the bathroom, I begin arranging what will be my operating room. I want to get started before my hands begin trembling, before I lose my nerve. I stare out the large windows that look out onto the bay and downtown Miami. Miami's distant towers are partially blocked by the concrete profile of Christopher Columbus, on whose broad shoulder this corner of Overtown rests. That hooked, asymmetrical nose... I could perfect it, given enough time.

Margo joins me at the windows. We stare at the colossus together. "Isn't it ironic," she says. "Thirty years ago, when Overtown was first being built, preservationists fought it like it was the end of the world. Now that it's become a blight, a slum, those same preservationists say it's as sacred as, I don't know, the Great Wall of China."

She walks into the next room, then returns carrying a large mirror from atop the dresser. She leans it against the couch.

"What's that for?" I ask.

"I want to see what you do, watch it all happen. So don't even *think* about knocking me out."

"Total anesthesia isn't necessary." I smooth out the sheet I've spread over the dining room table. "Climb aboard. Lie down on your stomach and pull your robe up around your waist."

She does as I instructed, raising her rear end immodestly — provocatively? — as she wiggles her robe into a bunch around her midsection. I concentrate on my tools. I've decided against an IV drip; I'll be removing only a small volume of tissues, between half and three-quarters of a pound. There's simply not that much there to remove.

The components of my cannula, suction unit, and power supply screw together smoothly, almost organically. I ask myself one last time: Should I have tried harder to bargain with her? Offered her money (or pastries) in place of this operation? But then I look at the places she has exposed for me, young white flesh where Trotmann has left his mark, and all objections and recriminations die unvoiced in my throat.

It's not as bad as it could be. Nowhere near the magnitude of damage he inflicted on Julia Bonnabel. Trotmann only operated on Margo once; maybe he was just breaking her in, waiting until her methodical gluttony could overcome her genetic predisposition toward gauntness. Bad enough. Staring at his obscenely amateurish incision, the way he cavalierly, cruelly left her two cheeks uneven in size and shape... I want to hurt him. I want to plunge my cannula into his chest like an ice-pick, then suck out his atrophied heart.

This is no frame of mind to be in before picking up a scalpel. "Margo," I say, struggling to keep my voice even. "These... irregularities on your left buttock cheek. I can correct them. I can inject lipids I'll be extracting from another part of your body into the damaged areas."

"The marks on my rear end?" she says, turning her head so she can see me better. "They don't matter. Just remove the fat, okay? Once you've sucked it out, I don't want you injecting any back into me."

A thought races through my head: *I didn't request your permission.* I do it right, or I don't do it at all. I rub an antiseptic solution on my hands and forearms, then pull on a pair of sterile gloves. I begin applying the pre-operative ointments to the areas I'll be working on, her buttocks and upper thighs.

In the mirror, I see her eyes following my hands. "What are you doing, Doctor?"

"I've applied an antiseptic to the areas where I'll be making the incisions. They'll be very small, just wide enough for me to insert the cannula through. I'll hide the incisions in the folds between your buttocks and thighs."

"What is all that other stuff you're slathering on me? It's cold."

"It's an anesthesia cream. The numbness lasts several hours."

Her face in the mirror grows hard. "Wipe it *off*. I told you you could give me a little shot where you'd be doing the cutting, not baste me with numbing cream like some Thanksgiving turkey. I need to feel what you're doing. Those are my *sins* you're sucking out of me. How can I achieve real expiation if I can't feel the pain? Hurry! Go get a towel and wipe me off!"

"I will *not* inflict needless pain. I don't know what kind of sadism you've become accustomed to. But if you refuse local anesthesia, I refuse to perform the operation."

"Even if it means never finding what you're looking for?"

I walk to the windows and stare out at Columbus's nose. Behind me, Margo sighs heavily. "All right," she says. "Do it. The way you want to."

I finish applying the anesthetic, then inject a solution of hyaluronidase and sterile salt water into her right buttock cheek.

"What is that, Doctor?" Her voice is softer now, almost apologetic.

"It's a solution that lowers the viscosity of hyaluronic acid, the cement that holds your internal tissues together. It allows the suction to be more effective. It'll be a few minutes before the solution takes effect. If you'd like, I could leave the room until then."

"Why? What for?"

"I thought you might need privacy, for... well, whatever."

"Are you asking if I want to pray?"

"Something like that." I check my watch. Ten minutes should do it.

I see her smile in the mirror. "No, I'd much rather you stay. It's a little weird, not being able to feel my thighs or my behind. About what I said before... not wanting the anesthesia? I'm glad you didn't let me bully you. I'm glad you insisted." She squeezes my hand, then lets the contact linger before pulling her arm back to a more comfortable position. "It was kind."

Amazing, the effect a single word can have. I feel those parts of me that were guarded and wary untightening, melting under the warmth generated by that one word. *Kind.* I uncap a body marker and begin outlining those contours of her body I plan to modestly reshape. As I draw ovals on smooth white skin, I sense small, hidden clumps of fatty tissues far beneath the nub of the marker, mysterious islands floating deep beneath her dermis, nourished by a sea of blood. I wish I had a fiber-optic camera to attach to my cannula so I could see those islands, visit them before suctioning them into a liquefied, undifferentiated mass. But I am a surgeon of the old school. I will know the islands by touch, by touch alone. The bright yellow ink shimmers on the skin of her right buttock like a golden tattoo, a constellation. A promise of blessedness?

"Doctor?" Her voice is completely relaxed now. I'm pleased. "Won't you tell me what it is you're looking for? I could be a lot more help to you if I knew."

The marker freezes in my hand. How much does she need to know? If her loyalty still lies with Trotmann, telling her about the Elvis could ruin everything. But if she can show me where he keeps it, my job becomes a hundred percent simpler. And telling her might magnify her trust in me.

"Margo, if I tell you what I'm looking for, and why, will you swear to keep it between us?"

"You're my Reductionist now," she says. "I'd have to be an incredibly evil person to do anything bad to you."

She sounds completely sincere. But a small, shrill voice in my mind reminds me: *Trotmann was her Reductionist until now. If she'd turn on him, why not you?*

Because I'm better than he is.

"What I'm looking for," I say, closely watching her face in the mirror, "is the preserved adipose fat of Elvis Presley, extracted by my father a few weeks before Elvis died."

Her eyes widen. "Your *father* was the evil doctor? Your last name is *Shmalzberg?*"

I expected her to be surprised. But not this way. "'Evil doctor'? What kind of nonsense has Trotmann been feeding you?"

She pulls words from memory, a kid reciting catechism. "Elvis was the first of us to ever seek expiation of sin in our special way. But he was tricked into choosing the wrong Reductionist, and he died soon thereafter because of that Reductionist's evil nature. Dr. Trotmann said that Elvis's spirit went to Heaven anyway, because of his saintly intentions. And ever since, his spirit has watched over his earthly fat, keeping it unspoiled, to provide us a holy example to follow."

Wonderful. According to Margo's theology, my father is Satan. Which makes me son of Satan.

I tell her the whole story. My father's story, and the story of my most recent ten days — the inquiries and threats from Muthukrishnan and the Ottoman that first made me want to reclaim the Elvis; and my desire to present it once more to my father before he dies.

"Trotmann isn't worthy of having it," I say, my throat raw. "The Elvis — I may not agree that it's holy, but it *is* something precious. It's... practically a member of my family. For Trotmann to have it, for him to use it to slander my father's name — it's an *abomination.*"

Is she with me? I can't tell yet. "My father's behavior wasn't beyond reproach," I admit. "His puncturing Elvis's stomach cavity was a bad mistake. But he fixed it. If Elvis had laid off the amphetamines and tranquilizers like my father instructed, he wouldn't have suffered the internal bleeding that killed him. Compare that to what Trotmann did to your friend Julia Bonnabel. He's maimed dozens of women, without a qualm. The man is a *serial disfigurer.*"

What is she thinking — *The words of the devil are sly and insidious, like honey-laden venom?* "Margo? Whom do you believe?"

She rolls onto her side. Her gaze is even and cool. "I told you before, you're my Reductionist now. In for a penny, in for a pound. Although in our case, it's going to be pound after pound."

"What about that business with my father? The 'evil doctor'?"

She purses her full lips. "That was never a part of the religion that made much sense to me. I mean, if your father was the first Reductionist, and what he did allowed Elvis to go to Heaven, what's so 'evil' about that? If Elvis died, that must've meant he was finished with his work here on earth. Maybe it was more important that his spirit be up in Heaven."

Good girl. Let the Reformation of the liposuction cult begin today, here in this room. We'll nail our ninety-five theses to the church wall together, using my cannula for a hammer.

"So let's get on with it," she says, rolling back onto her stomach.

I give the faded green button atop my cannula's hand-grip a test press with my thumb. The suction unit purrs and vibrates like a satisfied cat. "We're ready to begin now," I say. "When I make the first incision, you won't feel any pain; only a slight pressure."

I've read that before a Plains Indian would kill a buffalo, he would first beg its forgiveness. He approached his work with great seriousness and awe. This is how I approach this buttock, this lovely globe. To deface its perfect white smoothness with an incision seems a crime beyond measure. But what I remove from the one can be used to restore the other. I stretch Margo's skin between my gloved fingers and make a tiny, neat slice, just wide enough for my cannula. Forgive me.

With my cannula's familiar weight in my hand, my arm feels complete, magically made whole. I insert its blunt-tipped aperture into the incision, beginning my probe of the mysterious spaces beneath the dermis, as alien as the dust clouds between stars. I must be careful to shield the fatty layer just below the outer skin; removing that would be like knocking the colossi from beneath the corners of Overtown.

From the corner of my eye I see Margo twisting her neck in a desperate attempt to view my every movement. "Is it in? Is it in?"

"Yes. You must remain absolutely still. The cannula can hurt you unless I control it perfectly."

"I believe in you, Doctor Shmalzberg."

With that strange emphasis on my surname, I can hear her building new mythologies from this encounter. I push the cannula deeper, feeling for the deep substrata of fatty tissues that underlie her right buttock. It's hard, physical work. For the muscles of my right hand, it's the redreaming of an old, recurrent dream.

God, how I've *missed* this! I hadn't realized how much.

At last I sense the subterranean island I've been seeking. I push the green button on the cannula's handle, and the machine hums to life. A viscid flow of red, yellow, and white races through plastic tubing toward the storage canister. Margo's green eyes follow the spiraling flow, hypnotized by its ever-mutating beauty.

Her lips form soundless words. I can't tell what she's saying. But her earlier words repeat themselves in my mind:

I believe in you, Doctor Shmalzberg. I believe in you.

Ten minutes later, the procedure is nearly done. I've positioned myself so that Margo can't see the repair work I'm doing on her left buttock. I re-inject slightly more than half the lipids I've removed from her other cheek; about 250 cubic centimeters, or half a pound. Already, I can see the furrows beginning to disappear. I sutured the right-hand incision quite elegantly, and now I do the same on the left. In telling contrast with Trotmann's work, my incisions will leave no visible scars.

I unfasten the storage canister from my suction machine. My net subtraction was 190 cc's of subdermal fat, little more than a third of a pound. As I heft the diminutive weight in my hands (the weight of a small bag of chocolates, or a child's heart), I am overcome by a piquant sense of tenderness. My fingers embrace a small but significant portion of Margo.

How long did it take her to grow this third of a pound? How many furtive, lonely meals at Lansky's? My heart skips a beat — haven't I just suctioned away part of her fortification against the Metaboloft effect? But then I remember my trunkload of illegal desserts. For now, I can protect her. Metaboloft will reach the foreign fields where those ingredients were harvested, too, eventually. But in the meantime, Margo and I will wax fat as the world shrinks around us.

I hold the storage canister up to the light. The Margo tissues swim in their warm salt sea, glowing like luminescent jellyfish.

"Doctor? May I... may I see it?"

She sounds weak. "In just a minute." I pour her a large glass of orange juice to replace the fluids she's lost. "Here. Drink this, then I'll pour you another glass."

Only after she's downed the second helping do I place the canister in her hands. "It's... really kind of beautiful," she says. "So long as

I don't think about the sins that pollute it." She rotates the glass container in her hands. "It's so strange, to look at this and think that, just ten minutes ago, this was a part of me. Not just something foreign inside me, like an undigested piece of steak, but actually a part of *me,* something my blood flowed through."

"What do you intend to do with it?"

"I'll bury it later, before the sun sets."

"Oh." I'm not surprised, but I am disappointed. In some dim corner of my mind, I'd hoped she might let me keep it. To distract myself from such thoughts, I prepare the dressings I'll apply to her affected regions, while launching into what once was my standard post-operative monologue. "Leave these elastic dressings in place for the next three days. Don't get them wet. You'll experience some soreness over the next two weeks; stick to non-aspirin pain killers..."

Her emerald gaze is transfixed by the part of her inside the canister.

"Margo. Do you have any questions?"

Her eyes widen before focusing on my face, as if she's startled to see I'm still in the room. "Will I still be able to gain weight in my rear end?"

Already she's thinking about her next procedure? "The number of fat cells in your buttocks has been significantly reduced. Any weight you gain in the future will likely tend to accumulate in other areas, your abdomen, hips, thighs, or upper arms."

"How long might it be, Doctor? How long before I'm ready for the next operation?"

"I — there's no way of knowing. You've already learned that, given your genes, weight gain is an up-hill struggle." The air feels thick in my throat. Will she never be satisfied, never know peace? "As you continue overconsuming calorically rich foods, it's very likely your metabolism will begin slowing down, helping you to gain." My first real lie to her — there's a good possibility Metaboloft won't let any of us grow older, much less allow our metabolisms to lag. "In the meantime, it's best that we not overdo the liposuction."

The eagerness disappears from her face, quickly replaced by cold calculation. "I could always go back to Dr. Trotmann, reconsecrate myself to his church..."

"No!" I'm losing it, letting her play me like a tin flute. Or are we playing each other? "Margo. You have to promise me never to go back to Trotmann. He's never to lay scalpel or cannula on you again. Promise me that."

"Promise me you'll build me a church," she says.

I don't know how to answer her.

"I don't mean a physical building," she says. "At least not at first. When I say 'build,' I mean build it in your head, and in the heads of other people — the women who are still involved with Dr. Trotmann. A church without favoritism, or cruelty, or pain. There's so much that's good in Dr. Trotmann's church, but there's an awful lot that's bad. You could be the man to make it *all* right. The *good* Reductionist."

When I still don't say anything, she blushes slightly. "You don't have to give me an answer right now. But think about what I've said. Because I know one thing for certain now. You're the one who should have the Elvis fat."

My heart stutters. "So you've seen it? You know where he keeps it?"

She nods her head. "I've seen it. Lots of times. He usually takes it out during services. Between services, he keeps it locked up."

"At his church?"

"Yes." She winces slightly; the anesthetic cream might be wearing off. "But there's something else you need to know. It's not just locked up. It's guarded. By a ghost."

"What kind of ghost?" I smile. Maybe Trotmann has hired an Elvis impersonator and coated him in luminescent makeup?

"I don't think he's a ghost, myself. That's just what some of the other women call him. He's too solid to be a ghost. Dr. Trotmann performs a reduction on him at every service. It's part of the liturgy; the whole wall behind the altar is lined with jars of his fat. He's enormous, the biggest man I've ever seen. Dr. Trotmann says he's the resurrection of a famous man who died in a fire during GD2."

Suddenly, this isn't so funny. "What's his name, Margo?"

"Uh, Walter... Walter something..."

The remnant of my smile dies on my face.

"Hud Walterson," she says.

*

What should I make of Margo's revelation? Hud Walterson hasn't been a widely recognized public celebrity in almost twenty years. Even then, it wasn't his name that people remembered, it was his *body,* that great, lumbering mound of televised flesh, expanding and deflating like a Macy's Thanksgiving Day Parade balloon.

I'm sure the women in Trotmann's church, if they've seen Hud Walterson at all, remember him only from vid-9 documentaries. If Trotmann's been able to locate a man with Hud's congenital condition, the same type of glandular mutation, it wouldn't be hard for that man to pull off a convincing impersonation. He wouldn't have to look much like Hud at all. If the lighting is dim enough, even a prosthetic fat suit might be passably convincing.

I leave Margo to recuperate while I go in search of a cutting tool to liberate the Elvis. I remember passing a handful of pawnshops when I drove across the causeway that connects the Deco District to mainland Miami. I park in front of South Beach Pawn. The breeze whipping off the bay is cool and salty. Much fresher than the stale air inside the shop, a bouquet of dust, smoke, and sour body odor. The proprietor directs me to a shelf of industrial tools at the back of the shop. I pause next to a glass display case stocked with handguns. The Colts, Smith & Wessons, and Brownings are marked with small American flags.

"You need a gun?" the owner asks. "Today's the last day of our after-Christmas firearm sale."

A gun? Elvis was a gun collector, wasn't he? He collected police badges and police guns from all over the country.

"Which handguns do police use?" I ask.

"Lots of cops still use Berettas," he says, unlocking the case. "I got one of them right there."

"That's a foreign make, isn't it?"

"Yeah. Eye-talian."

"I want an American gun."

"A cop gun that's American made?" He reaches deep into the case for a black snub-nosed revolver. It looks like it was carved from a hunk of hardened lava. "Smith & Wesson .38 Special. The caveman of handguns." He stares dubiously at my slender physique. "You ever handle one of these before, Pops? It's got a kick that'll take your arm off. A Beretta'd be a lot more manageable for a guy your age —"

I shake my head.

I leave the pawn shop five minutes later with a hand laser and the Smith and Wesson police revolver.

Elvis used to shoot the screens out of television sets.

What will I shoot up? Hud Walterson's ghost?

CHAPTER 13

The Overtown building where Trotmann's church has alighted is only a half-mile from my hotel. Thirty stories tall, a towering gray tombstone for the ambitions of the men who built this city above a city. Margo tells me the building was planned as a luxury hotel and conference center. The combination of space, obscurity, and cheap rent must've been irresistible to Trotmann.

I wanted to break into the church in the middle of the night and be done with it, but Margo insisted that I attend a service before stealing the Elvis. Her logic, that watching a service will let me see exactly where the Elvis is stored, was undeniable.

Wholesalers make use of portions of the bottom stories as warehouse space. It's dark now, and they're gone. Margo and I enter the building through a small side entrance, for which she has a key. She's bought a white hooded rain jacket for me, identical to the one she's wearing. Plenty of the other congregants will be wearing them; down in the Deco District, with its nightly condensation showers, they're *de rigueur* fashion. In Trotmann's church, the white hooded jackets are becoming a sort of sacred uniform. Maybe small golden cannulas worn on necklaces will be next?

She leads me up two flights of stairs to the mezzanine level. Lighting is dim and distant, coming from a few auxiliary lamps in the seams between walls and ceiling. We enter the auditorium two minutes apart. I immediately head for the opposite side of the tiered seating area from where Margo has seated herself. I don't want anyone making a connection between us.

Only the first three rows are filled. I'd guesstimate about forty congregants are present. I take a seat on the edge of the sixth row, next to an emergency exit. The service hasn't started yet. Apart from a hum of soft conversation, the room is quiet. No music. I smile when I realize I was expecting organ renditions of Elvis's greatest hits; maybe a rousing choir version of "Burning Love." It's here. So close. My legacy.

Dozens of reflective objects on stage catch glints of light from small revolving lamps. As my eyes adjust to the subdued lighting, I realize what I'm staring at. Glass jars. Row upon row of glass jars sitting on shelves arranged on either side of a tabernacle, behind the lectern and a waist-high, eight-foot-long platform. Vacuum jars, each filled with a yellowed mass of what is undoubtedly human fat.

Two women climb to the stage and light a pair of large candles. I expect to smell some kind of incense. Instead, the scent that reaches my nose is gamey. The odor of — burning human fat?

A pin-light spot pierces the dusty air. Eric Trotmann steps out from the wings. He's much *smaller* than I thought he'd be. Bent severely with lordosis, shuffling across the stage with the aid of a wheeled cane, he's not even five feet tall. Dressed in maroon robes and a golden sash, puffs of white hair like cotton balls glued to his skull, he looks like a small-town college dean gone to seed. What was I expecting? A Savonarola the size of a funnel cloud? Even my father, withering away, is a more physically impressive specimen.

The two women who lit the candles now help Trotmann mount the podium. "Behold, my supplicants!" he says with a dramatic upward sweep of his thin arms. "Behold this miracle which my piety has brought to you this day!" His voice, unamplified, is surprisingly strong. The two women step away from him. "Sin which had been trapped, insidious, cancerous sin, now rises freely to the heavens, borne aloft by the cleansing kinetic frenzy of fire."

"Borne aloft, never to return." The response springs from the combined voices of forty congregants. Margo included.

Trotmann reaches across the podium, beseeching the women with his right hand, the hand that wields his terrible cannula. "Pray for the holy day on which your sins will be extracted from your body."

"We will pray for that holy day. We will strive to make ourselves worthy."

"No one can defeat sin by wrestling alone with it. Even the stron-

gest among us, fortified by good intentions and good works, may easily go astray without the proper example to guide them. And such an
example is here among us, eager to show us the true way."

He turns his head in my direction. Is he talking about *me?* Does
Trotmann somehow know I'm here? But he isn't looking at me anymore. The weight of his gaze falls on the opposite wing of the stage.

"Twenty-five years ago, he perished in the inferno of his own tragic
error — the error of wrestling sin on his own, of trying to starve sin
through abstaining from the rich, holy bounty which God has provided. But you can't starve sin! You can't jog it away, ex-cer-cise or
ex-*cor*-cize it! Sin, once entrapped in the fat of our bodies, must be
extracted by the holy cannula. And this man made the error of running from the cannula. And so when the burden of sin became too
much for him, when he hungered in his soul for his sin to be sent to
Heaven, to be borne aloft on wings of fire, he had no *choice* but to con-
sign *all* of himself to the cleansing inferno. In his zeal, he offered up
the wrong sacrifice, a burnt offering whose savor was not pleasing to
the Lord. And that was this man's error.

"But the holiness of this church is great enough to stir even the
dead. Hud Walterson has returned to us for the great and holy purpose of *renouncing* his error. Of *accepting* the dominion of the cannula over sin. Of providing with his own awesome, blessed, and resur-
rected body a holy *example* for each of you to follow.

"Hud Walterson, step *forth!*"

The great shadow lurking in the far wing of the stage moves. I can
hardly wait to see how good a fraud Trotmann has conjured up. The
man who emerges is certainly gargantuan enough. He must be close
to four hundred pounds. Poor lighting keeps me from getting a good
look at his face. He walks haltingly, leaning on a metal cane reinforced
by four heavy-duty buttresses; with each slow step, the folds of his
robes sway and part, revealing quivering, pendulous masses of flesh
drooping from his thighs and calves.

A second spotlight brightens his bulk as he approaches the long,
low platform near the center of the stage. Eerie — his skin tone, it's jar-
ringly similar to the real Hud Walterson's, a ruddy almond tone that
bespoke his mixed heritage as the son of Samoan and Jamaican immi-

grants. That heavily furred brow; the slight Hawaiian cast of his eyes; the long, straight black hair pulled back into a thick ponytail – either Trotmann has been meticulous with his homework, or, or...

Or *nothing*. It can't be him. The real Hud Walterson, *if* he'd somehow survived, would be almost sixty years old. This man looks to be in his mid to late twenties, younger than Hud was at the time of his death. I don't believe in ghosts. And I don't believe in resurrections. He's an incredible *doppelganger,* but that means either Trotmann was amazingly fortunate in finding him, or he put all those decades of experience in reconstructive surgery to effective use.

The *doppelganger,* with the help of the two women who had assisted Trotmann earlier, clambers onto the platform and lies on his back. The women open his robe, allowing his almost liquid belly to ooze out. The spotlight glints off the shiny, reddish-brown scars of dozens of prior incisions. The scars infest the flesh of his stomach, thighs, and upper arms like a multitude of bloated leeches.

"Our Exemplar has shown his willingness to accept the cannula," Trotmann intones, his right hand now holding his self-invented cutting cannula. He brandishes it, the wand of a pagan priest; its stainless-steel cutting heads click and whir like the mandible-crunching of an army of insects on the march. "How great is his body! How great the quantity of sin his fat has encased! So magnificent is his love for this poor, fallen world that he has taken on a triple, a quadruple, no, a *ten-fold* portion of sin for us. And now, in the sight of all this holy congregation, let us place the capstone on this blessing by extracting a portion of trapped sin."

Trotmann opens a drawer lined with scalpels and the other components of his cannula. Within seconds, he's screwed it all together with a practiced ease I can't help but envy. Then he dips several cotton wipes into an antiseptic solution and swabs down a small portion of the faux-Hud's stomach.

No anesthetic. I wince when Trotmann makes his incision. But the patient doesn't even whimper. I watch his face as Trotmann inserts the cannula and presses the button that activates the cutting heads. This *doppelganger*'s tolerance for pain is extraordinary, almost supernatural. His broad forehead shines with droplets of sweat. I can see

his jaw tremble, the tendons of his neck thicken like steel cables surfacing through the fat framing his face. I want him to cry out. What
kind of confederate has Trotmann recruited who can withstand such
torture, who *willingly* subjects himself to this?

I tear my gaze away from the operating table. Many of the women
surrounding me, and two or three of the few men among them, have
looks of rapture on their faces. They're hungering for what the faux-
Hud is being given. But how many of them could stand for even a second what he's enduring?

The electricity in the air, it's like what I remember sensing at the
early Good Humor rallies, or at the junk food riot that erupted the
night of Hud Walterson's immolation. Finally, it's over. Trotmann
sutures the incision. He slips his patient a pill or two, hopefully a
coagulant and a pain killer. He disassembles the cannula, and then the
women help him back onto the podium, carrying also the jar of newly
extracted fat.

"This congregant has been cleansed," Trotmann says. "Like a ripe
olive squeezed in a press, he has surrendered his oil."

"He has surrendered his sins."

"For the fat is the gathering place of sin. It is the sponge that pulls
sin into itself, gathering impurities and darkness from the innermost
to the outermost, to a place where they can be expunged."

*"From the innermost to the outermost. Deadly mercury, once ingested,
gathers in the fatty flesh of fish."*

"Yea, and the pesticides of the earth are to be found in the fat of children. For the fat is the gathering place of sin. And now our Exemplar
will lead us in the adoration."

The faux-Hud rises from the platform. I'm stunned — he should
barely be able to move. But he grasps his cane and walks slowly to the
tabernacle.

He opens it. Sitting on a shelf of dark wood is the glowing, molten
core of my childhood. The healing balm I used to banish my mother's
pain. My father's semi-secret glory; the legacy he entrusted to me. My
past, my present, and somehow, in a way I don't yet understand, my
future.

The Elvis.

It's still in the decorative crystal vacuum jar, the one my father had custom-made after he'd freeze-dried the Elvis for long-term preservation. The crystal jar I spent hours staring at as a boy, reading the etched lyrics to "Love Me Tender" over and over, like a prayer, while I stared at Elvis's etched visages. I used to think his still-beating heart was in that jar, hidden within the yellow fat and bits of partially digested food. The sacred heart of Elvis.

The giant grasps the jar and lifts it high over his head. With each passing second, he seems to draw more strength from it, standing straighter and taller. He takes a great breath, gathering himself to speak:

"Here is the beautiful one!"

That voice —

"Here is the father of us all!"

My God, I *know* that voice, I *remember* that voice —

"He was the man with the golden voice, the man with the golden body, beloved of women. From a willowy youth he built himself up, and the greater he made himself, the greater was his beauty. In the years before his end, even the sweat of his brow was prized. The most beautiful women of America fought and clawed for scraps of cloth which had been dabbed with his sweat."

The accent is different — the subtle Jamaican singsong has vanished — but otherwise, this man speaks with the voice of Hud Walterson.

"He showed us the way to be freed of sin. And then he ascended. But he has not left us. He will never leave us. His beauty, his example, his *voice* will live on forever!"

And suddenly, the voice is *here*. Elvis's voice, booming from loudspeakers all around the auditorium. "Amazing Grace." It's like warm oil being poured in my ears. It's too much, these two voices at once. The voice of Elvis — didn't I close my ears to it when I sold my birthright? And it was the voice of Hud Walterson that I turned to in my grief, losing myself in building a movement that was the reification of Hud's mania.

All through this journey, I've been afraid to listen to the voice of Elvis, afraid I wouldn't be ready. But I'm *hearing* it now, truly hearing it. "Amazing Grace"... he's singing it directly to me. To *me*. *To save a wretch like ME*... *I* was a wretch, a miserable wretch who helped start a movement that is destroying this country, that has made our women infertile, that has hollowed out our nation.

What would you have me do? Strive to tear down what I helped build? But what is the *sense* in that? With Metaboloft spreading through the food chain, isn't tearing down the Good Humor movement *futile?*

What do you want of me?

I clench my eyes shut, but not soon enough to stop the tears from escaping. *What do you want of me?* I press my hands against my ears. But I can't hold back the voice. Are you telling me that futility is no excuse? Is that it? That so long as there's still breath in my body, I'm not allowed to despair? That giving in to the forces which eat us is not an option? *Is that it?*

The music ends. The vibrations of his voice fade from the air. But they don't fade from my mind. I wipe my eyes. *I was blind, but now I see.* I want to see. I want so much to see. I will make your mortal remains my talisman in this struggle. My unavoidable struggle to undo the evil I've done, even in the face of the end of everything.

The congregants are filing up the steps onto the stage. Toward Trotmann at the podium.

"Go on," the woman closest to me says. "It's time for the marking."

The marking? Maybe I should head for the exits, mumble something about needing the bathroom? No, I couldn't duck out now without calling attention to myself.

I head for the steps. He hasn't seen me since I was a little boy. Surely, after all these decades, I'll be merely a stranger to him.

Trotmann reaches down and touches the young blonde woman ahead of me on the forehead, saying something to her I can't hear. Then she walks to the opposite stairs. Just a few seconds. That's all. Then I can hide myself until everyone is gone.

My turn comes. My heart feels like it's beating in the center of my skull. Trotmann leers down at me like a liver-spotted gargoyle. He dips his right forefinger into the jar of fat, the fat he's just extracted.

He reaches with that glistening finger for my forehead, but then stops, his eyes focusing on my face. "I don't believe," he says, "that I've seen you in church before."

"No," I say, smelling the sourness of his breath. "I'm new."

"Who is your sponsor?"

Should I mention Oretha Denoux? Does she even know about this church? "Uh, Betty, Betty — oh, Christ, I can't remember her last name now, and I don't even see her here tonight —"

He squints at the line of congregants waiting for his touch, then looks back at me. "We'll have to speak later, sir. Always good to... welcome... a new member to the church."

He reaches down and smears the fat on my forehead. "Carry this reminder," he says, "that the burden of sin may only be lifted through the holy cannula."

The touch of his leathery finger, the warm, cloying weight of the drip of human fat on my forehead (the fat of Hud Walterson!) — it's *revolting*. This must be what medieval Jews felt when Crusaders forced them to eat pork — a foulness, a personal desecration, a growing stain that can never be washed away.

But I force myself to murmur thanks. Then I walk away, passing Margo as she comes for her marking. I want to grab her, pull her away before Trotmann can lay his befouling finger on her. But instead I clench my fists and let her walk by.

At the back of the auditorium, a pair of women stand behind a folding table, assembling sandwiches. Peanut butter, banana, and bacon sandwiches. Of course. Elvis's favorite. Maybe the peanut butter and bacon are even real.

The loathsome fat gets smeared across my rain jacket's sleeve as soon as I'm out the door. I find a bathroom and try to ignore the brown, stinking water that spurts from the tap as I wash my forehead. There's a small utility closet behind the stalls. Faint ammonia fumes make my eyes water when I shut myself inside. I set my watch's timer for ninety minutes from now. Nine-twelve. That's when I'll reenter the auditorium.

So close. It's so very, very close now.

I leave my hiding place. The building is silent, apart from the skipping scratches of tiny rodent feet across cardboard boxes. The rats stay clear of my flashlight beam. The entrance to the auditorium is locked, but my pocket laser makes short work of the lock. I shine my beam on the tabernacle. Not much more than a tall wooden box, the tabernacle is sealed with two large padlocks, one at waist-level and the other a foot above my head. Their hasps are as thick around as my middle finger. Not impervious to my laser, but melting them will take longer than disabling the auditorium's weak lock did.

Top lock first. The band of metal begins to glow. First red, then orange, then a bluish white. A droplet of molten steel falls like a tiny meteor, sizzling when it lands. After another minute, the right side of the hasp's U is breached. I nudge the padlock with the barrel of my gun until it falls.

Stupid — the impact of it hitting the floor echoes through the auditorium like a rifle shot. Too eager —

Footsteps. Coming from the left side of the backstage. Slow, heavy, punctuated by another sort of muffled thudding; a cane? The Hud Walterson *doppelganger*. He won't stop me. I quickly train the laser on the bottom padlock, using my left hand, keeping the gun in my right.

The elephantine footsteps grow closer. He's slow; even holding the Elvis, I can easily outrun him. If he's got a gun, bad news; he's in the dark, and I'm lit by the laser's glow. But if I kneel down — carefully, carefully — I can partially put the corner of the tabernacle between us. And he's a much bigger target than I am...

"Louis, uh, Shmalzberg. Step away from the holy tabernacle."

How does he know my *name?* Even the real Hud Walterson never knew my name.

"Do not defile this holy place." He steps out of the darkness, leaning on his multi-stalked cane. He's not carrying a gun. "You should never have come here. You gave up any claim to the sacred extractions of our blessed Exemplar the, uh, the day you sold them to the Graceland circus for profit."

He's different than he was before. He's speaking so haltingly, as if he's being fed his lines... Could his voice be electronic? Could Trotmann have sampled the real Hud Walterson's voice from old newscasts and infomercials? But then why would the accent be different?

He takes another step closer. "I have a gun," I say. "I'm... I'm not afraid to use it. Stay where you are."

He stops. I take advantage of the respite to glance back at the lock.

It's beginning to glow. Another ninety seconds, maybe.

"You'll never escape with the sacred extractions," he says. "Your father is evil. The extractions will... if you touch them, they will burn your hands with... holy fire."

Hearing him mention my father makes me shiver. "Who are you?" I say, keeping the gun pointed at his mountainous stomach. "Who are you *really?* Some glandular case wearing a hidden loudspeaker?"

"I am Hud Walterson, returned from the next world."

He blinks quickly, his long, thick eyelashes fluttering like the wings of a hummingbird. He's lying.

Splitting my concentration between him and aiming my laser, I fail to hear the steps behind me, until the scrape of a shoe on concrete makes me turn.

Too late — my head bursts. Glowing padlock fades... to black....

CHAPTER 14

The first thing I see, when I open my eyes, is the Elvis. It's sitting on a wooden deck that surrounds a pit, on the opposite side from me, about fifteen feet away. An odor like sour milk rises from the dark abyss.

My head throbs. My hands — I can't move them. I'm tied to a chair at the edge of the pit.

"So the younger Dr. Shmalzberg is with us again. I was afraid you might sleep through our festivities."

It's Trotmann, sitting behind me and to my right. Where am I? The auditorium? No, must be another room like it. This pit and the deck that surrounds it are up on a stage; I'm facing dozens of rows of theater chairs. I test the cords tying my hands and arms. Snug. Painfully so.

"Did you really think I wouldn't recognize you?" Trotmann says. He walks halfway around the rim so that he's standing next to the Elvis. "Your father's face is indelible in my memory. Do you know how many hours I spent staring at his sanctimonious, hypocritical features while he testified against me at those detestable hearings? I memorized that face. And you resemble your father very much, young Dr. Shmalzberg."

"My... oversight," I manage to mutter. My mouth tastes like copper and dust.

"The wheels of justice, they turn slowly, but they turn. Your father was the golden boy, wasn't he? Took another man's techniques and innovations, Illouz's, and spun them into a brilliant career. Killed the god of rock and roll but made that work for him, too. Became the biggest moneymaker among the below-the-neck men of Beverly Hills.

"And me? *I* was the innovator, the *real* prodigy. *I* was the one who stole fire from Prometheus so my fellow physicians could make their fortunes. And how was I repaid? By being hounded from city to city, country to despicable, flea-circus country. And the crowning indignity? That I should be stripped of my license due to the efforts of such a bounder, such an intellectual nonentity as Walter Shmalzberg."

He pats the top of the etched vacuum jar as if it were a prize-winning show dog. "But where are we now, Walter and I?" He smiles, flashing nicotine- and coffee-stained teeth. "Your father is rotting away in a giant nursing home. The last I heard — and I do check on these things, I have my sources — his mind is mostly gone. He's buried alive in his own body, flailing for anything that connects him to his living past. That's why, in one of his more lucid moments, he sent you out to retrieve the Elvis remains."

"My father didn't send me for the Elvis."

He ignores me. "And where am I on fortune's map? In a much sunnier place. I still have my mobility, my mind. I have women! More women than in all my younger years combined! I'm worshiped and respected like a minor deity, young Louis. And I have a patron, a very powerful patron. A man who moves levers, who has the grasp and the will to change the world.

"But you want to know the best reward of all?" Steadying himself with his cane, he slowly bends his knees and plants a loud kiss on top of the vacuum jar. "I have your father's TROPHY!"

That boastful, smug gesture does as much to make me hate him as his past desecration of Margo's body.

I hear a rumbling to my left. The *doppelganger* emerges, pushing a multilevel cart weighed down with jars. Jars of fat, probably the ones that were stored in the other auditorium. He pushes the cart slowly up the ramp, to the edge of the pit. He takes care not to meet my eyes as he begins opening the jars. One by one, he tips their contents into the pit, shaking them to ensure that every last oily trace of lipids falls.

The flaccid splat of those fatty blobs, once part of the *doppelganger* and the congregants and maybe even Margo, hitting bottom makes my stomach twitch. The last strands of fogginess leave my brain, freeing me to wonder just what Trotmann intends to do with me.

"Do you know where I first met Hud?" Trotmann asks. "I met him at Graceland, six years ago."

Graceland. Why am I not surprised? "You went to see if you could buy more parts of Elvis's corpse?"

He smiles. "I already had the only piece of Elvis I ever wanted. I went to see their new Elvis-centered churches. Find out if any of them were interested in franchise deals. Given the asset I already owned, I figured starting my own Elvis church would be less risky and more lucrative than black-market plastic surgery.

"I wasn't able to connect on financials with the Graceland people. But I gained something far more valuable on that trip. I found Hud. He was in terrible shape, filthy, penniless. I recognized him immediately, of course, just as you would have. He had come to Graceland because... how did he put it? *Heh*... because Elvis was the only fat man in America who'd achieved the loving worship of women. 'An American singing-Buddha,' I believe he called him.

"Meeting Hud was a portent. I'd followed your career, just as I had your father's. I knew all about your early involvement with the Good Humor Men, how you'd built a movement around the life of Hud Walterson. And here he was, Hud himself, returned somehow from his famous death, speaking with me in the back of an Elvis church. A miracle, wouldn't you say? I knew I could do better than you, Louis, just as I'd bettered your father. You had the memory of Hud. I had the real thing. Why franchise an Elvis church, when I was being called to build a glorious church of my own? Hud returned to Miami with me. He's astoundingly creative, that boy. I credit him with the bulk of our liturgy."

"Hud" empties the last of the jars into the pit. The fat is deep enough to drown in, if one's hands are shackled. "What are you thinking of doing with me, Trotmann?" The final globule of congealed lipids splats onto the surface of the pool. "I have money. A lot of it. And I have Elvis's famous belt, the one he personally gave to my father, the World's Championship Attendance Record belt. Let me go, and we can work a deal."

He flashes those yellowed teeth again. "Why, that would be just fine, if I wanted money, or a World's Championship Attendance belt. Oh, that belt might be nice. But it's much, much nicer to have *you*. I never had the opportunity to have a son, you see. Your father's persecution of me ensured I never got the chance to settle down."

He hobbles over to me, squeezes my knee like a lewd elderly uncle. "I haven't yet told you about our wonderful liturgical practices. Once a year, we have a holiday where we take all the fat I've extracted and do a mass expulsion of the sin trapped inside. It's rather like Yom Kippur, but much more... bacchanal. Normally, we wouldn't be celebrating this holiday until the anniversary of Hud's death. But given your providential arrival, I believe I can justify a slight rearrangement in our calendar."

He turns to the *doppelganger*. "Hud, if you'd be so kind as to light the pilots on the gas burners, please. And then buzz the ladies, let them know it's showtime."

Gas burners... my God. Trotmann doesn't want to drown me. He intends to deep-fry me.

"You... fucking... *monster!*" I lunge forward, succeeding only in sawing the ropes into my wrists. "You're... you're *worse* than any horror story my father ever told about you."

He clasps his hands together, genuinely pleased. "Ahh, young Louis, you've made my day. Please rest easy in the knowledge that you'll expire in almost precisely the same way that Hud here did. Given that your Good Humor movement had its origin in that death, I'd imagine this should be a source of contentment."

The giant hasn't moved. "Hud," Trotmann says, a hint of irritation in his voice. "Didn't I tell you to light the gas burners?"

The big man rolls his cart back and forth a few inches, making the empty jars clatter. "I... I don't want to do it, Dr. Trotmann. It doesn't feel like a, like a right thing."

Trotmann slams the deck with his cane. "Not a 'right thing'? Don't you know who this man *is?*" He points at me, his wrinkled finger trembling with the force of his hatred. "He's a bad, bad man. As bad as his father. You watched him try to steal the holy Elvis remains. The Elvis remains that you *venerate*. Don't you think he *deserves* to burn?"

The *doppelganger*'s eyes — beautiful eyes — seem to plead with me before they look back to Trotmann, as if I can somehow extricate him from this terrible dilemma. "May-maybe," he says. "But couldn't you put him in an alone-room instead? Maybe beat him some, and then put him in an alone-room, where he can't steal anything —"

"How DARE you question me!" Trotmann swings his cane against the giant's meaty shoulder. The struck man doesn't flinch from the weak blow, only closes his eyes; but when he opens them, tears roll down his ample cheeks. "After all I've done for you! I rescued you from filth and hunger, gave you a home, a *purpose* for your miserable life!"

"I'll tell my, my brother what you did..."

His snuffled mumble makes Trotmann raise his cane again. This time, however, he strikes the deck. "You'll do no such *thing!*"

Tell my brother...? The real Hud Walterson was an only child.

Trotmann takes a deep breath, struggling to control his fury. "Now, unless you want me to let sin build up in that bloated body of yours until you burst from it, you'll heed me and start those burners. And don't forget to call in the women."

"Buh-but..."

"Sin, Hud. You're *bulging* with it. And I'm the only man alive who can take it away."

Head drooping, the giant backs the cart down the ramp. A moment later, I hear the hiss of released gas, then a muffled roar as it ignites beneath the pit. Trotmann smiles at the sound. "I'm going to make an example of you, young Louis. Today will become another holiday in our church's calendar. The day we fried the son of the devil in the heat of banished sin."

"You must be proud of yourself," I say. "It's quite a feat to bully the feeble-minded."

"Hud?" Trotmann chuckles. "He's not feeble-minded. Not at all. But he knows which side his bread's buttered on."

A loud, wet popping sound rises from the pit. The fat is beginning to bubble. Waves of shimmering warmth, visible in the dusty air, envelop my knees. The doors at the back of the auditorium open. About a dozen women file in. My only chance for survival is if Margo is among them. It's hard to see — but that tall one, it's *got* to be — Yes. It's her.

She stops walking. Our eyes lock. I can't read her face. For a half-second, my stomach plunges — was she Trotmann's confederate all along?

But her body language is easier to read. She visibly stiffens, then looks quickly from side to side, sizing up my predicament. She must've realized something was amiss. She lets the women behind her in the aisle pass her.

Margo, please be as clever and cunning as I think you are. She backs toward the entrance, her body still stiff. Then she swivels and slips through the partly open doors.

She's plotting my rescue.

Or she's panicked and can't bear to watch me die.

Be brave, Margo. Be cunning. Be loyal.

To me.

White smoke rises from the pit. A carbonized bacon stench hits my nose as some of the fat at the bottom begins burning. The women climb the ramp to the circular deck. Do they have any idea what's going on? They stare at me like I'm a squid in a tank, then glance nervously, questioningly at one another.

The deck quivers as the man who claims to be Hud Walterson ascends the ramp and stands next to Trotmann. We form a rough triangle atop the circle of the deck — the women at one corner; Trotmann and "Hud" to my left; and me facing both the Elvis and the doors.

"Today is a great day!" Trotmann announces. "Great are the workings of Heaven and the surprise blessings they bring! I know you all are wondering why I've called you back so soon after our service earlier tonight. Wondering why the cleansing fires have been lit when the Day of Joyful Banishment is still two months away."

He points at me. *"There* is your answer! The Anti-Elvis himself has been delivered into our power! That man is Louis Shmalzberg, son of Walter Shmalzberg... yes, the wicked Reductionist who tricked Elvis and then slew our blessed forefather with his poisoned cannula. The son has proven his own wickedness. He was caught in the blasphemous act of stealing the holy remains. He was prevented from carrying out this heinous deed by our blessed Exemplar, Hud Walterson. And very soon, in a display of Heaven's righteous vengeance, Hud will cast this Anti-Elvis into the cleansing fires.

"Hud, your followers call upon you to smite thy enemy in thy righteous rage!"

I search the faces of the women. Two wear expressions of thrilled anticipation. The others appear acutely uncomfortable; one is pale white and trembling. But peer pressure, the herd instinct, will keep any of them from intervening.

The popping in the pit grows louder. The lumpy giant walks slowly toward me. I've got to buy time for whatever Margo is planning. If she's planning anything... "Hud, you don't want to do this," I say. "Listen — you're no murderer. I remember you from your first incarnation. You were a sweet, gentle man. A man who went out of his way not to harm anyone —"

"The words of the Anti-Elvis are honeyed and smooth," Trotmann says. "But they drip poison."

The giant doesn't seem to hear his master. He stops and stares at me, his beautiful eyes full of a hope he's almost afraid to express. "You... you *knew* my father-mother?"

"Hud, be quiet!" Trotmann barks. "Do your duty!"

Father-mother? I have no idea what that means, but it's a lifeline I eagerly grab. "Yes, I knew him, I knew your father-mother," I say. "He devoted his life to other people's welfare. All the fast food restaurants and factories he burned, he burned them after hours, when no one would be trapped. The only man he ever killed was *himself.*"

"So he was a good man? A *good* man?"

"Hud, *shut up!*" I hear Trotmann's cane break on the giant's back.

"Yes, he was a *good* man, he inspired the whole country; he inspired *me.* Maybe some of the things we've done in his name have gone too far. But that wasn't his fault. He was a good man, who sacrificed himself for other people, people he didn't even know. He wasn't a murderer. Do you understand, Hud? He *wasn't* a *murderer.* And *you* aren't a murderer."

"Hud, *goddamn it,* PUSH HIM IN!"

A shroud of peacefulness descends on the giant's tortured face. "My name... my name is Benjamin," he says. "*Benjamin* Walterson. Not Hud. Benjamin." He steps, not toward me, but toward the edge of the pit. What —?

A sharp blast, painfully loud. Flecks of plaster — from the ceiling? — hit me in the head. The door in the back. It's open. A second blast.

Gunfire. Trotmann screams. Some of the women scream.

Benjamin, face blissful, totters on the edge of the pit, then falls forward in slow-motion like a dynamited obelisk.

The lights go out.

Benjamin hits the bottom of the pit. The sound is like rubber slapping jelly. Specks of boiling fat hit my legs, my chest. I shout in pain, but Benjamin — there's not a sound from him, no crying out in his agonizing death.

Another shot hits the ceiling, raining plaster. This third shot frees the women from paralyzing shock. Their shoes beat a panicked rhythm on the deck as they run for the ramp.

I hear Trotmann moaning. Then I hear someone bounding up the ramp. I hear her tight, excited breathing and feel her presence behind me.

"Don't move your hands," Margo says, "or you might lose them."

She clicks on a flashlight, which casts my elongated shadow across the deck, the pit, and Trotmann, writhing in a small but spreading pool of blood that leaks from his shoulder. My shadow touches the Elvis, which gleams, jewel-like, in the flashlight's beam.

I feel a sudden heat at my wrists; Margo is using my hand laser to cut the ropes. "Did you shoot Benjamin?" I ask. I feel guilty asking her this. But I have to know.

"Shoot who?"

"The giant. Hud."

"No. I shot the ceiling twice. I shot Dr. Trotmann. But I didn't shoot Hud. He jumped, didn't he? Or fell. Horrible way to die. I'm glad it didn't happen to you."

He jumped. But why? Did he sacrifice himself to save me, emulating the real Hud's death?

I'm suddenly able to move my hands. "There," Margo says, a fierce satisfaction in her voice. "I'll have your feet free in a minute. Thank God I found your things in time."

She's saved my life. How do you thank someone for that? "You saved me, Margo. You came back. I don't know what to say, except... thank you."

"You're my Reductionist," she says quietly.

The ropes grow slack around my feet. I take the flashlight and shine it into the pit. Benjamin's body, face down, covers the bottom like a huge plug. His only movements are involuntary shudders and ripples, caused by the pent-up fury of the boiling fat beneath him. There's nothing to do for him now. Except remember him.

His veneration of the Elvis gives me one more reason to do something healing and hopeful and miraculous with it. I step over Trotmann's writhing body to reach the relic I've crossed the country to reclaim. His eyes, squeezed shut with pain, snap open. His good arm moves like a striking rattlesnake, and his hand clutches my ankle. "Not... yours," he says. "We'll regroup. Hunt you down like a dog."

His wound doesn't look too serious; as best as I can tell, the bullet exited his shoulder cleanly, just beneath the collarbone. Still, the loss of blood could plunge him into shock. "Tell me who Benjamin was," I say. "Tell me, and I'll take you to a hospital."

His eyes narrow. "Fuh... fuck you. Not telling you a... goddamn thing, you son-of-shit."

I yank my ankle loose, then stomp that grasping hand as hard as I can. The hand that's guided his terrible cannula, that's violated Margo.

Then I turn away, blocking out his cries, ashamed that I've let him push me into striking a ninety-five-year-old lying in a pool of his own blood. The shame only lasts a few seconds, though. Because the Elvis is waiting.

Margo, who went the other way around the pit, reaches it first. She kneels down and picks up the engraved jar. She's beautiful... a priestess returning a lost relic to its rightful place in the order of creation.

"Here," she says, handing it to me. "This is yours."

Mine. Mine again, after twenty-seven years and more strangeness than I thought possible. I grasp the jar, sensing the etchings of Elvis's image with my bruised fingertips. Feeling the weight of those eleven pounds of him.

Margo stares at me expectantly. I wait for something to happen, some bolt of lightning to crash through the ceiling and transform me. Elvis adored the adventures of Captain Marvel Jr.

No lightning bolt strikes. I'm not transformed in the slightest. God help me, this isn't the finish line. Because now I'm forced to answer the sixty-four-thousand-dollar question:

What do I do next?

PART III
Viva Lost Vegas

CHAPTER 15

The equipment in this lab I've rented is top-notch. I'm about to uncloak a mystery: which drugs were in Elvis's system during his last week on earth. The jar containing the Elvis is inside an isolation box, sheltered from dust, pollen, even air. I begin opening it, slowly, with thickly gloved hands, my arms encased in plastic sheathes built into the sides of the box. Margo, wearing a starched white lab coat, watches wide-eyed from atop a stool, her expression a mix of anxiousness and trust.

Two days have passed since I recovered the Elvis. My physician's credentials and the Ottoman's money have proven indispensable again. We've rented this lab from the University of South Florida's biochemistry department.

Nearly have it open now... exasperating, having to work within these constraints, almost like making love while wearing a suit of armor. The last seal finally comes loose. I pick up a long-handled sample extractor from the floor of the isolation box, cut a tiny piece of the fat, and place it in an examination dish. Then I scrape away about half a gram of the stomach contents, distinguishable from the fat by its different texture and blood-red color, and set that in a separate dish.

"How long will the analysis take?" Margo asks.

I extricate my arms from the long gloves. "I'm not sure, really." I dab sweat off my forehead with a sterile wipe. "The fat may not reveal as much as the sampling of the stomach contents will. The pharmaceuticals that'll show up in the fat are those drugs that he'd been taking long-term, at least the ones that were fat-soluble. The stomach contents should reveal what he'd taken the morning of the operation or the night before. With a habitual opiate user, digestion is slowed, so not all the pills he took would have dissolved before the operation."

My own stomach rumbles. I haven't eaten since — when? Yesterday? Didn't American Indians deprive themselves of food and water before a vision quest? That's what I've embarked upon: a vision quest to decipher the messages buried within the Elvis.

I've got to find out what I'm supposed to do now. I'd hoped listening to his recordings would make it clear. Over the past two days, I've spent hours inside my car, listening to those old CDs over and over. But I've got to go deeper. I've got to penetrate the Elvis itself, force it to tell me how to simulate the man's state of mind.

I must achieve Elvis consciousness.

The more sensationalistic biographies have claimed that as many as fourteen different controlled substances were detected within Elvis's corpse. Soon I'll know exactly what was in his system the morning Elvis offered himself to my father's cannula. I carry the fat sample across the room to the chemical analysis unit. I place the tiny glass dish on the sample-holder tray; it's like putting a scrap of unicorn meat on the extended black tongue of a dragon, who promises me knowledge of my future in exchange for this rare delicacy. I select the most coarse level of analysis, not wanting the computers to break down complex compounds into their more basic elements. I also request that the printout list the non-organic, pharmaceutical compounds at the top.

By the end of the day, I'll have the components for an Elvis cocktail. A moveable feast that will help attune my thoughts to his. So that when I partake of it in the proper place, his message to me will thrill the air like the strummed chords of a Stratocaster.

We reach Orlando at dusk. Our trip was uneventful, except for the few sweat-inducing moments when I spotted a familiar-looking black sedan behind us on the highway. It trailed us by a quarter-mile for a few minutes, before we turned off for a recharge and some liquid fuel. When we returned to the road, the black sedan was gone.

I check us into the Castle Towers Hotel, where we register as Mr. and Mrs. Jesse Garon. The hotel is located in the heart of what was once Walt Disney World, now MannaSantos's Worlds of Wonder.

One of the questionable "improvements" MannaSantos made to the Magic Kingdom was to build this circle of medium-rise hotels around Cinderella's Castle. The newer buildings resemble nothing so much as a row of public housing blocks in Soviet-era Moscow.

Late this afternoon, we purchased the components for my cocktail at the university pharmacy in Tampa. Not surprisingly, the recipe turned out to be complicated. Its base is downers: ethchlorvynol, brand name Placidyl, a sleeping pill, and secobarbital, Seconal, a barbiturate known among the abusing community as the "red devil." Flavor is provided by two types of opiate pain pills: little yellow Percodans, and hydromorphone (Dilaudid), a narcotic seven times stronger than morphine. The cocktail will get its fizz from little heart-shaped "dexies," Dexedrine, the orange-colored upper that perversely looks just like Valentine's Day candy.

My vision quest will take place in the park. Not in a desert sweatlodge, and not on a mountaintop. I've thought this through very carefully. Elvis was the quintessential American. At its pinnacle, America was an amusement park, the dream factory for much of the rest of the world. And this place was the nation's greatest amusement park. Elvis loved amusement parks. He rented out Libertyland in Memphis several nights a year for his exclusive enjoyment. Without a doubt, he spent many of those nocturnal joy splurges stoned out of his mind.

I can't say I'm unafraid of what I plan to do tomorrow morning. I'd hoped crawling into bed next to Margo would help take my mind off tomorrow's dangers, but I can't make myself relax into sleep. It seems like a lifetime since I've lain in a bed next to a woman. Although it's hard for me to think of Margo as a woman, per se. She's so coltish, so girlish; so... unfinished. My arm is around her, cradling that place where a mature woman's breasts would be.

Margo was open to more than just sharing warmth. Even after all those years alone, I could tell that. Maybe with someone else, she wouldn't have hesitated being the aggressor. But she hung back, waiting for me to make my intentions fully clear, both to her and to myself.

I feel her stir. "Are you awake?" she asks, voice husky and indistinct.

"I haven't been able to fall asleep yet. How are you feeling?"

"I'm fine. I'm hardly sore, even when the pain pills wear off. You do good work."

"Thank you." She shifts, pressing more closely against me. "Have you been able to sleep?" I ask.

"I've been thinking stuff, and then maybe I drift off for a while... but whatever I dream is just a continuation of what I've been thinking about. So I'm never sure whether I'm awake or asleep."

"What have you been thinking about?"

I feel her back stiffen. "My father. I've been thinking about him a lot the past couple of days." Not so surprising, that. Her father's probably about my vintage. I may remind her of him in a hundred different ways; the scent of my aftershave, the topographical maps age has created on my face and the backs of my hands. "He taught me how to use a gun."

"Really? I was surprised you were able to handle my gun the way you did. I probably would've shot my own foot off."

"Yeah. Well, my father used to take me to the firing range pretty regularly. I shot off revolvers, automatics, deer rifles, the works. All while wearing these frilly dresses, little girl dresses like you'd wear to First Communion or a fancy birthday party. That was my whole wardrobe, pouffy little-girl dresses, hair ribbons, shiny white leather buckle-top shoes. When my mother couldn't buy the dresses in my size anymore, she started sewing them for me. I never owned a pair of jeans until I left home, when I was twenty-three. Six years ago."

She stops talking for a while. "Is your father still alive?" I ask.

"Yes." Pause. "As far as I know."

"You don't talk with him?"

"He and my mom split about a year after I left." She rolls out of my grasp, then turns to look at me. The lights of Cinderella's Castle, diffused through translucent pink drapes, barely illuminate the chiseled contours of her face. "I was the glue holding them together, I think," she says with a quiet edge of bitterness. "They didn't want me to ever leave. They wouldn't pay for college unless I went to Mount Carmel and lived at home. I hated it. When I finally got the balls to make a break for it, it was like I let all the air out of their marriage. And them, too."

I reach for her hand. "It wasn't your fault, Margo."

"I used to beg my mother to have another baby. So all their attention wouldn't be on just me. It's not like we were poor. But they always said they couldn't afford a brother or sister for me. So I was their everything. The baby doll. The son he took target shooting."

"I was an only child, too," I say. Didn't my own father try to bend me into the shape he'd planned for me? And didn't he mostly succeed? But at least he didn't specify my genetic characteristics prior to handing his sperm over to a technician. "You were right to leave."

She seems to relax some. "I was wondering something," she says. "Are you afraid? About tomorrow?"

I glance over at the dresser, where my pill bottles are lined up next to the Elvis. How many doctors have flushed their careers and themselves down the toilet by dipping too deeply into the medicine cabinet? This is a one-time event, I've told myself. I requisitioned micro dosages, since I'll be ingesting so many compounds at once. Elvis had built up an almost supernatural drug resistance by the time he died; my constitution isn't anywhere near as robust as his was. Am I afraid? I'd have to be already drugged not to be.

"Everyone's at least a little afraid of the unknown," I say, trying to belittle my fears.

"I didn't mean to make it sound bad, you being afraid. It doesn't make me think any less of you." She moves closer, kicking away the covers. "If you'd want... I could take them for you. My father was a doctor. There was always stuff in the house. I've taken some of the drugs you bought. I could try to have the vision for you."

"No, Margo." I pull her to me, tightly, feeling a tenderness so sudden and intense it's almost painful. "No. You don't know how much that means to me. But I have to take the pills myself."

The solo buffalo kill. The initiation into the mysteries of the tribe. Something I have to do myself.

One of the privileges of being a guest at the Castle Towers is a complimentary "character breakfast," followed by an early admission to the park. So I carry the pills downstairs with me to the dining hall. I also carry the Elvis, nestled securely (and heavily) against my chest in a soft denim baby carrier. I wasn't about to leave it alone in our room, and it wouldn't fit in the hotel's safe.

"Oh, *look!*" Margo squeals.

The characters are waiting for us when we step into the dining hall. The big-headed costumes are showing the combination of wear and neglect. But all of them remain instantly recognizable, particularly to someone my age. The Mouse is here, and the Duck, and the Mouse's Wife, and the Mouse's Dog. Even the Mouse's Best Pal Who Might Be a Dog (or Might Not).

I wonder if Margo could name any of them? She was a baby when the old Disney empire was dismembered and MannaSantos grabbed up the theme parks (I've always wondered how this fit into their over-all business plan). We get in line at the buffet tables. What's truly striking is the lack of children. Only a third of the younger couples have a child with them. I don't spot a single family with more than one youngster.

I load up my tray with orange juice and Leanie-Lean sausage and bacon, following Harri's suggestion to stick to meats. Eggs, too, might not yet have been adulterated by Metaboloft, so I don't object when Margo loads up her plate with fluffy yellow mounds. I haven't told her yet about Metaboloft. I haven't had the heart to. Who wants to tell someone they love the world is coming to an end? Particularly when there's not a damned thing one can do about it?

Or is there? The weight of the Elvis drags on my shoulders, but it lifts me up at the same time. Ever since I regained it, I've felt a feeling I haven't had for the longest time. Hope.

I eat my breakfast, not wanting to take all those powerful pills on an empty stomach. While assembling the elements of my Elvis cock-tail on my plate, I sense bulky presences crowding behind me. The Duck and the Mouse's Wife. Margo smiles wickedly, then reaches in her purse for a camera. "Daddy's taking his heart medications," she says. "He's got so, so many pills to take. But he's such a good boy about it."

Furry arms reach around my shoulders. I reach for one of the pills. Now, with the Elvis resting on my lap, I'm not afraid anymore. Even though there'll be a whole lotta shakin' goin' on, everything, somehow, will be all right. I pop the Percodan into my mouth, then down it with a slug of Florida's finest orange juice.

Margo raises the camera to her face. "Smile, Daddy!" she says.

By the time a hotel porter arrives with the wheelchair Margo had requested for me, one of my key questions is answered. I had wondered which of the three types of drugs I'd swallowed, downers, opiates, or speed, would kick in first. Not the speed, that's for sure. I fall into the wheelchair like a sack of grain. It's not that my legs aren't capable of supporting me anymore, just that they aren't of a mind to.

"The wheelchair was a good idea, wasn't it?" Margo says, steering me out of the lobby.

"Def... definitely."

The blue, cloudless sky looks hyper-real. I feel my head tumbling forward. I arrest its fall just before my nose would've flattened against the top of the Elvis jar. Jesus. Have the barbiturates locked out the other drugs? Will I pass out? Or will I spend my day awake but helplessly drooling, every muscle in my body absurdly relaxed, including, possibly, my bladder and bowels?

This last thought hits me like ice water. "How're you doing?" Margo asks.

"Hanging in there," I say. My mouth feels like it's jammed with toffee. What I heard myself say was *Hann. Ging. Giin. Thairr.*

We roll past the entrance to Cinderella's Castle. I stare up at the highest spire, my mouth involuntarily flopping open. Rumor has it that Walt Disney's cryogenically frozen body resides in a penthouse apartment at the top of the castle, waiting for the day when medical science can return him to the fast-vanishing children of America.

As if she's read my mind, Margo looks up and asks, "You think he's still up there? Walt Disney? Or did MannaSantos take his body away?"

"May... maybe still there." Or maybe MannaSantos took him away, like they removed his name and likeness from this park he built. Did they ever meet, Disney and Elvis? Elvis would love Disney; Elvis loved nearly everyone. But would Elvis be welcome in Disney's world? Maybe certain incarnations; the movie Elvis, the pasteurized Elvis of

G.I. Blues and *Blue Hawaii*. But the other Elvises? Disney would take a horse-whip to them.

Margo begins rolling me down Main Street, U.S.A. It's time travel on the cheap, a small-town commercial thoroughfare lined with Victorian and Edwardian storefronts.

"I always wondered why this was here," Margo says. "What does any of this have to do with movies or fairy tales?"

"Re-creation... of Disney's Midwestern... hometown." Actually, it has a lot to do with fairy tales. Hitching posts, but no horse shit. Saloons, but no puking drunks.

"So this is Disney's ideal America?" Margo says. "It's Dullsville, U.S.A., that's what it is."

As she directs us toward some other land, I realize what the street is missing — if it aspires to be America, *all* of America, it needs the Warner Brothers characters. Bugs Bunny. Daffy Duck. Wile E. Coyote. The *ying* to the Disney cartoons' *yang*. The Disney characters were the modest, quiet ones, Midwestern as their creator. Rural, family oriented, mild as milk. The Warner Brothers characters, on the other hand, were big-city types, even when their backdrops were barnyards — immigrants, climbers, wise-guys. Braggarts, never averse to using a stick of dynamite to make their point. If the Disney characters were older-vintage Americans, then the Warner Brothers characters were Jews and Italians, Mexicans and maybe even blacks, immigrants who came later or who didn't start making their mark on the culture until the turn of the twentieth century.

As Margo wheels me into the outskirts of Frontierland and Liberty Square, I sense an awakening of the Dexedrines. I'd wondered whether the speed and the downers would simply cancel each other out. But that's not what's happening. Instead of diluting each other, the two types of drugs have layered themselves. The downers are on top, dulling my reflexes, slowing my sense of time. But just beneath them, the speed simmers. One good shove, and my interior world will flip over, the two drugs inverting themselves like a pair of wrestlers.

Ahead of us, a paddle wheel steamboat plays its calliope on an artificial lake. Puffs of smoke rise from the chimneys of rough-hewn log cabins, spreading a kind of frontier perfume. I pull the wheelchair's hand brake, reaching down into the seething Dexedrine for coherence. "Muh-Margo. I've got a question for you. Elvis — is he a Disney character or a Warner Brothers character?"

"Warner Brothers? What? You mean, like Tom and, uh, the little mouse guy? And Bugs Bunny?"

Thank God for pirated vid-9s. "Yes, that's them. The other pantheon of American animation."

"So you're asking me if Elvis was more like Mickey Mouse or like Bugs Bunny?"

"Sort of. Try to keep all the other characters in mind, too. Donald Duck. Daffy Duck. The Road Runner."

She purses her lips. "That's easy," she says, a satisfied smile on her face. "Elvis was a Warner Brothers character. Mickey Mouse wouldn't do the things Elvis did. Daffy Duck would. What do *you* think?"

A warmth appears at the base of my spine and begins spreading. "Elvis," I say, smiling, "is *both*."

"How do you figure that?"

"He was born Disney. English and Scots-Irish ancestors, Protestant, raised in a small, rural town. In some ways he stayed Disney all his life. Revered his parents. Adored singing with gospel quartets. But the thing that set him apart, that made Elvis *Elvis,* was that he was always reaching across the line, seeking to encompass the other America, the Warner Brothers America. Even as a teenager, he dressed with a style as way out as Little Richard's. He spent years studying the great Italian singers. Half his best friends were Jewish — in *Memphis,* of all places! On his mother's side, he had a Jewish great-great-grandmother and Cherokee ancestry. Disney *and* Warner Brothers — do you see it now?"

Margo nervously glances at the small crowd nearby lined up for keel-boat rides, some of whom stare openly at me. "What I *see,* Doctor Louis," she says with good-humored sternness, "is you not making much sense. How about we go see a show? Maybe afterward I'll take you on a water-flume ride. Cool you off."

She rolls me toward the Hall of Presidents. That spreading, angelic warmth I've been feeling has to be the Dilaudid kicking in. The experience — it's not just lying on a warm, gel-filled waterbed — it's *being*

202 | *Andrew Fox*

the warm, gel-filled waterbed. Inside, the hall looks just like Ford's Theatre in Washington, DC. Solemn-faced robots of our fifty-one presidents sit quietly on stage. The lights come up, and the robots jerk to life, clearing their throats, coughing, muttering like old men with bad prostates. Andrew Jackson pretends to notice that an audience has gathered while they were dozing, and Gerald Ford waves hello. Then Washington, Jefferson, and Teddy Roosevelt begin bickering over who has the handsomest carving on Mount Rushmore, with Abe Lincoln remaining above the fray. And so it goes.

They all look so damned Puritan sitting up there. Even John F. Kennedy, lover of pneumatic Marilyn Monroe, even *he* has the dead whiff of asceticism about him.

I feel like I'm suffocating. Like there's a horrible weight on me, not physical, but *spiritual*. This Puritanism — it's what's been suffocating this country for the past twenty-five years. Pleasure hating, judgmental. Where's William Taft? Where have they hidden roly-poly William Taft, our fattest president ever, the counterweight to all this god-damned pinched uprightness?

He sits quietly in the back row, pushed off to the side like a class dunce with William Jefferson Clinton, who also has a noticeable paunch and jowls. The two Slick Willies, slick with the grease of juicy hamburgers running down their chins. The forgotten presidents of Fat America.

Fat America! Yes, there was a Fat America once. Americans drove the biggest cars in the world. They lived in the biggest houses, launched the biggest rockets, ate supersized restaurant meals. They listened to the music of Fats Waller, Fats Domino, Fats Navarro, Al "Jumbo" Hirt. And Elvis. What was the frontier for, after all? The American frontier, ever expanding to make room for all our stuff, our superhighways, our franchises and mega-malls and theme parks. And, yes, our expanding bodies.

Fat America dreamed it, and Thin America designed it, and together they built it and lived in it. Maybe they didn't really like each other, but together, the ascetics and the gluttons, the Calvinists and the Mardi Gras Catholics, they made America the dreamland for the rest of the world, the place where streets were paved with gold.

But the partnership between the two Americas cracked apart. Thin America consumed Fat America, but it achieved no fullness. We've been shrinking ever since, withering and shrinking. The incredible shrinking dreamland...

Margo touches my shoulder. "Are you seeing anything? Are the drugs working?"

Am I seeing anything? I'm seeing Presidents Dwight Eisenhower and Jerry Ford trade quips about their golf games as if nothing's the matter. And still William Taft sits in the back, silent, a husk.

My vision clouds with tears. If only he'd say something! If only he'd take command of the stage, assert himself, it might make a difference —

"President Taft!" I struggle to rise from the wheelchair. "Speak out! Don't let them silence you! A shrinking America is a *dying* America!"

Heads turn. Struggling with the weight of the Elvis, I gain a visceral new appreciation for Elvis's own struggles with his weight, how the once lean, hungry boy, now saddled with a sagging paunch, must've wrestled with the changes in his body and the smirks of the national media. The hell with them! He overcame, he learned to bear up under his weight like Atlas carrying the world, dabbing his sweat on hundreds of scarves that he threw into a sea of outstretched hands, to those who'd loved him thin and fat, boyish and middle-aged, angelic and devilish both.

I grab hold of the seat ahead of me. I *will* rise. I force my legs to straighten. Icy hail cascades from my hips down to my feet. I'm blind, my sight clouded by a whirlpool of colors and pinpricks of exploding light.

And when it clears, I see, I see —

I see a valley with great mountains on both sides, and the valley is split by a growing fissure. It's the Continental Divide, and it's growing wider, deeper, more terrible. The foothills of the mountains are beginning to tumble in, chunks of granite falling into an abyss that stretches to the earth's core.

And then Elvis comes. His head is high as the clouds. Somehow he's all the Elvises at once, Sun Studios Elvis and Army Elvis and Hollywood Elvis and Vegas Elvis, his face and body and costumes changing faster than my eyes can follow. He straddles the chasm, planting a colossal boot on each side. And then he begins flexing his mighty thigh muscles, straining to pull the two crumbling faces of the fissure closer together. He won't let this happen. He won't let us be pulled apart. But despite his groans and golden sweat, the chasm continues to grow wider, spreading his feet farther apart. Wider and wider, and wider still, until Elvis's pants begin to split and the cataclysm sounds like the fabric of the Milky Way being torn asunder.

But then there is another sound — (impossible, unbearable, rapturous) — all of Elvis's Top Ten Hits being sung at once by the same voice. And the face this sound emerges from — Elvis's face — it's red and jowly and shining with sheets of sweat, eyes staring heavenward for new sources of strength. And the earth quakes, for with a mighty thrust of his pelvis, Elvis halts the growth of the chasm. And then, as the hundred commingled songs grow louder and louder, yet ever more sweet, Elvis begins reversing the outward flight of tectonic plates — he's bringing them together, bringing *us* together, Disney America and Warner Brothers America, Thin America and Fat America —

"He's saving us! He's saving the country! He's healing the rift, binding up our wounds —"

Hands push me back into the wheelchair. Margo is arguing with someone in a Minuteman costume. "Can't you hear it?" I ask the Minuteman. "Can't you hear him *singing?*"

The final vibrations of Elvis's voice buzz around my cranium, petering out like the fading fragments of a meteor shower. He's going away. It's all going away.

"I'm very sorry, sir. I'm afraid you'll have to exit the attraction —"

"What is this," Margo snarls at him, "Liberty Square or Fascistland?"

"No," I say, waving weakly, "no, it's all right. We'll go. Let's just go."

I take one last look at William Taft, still sitting quiet as a medicine ball, but possibly with the tiniest of smiles peering out from beneath his walrus mustache. Then Margo, muttering angrily, wheels me back out into the sunlight.

"Those *assholes,*" she says. "You weren't bothering anybody. It's just a bunch of dumb robots in there. If anyone missed any of that amazingly clever dialogue, they could've just sat through it again —"

"It's all right," I say, reaching up to pat her hand. Her skin is as warm as a winter campfire. The distant January sunlight wraps everything in a fine mesh of translucent gold.

She parks the wheelchair facing a bench, then sits. "You saw something, didn't you?"

"Yes."

"Can you tell me about it?"

Its sheer overwhelmingness is already dimming in my brain. Losing the realness of it, the sense of *presence,* is immensely sad. "Yes. I want to tell you, I want that very much, but —"

She leans in closer. "But what? What's the matter?"

"But..." I feel squeezed, tight. There's a pressure inside me, pushing, insistent. Then I remember my own body. All that Florida orange juice I drank. "But first you need to get me to a men's room."

"Oh. Okay."

Priorities. Even Elvis himself was known to walk out on a concert when the call of nature became too insistent. Liberty Square shifts to Adventureland before we spot a sign for a men's room. Margo looks at me questioningly. "So how do you want to do this?" she asks. "Do you want me to, uh, you know, go inside with you? Help out?"

My pride, assaulted by images of my father, dependent on nursing aides for the simplest of personal tasks, rebels at the notion. Actually, I'm no longer a bowl of overcooked noodles. "I think I'll be all right," I say, rising without a stumble from the wheelchair.

"You're sure?"

"I'm sure."

She stares at the rounded burden hanging on my chest. "Won't that kinda get in the way? I'll hold it for you."

Let go of the Elvis? The last time I let go of it, I was cursed with twenty-six years of unhappiness.

"Louis, please don't look at me like that. Go pee with the Elvis hanging on your chest. But someday... you're gonna have to trust me."

She's absolutely right. She's done nothing but show me again and again that she's worthy of my trust. I slip the carrier off and hold it up so Margo can put it on.

"You're sure you're okay with this?" she asks.

My heart is pounding twice as fast as it should be. "I'm okay with it."

"Thank you, Doctor Louis." She leans over and kisses me on the cheek, pressing the Elvis into both our chests.

I push open the bamboo doors. The bathroom seems to stretch on forever: a trans-Atlantic tunnel lined with white and green ceramic tiles and gleaming porcelain. Disorienting. At the far end of the bathroom there's another exit, so distant it looks like a door for Cinderella's dwarfs.

I'm alone. Twenty urinals to choose from, my bladder on the edge of bursting, but instead of choosing the closest one, I walk down to one in the middle. Typical male precaution. Few situations evoke more vulnerability than when you're trapped facing the porcelain piss-catcher.

Ah. *Ahhh.* Yes. As satisfying, in its own way, as the vision of the Colossal Elvis. Or *was* my vision satisfying? I didn't see the end of it. What would've happened when Colossal Elvis's boots touched, when the walls of the chasm were forced together? Will I ever learn the secrets that would've been revealed?

I was *robbed*. By some clown in a Minuteman suit. I abandoned my home, made the quest, liberated the Elvis, took the drugs — all for *half* a vision. As useful to me as half a toothbrush, half a rowboat, half a goddamned *urinal* —

A thud, behind me. The sound of a stall door swinging open and banging into the stall next to it. I thought I was alone in here.

Well, no matter. In a couple of seconds, I'll hear him turn on a faucet, rub his hands under the water, then turn on a hand-drier.

Except... except I don't hear anything. Not even a footstep. He's standing there, by the stall. Behind me. Watching me.

My stream has slowed to a trickle. One more second, two, I'll be able to shake myself off, reinsert myself, zip up.

I turn around.

It's Elvis.

A normal-sized Elvis, staring at me with a blank expression. He's wearing a white jumpsuit with a bald eagle embroidered on it. His body is full, well-padded, the body of late Elvis, 1977 vintage. But the face, partially hidden by dark sunglasses, is thinner; the face of Elvis circa 1969. Maybe this is a continuation of my earlier vision — the Elvis that bridges the gap between Thin America and Fat America? Will he show me the vision's ending now?

I wait for him to say something. My image of him is amazingly sharp and clear. The earlier vision seemed real, too; but dream-real, not like this.

His silence is disconcerting. "Speak to me, Elvis," I say, my voice barely a whisper.

He tugs on the gold pull-ring at the neck of his jumpsuit, unzipping it. The unzipping reaches the great bulge of his belly, then stops just above his crotch. Across the mound of his stomach, his golden shirt is massively stained. Dark blotches, still wet and glistening.

"Gimme it back," Elvis says.

Blood.

"Gimme back what your daddy stole from me."

I *reject* this vision. This is a flashback to my childhood guilt that my father had killed the King.

"Gimme back what your daddy stole from me," the false vision repeats, more insistently.

I can prove this isn't real. All I need do is poke it, push my finger through its nonexistent substance, and it'll vanish.

I walk toward the open stall. It could've just drifted open due to metal fatigue. I reach for the place where my eyes falsely tell me I see blood.

My finger touches something solid.

It's not blood. The "flesh" my finger pokes into isn't flesh, either. It's some kind of padding.

I'm being scammed.

"Elvis" grabs my hand. Instead of pulling away, I push against his chest. He stumbles backward, into the stall. His head hits a pipe.

Two other stall doors swing open. Two more Elvises. Young Elvises, pink shirts and Western jackets. No padding.

My body is afire: the Dexedrines take over. The false Elvises move in slow motion. I run toward the doors I came in through. Then realize I can't lead them to Margo and the true Elvis.

I stop. One young Elvis is almost on top of me. I reach up, grab a handle on the wall and yank. A baby-changing platform crashes down on his head.

I'm rewarded with a moan. His partner stops to help him up. I run past them, toward the other exit. Slam the doors open. Brace myself in case there are other Elvises waiting outside.

There aren't. The sun is blinding. People all around. Where do I go? Try to blend in with the crowds? The doors slam open behind me. Run.

I elbow people aside. Shouts, curses, surprised dismay. I'm Charlton Heston in *Planet of the Apes,* running from the gorillas, fleeing through Ape City. No one will help me. Everywhere I turn, apes apes apes —

Hands grab at me from behind. Faster! Up ahead, hanging bridges swinging between rooms in a giant tree — the Swiss Family Robinson Treehouse. Maybe I could hold off the Elvises until security guards arrive?

I push through a line of twenty people. Nobody tries to stop me. I run up rough plank steps. Behind me, more commotion in the line. Louder outcries — the Elvises are being rough. Who are they? Who sent them? Trotmann? The Ottoman? Could Swaggart have sent them? Have they been tailing me since I left Graceland?

First room is a play room, full of toys made from coconuts and twigs. Up. Nearly twist my ankle. Christ. Clamor of steps behind me. The exertion. Feeling it in my lungs. My heart.

A library. Shelves, books, parrots. Weapons? I yank on several of the books. Then the bookcases. Bolted down. No good. Shit.

Higher. Across a swinging rope bridge. A kitchen next. Oven made from a ship's boiler, hand-cranked bamboo carousels to wash dishes —

Lungs burning. Have to stop. But they're right behind me. I stumble into the next room, bombs exploding behind my eyes. Long wooden table. Get around the far side — I can keep it between them and me. If there weren't two of them...

Up feels like down. I stare at the plates on the table. Seven of them. They swirl around, leafs in a whirlpool. When they stop moving, I see what's on them —

Peanut butter, bacon, and banana sandwiches. Seven peanut butter, bacon, and banana sandwiches.

Oh. Oh, God. Oh my God.

It's the second half of my vision. The missing piece.

I close my eyes, then look again. What's on the plates are plastic pork chops and turnips. The false Elvises storm into the room. But I've got my second wind. Enough of a second wind to breathe life back into America. If I get out of here.

They split up, stalking me on opposite sides of the table.

"Love me tender," the first one says.

"Love me true," says the second.

The plates are glued to the table. I yank one loose, fling it like a frisbee at the Elvis coming at me from my right. It careens off his temple, takes a fake sideburn with it.

"Aahh! Fuck!"

I pull two more plates off the table, brandish them like discuses. "Tender" rubs his bruised head. I feint a toss at "True." He flinches.

"Vernon, don't be a wuss!" the first Elvis shouts, checking his fingers for blood, after touching the side of his face. "He's just an old guy. Let's rush him. On the count of three —"

Distant clamor. Men rushing up the path?

"— three!"

I swing wildly with the plates, but they're on top of me. A fist buries itself in my stomach. Can't breathe — knees hit the floor, then my palms. Bad bad taste in my mouth...

"Oh *disgusting,* he's *puking —*"

"So don't step in it, okay? Just grab him, help me pull him over near the edge —"

"Don't want no old-guy puke on my new denim..."

I feel wind on my face. When I heave again, I don't hear a splat. I open my eyes. My vomit falls like chunky rain, to the ground fifty feet below.

"Now tell us where you've stashed the fat —"

"Or you're followin' that puke down to the sidewalk."

The great height sharpens my thoughts. They can't drop me. If they do, they'll never get what they're after. So long as they aren't too stupid to realize that, I'm fine.

Four stories below, in the middle of the crowd, I think I see Margo. Yes, it's her, the Elvis nestled against her chest. Trying to get my attention. Pointing to my left —?

Ah. A clamor of boots. Park security. If they can just do this without gunplay —

"Stand away from the ledge!"

"No sudden moves!"

Rent-a-cops. Now I'm frightened.

The Elvises drop me. My rib cage hits a restraining rope. Losing my balance — I grope wildly, but I'm sliding *over* —

Screams from below. Hands grab my legs. I'm moving backward instead of forward. A good thing. A very good thing.

I hear the Elvises putting up a fight. It doesn't last long. Someone helps me down the tree. Someone else wraps me in a tufted jacket that smells like a locker room. Numb. I'm numb all over.

There's an electric cart waiting for me at the bottom. And Margo. It's so good to see her. She squeezes me tightly, then helps me lie down on a platform in the back of the cart. She sits next to me as we pull away.

"I had a vision." Forming each word is like pushing a dull needle through thick oilskin. "The rest of my vision. We have to get to the car."

"Who were those men? They wanted to steal the Elvis?"

Passing rows of turnstiles. We're near the parking lot. "We have to get to the car." I feel myself slipping away. "The printout's there. In the car. Might mean... everything."

Everything...

I awake to something cool and wet being pressed on my forehead.

"How are you feeling?" a woman's voice asks. Not Margo's. A nurse stands over me. I glance around for Margo. "Better," I say. "Margo?"

"I'm here," she says, rising from a chair that was just outside my line of vision. "Are you really feeling better?"

"Where are we?" I sit up, slowly.

"You shouldn't be sitting up just yet," the nurse says, firmly pushing me back into a prone position. "Our paramedics brought you to the infirmary outside the front entrance of the park. Our on-call physician is coming in to have a look at you. We'd like to keep you under observation for a while. And the chief of security has some questions he needs to ask."

No. We can't get entangled in this. "We need to leave. I've done nothing wrong."

"I'm afraid leaving is out of the question. You need to rest. And the officers will want to know your connection with those other men."

"I was attacked. Randomly attacked. I'd appreciate recuperating in my own hotel." I sit up again, feeling somewhat stronger. "The officers can reach me at the Royal Citrus Resort on International Drive. Last name Merlin, M-E-R-L-I-N."

She edges toward a phone. "I'm so sorry, but if you try to leave, I'll have to call security."

The third Elvis is still out there. And this entire park is a MannaSantos facility. I have to see that printout. I glance desperately at Margo.

"Daddy's heart medication is out in the car," she says. "He was supposed to keep it with him, but he left it in the luggage. If I could just pull the car up —"

"I'll have security accompany you to your car," the nurse says.

"All right, enough of this shit," Margo says, pointing our gun at the nurse. Our big, cruel-looking gun. "We're out of here."

It's good to have such a decisive companion. I don't like frightening this undoubtedly honorable woman, but her fright is a small price to pay for the world's survival. Margo holds the gun while I strap the nurse to a chair with surgical tape.

The parking lot is a Sargasso Sea of cars. My stomach churns violently, evidence of more pills that want to come up. Let them come. They've already done what I needed them to do.

We reach the car. I trade Margo the keys for the Elvis. I barely get my door shut before she stomps the accelerator, pushing my little Nash for all it's worth.

"Where are we going?" Margo shouts.

"I — I don't know yet. Just get us away from here." I won't know where to head until I see that printout. Why the hell did I throw it so carelessly in the back seat? I dig through piles of clothes and CD cases. Did my father ever tell me what he accidentally sucked out of Elvis's stomach? Did I overhear it as a child? Was that bit of knowledge stashed in the attic of my brain, waiting for this moment?

Paper. Crinkly, smooth-grained paper. I dig it out from beneath my shirts. Begin scanning the long list of chemical compounds and substances. The drugs had been all I was interested in. Didn't bother reading past the list of drugs —

At the beginning of the second page... there it is.

Grouped with the stomach contents, just where I prayed I'd find it.

"Margo, I need to make a phone call." My throat has constricted to the width of a pin. "Find a pay phone."

She digs into her purse next to her seat. "Here, here's my cell phone. I don't want to stop — we're barely a mile outside the park —"

"No! The call has to be secure!" I accidentally knock the phone from her hand, and it slides beneath my seat as we round a corner. "I'm sorry, but it has to be a pay phone! Pull over as soon as you see one!"

It's 11:20 A.M. here, so it's 8:20 A.M. in Las Vegas. She'll already be at work. But I can't wait. I've got to share this.

Two or three miles later, we see a produce stand. And a public phone. Margo pulls over, gravel crunching beneath the Nash's skinny tires. The phone's push buttons are sticky with citrus pulp. I dial Harri's home number from memory.

Her recording picks up. "You've reached the residence of Harriet Lane. Wait for the tone, then you know what to do."

Yes, I know what to do.

— *beep* —

I know what to do now.

"Harri, this is Louis. I have your twentieth-century bananas."

CHAPTER 16

"Harri, this isn't a joke."

My evening phone conversation from my motel room near the Pensacola airport hasn't gotten off to the best of starts.

"I appreciate your effort to relieve my stress, Louis. Look, I'm really glad you recovered your family heirloom, and I hope it gives you much pleasure in the time we have left. But let's not try to make this more than it is."

"I'm not."

"Louis, salvation doesn't hide in a jar of fat. Didn't you suffer a blow to the head recently?"

Three minutes later...

"Okay, Louis, I'll at least concede that *you* believe what you're telling me."

"I performed the analysis myself —"

"Right before you took a fistful of narcotic drugs, correct?"

"I'm sorry I told you that. Do you want me to fax the printout to you? I'll be happy to." Then I remember something. "Muthukrishnan. The USDA man you said you were working with. Why would someone from USDA be looking for *me?* He must've somehow found out that non-bioengineered bananas might be preserved along with the Elvis fat. Call him. Verify what I'm saying."

Forty-five minutes later, she calls me back. Her tone is so changed that she sounds like a different person (salvation *does* hide in a jar of fat). However, skepticism is hardwired into her DNA, so I listen to ten minutes of her qualms about the viability of the banana-matter after exposure to stomach acids, and whether the analysis machine gave a false reading. If she were on her deathbed and met a welcoming angel, she'd insist on examining his credentials.

Still, I call the airport and book a flight to Las Vegas for Margo and me for tomorrow afternoon at 2:25 P.M., the earliest available. I'm uneasy about landing on MannaSantos's home turf. What Harri told me about possible sabotage of her team's efforts — inside sabotage — is profoundly disturbing.

When I call her back with the flight information, she puts Muthukrishnan on the line. "Dr. Shmalzberg, it is very good to hear from you again. I apologize for being so circumspect when we first spoke. But now all is turning out well. You are to be commended on what I understand was a difficult retrieval of the biological remnants. I wish that I could have offered some assistance."

Is he for real? It's impossible to tell over the phone. I mention my uneasiness regarding the corporation his department is in alliance with.

"I will not lie to you, Dr. Shmalzberg — the matters you speak of are of great concern. I can offer some reassurance regarding your personal safety, however. The Bureau of Investigation has detailed a team of agents to support my group in Las Vegas. I can offer you a pair of armed agents to serve as bodyguards during your time at MannaSantos. They will also ensure the security of the biological remnants. These agents will greet you at the airport, along with Ms. Harriet Lane and myself. Is this satisfactory?"

It should be. It would be, if I could be absolutely sure that Muthukrishnan is who he says he is. "It'll do," I say, not having much choice but to go along. "One more question. How did you know what you know about the Elvis?"

"Ahh," he says, a hint of laughter in his voice. "That, as they say, is a long story. Let me share it with you over a good cup of coffee. Have a good evening, Dr. Shmalzberg. I look forward to seeing you tomorrow."

I tell Margo about the conversation. She's on the bed next to me, with the bedspread pulled up to her chin. She's been complaining of stomach cramps for the past hour. I offered her a Dexedrine, but she refused it; she wants to stay clear-headed. "It doesn't feel right," I say. "Walking into MannaSantos's main campus... I feel like a mouse sniffing cheese at the edge of a mousetrap."

"Even with two FBI agents watching your back?"

"Even so."

"But you can't back out of this, can you? MannaSantos is the only company with the know-how to use the Elvis to wipe out that Metaboloft gene."

"They're also the ones who caused the disaster in the first place."

"An accident, right?"

I'm quiet for a few seconds. The thought that scientists at Manna-Santos could have deliberately released this scourge is almost too frightening to contemplate. "Probably. But being attacked today at a MannaSantos property... doesn't increase my confidence in the company's good intentions."

She winces as another cramp hits. "Couldn't that — ugh — be a coincidence? You've told me that other people have been after the Elvis."

Do coincidences exist? I've never been much of a believer in fate, but after what I've learned — that my father's worst incident of malpractice may provide the key to averting the mass extermination of all mammalian life — I'm not so sure anymore.

"Maybe you should've asked Muthukrishnan to send agents to stay with us until we get on that flight," she says. Her eyes flit to the gun on the nightstand. "Those fake Elvis guys... they could've followed us to Pensacola."

"For all I know, those 'fake Elvis guys' could *be* Muthukrishnan's agents."

Her pretty green eyes grow big. "What makes you think *that?*"

"I don't know... it's just that, with so much at stake..."

"You don't want to fuck up."

"Right."

"You need backup," she says. "More than just me. What about that woman over in New Orleans you'd gotten friendly with? It sounds like she has bodyguards to spare."

Oretha Denoux? It's a thought. It's her world, too; all the éclairs and chocolate turtles in existence won't stave off Metaboloft for long.

I pull the card with her private number out of my wallet. It's wedged next to my Good Humor Man badge, which now seems as abhorrent to me as an ID for the Nazi Party. But throwing it away wouldn't feel right, either. I've got too much personal history bound up in that badge.

Ms. Denoux picks up on the fourth ring. "Ahh, King Creole, good to hear from you again," she says. "How is our friend, Elvis? Is he once more nestled in the bosom of your family?"

I bring her up to date.

"So allow me to summarize," she says once my tale has wound down. "Because Elvis was willful and would not follow your father's instructions, and because your father was unskilled at liposuction, and because — forgive my bluntness here — because your father ghoulishly decided to retain a keepsake, you now have an opportunity to save the world."

"In a nutshell, yes."

"Doctor, do you believe in destiny?"

"I've been asking myself that all afternoon."

"I am a believer in destiny. Your flight to Las Vegas leaves tomorrow afternoon at 2:25?"

"Yes."

"Three of my men will meet you at your motel no later than noon. Keep them with you as long as you deem necessary."

"That's very generous of you, Ms. Denoux."

I wait for her to mention her quid pro quo.

"Thank me by saving our world, Dr. Shmalzberg," she says.

I help Margo relax into sleep with a deep tissue massage. I let my fingers drift along her sides, around the subtle swellings of her hips, down her long, slender thighs. It might be my wistful imagination at work, but her body seems less girlish than the first time I saw it. When her breathing takes on the slow, even rhythm of slumber, I lightly kiss all those places my fingers had touched.

Morning. A thin beam of sunlight strikes my face through a seam in the curtains. Margo's still sleeping soundly. Remembering her cramps, I decide to get her some medication for the long flight, and find some light breakfast for both of us. Ms. Denoux's men will arrive two or three hours from now, but I don't want her to be in pain that long. There's a drug store just up the road, about five blocks away.

I write her a note telling her where I'm going and place it on the nightstand, next to the Elvis. Maybe I should ask her to watch over it while I'm gone? No; she needs her rest. I'll take it with me. The gun, too.

I step out into the morning. The last hazy remains of a winter fog are burning off, revealing a long strip of low-rise industrial parks along a four-lane highway. I place the Elvis in the trunk of my car. My fuel gauge shows only a tenth of a tank left, and my charge is low. Doesn't matter. The airport's barely three miles up the road, and the car will wait there until we return from Las Vegas.

First time I've ever walked into a drug store with a gun in my pocket. I buy a bagful of over-the-counter stomach remedies, then walk a few doors down to a small take-out restaurant. The weather-beaten sign announces Vietnamese food, American food, and Fast Breakfasts. I stare in through yellowed, smudged windows. The only person inside is a short Asian man behind the counter, reading a newspaper and smoking a cigarette.

I step inside. The acrid scent of jet exhaust from the nearby air-port mingles with the aroma of artificial fat browning on a range. The man behind the counter looks up from his newspaper. "Help you with something?"

Margo shouldn't take her medications on an empty stomach. "I'll have two breakfast specials to go, please. Eggs well scrambled. Double meat on both."

"That'll be just a few minutes. Have to reheat the grill."

He disappears into the kitchen through swinging doors. I sit down in the booth by the window, so I can keep an eye on my car and the Elvis.

Another customer's coming. The owner will be pleased; he'll get to sell another couple of eggs...

My God. It's *Mitch.*

"Hello, Lou." No smile. He eases the door shut behind him.

"Mitch — how — how in the world did you *find* me?"

"That doesn't matter none." He hovers at the edge of the table, blocking me from the door.

My stomach turns as sour as a green grapefruit. "Why did you follow me all the way across the country?"

"You're in a shit-load of trouble, Lou."

"With the Good Humor Men?"

"Yeah. But that's not the worst of it." His eyes drill me with contempt and sadness. "What the *hell* got into you? Did you crack up? You want to know why I've followed you across the country? Because you were my best friend. Because I feel like I should've protected you better. And because I'm scared for you, Lou. Scared of what you've gone and gotten yourself into."

Does he know what I did in New Orleans? The scam I pulled on Severald? I slowly slide my right hand into my jacket pocket, feeling for the cool steel there. "Tell me what kind of trouble I'm in, Mitch."

"You practically started an international incident!" He half laughs. "Jesus Christ... you quiet guys... when you go off the road, you do it in a big way. Assaulting the ambassador of a foreign country. Stealing from him. Trussing him up like a lab rat. And you want to know what kind of *trouble* you're in?"

The Ottoman. He must've found the Ottoman when he went looking for me. And the Ottoman convinced him to somehow follow me as I chased the Elvis.

I pull the gun from my jacket pocket. This'll only cement his belief in my guilt, but it can't be helped. "I'm going to walk out of here," I say. "And you aren't going to stop me or follow me."

I slide out of the booth, keeping the gun trained on his broad chest.

"You won't use that on me," he says, remarkably calm. "I'd bet a thousand bucks you've never fired that thing before."

He'd win the money. "Mitch, you have no idea what you're getting involved in here." Am I capable of shooting him? I'd know where to place the slug so it wouldn't kill or cripple him... "Your friendship helped keep me alive, those years after Emily passed. But the future of the whole world depends on my catching a flight this afternoon."

A flicker of doubt shows on his face. "Tell me what this is all about, Lou."

"I don't have time."

"But you have plenty of time, Dr. Shmalzberg." *Behind me* — "Place your weapon on the table. I am a much more accomplished marksman than you are. My first shot will not kill you, but it will be most debilitating."

It's him, standing in front of the swinging doors. Thick black mustache, giant hands that make the silenced pistol he's pointing at me look like a flimsy toy. "Be obedient, Doctor," he says. "You would not be wise to give me cause for doing to you what I would most enjoy. On the table, please, where your friend can reach it."

I'm no gunfighter. And I'm no good to anyone if I'm dead. I push the gun toward Mitch. "Don't do this for him, Mitch. I don't know what he's told you. But helping him is the biggest betrayal of America imaginable."

He picks up the gun. The Ottoman advances on us. "I'll take that, Mr. Reynolds, if you please."

Mitch doesn't hand it over. "Just a second here. I want to hear him out."

"He has nothing pertinent to say to you," the Ottoman says. "Betrayal? He has betrayed his country by disgracing it. He has stolen my money and my property, property which I brought to him in order to verify its authenticity. You saw how he left me, Mr. Reynolds."

"He's lying, Mitch. He threatened my family. The Elvis wasn't his. He tried to force me to give it up or tell him where it was."

Behind the Ottoman's smile is a cold anger. "Do you deny that you stole my money, Doctor?"

"I don't deny that."

Poor Mitch was never the swiftest train out of the station. Befuddlement is creeping up on him, and he doesn't like it. "Look," he says. "Mr. Quant promised that if I helped him find you, if I convinced you to return his stuff, he'd let this all drop. No cops, no secret police. That sounds like a good deal to me, Lou. You could start over. Maybe I could even smooth things out between you and the Good Humor Men. You could go home."

"There won't be a home to return to," I say, "if you don't let me get on that plane." I turn toward the Ottoman. Sweat droplets glide down my sides like damp snails. "Mr. Quant, I can't give you the Elvis. If I don't turn it over to the Department of Agriculture, every person on Earth starves to death within four or five years. There's a rogue gene that's spreading from the American Midwest. It's called Metaboloft. A creation of the MannaSantos Corporation. It was designed to raise human metabolic rates. They intended to insert it in only a few select crops. But their design was faulty. Now it's infiltrating thousands of other types of plants and crops, spreading on the wind."

I turn back to Mitch, who's still holding onto my gun. "Don't you remember the deer, Mitch? It's Metaboloft. It affects all mammalian metabolisms, not just humans. It's gotten into the leaves and grasses they eat. We're higher in the food chain, but we've started melting away, too. Look at yourself. You've been losing weight these past few months. Haven't you?"

He turns pale. "Jesus Christ... I sure have. Thought I was sick or something..."

"Scientists at MannaSantos are trying to create a countergene. And the Elvis — the liposuctioned belly fat my father saved from the operation — it contains *bananas,* real, old-fashioned bananas, which may be just what the gene engineers need to build their counteragent. My father punctured Elvis's stomach with his cannula, accidentally sucked out his partially digested breakfast. Those bananas have been preserved in a vacuum jar for the past sixty-four years."

The Ottoman grunts with dry amusement. "Doctor, I would not have expected you to be such a talented fabulist. That story could command a place of honor among the tales of the Arabian Nights. Return my money and my property, and you will be free to concoct any tales that please you."

An idea seizes me. A Solomonic idea. "We can split it," I say. "We can take the Elvis to a lab facility and I'll divide it up. I need the stomach contents. Your emir wants the fat. We can both have what we need."

The corners of the Ottoman's mouth jut out from beneath his mustache for the briefest of seconds. "I don't think so, Dr. Shmalzberg. I don't bargain with lying infidels."

Blood colors Mitch's face. A good Baptist, he took that insult more to heart than I did. "Is this on the level, Lou?"

"Every word," I say.

Mitch puts himself between the Ottoman and me. "I'm not real sure who stole that jar of fat from whom," he says. "But that doesn't matter anymore. Lou's solution — that sounds like the right one to me."

"Mr. Reynolds," the Ottoman says, "you have no authority in this. It would be best for you if you give me Dr. Shmalzberg's gun."

Mitch's ears turn red. "Fuck you."

"Americans..." the Ottoman sighs. His gun makes a sound like a burst of compressed air. Mitch shouts and stumbles backward.

I dive for my gun. The Ottoman kicks it into a far corner. It disappears into a pile of boxes. His next kick sends me sprawling against a booth.

When my vision clears, my fingers come away from my head bloody. Mitch looks much worse. The bullet tore into his stomach. The restaurant's floor is turning dirty red. Mitch squirms into a fetal ball and weakly moans.

The Ottoman places himself between me and the door. "Give me the fat, and I will allow you to summon an ambulance for your friend. Refuse, and together we will watch him bleed to death."

I kneel by Mitch, roll him onto his back, tear open his soaked shirt. Blood spurts from a hole just below and to the right of his sternum. Missed the spine. Possibly punctured the liver. "He freed you," I say. "He helped you."

"I do not need his help anymore. And he was poor company in the car."

I tear strips from Mitch's shirt. Roll one up and press it into the broken lips of the wound, then wrap two others around his midsection, tying them as tightly as I can. I wad up my jacket and shove it under his tailbone, trying to elevate the wound above his heart.

"An admirable effort," the Ottoman says. "Even so, your friend will soon glimpse Paradise, though its gates are shut to unbelievers."

"Why?" I pull Mitch's belt out of its loops, tie it around my makeshift dressing. "Why does your emir want the Elvis so goddamned badly?"

"My master studied in America as a young man. He heard the Blessed Troubadour sing, and it was a moment of illumination for him. He is old now, and wealthy almost beyond mortal imagining. He directed me to acquire Graceland, transport it across the oceans, timber by timber. My offer was rejected most discourteously. Insultingly, in fact. As you have insulted me, Doctor."

"So he went after the fat as a consolation prize? How did he even know it existed?"

He raises eyebrows in honest surprise. "Was not its existence revealed in your national newspapers? The *Enquirer*? The *Star*? The Caliphate's intelligence service searched all information databases for word of such relics. But this relic is a prize beyond all others. For it will allow us to midwife the birth of the Islamic Elvis."

Midwife the birth — "You mean you want to *clone* him?"

"I believe that is your American term, yes."

I laugh. My hands are stained with my best friend's blood, a foreign maniac has a pistol pointed at my head, and I'm laughing so hard tears spill out. "But that — that's *ridiculous!* Even... even if you could do it, the clone wouldn't be *Elvis!* He'd have a certain amount of genetic singing ability, perfect pitch, sure... but he wouldn't have Elvis's upbringing, all the things that made Elvis *Elvis*. There'd be no Gladys, no poverty-stricken childhood in Tupelo, no black gospel choirs for him to hear, no Grand Ole Opry —"

"My master has arranged for the proper influences. The lad will be raised in the light of the Prophet. Nourished in the wisdom of the Book, our Elvis will extinguish all memory of his Western predecessor."

Mitch is bleeding through my dressing. I pull off my shirt, wrap that around him. "You want to clone Elvis? Fine! Do it! You only need a few ounces of the fat. Let me keep the rest. The Metaboloft gene — it won't stay isolated in North America. Your Caliphate won't be safe. Let me save your country at the same time I save my own!"

His eyes, cold and black as marble in winter, narrow to contemptuous slits. "Perhaps when we first met, Doctor, such an appeal might have moved me. Before you forced me to endure the indignity of lying in my own filth. If what you have told me is true, I will rejoice in the wasting death of America. And Allah will protect my country —"

The kitchen doors creak open. The Vietnamese cook, blood flowing from a long wound above his left eye, pumps a short-barreled shotgun. But Quant is faster — his bullet hits the cook's upper torso before the Asian man can get off his shot. Flung against the wall, the wounded man finishes squeezing his trigger. The blast goes deafeningly awry. It hits the ceiling, showering the Ottoman with debris.

I grab a metal napkin dispenser and hit him in the head with it as hard as I can. It barely staggers him.

Still dizzy, I knock aside some of the boxes, dig wildly through mounds of plastic forks and ketchup packets for my gun. Can't find it — I hear him behind me, grunting with pain and anger. And I pull the door open and run.

I run past what might be the Ottoman's car. Silver; not black? If I had my gun, I could flatten his tires. If the queen had balls she'd be king.

Almost to my car now. The Elvis is wrapped in a blanket in the trunk. Way behind me, the restaurant's door slams shut. I won't hear his silenced gun when he fires. Just feel the slug splitting flesh, pulverizing bone.

Keys. If I put my keys in my jacket pocket, I'm fucked. No, they're in my pants pocket. I'm not dead yet.

I duck low, unlock my door, and then I'm stunned by a boom like a truck back-fire. Suddenly my seats are covered with chunks of safety glass. I jam the key into the ignition. A bullet slams into a body panel. My tires crunch glass as I pull away.

I'm out of the parking lot. Onto the access highway. Where to now? A police station? I wouldn't know where to look.

Check the rear-view mirror. There he is. Pulling onto the access road. His car's bigger than mine. Probably faster. Signs point to Interstate 10. The coastal highway that runs west to New Orleans. Five, six hours away. If only it were closer... there, I'd know where to run to.

At least I'm leading him away from Margo. He won't shoot at me while my car is moving. He must realize there's a chance I've got the Elvis with me. Shoot out my tires, shoot me, the car rolls and burns and then the Elvis is barbecued fat, no good to anybody. I'm invulnerable so long as I keep moving.

224 | *Andrew Fox*

A yellow caution light blinks on my dashboard. My fuel gauge. Fucking hell. Forty miles of invulnerability are all I've got left.

He's right behind me, his big silver sedan charging like an enraged rhino. He smacks my bumper, jerking my head into the seat back. Trying to intimidate me into pulling over.

Something slides out from beneath the passenger seat. Margo's cell phone! I scoop it up. Call the police? There'll be a warrant out for me, too, thanks to the World of Wonders mess. They might confiscate the Elvis. No good.

We merge onto I-10. The highway's practically empty. A sign says it's 280 miles to New Orleans. Won't make much more than a tenth of that before running dry. But part of New Orleans, an armed and dangerous part, is coming to me. Somewhere west of me, on this very same highway.

I dial Oretha Denoux's number from memory, get an assistant. I say it's an emergency. The clamor of the Ottoman crashing into my rear puts an exclamation point on it. Oretha gets on the line. I explain my situation as succinctly as I can. She puts me on hold. One very long minute; I spend it staring in the mirror at Quant's face, hard as the visage of an Easter Island statue. She clicks back, tells me her men are less than ten miles from me, on the far side of the Florida-Alabama border.

Another click, and I'm talking with a Mr. Sherman Johnson. "You're being tailed?" he says.

"Tail*gated* is more like it," I say, gritting my teeth as I brace for another impact.

"And you want to shake this guy? Permanent-like?"

This isn't a cartoon. They won't lift his car from the highway with a giant electromagnet, then fly him back to their secret hideaway. By calling in their help, I've commissioned a murder.

I look again in my mirror at the stone face of the man who would kill me. Who may have killed Mitch. Who would happily doom all America to mass starvation. If the law of self-preservation doesn't apply now, it never will.

"Make it as permanent as you can," I say.

"Describe your car. And his."

I do that.

"We're in a black stretch LaSalle," Johnson says. "When you see us comin', try to get at least three car lengths ahead of your tailgater."

Is the Nash up to it? "I'll do my best."

The highway is an empty concrete ribbon. Far off on the western horizon, where the two sides of the highway merge into a single vanishing point, I see a black dot. It grows larger, into a stretch LaSalle.

I jam my accelerator to the floor. The Nash whines with annoyance. Still, I begin to slowly, slowly pull away from the Ottoman. Maybe he's toying with me, letting me get a little ahead before gunning it and slamming into my rear again.

Too bad for him.

When the LaSalle is almost even with me, I see four chrome pistols flash in the sun. Their whiplike cracks Doppler away behind me. In my mirror, the Ottoman's car swerves to the right, leaps the shoulder of the road. It lands on two tires on the grassy slope, rolls and bounces and rolls. I feel a disturbing exhilaration when it bursts into flames.

Islamic Elvis, you're stillborn.

I call 911 for Mitch and the Asian cook. I hope they pull through. Especially Mitch.

We make the gate at the airport just before they're ready to seal up the plane. Me, Margo, Sherman Johnson, and three other black men big enough to merit their own zip codes. We ran late because of one last precaution I had to take. The Elvis is back in its carrier, hanging reassuringly against my chest. I lost the remedies for Margo, so I had to dope her up with half a Dilaudid. She's groggy, but at least the flight shouldn't be unbearable for her.

Margo asked me why I need to go to Las Vegas, why I couldn't ship the Elvis or have Muthukrishnan collect it here. It wasn't easy to explain why I need to personally see this through. I've been singled out for a special destiny. The events of the past three weeks — hell, the events of the past sixty-four *years* — have proven that beyond any doubt.

The plane's seats are discolored with decades of sweat and spilled beverages. I slide into a window seat, Margo beside me, her eyes fluttering in a losing struggle to stay open. Two of our escorts sit in front of us, two behind.

A helicopter lands on the next runway over. A pink helicopter. With a lightning bolt insignia on its tail assembly. I can just make out the letters surrounding the bolt – TCB. Taking Care of Business. It's from Graceland.

Four men emerge from the copter, all dressed in gold lamé suits. Thugs impersonating the King. Maybe the same ones who cleaned my clock at Worlds of Wonder.

Our plane begins moving. You're too late, you bastards. Too late. Tell Swaggart I hope his new nose sinks into his face.

As soon as our wheels leave the ground, exhaustion envelops me. I glance over at Margo. Mouth open, asleep. I pull a pillow down from the overhead compartment and arrange her so that she won't wake up with a stiff neck. Then I recline my own seat and close my eyes.

One puzzle's answer comes to me as I slide toward sleep. How Mitch was able to track me across the country. The Good Humor Man badge in my wallet. It's embedded with a geo-positioning chip.

If I'd discarded the badge after New Orleans, he couldn't have followed me. I hope he makes it. Two deaths on my conscience are more than enough...

"Sir, you need to bring your seat to its full upright position."

My eyes flicker open. "We're landing? We're in Las Vegas?"

"You must not have heard the captain's announcement," the attendant says. "We've been diverted."

I push myself to full wakefulness. "Diverted? Where? Why?"

"It's no cause for concern. There's been a runway accident at McCarran International. We're landing at a private airport on the other side of the city. Buses will take you to the main airport so you can make your connections. There shouldn't be too much delay."

Paranoia stirs in the bottom of my stomach. Harri and Muthukrishnan and the FBI agents are supposed to meet us as soon as we step off the plane. "Miss," I call after her. "What field is this we're landing at?"

She doesn't hear me. Margo is still asleep. I lean forward and touch

Sherman Johnson's shoulder. "Did you hear what's going on?"

"Nothin' to be concerned about," he says without turning around. "You've got four good men watchin' out for you and the miss. We'll get you where you need to go."

The landing gear whirs. We're flying low over sandy-brown foothills. I see the control tower and a lone landing strip ahead, growing larger each second.

There's a hanger alongside the landing strip, large blue letters painted on its wide roof. I read them as we make our final approach.

MANNASANTOS, INC.
MERGING NATURE AND SCIENCE
TO FEED A HUNGRY AMERICA

CHAPTER 17

The jet touches down on MannaSantos's runway. The old plane's tires bounce twice, jamming the Elvis into my solar plexus.

A mobile staircase drives toward the plane's hatch, followed by a bus. My blood pressure settles down — maybe the flight attendant was right, and this is just an innocent diversion?

But then two other vehicles drive onto the tarmac. Big Suburban-like trucks with MannaSantos markings, police-type light bars, black-tinted windows.

Margo puts on a groggy smile as she unbuckles her seat belt. I don't want to panic her. But she senses my mood as we head down the aisle; she strains to see what I'm staring at through the windows. Sherman Johnson and his lieutenant are ahead of us, the other two men immediately behind. Whatever weapons they brought are stowed in their luggage, now being transferred into the bus's cargo hold.

"Those trucks," I whisper to Johnson. "They give me a bad feeling —"

"Don't worry," he says, too quickly. "We got your back."

Hearing the stumble in his voice frightens me worse than anything.

Margo clutches my arm as we descend the rickety metal stairway. The sun assaults us, rebounding from the plane's fuselage, glinting off the trucks' chrome bumpers. I don't see the men and women emerge from the two trucks until I'm on the tarmac.

They cut me and my companions off from the rest of the passengers, who are led toward the waiting bus. The men wear security uniforms emblazoned with MannaSantos's logo. The women — they're wearing hooded white robes. Like what Margo wore when she was one of Trotmann's acolytes.

230 | *Andrew Fox*

We're quickly surrounded, outnumbered more than two to one. One of the uniformed men places himself confidently in front of Sherman Johnson. "We need to speak with Dr. Shmalzberg," he says. "Privately."

"Dr. Shmalzberg doesn't go anywhere without us," Johnson says.

I hear Margo gasp. I glance over in time to see her face go white. "Mildred," she asks one of the women, "what are you doing here?"

"Striking a blow for the true Church." Before I can raise a hand to protect Margo, the tall woman decks her. "Traitorous *bitch*."

I kneel to help her. She's stunned more than hurt, thank God. Johnson and his lieutenant immediately move to restrain Margo's assailant, but that's when she and the others reveal their guns.

"Isn't it a shame," a familiar voice asks, "that the airlines have such persnickety rules about carrying weapons on board?"

I hear the approaching whir of an electric motor. Staring through a forest of legs, I see a figure in a wheelchair rolling toward us.

It's Trotmann.

A thick bandage puffs up his left collarbone beneath his jacket, marking where Margo's bullet passed through his frail body. Likewise, his right hand is lost inside a glove of plaster. My handiwork. I should've done worse.

I help Margo off the tarmac. Seeing Trotmann here hardly surprises me. All the forces of darkness are gathering against us.

Trotmann leers up at me, pats the Elvis with his good hand, then shares his leer with my four bodyguards. "I've always wondered how heroic gunsels are without their guns," he says.

I've been wondering the same thing. The shame-faced expression worn by Sherman Johnson tells me all I need to know.

Margo grabs me tighter. I return her embrace. "Trotmann, you've got no idea what you're doing," I say. "This isn't about you and me and my father anymore. If you love your country — if you love the world — you'll let us give the Elvis to the scientists who need it —"

He cuts me off with a sharp gesture. "Oh, no need to tell me your tale of woe about the wasting plague and sixty-five-year-old bananas. My patron has explained everything. You were much less discreet than you thought, Mr. Would-Be-Messiah." He fondles the Elvis's glass jar, still nestled securely in the carrier against my chest. His leer absolutely disgusts me. "I can't tell you what joy this turn of events has given me. One of the horrors of old age is knowing that the world will continue blithely on after you've died. But now, not only do I collect my precious property, but I ensure that no one will dance on my grave. We all go down into the pit of nothingness together, eh, young Shmalzberg?"

"You're insane..." How can his guards listen to this and still follow his orders?

"Insane?" He tilts his head; tufts of coarse gray hairs sprouting from his nostrils make him look subhuman. "No. Just petulant. And childless, thanks to your father. Maybe if he hadn't persecuted me, I'd have a connection to the future, and I wouldn't be so pleased to let the world choke on its own bile. We'll have lots more to talk about once I introduce you to my patron. He's eager to meet you."

Margo hugs me tighter. "Take me, too," she says to her former Reductionist.

Trotmann whistles appreciatively. "Brave girl. Braver than these slabs of muscle you brought with you. But the sponsor of our festivities gave me strict instructions that I was only to fetch the junior Shmalzberg. Besides, it'll be a worse torture for you to be separated from your new Reductionist, wondering about his fate until your flesh melts from your bones."

He turns to his followers. "Take them. Keep them confined for forty-eight hours. Then let them go. By then, Dr. Shmalzberg won't be a concern to anyone."

A MannaSantos security guard pulls Margo away. *Louis!* I don't want to leave you —!"

"It's all right," I say, praying I'll survive to repay such loyalty. And love. "Johnson — keep her safe. If you can't help me, at least do that."

Oretha Denoux's foot soldier barely meets my eyes. "I'll — do what I can."

Half of Trotmann's entourage shepherds my companions toward one of the trucks. Suddenly, I wish the Ottoman were still in the game. That human bowling ball would come in handy now. If he were alive, he could still track me... through the card in my wallet —

232 | Andrew Fox

"Margo!" She turns, resisting being shoved in the truck. "Tell Muthukrishnan — tell him a Good Humor Man is never lost!"

I catch the look of bewilderment on her face before she disappears. I glance at Trotmann. Far as I can tell, he thinks my outburst was merely emotional bravado, not code. I pray Margo will repeat those exact words when she sees the feds. I pray the FBI agents will guess I've still got my card on me.

I pray I can stay alive long enough for them to find me.

Nightfall is still an hour away. The outskirts of Las Vegas look to be as much of a ghost town as Albuquerque. I'm squeezed between two MannaSantos goons, facing Trotmann in his wheelchair. He hasn't taken the Elvis away from me yet. Maybe prying it away from me is so exquisite a pleasure that he doesn't want to rush it.

There's so much I need to know. "The Metaboloft breakout... did the heads of MannaSantos know it would happen? Was unleashing the plague an intentional act?"

Trotmann rubs his left shoulder; the dressing on his wound is matted with dried blood. "Oh, it was an intentional act, yes. But not on the behalf of the legitimate, visible corporation. Most of MannaSantos, including your friend, Harriet Lane, thought they were rolling out just another in a highly profitable series of products. But there is a visible MannaSantos, and there is an *in*visible MannaSantos, dust bunnies that blew under the bed and were forgotten. A subterranean MannaSantos has been pushing the buttons all along, quietly laughing as hapless nonentities like your Harriet Lane have tried getting the genetic genie back in its bottle."

"Why would anyone want to starve the world?"

"You'll have to ask my patron that. You've been so involved with his 'family' over the years, he practically considers you an uncle."

I turn to the guards. Have they been listening to what Trotmann's been saying? "Do you understand what you're a part of?" I ask them. "Do either of you have children? They won't live to see their adulthood unless I deliver this biological sample to the government."

They don't answer. "You're talking to a wall," Trotmann says. "They think I'm a harmless loon, but they've been told to follow my instructions. Decent paying jobs in Nevada are about as common as icebergs in the desert. A MannaSantos paycheck is a prize to be lusted after. Isn't that right, Jack?"

"Absolutely, Dr. Trotmann," the guard to my right says.

"And don't even consider trying to win over any of the women. They *don't* think I'm a loon, but talk of apocalypse doesn't faze them. It excites them. A melting away of all flesh fits quite delightfully with their mind-set."

We reach the edge of the fabled Las Vegas Strip. "Since you're stuck with me, young Shmalzberg," Trotmann says, "you might as well enjoy the ride. Behold the ruins of Las Vegas!"

The Luxor casino's gigantic black glass pyramid is still impressive, even though its once geometrically pure lines have been made jagged by the ravages of vandalism and weather. Guarding the boarded-up entrance, the concrete Sphinx and statues of Ramses look as ancient and decayed as the originals.

"The American pharaohs didn't build as well as their Egyptian predecessors," Trotmann says. "That pyramid won't last even one century, much less fifty centuries. Ah, look there — New York New York was always one of my favorites. All those years when I didn't dare set foot in Manhattan due to legal concerns, I could come here and stare up at one-third scale mockups of the Chrysler Building, the Empire State, the Brooklyn Bridge."

He snorts, then wipes his nose with his good hand. "Actually, you and your friends are responsible, at least partly, for the somnolent state of Vegas. Didn't your Good Humor movement help usher in the new age of American Puritanism? In banishing gluttony, didn't you also burn up some of the other Seven Deadly Sins with your ridiculous flamethrowers?"

He coughs so hard I expect to be hit with bits of lung tissue. I can't help but look again at the filthy dressing covering his wound. "Trotmann, you need to get your wound cleaned. You'll die of an infection —"

"So *what?*" he snaps, kicking off another bout of coughing. "I'm die — dying anyway. We're all dying, some faster than others. But some lucky ones get to move to the front of the line."

234 | Andrew Fox

We turn off Las Vegas Boulevard onto a long entrance road leading to one of the massive gaming and hotel complexes. The road leads
beneath the spread legs of a colossal statue at least a hundred feet tall.
The sun is almost beneath the horizon, so the statue's face is obliterated by the day's final glare. But its stance, guitar, and jeweled jumpsuit are unmistakable. It's Colossal Elvis, straight from my vision.

"Trotmann, this place you're taking me — what —?"

He's delighted by my awed expression. "Yes, my precious property is coming home in more ways than one. Welcome to the Viva Las
Vegas-Graceland Casino. Formerly the Flamingo, one of the Strip's
earliest gambling resorts."

I stare behind me, watching the fading sunlight form a corona
around Colossal Elvis's black curls. "Elvis and Ann-Margret came
here in 1963 to film *Viva Las Vegas*..."

"It's gone through many expansions since Bugsy Siegel built it.
There's a little statue honoring Siegel, in a courtyard next to a dead
rose garden. A memorial to a murdered Jewish gangster... I'm surprised those officiously pious twats from the Graceland Corporation
didn't take a sledgehammer to it when they bought the property."

The truck comes to a halt next to one of four hotel towers surrounding a central auditorium. None of the buildings appear occupied. The
front two towers have some kind of rippling lattice work winding
around them. The guards yank me outside. What I thought was deco-
ration is actually the structure of a roller coaster that surrounds two of
the towers. The tracks rise and plunge through monumentally scaled
scenes from Elvis's movies: the Bourbon Street honky-tonk from *King
Creole*, the emerald breakers from *Blue Hawaii*, the massed race cars
of *Speedway*.

The wheels of Trotmann's chair strike the concrete behind me.
"Can you smell the scents of decay? This wasn't a good investment
for Graceland. They sank over two hundred million dollars into this
complex just before GD2 steamrollered the economy, and then they
were able to keep it open barely more than a decade. It's been fifteen
years since any thrill seekers have taken a spin on Elvis's Whole Lotta
Shakin' Goin' On roller coaster. Care to go for a ride?"

He's bluffing. "If it's been fifteen years since any maintenance was done on this ride, none of the hydraulics will work. Your men can strap me into a car, but it won't move."

"Smart boy. But what you can't see too well in this light is that one of the cars is stopped just before the first big drop. We can get you up to that car through the hotel tower's windows. One good push could be all it takes to get it rolling. And then you'd have maybe ninety seconds to wonder just where metal fatigue has taken its toll. Will you scream for Elvis to save you as his rusted pelvis breaks away and you are ejected from mangled tracks twenty stories high?"

He squeezes my hand. "But that's a daytime game. It's night, the time for adult entertainments."

The guards pull me toward the security fence that surrounds the towers. One of the MannaSantos men unlocks a gate. The entrance courtyard is lined with dead trees and statues of Elvis: bronze figures, dulled by a green patina, portraying him at every stage from boyhood to his final performing days in Memphis.

We enter the arena. I'm ushered past acres of silent, dusty slot machines, lit only by dim emergency lighting. We climb two sets of unmoving escalators to a third level above the gaming floors; a guard carries Trotmann's wheelchair, and two of the old man's followers help him up the steps.

"What casino was complete without a dinner theater?" Trotmann asks. My eyes are stunned by what looks like the entrance to a 1950s-style movie palace. Ribbons of pink and aqua neon, startlingly bright after the dimness of the rest of the complex, coil around the empty box office. The marquee blazes with hundreds of light bulbs that spell out THE VIVA LAS VEGAS EXPERIENCE. "I believe you'll find the performance quite... nostalgic."

Inside, the theater looks like a gargantuan cabaret, with dozens of small round tables. The walls are covered with drapes of pink velvet, and the ceiling is lined with what looks to be tufted emerald leather. Oddly, there's no stage. Except for us, the big room is empty.

Loudspeakers crackle all around me. "So you've returned with your playmate and celebrity souvenir, Trotty-Trot," a voice booms.

Not just any voice — the voice of Hud Walterson. And also Benjamin, who plunged face-down into a cauldron of boiling human fat.

236 | *Andrew Fox*

Trotmann's grinning like a cat who swallowed an ostrich. "Some people just won't stay dead, eh, Shmalzberg?" he says.

"I'm not impressed with your ghosts anymore," I say, half expecting an enormously corpulent man — or a rubber facsimile — to rise from the floor. "Especially not in a theater that's probably wired up with a thousand tricks."

"I'm not a trick, Dr. Shmalzberg," the amplified voice says. "And I'm not a ghost. Unlike almost everything else that can be experienced in this theater, I am a thing of substance, great substance, and regrettably real. You wish to see my true face? It's the last thing you will see. But I have much to show you before then. Put the RM on him."

My two escorts force me into a chair by one of the tables. One of them ties my wrists behind me. Trotmann rolls himself to the table's edge and presses a button. A tray slides open. He pulls a banded headpiece from the tray and unfolds its spidery arms, then slides it onto my head. The touch of its silver titanium makes my scalp tingle. Nerves all over my body are jumping with anticipation. The spider nesting atop my head isn't unfamiliar to me. It's a more sophisticated version of the personal *Réalité Magique* device I used hundreds of times to bring Emily back to me.

My vision grows hazy, as if someone has stretched my optical nerves and twisted them like strands of melting licorice. I wait for the headache... yes, there it is, accompanied by a brief flittering of nausea. Both headache and nausea disappear quickly, much more quickly than I remember. This system is generations beyond the primitive unit I paid to have jury-rigged twenty-five years ago.

My vision suddenly unclouds. The theater still looks like the theater. Only now I see things with unsettling clarity, as if every grain in the green leather on the ceiling is in perfect focus. And the men and women clustered around me all look like Elvis and Ann-Margret. Even Trotmann; although he's a wizened, octogenarian Elvis.

I hear puffs of compressed air high above my head. Floating near the ceiling, an Elvis blimp, roughly man-sized, slowly navigates in my direction, the propelling puffs of air apparently issuing from its posterior. Its face, bloated round as a trash can lid but still recognizably Elvis, talks to me in the voice of Hud Walterson.

"This theater is a lost treasure," it says. "Probably the most power-ful *Realité Magique* installation ever constructed in North America. The technology was outlawed soon thereafter for health reasons — just like most pleasurable vices have been."

The blimp hovers above my table. Its broad forehead glistens with moisture. Droplets fall, glittering in the theater's spotlights. They hit the table and spatter, striking my face, smelling like ripe human sweat.

"This theater has provided me with some of the only pleasures I've ever known. Perhaps once we are all reduced to bones, the crawling and creeping things of the earth will know pleasures which we have denied them by our selfish, cruel lives, free at last to navigate our corpses. Do you think so? My father discovered this place. When he knew he was dying, when it no longer mattered that he'd burn out his nervous system utilizing this technology, he brought me here to show me things. Foreign capitols he'd visited as a young man; mountains climbed; the few women he'd known in a carnal way."

The blimp begins to descend, expelling gas all the while. By the time it reaches the ground next to me, it's taken on the aspect of an obese but decidedly non-blimplike Elvis. "Disorienting, isn't it? All of the theater's default templates come from old Elvis musicals. But the genius of this setup is its multithreaded interperceptivity. A male cus-tomer didn't merely experience his wife or girlfriend as Ann-Margret; he experienced himself as Elvis — Elvis singing, Elvis driving a race car across the top of Hoover Dam. And all the members of his party shared that perception of him as Elvis and themselves as Elvis or Ann-Margret. The system's neurological radiations are powerful enough that many of the effects can be experienced even without a headset, although a headset's modulation provides a richer illusion."

Elvis is still losing air. He's dropping substance by the second. His skin hangs loosely from his frame, as though something is eat-ing him from the inside out. "The most dangerous and exhilarating aspect of the technology is that transmissions can be pushed in both directions — both into the brain, and from the brain, outward. A dis-ciplined mind, at considerable risk to itself, can take hold of the tem-plates... and make of them its own creatures." Elvis's famine-stricken face caves in like a ball of Silly Putty crushed by an invisible fist. When it reforms, it is the face of Hud Walterson and of Benjamin. Only now the familiar almond-shaped green eyes and strong dark brows are puckered by extreme emaciation.

I close my eyes tightly. Shockingly, this gives me no relief — my lids might as well be glass. "Why make me sit through this production of *Andy Warhol's Elvis*? Trotmann wants to kill me on a broken roller coaster. That I can understand. But not this. You can take the Elvis remains any time you want. Why not get it over with?"

"I want you to know me," he says, coming close. His breath smells of things dying. "You're an important man to me, Dr. Shmalzberg. That's German, isn't it? *'Fat city'*... that would've applied to my brothers and me at one time, but not to you. You're important to me because you helped give my progenitor's life and death meaning. That movement you helped found made him a legend. And you caused my brother Benjamin's death —"

"He committed suicide," I say. "Jumping into a vat of boiling fat was preferable to suffering more of Trotmann's torture."

"Liar! Liar!" the ancient Elvis/Trotmann screams.

"No matter," the walking skeleton says. "What matters more is what you intended to do with that glass container of freeze-dried fat. I want to melt myself from existence, Doctor. And at the same time, I want to melt every other human being from existence, too. And you want to use your magical old fat to put flesh back on humanity's mean *fucking* bones. That makes you my nemesis, doesn't it?" He smiles, showing blackened gums that have pulled away from the roots of the few teeth still hanging in his head.

My stomach lurches. Suddenly I'm lying on my back, surrounded by some kind of translucent plastic box, open on top. I can move my arms, but they're strangely weak and uncoordinated. All I can do is flop them up and down. I try to sit up. My muscles won't lift me. I can't see past my own chest — my view is blocked by folds of fat, folds of my own neck fat. I try to say something, but all that comes out of my mouth is a wail, muffled by my own blubbery cheeks.

"Welcome to life as an eighty pound infant." My self-proclaimed nemesis lurches into view above the box, now dressed in a researcher's white lab coat. He reaches a rubber-gloved hand into the crib and tickles my chins. "No woman gave birth to you; you came to term in a vat of artificial amniotic fluid." He presses a button, and the rear part of the crib raises up hydraulically, pushing my torso into a sitting position. He forces my jaws open, then shoves a plastic tube into my toothless mouth. "Feeding time, little man."

A sweet, milky liquid begins flowing into my mouth. I can't help but swallow. The faster I swallow, the faster the substance flows. I'm constantly on the verge of choking, but somehow the machine senses exactly the maximum volume I'm able to force down. My nemesis watches me eat, a sardonic smile alternating with an expression more forlorn and haunted.

"MannaSantos was formed during GD2 from sixteen smaller companies that staved off bankruptcy by merging," he says. "One of the companies was DietTeck International, the weight-loss firm that boasted Hud Walterson as its most prominent celebrity client. They preserved his frozen tissue samples. I can only imagine how delighted the MannaSantos scientists were when they discovered what they had in their inventory: the genetic material of a man with one of the most severe cases of congenital obesity on record. An ideal source of test subjects for their planned line of genetically modified weight-loss foods."

My stomach aches. But the rate of flow still increases. God help me — I can't stop sucking it down. Even when tears of pain begin flowing down my obese cheeks, I can't stop sucking it down.

"Human cloning had been outlawed years before. But they did it anyway. Federal regulators were never much of a concern." He leans down to wipe a tear off my cheek, but keeps the feeding tube firmly lodged in my mouth. "They made twelve of us. Someone had the notion to name us after the twelve sons of Jacob. You met my brother, Benjamin. My name is Joseph — the one who rose from slavery to become the power behind the pharaoh."

My crib winks out of existence, replaced by a sturdy institutional bed, surrounded by bars. "You're now six years old and 220 pounds. You suffer from childhood-onset diabetes and an enlarged heart. You've never been hugged or caressed or kissed; you've never played with another child, not even one of your eleven identical brothers. The only toy you've ever seen is a sock monkey that was placed in your crib, now tied to the bars of your bed. You think that sock monkey is God, because it's the only vaguely human thing you've ever seen that hasn't stuck you with a needle or shoved something vile down your throat."

It's hard to breathe. Joseph must've suffered from asthma, too. A machine above my head hisses. My left forearm, pudgy as a fire hose, stings as a purplish liquid enters my veins through a shunt. A technician stands over me. He attaches a tube to a shunt in my other arm, then presses a wooden dowel into my right hand and forces me to squeeze it, again and again, heedlessly crushing my fingers. I watch my blood run away from me, filling the spirals of a plastic tube as if it's eager to escape the disaster that is my body.

The lights dim. The only sounds I hear are the humming of the equipment, my brothers' snores, and the desperate puffs of my own breathing. Footsteps now. I smell an unfamiliar cologne. A tall, dark silhouette stands above me. Hands lower the rails surrounding my bed. My body involuntarily tenses, anticipating a wound, but the man lays a cool hand on my forehead. The kindness in his touch is electric.

"No, Joseph," he says. "I haven't come to inject you or take a sample. My name is Theodore. I'd like to become your friend." I've never been spoken to before; spoken about, but never *to*. His voice is a thousand times more nourishing than the MannaSantos nutrient shakes. "I just started working here. I thought you might like to hear a story." He pulls a chair to the side of my bed. " 'Once upon a time, deep within the Hundred Acre Wood...' "

My visitor continues reading, but his voice is replaced by Joseph's. "His name was Theodore Weiss. He'd been ordered to shape the data gleaned from us clones into practical applications. He and his wife, a fellow biologist, suffered moral qualms when they discovered how we were being treated, but their protests were ignored. Weeks before I first met her husband, Mrs. Weiss was killed in a car accident. They'd had no children. Dr. Weiss decided to personally better the lives of as many of us as he could, as a memorial to his wife. This is the story he wove for me, feeding it to me along with tales of the Hundred Acre Wood and Beatrice Potter.

"Over the course of many nights together, we discovered something quite amazing. Amazing to me; less so, as it turned out, to my benefactor. My mind, cruelly unexercised to that point, absorbed knowledge and new skills like a proverbial sponge. My progenitor Hud Walterson had been an intellectual nova, a genius, but his light was annihilated by the black hole of his obesity. He didn't attend school past the third grade, trapped in his bed by the shackles of his flesh. If he'd had access to teachers, books, a computer... he could have accomplished anything. *Anything.* He would've been remembered as one of the great minds of his time, instead of a freak who sparked a vigilante movement."

My body changes, grows. I'm a teenager now, inhabiting a much larger bed, restrained by leather straps. They cut deeply into my pillowy flesh. I'm now somewhere beyond six hundred pounds. My mind is afire with concepts and data I can barely comprehend, higher mathematics and molecular biology far beyond what I was taught in medical school. But I sense this blizzard of cogitation is a blind, a curtain I'm trying to draw to block something I can't bear to see.

At the far end of the long, darkened room is a thick window, reinforced with wire, about two feet square, that looks into a bright operating room. An autopsy is being performed on the far side of that window. I want to look away, but I can't. Doctors are taking a gigantic body apart, organ by organ, slicing through folds of blubber with electric scalpels. Dismembering a body that looks exactly like my own...

"'Project Walterson' was brought to a premature end eight years ago, Dr. Shmalzberg. Hints of illegal cloning had been leaked to federal regulatory agencies. MannaSantos hastened to cover up their tracks, destroying all evidence of the project. Including, of course, us — we eight clones who remained. But before they cremated our enormous euthanized bodies, they performed autopsies, gathering whatever last scraps of data they could. The project's shutdown was hastened by the escape of one of its subjects during a power failure — my brother Benjamin, who was more ambulatory than the rest of us."

Joseph's almost emotionless patter belies what I'm feeling, what he remembers feeling, what he now forces me to feel. My oversized heart beats with terrified urgency, as if it could supply this body with strength to snap its bounds.

But then those bounds loosen of their own accord. Theodore Weiss and another man help me onto my wobbly legs. "Joseph," Weiss whispers, struggling beneath my arm, "I won't let them butcher you. I'm taking you home. I can adjust the records, make them believe you've already been disposed of..."

The dormitory blinks out, replaced by a spartan room filled with computer equipment and furniture sized for a Walterson. "He made me disappear," Joseph's voice continues. "He was in a position of high enough authority that he could alter secret files and leave no fingerprints. The final disposition of the clones was a hurried, almost chaotic affair, and our corpses were virtually indistinguishable. Dr. Weiss lived in a house at the edge of MannaSantos's enormous desert compound. Even then, his health was beginning to fail. He performed more and more of his work from home, rarely making the seven-mile drive to his office. My education accelerated tremendously. I required little sleep, laboring at his computers for up to twenty hours a day. Every new byte of knowledge, I consumed voraciously.

"I soon reached the point where I could assist Dr. Weiss with his work. I tried erasing from my memory all thoughts of my inhumane genesis and the brutality that followed. I pretended that Theodore Weiss was my father, that my life had started the night of my exodus from the research center. Dr. Weiss made the transition from treating me like a student to a junior colleague, and then to his respected equal. During the eighteen months leading to his death, he came to view me with a measure of awe. The more I applied myself to his projects, the higher his star rose within MannaSantos. His increasing penchant for privacy was viewed as an acceptable eccentricity, given the profits his researches were adding to the corporate coffers.

"The final project we worked on together was the Metaboloft gene."

Now I'm standing in a simple bedroom, staring down at the husk of Theodore Weiss. "He was diagnosed with spinal cancer. The tumors were inoperable. Radiation was ineffective, and chemotherapy drained too much of his strength. He eschewed further treatment, hiding his impending death from the company, eager to complete with me what he considered his life's crowning achievement."

The distant sun of winter looks smaller than the faded, midday moon. I have a shovel in my hands. The blade, with my weight pressing it, penetrates the dry earth easily. I'm burying Theodore Weiss, straight into the red, sandy soil.

"I had to hide my existence. No one could know that Theodore Weiss had died. It was simple for me to assume his identity and responsibilities as the project's lead geneticist. I already knew his clearance codes, and much of what he'd passed off as his own work had actually been mine. Utilizing old lecture disks, digitally altered, I was able to participate as my deceased mentor in video conferences. His work had been his life; no friends or relations would come seeking him.

"And then I decided to use those clearance codes to learn more about my adoptive father, the man who had been Buddha and Moses and Jesus to me. My savior. My god."

The desert gravesite shimmers and fades. I'm back in the theater, back in my own body. The skeletal Joseph stands before me. The muscles and tendons of his face harden, a topographical map of grief and betrayal. "Foolishly desperate to regain a sense of intimacy with him, I accessed his journal and private correspondence. What I found..." His voice goes soft as a sleepy child's, but volatile as nitroglycerin. "What I found were *lies*. He hadn't been a junior scientist reassigned to the Walterson Project. He was the project's director, the *initiator*, the man who'd commanded that my brothers and I be created from frozen cell scrapings. Just as he later commanded that all evidence of his work be destroyed. And his saintly wife, the woman whose death had inspired him to uplift me? She hadn't died. She'd divorced him three years before I met him. She remained very much alive, still working at MannaSantos as director of public relations."

Oh my God... Harri? She was married to Weiss?

"Human kindness is an illusion. Man is the cruelest of all beasts, because he adds the power to deceive to the power to kill."

His green eyes have become pools of darkness. "America wanted to grow thin? They paid men like Theodore Weiss to mutilate children — to mutilate *me* — so they could fit into smaller and smaller pairs of bluejeans? I would give them what they wanted, and more, and *more*, until they choked on their own vanity. Until ambulating flesh was a bad memory the grass and trees had forgotten. Metaboloft was the scourge Fate placed in my hands.

"Acting as the infallible Dr. Weiss, it was easy to convince the development team that the protein shield I'd designed was foolproof. But I knew the combination of environmental inputs which would unshackle the gene. I'd tracked the development of seasonal ozone holes over the Midwest. Metaboloft was a bomb on a precisely calibrated timer. And now it's a bomb inside each one of us, accelerating our basal metabolisms, becoming more voracious with each meal we ingest."

Have any of the security guards been hearing this? I doubt I could make an appeal to them — Joseph could easily make me mute.

The only person I can be reasonably sure will hear me is Joseph himself. He wouldn't have shown me all this unless he wants a response. Could he be subliminally begging me to convince him not to kill every human being on earth?

"Joseph... maybe the kindness Dr. Weiss showed you wasn't entirely venal. Maybe it was his attempt to atone. Didn't he bring you here to share with you the best experiences of his life? Would he have done that if he hadn't come to love you as a son? I know something about having done a great evil, and how hard it can be to make amends."

His fleshless death mask hasn't changed its expression. Maybe what reached Benjamin will reach him, too? "Your original brother, Hud Walterson, suffered just as you suffered. He was robbed of his potential, humiliated, forced to be a test subject for experimental science and quackery. He lashed out, just like you're lashing out. But even at his most destructive, he never harmed another soul. Even when he was burning factories, his goal was to lift people up —"

My mouth moves, but no sound comes out. Joseph doesn't want a debate.

"You are... an interesting man, Dr. Shmalzberg. It might be worth some of my time to see what is inside your head. If you reach the morning with an unbroken mind — a slender chance, but this is Las Vegas, land of gamblers and daunting odds — I will keep you alive until Metaboloft takes you. I might like to see my progenitor's face through your eyes. Come morning, if you're more than a husk, I'll teach you to project your memories using the RM —"

"Hell *no*, you won't!"

I jerk my head around. Trotmann, still Elvis but frothing mad, looks primed for a fatal embolism. "Shmalzberg's getting on that god-damned roller coaster! That was the deal! You'd screw with his mind some, then I'd take the Elvis fat and strap him into the big bang!" He stares wildly around at his handful of Ann-Margrets. "Isn't that right, girls?"

Joseph laughs. "Trotty-Trot, be careful you don't use up your value as light entertainment." His voice drips with condescension, sugar-coating a promise of violence. "You gave my brother a home, and a reason for existing. But you also treated him little better than a stray dog. Get on my bad side, and I'll show you what it feels like to plunge twenty stories."

"Shove your threats up your fat ass!" Trotmann, shaking with fury, wheels closer to his women. The acolytes stare at each other uneasily. "I don't have to take this from you! What do you care what happens to Shmalzberg, just so long as that fat doesn't end up in the hands of the government? We're taking the fat, and Shmalzberg's going on the god-damn ride!"

Joseph shakes his head. "No. You're the one going on a ride." He turns to the four MannaSantos security men. They're outnumbered by Trotmann's women, and only equally armed, yet their far greater intimidation factor seems to skew the scales in their favor. "Tie him to the seat next to Dr. Shmalzberg. Then put an RM helmet on his head."

Will the women fight? One reaches for her weapon. The other five look as frozen as the statues in the courtyard. If only I could get my hands loose —

A voice booms from the theater's sound system, a voice that isn't Joseph's:

"*Trespassers, drop your weapons on the ground.*"

CHAPTER 18

The voice echoing through the theater isn't Joseph's — but it *is* piercingly familiar. Joseph's projection flickers. He's as startled as any of the guards or acolytes.

"You are trespassing on property and abusing equipment which belongs to the Graceland Corporation. You are surrounded by Graceland security and Las Vegas police. Set your weapons on the ground, step away from the Elvis remains, and vacate the premises. Do this, and no charges will be filed."

That voice — of course I know it! It's Swaggart's. He and his Elvis-impersonating goons have been tailing me all the way since Memphis; he must've been the one who sent them after me in Orlando. I don't know how they found me, but I'm grateful as hell.

"You have ten seconds to put your weapons aside."

Only a few of my captors look cowed; the rest scan the theater for defensible positions. "You'd better do what they say," I shout, improvising furiously. "These are serious people — they control the whole city of Memphis like a Mafia syndicate, and they'll do whatever they have to to get what they want —"

"NO! Nobody gets the Elvis fat but *me!*" Trotmann grabs a pistol from the belt of one of his startled followers. He rolls toward me faster than I would've thought possible, then slams into my chair and paws my torso, reaching for the Elvis. Rolling away from me, it's like he's torn off one of my limbs.

The Elvis perched precariously on his lap (*Hold onto it, at least!*), he waves the gun uselessly with his bad right hand while propelling himself toward an exit. "You spineless fuckers!" he shouts at the ceiling. "You don't have the balls to shoot a helpless old man in a wheelchair! Ha! I DARE you!"

Someone takes his dare. Before the shot finishes echoing, Trotmann slumps over the Elvis. His wheelchair coasts to a halt ten feet from the door.

"You MORON!" Swaggart screams. *"You might've damaged the artifact!"*

The acolytes who were unnerved before, now sprint for the exits. The others either duck beneath tables or overturn them to use as shields. More shots shake the theater. Two MannaSantos guards fire back from behind upturned tables, aiming at the ceiling, where the gunfire seems to be coming from. There could be technical crawl spaces up there; Swaggart would have access to the schemata of this whole facility.

Suddenly the theater becomes the surface of Lake Mead, surrounded by distant canyon walls. I'm hovering just above the surface of the water; Elvis and Ann-Margret whiz past me on water skis, soaking me with their spray. Swaggart's doing? Or has Joseph's panic left the system without a hand on the tiller?

Even above the roar of twin speedboats, I hear the intensifying exchange of gunfire. I could catch a bullet any second, although the RM might make it taste like a rum and Coke and feel like a showgirl's caress. I've got to get to the floor. I start rocking back and forth. Can't tell if I'm making any progress — I can't feel the damn chair beneath my ass, can't tell if my balance is shifting, can't see anything but sunlight shimmering off the lake and Elvis's perfect hair and Ann-Margret's smile —

Whoa! I plunge through the surface of the water. Now I'm under the waves, swimming past a Technicolor reef with the ease of a manta ray (There aren't any reefs in Lake Mead — could this be a scenario from *Blue Hawaii*?). The sudden change in altitude must've been me tumbling over and hitting the floor. But the RM helmet wasn't dislodged; I'm still getting the complete, if rudderless, effect.

Now I'm back in the theater again, but it's a different theater, larger, with a conventional stage. I'm in the midst of an audience, in the front row, near the orchestra. I recognize all this: it's the Flamingo Casino employee talent competition from *Viva Las Vegas,* with Elvis battling Ann-Margret for the prize money so he can buy an engine for his race car. But the scenario is all wrong — Elvis and his dancers are dressed in zoot suits, dancing with tommy guns, as if they're performing a number from *Guys and Dolls*. Or *The Trouble with Girls*...

The dancers pivot and spin, holding their machine guns above their heads like batons. Trap doors open in the ceiling; gun muzzles flash, spraying the dancers with lead. Two of the dancers fall out of the line, clutching their breasts while they twirl to the floor. The remaining dancers leap and kick, then duck low as they fire their weapons in unison at the ceiling. Twin figures plummet from the trap doors, dangling from ropes like broken marionettes. As they twitch, their bodies gush fountains of bright red blood from dozens of wounds.

Two more trap doors spring open. Rope ladders drop to the floor. Two men scurry down them like fleeing spiders as the orchestra vamps toward a climax. One of the men has a bandage covering his nose. The two fleeing men run left, then right, blocked at each turn by menacing dancers. A trio surrounds one of the men. They all place the muzzles of their guns against his head and pull the triggers, and his head disappears with a resounding pop, like a soap bubble.

Elvis himself halts the second fleeing man, the one with the bandaged nose. He grasps his Tommy gun by the muzzle, winds up into a batter's stance, and swings. His opponent's struck head flies for the rafters. When it hits the ceiling, the whole theater flashes as dazzlingly as a pinball machine, the orchestra resounding with clangs and honks and blings...

And then I'm back in the real theater — I think — lying on my side on the floor, still tied to the chair. My ears are ringing. The air stinks of burnt gunpowder and blood.

Christ... they managed to massacre each other. Cries of pain push through my tinnitus. Ten feet away, a MannaSantos guard writhes on the floor, clutching a bloody knee, screaming an unending loop of profanities. Above me, a man dressed as an Elvis impersonator dangles from an access panel in the ceiling, his slack torso and arms forming a macabre chandelier. I think it's one of the men who almost pitched me out of the Swiss Family Robinson Treehouse.

"I'm glad to sense that you're alive and unharmed, Dr. Shmalzberg. I'd miss you terribly if you were already gone."

Joseph's voice in my head — *shit*...

"I'm sorry to disappoint you, but this bungled intervention won't be your salvation. I'm not certain these men are friends of yours, although one seems to know you. Shall we find out more?"

I try freeing my hands. The ropes are a little looser than before, but not loose enough for me to slip free. "Joseph," I shout. "Free me so I can help the people who are hurt. That man over there by the table will bleed to death from that knee wound. I can keep him alive until an ambulance comes. He's one of your own men —"

"That's an inventive ploy, Doctor. But I don't think I'll be setting you loose just yet. We've got lots of other things on our agenda, you and I. Mr. McNaley, go pick Dr. Shmalzberg off the floor please. Mr. Kelvin, place our new prisoner into the RM unit next to Dr. Shmalzberg."

I'm lifted from the floor and shoved roughly against the table. I spot Swaggart, his thin arms pulled behind him by a man bleeding from his temple. Swaggart's bleeding, too, more seriously. The right half of his pink velvet vest is stained crimson. His face has gone the color of plaster, even whiter than the mound of bandages crowning his nose job.

Kelvin pauses when he's a few feet from the man with the knee wound. His hard face grows indecisive; his eyes flit between his comrade and me. "If — if he's a doctor, and he can help Buckner, maybe we should —"

"Mr. Kelvin, what did I just *say?*" Joseph's voice booms.

"But there's still a chance to do something for him —"

"Mr. Kelvin, do you need to be reminded that I have complete access to your family's files? Would you care to know what my other employees will do to your elderly mother and father if you persist in being contrary?"

Kelvin shuts up. He ties Swaggart to the chair next to me and secures an RM helmet to his head.

The Graceland curator rouses himself from a nearly catatonic daze when he sees me. "Swaggart," I say, "why didn't you actually go to the police? Why did you try to force things yourself?"

He licks his lips, now coated with blood. "Wasn't... an official Graceland operation... going after you. I did it... on my own. If I'd gone to the cops... I couldn't have been sure I'd walk away with the Elvis remains." He smiles, his mouth twitching involuntarily. "Besides... I was tired of always being... supporting player. Wanted to be... the star. That's why I got... the nose fixed."

Joseph materializes on the far side of the table. This time, his image combines the standard, thick-jowled Walterson head with a Charles Atlas body, rippling with comic-book muscles. "So you actually are connected with the Graceland Corporation?" he asks.

Swaggart's face doesn't register shock or amazement, just agony. "I'm their... head curator of Elvis artifacts."

"A junk collector who plays with guns. What do you know about the Metaboloft gene?"

Swaggart shakes his head. "Never... never heard of it. Just wanted the fat. Like those other men chasing Shmalzberg. Like you..."

"*Not* like me. I'm not an obsessive, like Trotmann, or a dreamy fool like my brother." He dismisses Swaggart with a scowl. "I don't find you very interesting, Mr. Swaggart. But you're a historian of sorts, so you should find what I have to share fascinating — a personalized preview of the future history of mankind."

Swaggart's eyes roll upward in their sockets. He's been sucked into the RM world. Joseph's not letting me see what Swaggart is seeing. But the palpable pressure against the edges of my consciousness is his way of letting me know he can open the floodgates at any time.

Swaggart's shoulders twitch. His hands struggle against their bonds. He tries to roll himself into a ball, as if his stomach is on fire and he wants to smother the inferno. His face tightens until I hear his teeth crack. Then he screams. A high-pitched sound that obliterates the moanings of the other dying men. It makes me sick to my stomach.

After his vocal cords have been shredded to a pulp, Swaggart's head falls to the table. He's still shallowly breathing, but otherwise, he's a cinder.

"That little preview was also meant for your benefit, Doctor." Joseph's voice is omnipresent, coming at me from every direction. "Your Mr. Swaggart didn't have much in the way of reserves. No fat on him, either physically or spiritually. I didn't make him experience anything I haven't already personally endured. I've been eating

Metaboloft foods since a year before the gene escaped into the wild. I'll still be vanishing months after the last of my 'countrymen' have disappointed the worms with the paucity of flesh on their dead bones. And the last part of me to vanish, as I look out upon the empty cities, will be my grin, like the Cheshire Cat's."

He's going to do to me what he just did to Swaggart. How can I fight back? Despite his incredible technical accomplishments, he's basically still a child, an unsocialized, horribly abused child. Like Benjamin was. Except that, unlike Benjamin, he's an outraged child, angry enough to burn the world —

"Now, Dr. Shmalzberg, let's see if you are made of sterner stuff."

Nausea and vertigo hit me again. Then I'm in a strangely familiar bedroom, lying on a king-size bed, atop a velvet leopard-print bedspread. Multiple television monitors are built into the wall, early RCA models — this is Elvis's bedroom at Graceland. The theater must have this "set" coded as one of its templates.

A large mirror on the dresser tilts so that I can see myself. "I'm not without a heart, Doctor. I've decided to grant you what undoubtedly would be your last wish." I'm Elvis — naked, fat Elvis, spread-eagled, wrists and ankles tied to the four bedposts.

Joseph reappears. Four of him, all skeletal. They surround the bed, white doctor's coats hanging from their bony shoulders like shrouds. Good Lord... they each have a cannula, all four of Trotmann's design, with those fiendish cutting heads.

"With these devices," the Josephs say in unison, "you and others of your kind helped create the mania that helped launch MannaSantos. Which then created me. It's only fitting that we close the circle. And what loving son wouldn't want to relive his father's greatest moment?"

They switch their cannulas on. I hear the cutting heads clicking, like the mandibles of an army of marching insects. No anesthetic, no hyaluronidase — they're going to cut me straight up, like what Trotmann did to Benjamin. God. Here it comes —

Four cannulas dig into my flesh. The pain, agonizing, but... almost bearable? Cutting heads eviscerate my belly folds and flabby thighs. Blood splatters the four Josephs' white coats. I should be out of my mind with agony. The only possible answer — Joseph never experienced Trotmann's sadistic liposculpture himself. He's only heard it described. *If I can manage to hang on, maybe I can figure out how to deal with him...*

"How does it feel, Dr. Shmalzberg, to be on the receiving end of your own barbarity?"

"Trotmann's... barbarity, you mean. I treated every patient with dignity."

"Then it's a shame you can't be operating on yourself."

Operating on myself? In this Alice in Wonderland world, that could mean my salvation. I've overridden RM settings before. Those years I was clinging to Emily's memory... I almost burned out parts of my brain abusing the equipment. But I've never tried controlling a system of this power. And I've never had to compete with a rival controller much more skilled than me...

The Josephs turn up their cannulas' pumping rates. The flow of my fat and blood and effluvia into the collection jars doubles, then doubles again. *My body... it's shrinking.* The folds surrounding my middle grow smaller by the second. I'm starting to feel it now, what Swaggart must've felt — a horrible weakness, a hunger that slashes my organs with its claws.

I can't afford to wait any longer. I concentrate on the front of my skull, imagining invisible "hands" sprouting from my forehead and reaching for the four cannulas. I feel the beginnings of a tension headache. *I've partially reversed the direction of the RM's electrical impulses, forcing it into a two-way flow.* With those infinitely malleable "hands," I reach into my Elvis skin, sliding beneath the dermis to the shrinking layers of fat where the cutting heads are reducing me to bloody pap. I take hold of the cutting heads, hidden from Joseph's sight, and bend the metal, struggling to reshape it into much less malevolent forms, the shape of my own cannula's tip. The exertion soaks my faux form with sweat.

Almost there... I've got a leg up on him in that I know cannulas intimately. Ahh... the cutting has stopped. Now, if I can reach the suction units without his noticing, reverse the flow — I can pump the fat back into this body. With the dream logic this RM world seems to go by, that should pull me back from the brink of starvation. I have to distract him. What precoded scenarios would the theater have that might pull his attention —?

"Joseph, you've experienced some of the worst humanity has to offer. But human beings are capable of amazing kindness, as well as cruelty —"

"Hunger is making you babble, Doctor. You might as well recite the Canadian national anthem, for all the good it will do you."

Not babbling. It's here, in the theater's "library." I knew it would be — it's one of the iconic Elvis moments that everyone remembers. "Have you ever experienced selfless altruism, known the joy of giving with no expectation of payback? Let me show you —"

I "push" him into a second scenario. Let *him* be Elvis this time. The effort makes my head pound, but I'm rewarded by the echoing ripple of his amazement. He's so flabbergasted that he doesn't struggle against the scenario. He stands on the lot of a Memphis Cadillac dealership. It's summertime, hot and sticky. He's having fun, picking out Cadillacs to give away to friends and employees, walking around dozens of new Eldorados and Sevilles, telling the salesman which ones to prep for delivery to Graceland.

He's already picked out thirteen cars when he comes across a black family staring through the windows of the showroom. They've driven up in an elderly Ford, well-maintained but showing its decrepitude. The wife, a bank teller named Mennie Person, jokingly tells her husband that since her birthday is coming up in two days, how about that nice blue Eldorado there in the corner...?

I make Joseph feel what Elvis felt at that moment; the burst of endorphins the scenario stimulates in his brain makes it easy. Here is a mother, just like Elvis's beloved and long-gone mother Gladys. She's a member of a race to whom Elvis owes a debt of affection and gratitude, ever since his boyhood days of sneaking into the back pews of black churches to listen to the singing. He knows he can brighten her entire year through an act of unexpected and outrageous generosity, and maybe impress upon those youngsters the essential goodness of people, a goodness that can leap across racial boundaries.

"You like that car?" Elvis/Joseph says. "I'll buy it for you."

And while I let Joseph bask in that burst of endorphins, I'm reversing the flow on the cannula pumps, returning my stolen substance to me. But as I regain my strength, I wonder if I can do more than merely distract Joseph. Weiss taught him much about science and biology; but what did he teach him about morality?

The four skeletal Josephs, who've been motionless since I shunted him into the Cadillac dealership, now spring back to "life." *"That* was surprising," they say, appraising me with new wariness. "You're far more talented than the hapless Mr. Swaggart. But I don't see what you hoped to accomplish —"

Straining, I slam him into another scenario before he can see what I've done with the cannulas. He's Elvis again, this time returned to Tupelo to cut the ribbon on a newly built playground he's donated to the city. Maybe this scenario will stroke Joseph's emotions more — he's surrounded by poor children who've never had a decent ball field to play on, children as impoverished as Elvis once was. But he's fighting me this time, struggling against the theater's coding. Forcing him to stay inside the scenario is as strenuous as physically wrestling him.

"Joseph," I say, projecting my voice across the cloudless Mississippi sky. "This is part of what humanity is about, too. For every act of violence or neglect, there can be a countering act of healing kindness. You can choose to be on the side of kindness. Hud Walterson came from a desperately poor family. Members of his family, *your* family, could still be living somewhere in poverty, in need of the help you can give them. You could find your family, help them —"

"ENOUGH!"

The Tupelo playground and blue Mississippi sky shatter. My skull feels like it shatters, too. I make a feeble attempt to grab for another scenario to shunt him into, but he's learned how to block my access to the theater's library.

"How DARE you try to toy with my emotions!" the four of him bellow. "There is no 'kindness' in the human animal. 'Kindness' is the drug Theodore Weiss fed me so that he could steal the fruits of my genius."

Their attention falls on the fat collection jars, now empty, completely drained back into me. The four Josephs scream with pure rage.

The bedroom vanishes. I'm lying in loose dirt, staring up at a merciless desert sun. Distant reddish hills block the horizon. I pick myself up, surprised I'm not chained or shackled. I'm back in my own body, a few dozen yards away from a solitary ranch house.

"This is where I buried Dr. Weiss." I whirl around. Joseph is behind me, just one of him now, but an imposing giant of at least four hundred pounds. "And this is where I will bury you."

My flesh contracts again, and I don't have Elvis's eighty pounds of extra adipose to act as a buffer. He's not using any fancy symbolic modelings this time, just a brute projection of his own memories of starvation. I double over. Deprived of its fat stores, my body begins leeching nutrients from my bones and organs. My metabolism races — I'm burning with fever. I roll into a ball, trying to squelch trembling that threatens to bounce my eyes out of their sockets.

I try to parry with memories of my own, recollections of enormous meals, Passover Seders at my great-uncle's house, my great-aunt forcing one more helping of greasy matzoh farfel down my gullet... but Joseph swats this away.

He's going to kill my mind. There's no reaching or dissuading him. I have to hurt him, as badly as I can. God forgive me.

Conjuring a scenario from my own memories is infinitely more painful than pulling one from the theater's library. I feel something break behind my eyes. But a terror of death forces me on.

We're in the auditorium of Trotmann's church, on the edge of the pit. Waves of heat rise from the boiling fat to sear my face, and they sear Joseph's face, too, because he's occupying the body of his brother Benjamin. He's teetering at the edge of the pit. Mentally, he's fighting me like a wildcat. But this time I've shackled him to a body and mind almost precisely like his own, and that glue helps me maintain my hold.

He's still starving me. My heart is growing weak. I force Joseph to say his brother's last words —

"My name... my name is Benjamin. *Benjamin* Walterson. Not Hud. Benjamin."

And then I send him toppling face first into the fat. My memory of the burn I received from flying blobs of superheated fat — I stretch it over his whole body. I add a more distant memory, of second degree burns I received early in my career as a Good Humor Man. Those dying nerve endings add their screaming to the maelstrom. He's bucking, kicking, enormously strong. Forcing him into the memories is like trying to drown him — I'm straddling his thrashing body as I force his head beneath a pool of lava, burning my own hands...

By sheer force of will, he tears away my projection. I lie dazed on the hot sands, back behind Weiss's house. But Joseph is sprawled on the red earth, too, his unmoving bulk lying face down. Did I manage to —? No. He forces himself to his feet. All that effort, at unknown cost to my cerebral cortex, and I've only managed to stun him...

"Very... very good, Doctor. You're making this a contest. But you're merely... postponing the inevitable. I'm younger than you are. Stronger. With infinitely more experience manipulating this system. And lest you forget, I can have your physical body killed at any time, with just a word."

I've hurt him worse than he's letting on. He's shaking. His voice quakes, even as it echoes powerfully from the surrounding hills. But my own strength is nearly gone. And he's tensing for another assault —

My fever spikes. Blood feels like it's boiling. The sky whirls like a gigantic funnel cloud. I raise my arms, trying to ward off this wave of agony. I can see my wrist joints, the long bones of my forearms, as though I've stuck my arms behind an x-ray scanner. My organs are on the verge of collapse... my shrunken heart muscle thin as a stretched rubber band...

He thinks I've hurt him as badly as I can. That I've shot my last arrow. But I've got one left. I nock my arrow and let fly.

Conjuring the scenario is like swimming against a tide of molten lead. Binding him with the remaining shreds of my strength, I drag him back in time twenty-six years. To a burning candied popcorn factory on the outskirts of Los Angeles. I sense blood running from my nose and ears. The prelude to a cerebral hemorrhage? But there's no stopping this now. I'm standing in the middle of a crowd. We're waiting for the famous Hud Walterson, waiting for him to escape yet another junk food conflagration, confound another posse of lawmen.

But that's not going to happen. Not this time. Because his face appears in an open third-story window. Hud's face, and Joseph's face. That's right, Joseph. *I was there.* I saw your progenitor die. I feel his panic skyrocket as he recognizes the event I've nailed him to, just as I see Hud's/Joseph's expression crumble into despair as the flames fill the room behind him.

I know despair. I impale Joseph with something more elemental than memories of the searing of flesh. I make myself remember Emily's death, and I drag him down into that inferno pit of memory with me. I make him know what it was like to watch the person you love more than your own life be humiliated, crippled, and finally squelched by a cluster of cells that have gone on a senseless rampage. I make him know what it was like to have every bit of oxygen squeezed out of your soul.

I look up into Hud's face, and I remember his agonized expression of despair. I recognized that despair because I'd lived it, too. Now I make Joseph live it — the realization that everything you are will soon be ash, soaring into flame-driven updrafts to be scattered and lost. All tomorrows are gone. All possibilities for happiness, for connection, even for pain, all wasted. You've thrown it all away, and the gesture means nothing at all.

Your suicidal gesture means nothing, Joseph.

His hair and clothing ignite. But the worst of his agony is over, because he's beyond feeling. He topples out of the window, already stiff, a short-lived comet plummeting to the asphalt.

I let go of the scenario. It slips away from me like a whale carcass sliding off my boat just before the weight would capsize me. Back to Weiss's desert vista...? No. I'm returned to the casino theater. Thank God. Thank God. Whether the rest of my life is measured in minutes or decades, I will dedicate it to the opposite of despair.

There's no sign of Joseph, either inside my head or out in the theater. Something's wrong with my field of vision, though. I try to get up from my chair, stumble against the table, and discover that my hands have come loose from the cords. My wrists are bloody, rubbed raw. So my struggle wasn't entirely in my head.

Swaggart is next to me, flopped over the table. He still has a pulse, but otherwise he's completely unresponsive. McNaley and Kelvin, the two guards, sway on their feet like sleepwalkers. Their faces twitch as their eyes slowly focus on me, as if they're surfacing from hypnotic trances. How much of Joseph's and my combat spilled into the theater's ambient atmosphere, enveloping them despite their lack of helmets?

Awakening, they don't appear hostile; just dazed. "Do... do you have phones?" I ask them. It's hard to make my mouth work right.

"I... we... we don't..."

"Find a phone," I say. It's like talking with a mouth full of wet concrete. "Call an ambulance for your friends, and for the others. Joseph doesn't have any hold over you anymore. I don't think he's in any shape to hurt anyone ever again."

Suddenly, their faces lose their befuddlement and take on a profound fright. They're pointing above my head, behind me —

I turn around. The main entrance doors, a dozen feet tall, tremble, buckle, then burst open, flying inward with such force that they leap off their hinges and crash to the floor.

My God. It's the Ottoman. He's gigantic, easily nine feet tall. His suit is in shreds, pierced through by shards of his destroyed limousine. His face is a mask of blood. But his mouth still works well enough to scream my name:

"SHMALZBERG! You insidious Jew! You thought your African underlings killed me, did you? But Allah has declared my mission will succeed, and no force on earth can subvert His will."

He bounds into the theater. The floor trembles. He's unstoppable...

"I will remove the fat of the Troubadour from your friend Trotmann's corpse. You will come to envy him his easy death. Your body contains hundreds of bones, and I will reduce each to jelly in its turn."

He's towering over me now, blocking all light. He keeps coming back and back, like an indestructible movie monster, like *The Terminator* or the killer from *Halloween*...

Oh. Of course. Of course.

I make him hunch his shoulders and leer like Jerry Lewis in *The Nutty Professor*. For good measure, I give him horn-rim glasses and a set of outsized buck teeth. As a good Frenchman, I'm sure he appreciates the homage to one of his country's greatest cinema idols.

My hands feel for the helmet I'm still wearing. My brain, like a bee's stinger after it stings and detaches, has kept pumping away, injecting my senses with scenarios from my nightmares. I remove the spidery contraption. The Ottoman disappears.

I suppose his embassy will retrieve him, either from the hospital or the morgue. I should visit his grave or bedside someday, honor him for the quest he inadvertently sparked, for what he has given me.

McNaley and Kelvin have fled. The theater is quiet, apart from the weakening moans of the wounded. I walk over to Trotmann, hunched over in his wheelchair. He's gone cold, but he's done a good job protecting the Elvis from harm. The glass vacuum jar isn't even scratched. *You'll have to pry it from my cold, dead fingers, Shmalzberg.* That's something he would've said. Now I do exactly that.

I need to know what happened to Joseph. He could've been controlling the RM system from a distant site, but I'm betting the control facilities are inside the theater. I stumble toward the far side of the auditorium, to where the wall is lined with curtains. Something is broken inside me. I peel away the red velvet curtains. Sure enough, there's a whole other room back here, filled with control boards.

I find Joseph sprawled on the floor. A broken RM helmet lies next to his head. He doesn't look much different from his final projection, a human mountain, although only half as massive as Hud was at his zenith. I kneel next to him. His breathing and pulse are strong, but when I force his eyes open, they've turned up inside his head. He's in the same state as he left Swaggart... smothered in a coma, lost to himself.

There's something wrong with his face, a neuromuscular degeneration, possibly the result of a stroke. It makes the left half of his doughy face sag. I can't tell how recent the damage is. Did he suffer the stroke tonight, or had he already injured himself with the RM equipment before ever meeting me? Or did the MannaSantos researchers cause this degeneration years ago?

It doesn't matter. Hud, Benjamin, Joseph... I wish all three of you could've lived happier lives. And come to better ends.

Staring at his lopsided face, feeling its soft folds with bruised fingertips, I realize what's happened to my vision. My left eye has gone blind.

CHAPTER 19

I find a cell phone on one of the dead guards and call for an ambulance. Then I give what limited first aid I'm capable of to those men and women still clinging to life. Once I've done what I can, I go to meet the ambulances. I want nothing more than to lie down and sleep. But I'm afraid that if I do that, I'll never wake up again; or I won't wake up whole.

The sky is just beginning to turn a lighter shade of gray. Almost morning. That's a funny thing about spending time inside a casino; you lose all sense of time. I trudge down the long access road toward Colossal Elvis. The last time I saw him, the sun was setting on his head. Now the sun is rising between his knees.

I shelter from the wind by huddling against his gigantic blue suede shoe. I must've bitten my lip while mentally fighting Joseph. My blood tastes as good as a marbled prime rib from Lansky's. It's good to be able to feel or taste anything. *Anything.*

Muthukrishnan and his entourage arrive almost simultaneously with the ambulances. Margo has her arms around me almost before I see her door being flung open. Her hair smells of cigarette smoke. Right now it's the most wonderful scent in the world.

"Louis! Johnson and the others managed to overpower the guards before they could lock us away. But I was so afraid we'd be too late..."

"Not too late," I say, burying my nose and mouth in her hair. "I managed to pull my own fat out of the fire this time. So you figured out what I said about the Good Humor Man card?"

"Yes..." She looks searchingly into my face. "Louis? Your voice — it sounds slurred. Did they hurt you?"

Hearing the fright in her voice makes all the remaining strength go out of my legs. Muthukrishnan is there to help catch me. "Doctor, are you all right?"

I don't want to frighten Margo. But the faster I get treatment, the more chance I've got of retaining whatever faculties I'm left with. "I think I've suffered what we doctors euphemistically call a 'neurological event.' You've probably noticed I need to drop my membership in Toastmasters..."

My feeble attempt at lightheartedness fails to lessen Margo's shock. She whirls on Muthukrishnan. *"Get one of those ambulances back here! Right now!"*

"Of course, of course," he mumbles. He pulls a radio from its holster. She helps me to lie down, bundling her jacket beneath my head. I want to tell her not to worry, but suddenly I barely have the strength to do anything.

A pair of feds approach Margo and me. One of them kneels down next to me. "I'm very sorry, sir," he says, his voice gravelly and surprisingly sincere. "I'm going to have to retrieve that glass jar from you. I've been made to understand it's vital to national security —"

Margo's fury eviscerates him. "Leave him *alone!* That's not *important* now! Do you have any idea what he's gone through to get that back, what it means to him —?"

Although lifting my arms is like hoisting petrified logs, I try to soothe Margo. "No... it's all right... let him take it. I wanted them... to have it, remember?" I have to trust someone. And besides, I've taken precautions, in case my trust is misplaced.

The FBI man gently removes the Elvis from its harness. Suddenly he looks like a middle-aged Sam Phillips, the visionary owner of Sun Studios who recorded Elvis's first hit records, and I'm both comforted and reassured. I remember the miracle of the loaves and fishes... from a tiny morsel, Elvis will nourish the world.

Brain scans bear out what I already knew. I've suffered a stroke. Not a major one, but not one I'll soon forget. With months of therapy, I should regain reasonably normal speaking abilities. The blindness in my left eye, alas, is irreversible.

Muthukrishnan is good enough to hold off conducting my debriefing until after my initial treatment is done with. Then he and the lead FBI man shoo the nurses from my room. Harri and Margo are allowed to be present, since they are also being debriefed. I tell them everything that happened in the Viva Las Vegas Theater. With my good eye, I watch Harri's face. She hasn't aged well, sad to say. Her sense of horror and self-loathing as I tell Joseph's tale is as apparent to me as my own semi-blindness. She was more deeply implicated in all this than I ever would have imagined.

I don't like thinking of her that way. "Harri," I say, "what I brought for you, is it everything you need?"

"All of our initial tests have been positive," she says. She won't meet my one good eye. "If we work around the clock, we should be able to design a counteragent within the month. Have it field-tested within three or four, and, God willing, have it ready to run by the next growing season."

She tries to sound enthusiastic. But all I hear is exhausted, guilty relief.

"Dr. Shmalzberg, how sad that you chose not to trust me when we first met," Muthukrishnan says. "You could've avoided much pain and trouble."

"But we wouldn't have learned anything about Joseph," I say, concentrating on controlling the movements of my tongue and lips. "He would've remained free to sabotage the use of the Elvis, just as he did the rest of MannaSantos's recovery efforts."

Margo doesn't look well; she's pale, and all morning she's been much more quiet than usual. But now she interjects. "Mr. Muthukrishnan, every step of the journeys we take is necessary. Louis had to meet Ms. Denoux in New Orleans. He had to meet me and confront Dr. Trotmann. He had to suffer at the hands of... of that horrible Mr. Walterson." She haltingly takes my hand, more shy than she's seemed since we first met. Does Harri's presence make her nervous? "He still has great things to do. Without those painful steps he's taken, he wouldn't have grown into the man he needs to be."

Margo's belief in me still stuns me. I hear Harri's barely suppressed sigh, rich with irritation, and perhaps other emotions, too.

Muthukrishnan smiles; he looks upon Margo as though she's a charming child who's just delivered an adroit performance. "My devout Hindu parents would have expressed very much the same sentiments. They were quite disappointed when I decided to retrace an old family pattern and emigrate to the U.S. They believed I was predestined for other things, grander things. I, however, still believed in the tarnished promise of America."

"You can't very well blame me for mistrusting you," I say, "not after that visitation I got from the Caliphate's emissary."

Muthukrishnan sniffs. "I would think a man of your education and background would know better than to tar all 'foreigners' with the same brush. I was invited to your country to fill a vital position for which a native-born worker could not be found."

"Do you know what happened to the Frenchman who was chasing me? Is he dead?"

The FBI man, quiet for a long time, answers. "Mr. Quant is very resilient. He survived three bullet wounds, a broken sternum, and two broken legs. Caliphate embassy personnel sealed him off before we could learn more than his name. They intimated that his attempted assassination would spark an international crisis. But they stopped making noises when we let them know that one of his two shooting victims in Pensacola had also survived and is available to testify against him. Diplomatic immunity only goes so far. They bundled Quant onto the next available medical flight to Paris."

My heart jumped when he mentioned the Ottoman's victims. "Mitch Reynolds — is he alive?"

He nods. "As of last night, Reynolds was in stable condition. His doctors told me he wouldn't have pulled through without that first aid you gave him. Quant was a nasty piece of work, relying on Reynolds to track you across the country, and then cutting him down. By the way, those guys from Graceland traced you to the casino the same way we did. We were able to talk to one of them this morning."

"Swaggart?"

"Not him. He didn't pull through. One of the guys wearing an Elvis suit. He told us that somewhere between Memphis and Miami, they noticed their satellite radio picked up strange interference in its lower bands whenever they were within a mile of your car. Swaggart had mentioned that you were a Good Humor Man, and the other Elvis look-alike used to be one, too. He remembered the badges and their GPS locators. That's how they tracked you in Vegas."

Swaggart. I might owe my survival to that neurotic corporate toady. I wonder if it was worth it to him, all those years of sucking up to Elvis's descendants, trying to redeem his father's thankless career...

Dad. So much has happened in the last week that I haven't even thought about him. "Mr. Muthukrishnan, I have to call the Pacific Vistas Convalescent Complex. My father —"

Harri raises her hands to calm me. "It's all right, Louis. I called there this morning. He's doing fine. The dietary supplements you ordered are keeping his weight stable, at least for now."

My relief is deep, but fleeting. What about the millions of elderly Americans who don't have physician sons to bully their nurses into ordering dietary supplements? How long will it take for the ghost of Elvis's breakfast to saddle up and ride to the rescue? "Harri, once the counteragent is released, how many months will it take to spread throughout the food chain?"

Every furrow in her careworn face deepens. "We're still working on the models... It's taken Metaboloft almost three years to spread from the Midwest corn-growing regions to its current dispersion path. Right now, the primary infestation covers most of the continental U.S. Pockets of infestation have been rumored as far afield as Central America." She bites her lower lip. "We'll have the advantage with the new agent of being able to plant it in multiple regions, and we should be able to affix it to a variety of plant forms. But even so... under best-case scenarios, which we aren't assured of having, the earliest I'd venture to predict we could have Metaboloft completely squelched is two years."

"Two *years* — *!*" I can't get the gaunt faces of my father's ward-mates out of my mind. "There could be a bigger death toll than anything this country's seen since the 1918 influenza epidemic. You said the Metaboloft effect is self-reinforcing; the more a person eats it, the faster his basal metabolism accelerates. You can't let this go on for two years — crops have to be burned, foods have to be pulled from the shelves. Mr. Muthukrishnan, what does the government plan to do?"

"Certainly nothing like what you suggest." His face turns severe. "Do you realize the chaos such steps would bring? You fear the starvation of a few million? What about the starvation of *tens* of millions? Because that will surely be the result should word of this outbreak become common knowledge. No other nation on earth has the spare agricultural capacity to feed America in addition to itself. Start burning crops and the contents of supermarkets, and the ensuing panic and economic disruption will accomplish much of Joseph Walterson's goal a good deal faster than he had planned. The survivors will look back upon the GD2 years as a golden age, by comparison."

"But you can't sit back and do *nothing!*"

"I in no way meant to imply that we would do *nothing*. We already know that the elderly, young children, and the sick are in the most immediate danger. My agency will work discreetly to ensure that caloric supplements and drug cocktails which can retard metabolic rates are made available to the most vulnerable. America was the first nation to land astronauts on the moon. Certainly we can build a few dozen factories to manufacture weight-gain powders in the required time frame."

Maybe. But can you turn around a nation's destructive thought patterns in just a few months, without letting the citizenry know they're battling a plague?

Word of all this will get out. If not from my mouth, then a dozen others. Too many hands have already touched Metaboloft. Involving the nation's doctors, no matter how discreetly, ensures that a platoon of whistle-blowers will emerge to tell the tale, no matter what the consequences.

But if a certain amount of chaos is unavoidable, maybe I can make it work for the good of us all. Maybe what we need is a storm of nationwide panic to blow away what's turned rotten and malignant in the last twenty-five years.

"What does the government plan to do about the Good Humor Men?" I ask. "The illicit foodstuffs they burn are the very things that could be saving people's lives."

Muthukrishnan looks to the FBI man for a reply. The agent shrugs his shoulders. "The Good Humor Men are officially deputized by state and local governments. You want to get rid of them, you don't start with us feds. You'd have to get campaigns rolling in almost all fifty states."

"But the President and Congress could encourage state legislatures to reconsider the vigilantes' legal authority," I say. "The biggest stick Good Humor squads wield is their ability to confiscate health cards. What do you think would happen if Congress told the states they were withholding insurance pool grants to any state that continues sanctioning the food police?"

Muthukrishnan is momentarily quiet, but I can see that I've gotten the cogs of his sharp mind turning. "I will take your suggestions under advisement, Dr. Shmalzberg. But my agency's ability to sway the political process is limited. Congress will be emboldened to act on the issue of the Good Humor Men if there is a groundswell of public opinion demanding action. Given your passion and experience, I would suggest that you would make an ideal candidate to rouse such opinion."

Is he out of his mind? I just suffered a stroke, I'm half-blind... But the more I think about it, the less ludicrous his suggestion seems. What Margo said just a few minutes ago, words that even I dismissed as naive enthusiasm, now sounds like the preamble to a calling.

I've been called. I can't hide from that.

"I... I'll take your suggestion under advisement, Mr. Muthukrishnan."

"Very good." He gathers his recorder and papers into a briefcase. "We shall remain in touch, Doctor. Mr. Bergeron, do you have any final words for Dr. Shmalzberg?"

His companion rearranges his gun holster before putting on his coat. "If I were you," he tells me, "I'd take our directive of confidentiality very seriously. One word of any of this to the media, and you'll end up doing your rehab in San Quentin Federal Detention."

When the door closes behind them, Harri exhales with relief. "Lovely bedside manner," she says.

I don't answer her, because Margo has gone even more pale. Her forehead glistens with a sheen of sweat. "Margo, are you all right?"

She shakes her head. "I'll — I'll be fine. Don't worry. I just need a glass of water. Be back in a minute..."

She bolts out the door. That wasn't just a glass of water she's after. Harri comes to sit by my bedside. "You collect interesting friends, Louis." Her tone isn't entirely unkind.

"I'm worried about her. It could be all the stress of the last few days. But she hasn't been the same."

She clucks her tongue. "The same as what? How long have you known her? A week? For all you know, she could be like this all the time. An odd bird." She laughs, sounding both cynical and tired. "It's been a long time since I was that young and unformed." She stares at the door, then takes her glasses off and wipes them with a tissue. "I think she may be in love with you. Cradle-robbing never had pride of place among your perversions before. How do you feel about her?"

"She saved my life."

"That's beside the point. Do you love her?"

Do I? In little more than a week, I've memorized the sounds of her breathing, the scents of her skin and hair. Three times I've been reunited with her after I'd been close enough to Death to touch the hem of his cloak. Cannula in hand, I've shared with her the most intimate moments I can conceive. And she has shown me a path for the remainder of my days.

Emily, as much as I love you, as much as I miss you... I'm giving myself permission to love another.

"Yes," I say. "I believe I do."

"Oh." Harri smiles tightly and almost imperceptibly shakes her head. "Well. Good luck, then. I've always thought that... once we reach a certain age, we've made too many compromises, sold too many shares of our souls to truly connect anymore with the young. Good luck to you."

I tell myself she's trying to be kind. But her accusing tone disturbs me. "Harri, why didn't you ever tell me you were married to Theodore Weiss?"

Immediately, her wounded expression makes me sorry I asked. "That... wasn't a happy time in my life. If you and I had dated longer...

well, I'm sure I would've mentioned Ted eventually."

"How much did you know about Weiss's work? About the Walterson cloning project?"

Her cheek twitches. "I'm not going to lie to you," she says. "Although I wasn't on the team that Ted headed up, my team's researches benefited greatly from his work. He was proud of the project, but I could tell he was suffering from guilt, too. I did some poking around. I saw the test subjects myself, what was being done to them. I tried to convince Ted that what the company was doing was immoral. We fought about it for months. That was pretty much the final nail in our already wobbly marriage."

"Why did you stay with MannaSantos? Why didn't you quit?"

She stares at me anew, contrition replaced by anger. "Don't you dare accuse me, Louis! I won't take it, not from you. Not from a man who befriended a gang of thugs, justified their bullying of hundreds of innocent people, and for twenty years basked in approbation you knew you didn't deserve."

I deserve that slap. "I was running away from grief I couldn't face. I made an accommodation, a bad one. I'm devoting the rest of my life to undoing the harm I've done."

"Good for you, Louis. Well, I 'made an accommodation,' too." Her voice has lost some of its harshness, but she's still trembling. "You think it would've been easy to quit MannaSantos in the middle of GD2? You think I could've found other work in my field at even a *fifth* of the salary they were paying? As it was, I took a monster pay cut when I transferred to public relations. But it was worth it to not have anything to do with Ted and his project anymore."

"The leaker who reported the cloning to the feds — was that you?"

Her eyes grow cloudy. Tears leave wet tracks down her wrinkled cheeks. "I thought I was *saving* them. How could I have known — no, no, I *should've* known, I should've realized what Ted's bosses would do after I backed them into a corner..."

I reach for her, pull her into what I hope is a comforting embrace. She doesn't pull away. "Oh Louis, I *killed* them! When I alerted the feds, I signed the clones' death warrants. I might as well have dissected them myself..."

"No, Harri. You did the best thing you could. What happened afterward wasn't your fault."

"But it *was!* And the last clone. Joseph. The one no one knew Ted had spared. Would he have done what he did if his brothers hadn't been killed? Does this whole Metaboloft disaster rest on my head, too?"

"Of course not. No. No." How much of this emotion is genuine, and how much is meant to manipulate my feelings? "We can't see the ultimate results of what we do. An action undertaken with pure motives can result in terrible consequences. Or, like my father's experience, what begins as a disaster can prove to be the salvation of the world."

She pulls free of my hold. "So what are you telling me? That I need to stop beating myself up and trust in some Higher Power? I'm an agnostic, Louis. I had my mother pull me out of Sunday school because it was just too damn silly —"

The door opens. Margo walks in. She looks even worse than when she left the room a few minutes ago.

"No need to come up with an answer for me, Louis," Harri says, straightening her blouse. "Take care of your friend; she's looking a little peaked." She glances quickly at Margo before leaving. "And when you're feeling better, honey, you take care of him, too."

All my anxieties fade into insignificance when I let myself absorb the fright in Margo's lovely young face. "Margo, what's wrong? You've been feeling poorly ever since we were in Pensacola. Has it gotten worse?"

She stares at me with a stricken, forlorn look. "I — I don't want to worry you, Louis. You've got so much weight on you already."

"Darling —" The word slips out before I can stop it, but it feels right, and she doesn't look offended, thank God; "...darling, if you won't tell me what's going on, I'll crawl out of my skin. Come sit next to me and tell me."

She stumbles to the chair where Harri had been sitting. I take both of her hands in mine. They're cold and damp. "I think," she says, stammering, "I think there may be something seriously wrong with me. Oh, Louis, I don't want to believe it has anything to do with what you did with your cannula — I'm so grateful, and even if something did go wrong, I don't blame you —"

Now my hands go clammy. "Have you swelled up where I did the liposuction? Are you bleeding?"

"I —" She looks away from me. "Yes. I'm bleeding. I've been noticing spots of blood ever since I started cramping. Just earlier... Louis, my underpants were filled with blood."

I immediately hit the call button and yell for a doctor. A minute later, a nurse appears. I have Margo repeat what she just told me. The nurse pulls a curtain to cordon off the other side of the room and has Margo join her. She asks Margo to change into a robe. The fact that she doesn't call for doctors to assist calms me. The empathic questions she poses to Margo get me thinking, then hoping.

All those years of high-calorie meals at Lansky's... maybe they finally overcame her genetic predisposition to remain physically stuck in pre-adolescence. Maybe her eating the Carnival treats I brought from New Orleans pushed her body past the tipping point, into womanhood. The nurse's gentle explanation to Margo confirms what I want so much to hear. Twenty-nine years old, and it's her first period.

Despite feeling steady as a wet dish rag, I walk around the curtain. Margo sits on the bed, her robe bunched between her legs, her mouth forming an "O" the size of a ripe strawberry. She looks at me, eyes brightening. Slowly, deliciously, she begins to laugh.

All the ice inside me thaws in an instant. My arms are around her, and my fingers become Magellans, circumnavigating the incipient curves of the woman she's becoming. I'm laughing, too.

"Oh, Margo, darling, you aren't dying. Not at all. You're *living*."

EPILOGUE: CALORIE 3501

Today is my seventieth birthday. According to Jewish tradition, now that I've reached this age, the full span of a man's life, my odometer rolls over and I begin again; I can celebrate a second *bar mitzvah* thirteen years from now.

My first service of the day is scheduled to start in twelve minutes, and I still need to make sure my father is ready. I stand in front of the mirror and finish tying my tie, a collage of Elvis's record covers, then take one last gander at myself. For a newborn, I don't look too bad; even though my cousins insist the eye patch makes me look like Lafitte the Pirate. Pinching the thin skin surrounding my waist, I remind myself I've done well to maintain eighty-five percent of my weight this past year. Margo's done better than merely maintain, thank God.

Moving down to San Diego was a fine idea. Dinners at Cindy's are a never-ending pleasure, especially now that she's free to indulge her inner chef, and Will and Blair have made a habit of attending services now and then. It's been good for my father, too. Cindy is always a familiar face for him. Consuela has been a blessing; without her daily help, I couldn't maintain my father outside of a nursing home. Dad's never alone now. Consuela's always there, hovering over him like a Jewish mother, nudging him to *eat, eat.*

It's not a long walk to my father's bedroom. For the beginning of a new life, this modest home is perfect. I'm living like my great-grandfather lived, in a two-bedroom walk-up apartment above my storefront business. In his case, a butcher shop; in my case, a church. I poke my head into my father's bedroom. Consuela's dressed him in his brown suit, and she's helping him tie his shoes. The thirty-year-old suit billows around him as if he's made of twigs and wire. It could be a lot worse, though. "Consuela, how's Dad doing this morning?"

She looks up and smiles. "Oh, very good, Dr. Shmalzberg. Your father, he is a pleasure, a pleasure."

I give him a hug. It's so wonderful to touch him, to smell the same drugstore aftershave he's used for at least seventy years. He stares at my aqua and pink robe with habitual surprise. "Why are you dressed up?" he says. "Are we going to a parade?"

At least he's finally stopped asking me about the eye patch. I shake my head, give him my almost ritual answer. "No, Dad, we're going downstairs to services."

Confusion. "Do — do I have to bring my *tallis?* I can never remember where I put the darn thing —"

"That's all right, Dad. It's not that kind of service. You look just fine."

Consuela smoothes his jacket across his shoulders. "Yes. Very handsome."

He gestures for me to lean down so he can whisper in my ear. "That pretty young girl who comes around — is she going to join us? I like her."

"She likes you, too." Even though Margo isn't a face from long ago, still he remembers her, even if he can't recall her name. "Margo had a business meeting this morning, Dad. But she'll join us later."

Margo has displayed a talent for commerce that I think surprised even her. Oretha set her up as the company's Southern California sales rep, which certainly has proven to be no act of charity. Margo's commissions have made everything possible — getting the church started, maintaining my father at home, paying for my travels to dozens of state capitols to testify against the Good Humor Men.

"Okay, Dad. Take it nice and slow." Consuela and I guide him down the stairs. Step by step... not all steps have been without pain. Mitch hasn't spoken to me since I testified before the California State Senate. That's been a hurtful rupture. We reach the ground floor without a stumble. I'll have to make sure our next home has an elevator, or occupies a first floor. Already, the church has begun outgrowing its storefront rooms. The meals we serve may have something to do with that... I've heard more than one congregant refer to us as "the food church." But I'd like to think our growing popularity is based upon more than just physical nourishment.

Outside, I find a familiar figure waiting. "Consuela," I say, "why don't you walk Dad over to the entrance. I'll be with you shortly." I turn to my unexpected visitor. "Hello, Ravi."

Muthukrishnan allows himself a smile. "I am pleased we are on a first name basis, Louis. Your speech is much improved. Our investment in your therapy was not wasted."

"To what do I owe the honor of this visit?"

"I wished to offer my congratulations on your recent success with the California legislature. Convincing them to withdraw legal sanction from Good Humor squads, simultaneously decriminalizing the sale and consumption of high-calorie foodstuffs and granting amnesty to food offenders — that was a great victory."

That's gracious of him. "I wish the victories would come faster. Public attitudes about eating have years of inertia behind them. People actually welcomed signs of the wasting plague at first. Until thousands of their aged parents and grandparents began dying. Has your department had anything to do with containing the food riots?"

His smile fades. "That has been mainly the work of the National Guard. Institution of martial law in many urban jurisdictions has been a most regrettable necessity. My department's activities have been limited to distribution of nutritional supplements and combating harmful rumors. The drip-drip of leaks to the media, leading to massive unrest... this has been most disturbing to us. Disturbing to *me,* Louis." He glances at the crowd waiting by the doors of my church. "All that you have built here — it is most impressive. But indiscretion on your part could make it vanish overnight."

I knew he wasn't here for a mere social call. "I've had nothing to do with any leaks. All my testimony has focused solely on the Good Humor movement's abuses of power. I haven't mentioned Metaboloft once. I've held up my end of our agreement, and I'll continue to do so."

"I am glad to hear that." He stares again at the growing crowd. "I have been most fascinated by what I've heard of your church. If you would not mind, I would like very much to stay for the service."

"Please join us." Freedom of religion still holds in America.

Muthukrishnan may not be happy with certain elements of my service, but I've cloaked them in enough metaphor to uphold the letter of our agreement. Any action he might take against my church would land him in federal court, where the entire story would come out under oath — a consequence he's eager to avoid.

I do a quick head count while unlocking the church's front doors. Right around a hundred; not bad for a Saturday morning. I like to think our fellowship looks like America. Faces of all hues; Spanish and Vietnamese phrases intermingle with English. Elvis would approve. A clump of older Hispanic women gathers around my father and *kvell* and fuss over him. He's become a figure of no small reverence among the congregants. These people know the truth, even if I've swaddled it in a protective wrap of mythology.

I spot Mr. Lee at the edge of the crowd, pushing his mother in a wheelchair. He looks pinched and frail, but positively robust compared with his parent; the Metaboloft effect has burned away whatever reserves she once had. Only her eyes are fully alive, darting from face to face. I kneel down and embrace her. Her skin, so terribly thin, burns with heat. She smiles at me with cracked lips. "You hang in there a while longer, Mrs. Lee," I tell her. "Salvation is coming soon." How wonderful to say that, and to truly believe it.

I find her and her son a good spot near the front. Our stage is a simple riser made of aluminum and plywood, our tabernacle a wooden box much more modest than the one the Israelites carted through the desert for forty years. Consuela turns on our welcoming hymn, Elvis singing "You'll Never Walk Alone."

I see my cousins Will and Blair enter. "Louis!" Will says. "I'm glad we made it in time. I think I saw Margo coming up the road behind us."

"I thought you two were going camping this weekend. Not that it isn't a pleasure to see you..."

"Oh, we're still going," Will says. "But we wanted to catch your service first. And we certainly didn't want to forget your birthday."

"This is a big one," Blair says, giving me an especially warm hug. "Happy seventieth." She steps back and grasps my hands, an excited smile brightening her face. "We've got something special to share with you. It's a gift... for us as much as for you. More for us, actually.

We've, uh, we've decided to go natural."

Will slips his arms around his wife's middle. "Honey, don't be so shy. Make that past tense. We've *gone* natural. Planting season's over and done with. Harvest is, oh, about seven months from now."

My smile must stick out three feet from the sides of my face. "Oh, you two... my dears... I can't tell you how happy this makes me." I pull them both to me. "What did Cindy's face look like when you told her? She's been waiting for a grandchild for so long! I can't wait for you to tell Margo. Can you join us for the brunch?"

"Of course," Blair says, eyes shining. "We wouldn't want to go hiking on an empty stomach."

They find seats near the back, and I climb to the stage. Mounting the pulpit terrified me when I first began this. But a year and a half of talking to law makers and my growing congregation has done wonders for my speech and confidence both. The brain is a miraculous creation, routing its pathways around the broken places when called upon to do so with enough persistence. And faith.

"My friends, today's reading from Scripture comes from Exodus: God's provision of manna and quail to the Israelites in the desert of Sinai. As a symbol of our faith that God will provide us, too, with the manna which we require in our time, I invite Brother Chung Mow Lee and Sister Imelda Sanchez to open the tabernacle."

And there it is. The Elvis. Not all the substance my father removed from the belly of the great singer. Just the portion I placed in a separate vacuum jar in Pensacola, a hedge against the chance that my trip to MannaSantos would prove disastrous. Enough for us. Because even a tiny portion of Elvis will feed multitudes.

Just as I'm about to begin reading, Margo slips inside. She spots an empty seat not far from Will and Blair and tries to squeeze unobtrusively into the row. It's not an easy trick. She's not as lithe and limber as she was six months ago.

I think I'll save her the trouble of squeezing into that row. Blair and Will have me feeling inspired. A little improvisation is called for. "I'd like to invite my fiancée to join me at the pulpit."

She's surprised, but not displeased. I help her up the steps to the stage. She wears a hesitant smile, not sure what I'm up to. Two months from now, when she's eight months pregnant, she will be a bride few guests will soon forget.

We stand in front of the open tabernacle. I drop to my knees, causing the older ladies to gasp, and caress Margo's taut belly, swollen with burgeoning life. I kiss it, letting my lips linger, welcoming the future on this day my life begins anew.

Thank you, Elvis.

ACKNOWLEDGMENTS

Although the writing of this book predated the Hurricane Katrina disaster which struck New Orleans and the Gulf Coast in August 2005, I would be horribly remiss if I failed to acknowledge the dozens of instances of assistance, both large and small, which sustained my family and me during those harrowing months of potential homelessness. Such kindness and generosity can most likely never be repaid in kind. I only hope that, when I have the opportunity to step up to the plate myself, I will prove to be as giving. And I will do my damndest to teach my boys to practice the sorts of compassion and thoughtfulness which were shared with us.

When the temporary housing Dara's mother, Phyllis Levinson, attempted to secure for us fell through (unbeknownst to her, her condo in Hallandale, Florida, had become infested with mold due to a leak from the upstairs apartment), Larry Leibowitz and his family lent us the use of a condo in Surfside for September and October, probably saving me from going out of my mind. The unit we stayed in ended up being in the same building where Isaac Bashevis Singer had written many of his novels. My parents and my in-laws, the Hirschfeld family, put us up in hotels until Larry was able to settle us into the condo. My sister, brother, and sister-in-law collected enough clothes, toys, and essential personal items from their neighbors and coworkers in Tampa to fill an entire Dodge Durango, and Ric and Robyn drove this treasure trove to us across Alligator Alley. Old Miami friends whom I hadn't seen in years — Robert and Lori Haydu, Stanley and Mia Wong, and Jeff Jackson and his family — reunited with me, met my family, and gathered so much baby equipment for us that we ended up re-donating half of it to other families displaced by Katrina. My dear cousins, May and Joe Miller, babysat my two boys and let me use their

Internet connection for hours on end. Phyllis also helped Dara and me buy a van to replace our cars, feared lost. Family friend and handyman Butch Martin rescued our eight housecats, trapped for three weeks with little food or water; and Clyde Faust kindly housed them, free of charge, at his small animal shelter until we could return home.

The science fiction and fantasy community is truly an extended family, one I am especially proud to belong to. Fans and pros alike were breathtakingly generous to us. We were attending Bubonicon in Albuquerque, New Mexico, when the storm hit and we learned we wouldn't be able to fly home anytime soon. Jane Lindskold, Pati Nagle, S. M. and Jan Stirling, Yvonne Coates, and the members of the Albuquerque Science Fiction Society fed us and did their best to keep our spirits up. Craig Chrissinger and Wendy Jay gathered clothes for all four of us, and books, videos, and toys for Levi and Asher. Nina and Ron Else from the dealers room took up a collection for us. Knowing that my computers and backup files might have been lost in the flood, Steve and Jan donated a Dell laptop which they weren't using anymore. From Austin, Texas, Bradley Denton shipped me a copy of WordPerfect, my favorite word processor, and sent signed copies of all of his novels. Lucius Shepard, Adam-Troy Castro, and Gordon Van Gelder all mailed copies of books and magazines to fill up my hours (which ended up not being nearly so empty as I'd thought they would be, not with a toddler and an infant in tow, plus efforts to run a statewide food program in Louisiana from public library computers in Miami, Florida). Once we were down in Miami, Adam-Troy and Judi collected children's clothes, toys, and even a Cozy Coupe car from their neighbors, then personally delivered them to our hotel. Deborah Layne, an editor I'd met only very briefly, wired us money, as did Lou and Xin Anders. Perhaps most impressively, an ad-hoc committee of Gulf South science fiction fans, many of them victims of the storm themselves, tracked me and my family down in Florida and mailed us two care packages, even including groceries.

I also owe great thanks to my agent, Denise Dumars, who stepped in for me when Dan Hooker passed away and who continued to believe in this book, despite many disappointments; and to Marty Halpern and Jacob Weisman, who shared Denise's enthusiasm and faith.